THE JERSEY DEVIL

THE JERSEY DEVIL

HUNTER SHEA

PINNACLE BOOKS
Kensington Publishing Corp.
www.kensingtonbooks.com

PINNACLE BOOKS are published by

Kensington Publishing Corp.
119 West 40th Street
New York, NY 10018

All Kensington titles, imprints, and distributed lines are available at special quantity discounts for bulk purchases for sales promotions, premiums, fund-raising, educational, or institutional use. Special book excerpts or customized printings can also be created to fit specific needs. For details, write or phone the office of the Kensington sales manager: Kensington Publishing Corp., 119 West 40th Street, New York, NY 10018, attn: Sales Department; phone 1-800-221-2647.

ISBN-13: 978-0-7860-3887-9
ISBN-10: 0-7860-3887-X

First printing: September 2016

10 9 8 7 6 5 4 3 2 1

Printed in the United States of America

First electronic edition: September 2016

ISBN-13: 978-0-7860-3888-6
ISBN-10: 0-7860-3888-8

For Lori and Bruno

You know what they say, getting old ain't for pussies.

—RAYLAN GIVENS, *Justified*

Chapter One

Five years earlier

Jane Moreland couldn't believe how heavy Henry was, now that he was deadweight and starting to ripen. She should have done this last night, right when it happened, but she'd needed a clearer head. Polishing off the bottle of Knob Creek and passing out on the kitchen table hadn't helped matters much.

Well, no sense complaining. She'd been due a little *me time*.

She woke up after noon, unsure what had transpired the night before until she saw him, lying there beside the sofa, neck all twisted to one side and his face blue as a Smurf.

At least there isn't blood all over the place, she'd thought. Just a little at the corner of his mouth. None on the carpet. One less thing she had to worry about.

There was no way she could get him in the truck during the day without anyone seeing. To kill time, she took a long, hot bath, washed and dried a load of laundry, drank three bottles of Coors that had been tucked away in the back of the fridge, watched a Jimmy Stewart movie on TMC, and chain-smoked half a pack of coffin nails. The entire time, her eyes kept flicking to the clock, then the window, waiting for the sun to check out. She found some old jeans and a .38 Special concert T-shirt, put on her scuffed cowboy boots and tied her blond hair in a high ponytail.

When it was half past six, she dragged an old throw rug from the garage, laid it next to her husband and turned him into it with a whole lot of grunting and sweat. She'd thought it would be as easy as rolling up a burrito. Back when she was in high school, she'd worked at a burrito joint owned by a pair of Chinese brothers with deep Southern accents. She'd never been able to reconcile the words coming out of those faces. It was a time before Chipotle, when a burrito was a mushy thing you got at a Mexican restaurant that tasted like crap. The job, and the place, didn't last very long. In the two months she worked there, she became an expert at making burritos so fat, they were just about to bust out of their flour straitjackets.

A dead Henry, she learned quickly, was a hell of a lot more to handle than shredded beef, beans and rice. Once she'd gotten the rug around him and cinched off the ends with duct tape, she sat propped up against his cocooned body and laughed, wondering how many burritos it would take to equal Henry's total mass. Logic dictated that she should have been distressed at this point, perhaps freaked out or even, daresay, remorseful.

"You didn't earn my remorse," she said to the rug-encased corpse, giving it a hard slap as she stood up.

Good old boy Henry was a righteous bastard, a redneck from some pissant town in South Carolina who'd made his way to New Jersey via a construction job when he was in his twenties. They'd met at Dingo's Bar when she was still two years from legal drinking age. At first, she'd been entranced, as young, dumb girls will, by his sweet Southern accent. She'd heard him order a Jack and Coke over the din of meatheads and was immediately drawn to the rugged cutie with long hair and five-day stubble. He couldn't have stood out more if he had worn an alien mask and bikini.

They dated for six months, took a trip to Vegas and became a cliché. It took a whole year before the real Henry Moreland came out. He smacked her across the face in a drunken stupor one night because she didn't hand him the TV remote fast enough.

The rest is the same sad story that too many women confess to at shelters or police stations. After a while, Jane didn't know who she hated more—Henry for being an abusive asshole or herself for not having the guts to run away.

On nights she couldn't sleep, she'd let her mind linger on all the different ways she could make him disappear. That was her happy place. Poison his dinner, cut the brake lines in his truck, loosen the top step going down to the basement—the possibilities were endless. Thinking about it always settled her down. But that's all they were—private thoughts. Jane knew she was too chicken-shit to actually do anything. Hell, she couldn't even bring herself to jump in the car and just drive until she hit a border crossing, north or south. It didn't matter.

And then he came home last night so drunk he could barely stand. He'd parked his pickup on the front lawn, stopping just a few feet from the house. Jane had been reading in her favorite lounge chair—the one with the little head cushion—on the ground-level porch. It had been a nice night and even the bugs tapping against the overhead light didn't bother her . . . much. If Henry had applied the brakes just a hair later, he would have killed her. She should have been fuming at him.

No. It was the other way around. He stomped past her, bursting through the door screaming incoherently, a bottle of Bud dangling in his fingertips, sloshing suds all around.

"Henry, what are you saying?" she'd asked, tensing up for the inevitable. He'd cracked one of her ribs the week before. It was just starting to heal. She knew another shot to her right side would break the rib entirely, and he was not taking her to a hospital anytime soon.

When he swung at her, for what only Henry and God knew, she'd twisted away, protecting her vulnerable side.

That's when he kind of corkscrewed in the center of the living room. His feet went out from under him and he pitched forward, so drunk he didn't have the sense to put his arms out to break his fall.

His head thwacked the corner of the coffee table.

And just like that, he was dead. His neck swiveled to an angle the human spine is not meant to support. He was dead so fast, his body didn't even twitch. Jane heard a sickening crack, like marbles being smashed together. When she got the courage to get close to him, kneeling on the floor so she could see if he was breathing, she saw that the lights in his eyes had been turned off for good.

Henry was the second person to die in front of her. The first was her grandpa, who suffered a fatal heart attack during Thanksgiving dinner when she was eight. He was talking one second, asking her mother for more yams, and gone the next, his head on his plate, peas and carrots mashed under his cheek, staring at her with graying eyes.

Jane couldn't call the cops because all of Henry's

friends were on the force. He liked to tell them that if anything ever happened to him, Jane was suspect number one. Sure, they laughed it off when he said it, but she couldn't trust them any further than she could throw Henry. Henry knew that there might come a day when he pushed her to her breaking point. That was his way of letting her know she'd never get away with it.

"Bet you didn't see this coming," she said to the open trunk. The back of her old Honda sagged a bit from his weight.

It was going to take a hell of a lot to get him out of there, but she had plenty of time and no fear of prying eyes.

Jersey's Pine Barrens, or Pinelands as the locals called them, were vast and dark and sparsely populated. The moment Henry took that dive, she knew she'd end up here. The Barrens were an infamous dumping ground for bodies. Henry was just another log on the fire. The critters and wilderness would make quick work of him.

It was a two-hour ride from their house to this spot. She remembered it from the nature walks she used to take with her father. The trail was a mile from here. She found a break in the trees and drove as deep as she could. Decayed leaves crunched under the tires. They would cover up the fresh grave nicely.

She almost popped a vein in her neck getting Henry out of the trunk. His body made a soft thud when it hit the ground. Wiping her brow, she grabbed the shovel and flashlight and got to work.

As she dug, she thought about what she'd do when she got back. Dozens of scenarios swam through her head. Whenever she started to worry about being accused of murder, she said out loud, "Habeas corpus."

Not that she was any kind of law expert, but she'd watched enough *Law & Order* to have a little confidence in her assessment of the situation. *Corpus* had to mean corpse, and her husband sure fit that bill. Now the *habeas* part, she was just spitballing.

Without a corpse, they'd have to leave her be. Wasn't that the gist? Or was there another word for it?

No matter, she didn't care if it took a year for everything to die down and go away. She'd proven she was patient.

Lost in her dreams of a new life, the head-piercing screech that ripped through the still night air made her drop her shovel.

"What the hell was that?"

Jane grabbed the flashlight propped on the edge of the grave. The beam swept through the trees.

What kind of animal makes a noise like that?

She couldn't stop the hammering of her heart.

It was one thing to hear an odd cry during the light of day. Hear something like that in the dead of night, in the middle of a primeval forest, and it got your attention.

Jane picked up the shovel, now holding it as a weapon. She waited, her chest rising and falling faster and faster.

A soft breeze ruffled the trees. She saw hundreds if not thousands of twinkling pinpricks in the sky.

She didn't dare move or make a noise. Whatever it was, it either sounded as if it were royally pissed off or in pain.

Could have been an owl. They're supposed to sound like a woman screaming. So are deer when they're afraid.

Her body tensed.

What's out here that would scare a deer like that?

"I don't know, but it's scaring me pretty good right about now," she said, comforted by the sound of her own voice. The jolt of fear snapped her to reality for the first time since Henry had taken his fatal fall.

"Holy shit. I'm out in the middle of nowhere, burying my husband. What the hell's wrong with me?"

Grrrrrrlllllllllll.

"Oh, my God," she yelped, swinging the shovel in every direction in an effort to protect herself. The growl sounded near . . . and dangerous.

A river of cold sweat trickled between her breasts. She'd never been so scared in all her life, not even the night Henry broke the bedroom door down with the fireplace poker, trying to get at her because he was drunk and horny and angry as hell that the Yankees had lost the playoffs to the Tigers. "Beaten by nigger town!" he'd spat over and over again, even while he was on top of her, grunting and pumping too long because he had a full case of whiskey dick. She'd been terrified that night, but she knew he couldn't hump and swear forever. He'd eventually roll off her and pass out.

Now, she wasn't so sure what would happen.

"Stay away from me," she said with faltering conviction. She saw the rug with Henry wrapped up inside, and for the first time in over a decade, she wished he were here.

The flap-flap of wings whooshed overhead. Jane looked up but didn't see a thing.

Eyes flickering around her, a scream froze in her throat as she watched something swoop down and carry the carpet, and Henry, away.

There weren't any birds that could do that. Henry weighed over two hundred pounds. It would take a damn pterodactyl to get him off the ground.

"No, no, no, no, no!" The shovel clanged at the bottom of the grave as she struggled to get out. Her car was only fifteen feet away. She had to get inside. The soft soil crumbled in her hands. The more she struggled for a solid hold, the worse it got, like quicksand.

Jane tried jumping straight out of the hole, but she'd dug it too deep. She hit the edge hard with her chest, knocking the wind out of her. Her feet and hands fought to get any kind of purchase. It seemed as if everything gave way at once. She fell on her back, staring in horror as one side of the grave poured on top of her.

That insane flapping noise returned.

Maybe it's better I just stay in here and wait for it to leave. If it thinks I'm gone, it won't stick around.

Jane gathered more soil, covering her body from the neck down. She clicked her flashlight off, trying her best to steady her breathing so as not to make a sound.

When she heard another growl, she almost screamed. She had to clench her lower lip between her teeth, drawing blood, to keep from crying out. Hot tears dripped from the corners of her eyes.

You did this to me, Henry! I wouldn't be here if you hadn't turned into a monster. I kept telling you that drinking was going to kill you someday. Goddamn you! Goddamn you!

Jane wept as quietly as she could, holding on to her belief that it was Henry that put her in this position. Before she knew it, she was fast asleep, the stress of the past twenty-four hours having bled her dry of her last ounce of energy.

* * *

The flickering sun filtering through the trees woke her up. When she lifted her hand to block the rays, sand and dirt fell into her eyes.

She was cold. A case of the shivers hit her hard.

Birds chirped. A woodpecker hammered away on a nearby tree.

"Thank you, God," she whispered, emerging from the soil like she was in a cheap zombie movie.

Now that she wasn't in a panic and could see what she was doing, getting out of the hole was a whole lot easier. Any hopes that what had happened last night was a dream brought on by temporary insanity were dashed when she saw that Henry was still missing.

What the hell could have taken him?

Jane had heard that there were bald eagles in the Pinelands. Didn't eagles carry off baby cows? A baby cow could weigh as much as a man, couldn't it?

No, they weren't that strong.

She'd go online to check when she got home.

Home.

Where, for the first time, she could actually relax without the fear of madness to come.

Her hands shook as she fumbled for her car keys.

"At least that bird did me a favor. Hopefully, he took Henry someplace he'll never be found."

Dropping the shovel and flashlight in the trunk, she wondered if she should cover up the hole.

Nah. People see that, they'll think some kids were just messing around.

She didn't think she had the strength to fill it back up anyway. It felt as if she'd been cored and bled dry.

A shower, Valium, glass of wine and proper sleep in her bed, that's what she needed.

The car door opened with a loud creak. Henry was always promising to grease up those hinges.

A burst of wind washed over her just before a pair of sharp claws dug into her shoulders. In an instant, she was looking down at the top of her car. She tried to scream but nothing would come out.

Leathery wings flapped on either side, the cool morning air biting her flesh.

Up and up she went, until her mind saved itself by shutting completely down.

Chapter Two

"I hate this," Michael said, his mouth full of sunflower seeds. He spit gobs of shells out the van's window. "I really do. We don't know what the fuck's back there. For all we know, that shit is in the air giving us cancer or shrinking our dicks."

John shook his head, keeping his eyes on the road. They'd been surrounded by pine trees for miles now, without another car in sight. It was like driving in a nightmare—you kept going and going, never getting anywhere, never seeing anything but the same unbroken scenery, mile after mile.

He liked it better when they went to the site by the water, down south more. Getting to it involved some real overgrown terrain, but at least they could chill out at the nearby beach when they were done. The blue water and sand made up for the spookiness of the overgrown woods where they dumped the shit, usually under cover of night.

"How about this," John said. "Measure your dick now, and measure it again when we get back. Then you'll know if it shrunk."

Michael held up a finger. "One, I don't have a tape measure. Two, there's no need to be an asshole. You mean to tell me you like carting around barrels of chemicals, not knowing what they're made of?"

"There's worse ways to earn a buck. Look, quit crying. We've done this like half a dozen times already. Do you have cancer?"

"No."

"I rest my case."

"That doesn't mean it's not growing inside us, getting even stronger now because we're locked in this van with the stuff."

John laughed. "You're getting soft, Mikey. Maybe you need to stop eating seeds like a bird and try a steak every once in a while."

"Wait until you're married and your wife gets these crazy ideas in her head. You'll be a vegetarian, too."

"I don't think so."

"Yeah, we'll see. I know this little fad of hers won't last. It's easier to just go along."

"Even when you're not around her you're eating like the fattest rabbit in Edison. What do you say we go to Morton's for lunch? My treat."

Michael waved him off. "No can do. When you stop eating meat, you get like this super sensitivity. You can smell it on someone from a block away. If I have a steak for lunch, Gloria will know the second I walk in the door."

"You're outta your mind."

"I'm not fucking kidding you. Last week, I ate one of those sausage biscuits at McDonald's for breakfast. I didn't get home until midnight, and Gloria could still smell it. She stopped me before I could even kiss her hello. Next thing I know, I'm on the damn couch. I spent a lot on that custom sleigh bed upstairs and I intend to sleep in it as much as possible."

"You sure you're the same Mikey who used to knock back twenty White Castle sliders in one sitting?" John said. The turnoff wasn't far. He kept his eyes peeled for the marker—a red bandana nailed to a tree on the right side of the road.

"Ha-ha, single man. I can't wait until Julie gets her hooks into you. You talk a big game now," Michael said.

"That's not going to happen because that ring finger of Julie's is going to remain the way it is—ringless. I guess I gotta thank saps like you for saving me from myself."

That got a chuckle from Michael. "It's good to know I'm providing a service." He moved forward in his seat. "Look, there it is."

John had to squint to spot the smear of red. Michael always had incredible eyesight. *Must be getting even better with all those carrots he's been eating*, he thought.

He turned the van off the unpaved road. It barely fit within the narrow clearing. That was the point. No one was supposed to know about this spot.

The terrain was treacherous. He wished they could have used a four-by-four, but the van was the only thing that fit the containers. A couple of times, the van almost got stuck, tires spinning and kicking up the soft earth in muddy fountains.

"Home, sweet home," John said, pulling up to the second marker, a tattered blue bandana tied around the branch of a dying bush. The circular clearing was a shade over forty feet in diameter. The first time they'd come here, Michael had commented how it looked like a landing site for a UFO that'd punched down through the trees. John agreed that it looked pretty unnatural. He'd heard that a whole town used to be out here, built around some kind of factory hundreds of years ago. Over time, people left the town and its rotted structures gradually sank into the earth. He wondered if there was a house or general store right under his feet.

"You wanna start the digging?" John asked.

Michael shrugged. "No skin off my ass. Let's lug those containers out first. I don't wanna get tired from digging, then have to get them out of the van."

John got out, admiring the new Venuccio Brothers logo on the side of the van. The boss had hired a legitimate designer to come up with it. The sweeping letters reminded him of old-time Little League lettering they used to have on their jerseys.

They opened the double back doors, slipping on thick rubber gloves and white masks to cover their mouths and noses. The four black steel containers looked heavy. They knew from experience that whatever was inside was remarkably light.

Each grabbed a side of one barrel and hefted it out of the van. They made sure not to drop it on the ground. They'd been told time and time again to be very careful. Michael was so paranoid, he treated those things like they were newborn babies.

"Does the lid seem kinda loose to you?" Michael said as they shuffled in tandem to the clearing. Liquid sloshed about inside.

"No. If it was, I'd let you carry it yourself."

"You're really pushing it today."

They lugged it to the spot where they estimated the last batch had gone under, near the upper right edge of the circle. As they got closer, Michael pulled up.

"Holy shit, Johnny. What the hell?"

Three months earlier, they had buried six barrels of the waste material only Venuccio Brothers Carting would carry out of the lab in Elizabeth. They both knew whatever was in the barrels was illegal. If it was on the up and up, it wouldn't be in their van. They'd never been told how toxic the materials were, but it didn't take a genius to figure out it was probably some pretty bad stuff.

John's heart pumped faster when he saw that one of the barrels had been dug up. It was still nestled in the tight hole they'd placed it in, but all of the dirt had been removed from the top.

Worst of all, the lid had been pried open.

"Jesus, you smell anything weird?" Michael said, his eyes showing way too much of the whites.

John looked around, taking a few deep sniffs. "Nah, all I smell is trees."

"I'm not going near that, man."

"All right, all right, don't get yourself in a panic. We'll just bury them over there," John said, nodding to the other side of the clearing. "We haven't planted anything there yet."

"But what about that one? If we leave it like that and someone finds it, we're screwed."

Sighing, and now cringing with the start of a massive headache, John said, "Look, we'll just throw the dirt back on."

"And breathe in whatever's in there? No way."

"Then I'll do it."

In fact, that was the last thing John wanted to do, but he knew there was no way Michael was going to take one step closer.

Just get it done quick and get the hell out, he thought. *We'll have to tell the boss someone's been snooping around. Jeez, I hope it wasn't some dumb kids. What if they got sick?*

John and Michael were hard men who did terrible things from time to time, but they never, ever harmed a woman or child. John's stomach turned at the thought of that nasty sludge getting on some kid who just wanted to play in the woods. Best to cover it up quick and hope no one else tried to go digging for China.

They gently placed the barrel on the ground while John went back to get the shovel.

Michael was pointing. "Look, is that a boot?"

John peered at the other side of the exposed hole.

There was a brown cowboy boot in the brush.

"Looks like some hick ran out of his shoes," John said, trying to lighten their mood. "I don't see the other one, though."

He found the lid and flipped it with the end of the shovel on top of the barrel. Before it landed, he looked at the black sludge inside. It looked like used motor oil. *A tank of oil like that would weigh a ton. I wonder what it's made of?*

John quickly went about tossing the dirt back onto the barrel. He wanted it out of sight in a hurry. If there were toxic fumes rising from it, the less he breathed, the better.

It took less than a minute to cover it all up.

"See, that wasn't so hard, was it?" he said.

When he turned around, Michael was gone.

"Hey," he called out. "No piss breaks until we get these new ones planted. You hear me?"

He stopped, listening for the sound of his partner's heavy stream or the crunch of leaves.

"Mikey! Quit playing around. Let's get this shit done, son."

He waited a minute, checked the van to make sure he wasn't taking a nap inside.

"Mikey?"

A loud scream put him on instant high alert. It sounded as if someone had just shouted their voice box raw. John drew his gun from the holster he kept at his back.

If that's you, Mikey, you're gonna get shot.

It couldn't be him. Michael knew better.

John flew forward as something smashed into him from behind. His gun thumped underneath last fall's leaves. John howled. It felt like the back of his shoulder had been shattered. His right arm had gone numb, right down to the tips of his calloused fingers.

"You son of a bitch," he cursed, struggling to flip onto his back and face his attacker.

Twigs snapped as something stepped beside him.

He looked up.

"No way. No way. No! No!"

Chapter Three

The Pine Barrens claimed the Honda and the Venuccio Brothers van as its own, shrouding them from prying eyes. Over time, they rusted, the tires went flat, rubber and seals dried and cracked, until they looked older than the Barrens itself. The earth started the slow process of dragging them to its depths while plant life grew up and over them, twisting tendrils with lush leaves sealing the car and van in Nature's grip. They would never be seen by another pair of human eyes again.

Chapter Four

Present day

Sam Willet—Boompa to his family—woke up with an admirable case of morning wood. Scratching at his chin underneath the wild tangle of his beard, he looked down at his tented pajama bottoms and said, "Not bad. Now what am I supposed to do with this?"

Truth was, it *wasn't* bad, considering his eighty years on God's green earth and disdain for male enhancers. When he was a younger man of sixty, his sex life with Lauren had been better than when they were honeymooners. He'd assumed that things would settle down when he turned seventy. After that, there was no sense funneling PEDs to his pecker, chasing the poor woman around the house. She'd earned her peace. Then he'd pass away and bide his time in the ether waiting for her.

It wasn't part of the plan, her dying ten years ago and his body still champing at the bit to find some loving. Every time he woke up like this, he felt grim satisfaction that he still had it, and pain at the reminder that his days of strutting were long behind him.

There was a knock at his door.

"Boompa, you up?"

That was his grandson Daryl.

"Of course I'm up," he said. "I've been getting up before the crack of dawn more years than you've been kicking around."

Daryl gave a short laugh.

"You need me to help you out of bed, old man?"

He flipped the covers back, crossing the room in three heavy strides, his footsteps sounding like thunderclaps on the bare, hardwood floor. Throwing open the door, he barked, "How about I change your diaper, son? Lord knows I seen enough crap come out of you over the years."

Daryl jumped back, hands held up in surrender. He was tall and solid as a fireplug, just like his father. His frayed Mets cap was on backwards. Sam pulled it off his head, setting it straight, so the bill was facing front.

"I swear you do that just to hound me," Sam said.

Daryl's sad blue eyes sparkled for a moment. "You found me out." He happened to look down and said, "No need to salute. I'm not an officer."

Sam chuckled, covering his slight bulge with his shirttail. "Why don't you go downstairs and fix me some breakfast? Make yourself useful."

Daryl clomped down the stairs. "Same as always? Farina with prune juice and a Metamucil chaser?"

"Keep it up, kid. You won't be young forever."

Sam closed his bedroom door, gathered his shirt and overalls and went to the attached bathroom. He looked out the window. It was still dark out, but he could see a pink sliver of light on the horizon. The air drifting through the open window was chilly, but the weatherman said things would warm up by nine. The farm needed constant nurturing. It wouldn't be long before the place was overrun by his farmhands and family. Sam had been born and raised in the Bronx, and he never could get over how just an hour north from a city of concrete and apartment buildings, Pine Bush was as rural and countrified as the Deep South.

Giving himself a dry shave, he heard the dulcet tones of Frank Sinatra wafting from the stereo in the kitchen. The kid, and everyone else around Sam, knew all about his passion for the American standards sung by real men—Sinatra, Dean Martin, Mel Tormé, Tony Bennett, Bobby Darin and Nat King Cole. The smell of eggs and sausage coupled with the greatest music ever recorded got his old bones in motion. Daryl had become a hell of a cook, and he was Sam's favorite person to see first thing in the morning. Sam only hoped he could help his grandson find his way in the short time he had left. Farming just wasn't in him. He did everything they asked of him, but Sam could tell Daryl didn't have a passion for it.

He got downstairs before the rest of the family so he could sneak a sausage link.

"You want a slice of toast with that?" Daryl asked, working up a huge pan of scrambled eggs. He'd baked two loaves of bread the day before. The butter was also made right on the farm. Sam felt sorry for all the billions of people who didn't own farms and had no idea how incredible breakfast could be.

"I can wait," he said. "I think I'll check my e-mail first."

The old floor creaked under his weight as he walked to the living room. Sam was old, but he was still a big man, just over six-three, and spry as a man half his age. He found his iPad on the side table next to his lounge chair and turned it on.

The first thing he looked through were the multiple Google alerts that his granddaughter, April, had helped him set up when he got the tablet a year ago. He was not one to be left behind by the changing times. He'd bought a computer in the early nineties, using it mostly to keep records for farm business. When the Internet came along, he was hooked.

Can't believe all the stuff these tablets can do, he thought, marveling at the slim device in his thick hands.

He was about to click on the links for his *cryptid* alert when his daughter-in-law, Carol, swept past, patting his shoulder.

"Morning, Boompa," she said with a yawn. Carol was just shy of fifty and slender as a pitchfork handle, with a bosom that looked surgically enhanced, though she was as real as the day was long. He looked at her, silhouetted by the lamplight, and said to himself, *You picked a wonderful woman, Bill, even though you had to do your picking awfully young. Not many guys win that lottery.*

She tied her long, dirty blond hair into a ponytail while she looked out the big front windows. There wasn't much to see now, but soon enough, the entire farm would be lit by the morning sun.

"Mornin', dear," Sam said.

"Isn't it a wee bit early to be looking for monsters? I bet you haven't even had your coffee yet."

"I did have a bite of sausage," he replied with a wink.

"Bill will be down in a bit. Give me a shout if you find any," Carol said as she walked to the kitchen.

At his age, if he found what he was looking for, he'd do more than shout. He'd ring the damn bells at St. Luke's church. With each morning he woke up, he had less and less time.

But something told him big changes were blowing on the wind, just the way that scruffy Bob Dylan used to sing in his nasal whine. Like his old great Aunt Ida, he'd been looking deep into the tea leaves, and things were starting to stir again.

Six hundred miles away, Norm Cranston considered finishing the warm dregs sitting at the bottom of the bottle of Modelo he'd left on his back porch. He never was one for the hair-of-the-dog-that-bit-ya theory. Instead, he poured it onto his lawn, tossing the bottle in the blue recycling bin on his deck. It had rained overnight. The air smelled sweet, renewed.

He greeted the singing birds with an echoing belch.

Boy, he'd had too many last night.

Norm liked to drink alone, throwing one-man, one-cat welcome home parties whenever he'd been away for a spell. He'd returned yesterday from a weeklong stint in Ohio, following up on a rash of sightings of a Bigfoot–esque beast near the Cuyahoga Valley National Park. The Grassman tended to be a little shorter than your typical Sasquatch, with a tendency to track deer, its favorite prey. Though relatively quiet over the past several years, three sightings had been made by backpackers two weeks back. Word had spread and people were starting to fear going to the park. The Ohio Forestry Service had hired him on the QT to come out and follow up on the stories, hoping he'd find nothing and report it as simple misidentification. He'd gone so far as to camp out alone for six nights. As expected, he didn't come across the Grassman. What the backpackers probably saw were bears.

When he'd interviewed the witnesses, he wasn't

shocked to learn that they were all city dwellers with scant experience in the great outdoors. They weren't accustomed to coming across any wildlife bigger than a raccoon. Bear encounters were frightening, and easily misconstrued by a brain that was misfiring while allowing the bladder to empty its contents.

"Lions and tigers and bears, oh, my," Norm said, drinking orange juice straight from the carton. He'd spend the weekend working on a couple of articles, then a blog post, reassuring folks that the Grassman was not a threat to those seeking to bond with nature in Ohio.

Of course it wasn't. If there'd been an actual Grassman, Norm was pretty sure his ass wouldn't have been out there. At least, not alone.

"Hey, Salem, you mind g-going out to get some groceries? The cupboards are pretty empty," he said to his black cat, perched on the windowsill above the kitchen sink. Salem followed him with his wide, orange eyes. Norm's neighbor, Pam, always watched the lazy ball of fur when he was away. She made sure there was plenty of food for the cat. It wasn't lost on Norm that the cat was taken care of far better than he had ever been.

"Or maybe you'll share your Fancy Feast with me."

Salem made a contented cooing noise. Norm patted his head.

"You always were generous."

He put a Jimmy Dean frozen sausage and biscuit in the microwave. While he waited, he spotted himself in the small oval mirror he kept by the fridge. His eyes were bloodshot. His goatee that hung six inches from his chin was kept from going wild and woolly with a series of different colored rubber bands. Norm stepped back, rubbing what was becoming a considerable beer gut. He'd be forty-two in the fall. There were aches and pains that came with the age, but he could still motor when he had to. Hell, he'd just backpacked and camped in a mild wilderness for a week without any ill effects.

The Modelo was what was making him feel old today. He loved his beer, but it was starting not to love him back.

Norm plucked his straw hat from the kitchen table and plopped it on his head. The hat, for some reason, made him feel whole. He knew he looked like an extra from *Hee Haw*, but he didn't give a rat's ass. The hat had become part of his brand—the brash cryptozoologist who'd been featured on more cable shows than he could count.

His hook was his ability to remain impartial while still retaining his childlike wonder and fascination with tales and sightings of creatures both strange and mythical. When he was young, his father had pulled him aside one day and told him in confidence about his encounter with a Bigfoot while hunting in East Texas. He'd only mentioned it that one time, but it had been enough. Norm exhausted the library's stash of books on Bigfoot, lake creatures and Thunderbirds. When online bookstores came along, offering a worldwide library of tomes on the unexplained, he dove in headfirst. He went and got a degree in zoology so he'd have a broad knowledge base of all known creatures, their habits and habitats. With that in hand, it would be easier for him to separate the known from the unknown.

And now here he was, hungover but with a decent check in his bank account from the state of Ohio, talking to his cat while wearing a straw hat.

The microwave dinged. He set the sausage aside to cool. His stomach growled. He wasn't sure whether it was from a craving to tear into the patty of processed meat or a growing need to expel last night's party.

"Let's liven this day up a little, sh-shall we, Salem?"

The cat crept down from the window and made figure eights around his legs.

Norm booted up his laptop, opened his iTunes account and clicked Play on his Shooter Jennings playlist. Waylon's wayward son growled out his mix of country and Southern rock while Norm bit into the sausage.

"Jimmy D-D-Dean, where did you go wrong?" Norm dropped his breakfast onto the plate with an eye roll.

He must really be awake now. The stutter came back as sure as night follows day the moment he was truly and fully awake, as if his awareness of himself and his place in the world was enough to smack the confidence straight from him.

Salem jumped up on the table, putting a paw on the laptop.

Opening up his e-mail, he saw over four hundred messages. Sure, a few were spam, but he got a lot of e-mails from believers and skeptics alike. Being unplugged for a week wreaked havoc on his in-box.

"Why don't w-w-we write to Sam first?" he said. Salem meowed.

Norm and Sam Willet had been friends for the past ten years, ever since he'd gone to Pine Bush in New York to film a piece on big cats roaming around the farms up there in a place where there should be no big cats. He'd met Sam Willet when he and the crew visited his farm to take some B-roll. It turned out the old man had an incredible story of his own to tell, so long as the young cryptozoologist kept it hush-hush. Norm had proven himself a worthy confidant, and the two had been corresponding by e-mail ever since.

Whereas Norm had an interest in a wide range of cryptids—land, air and sea—old Sam was fixated on one particular nasty little creature. Norm had promised to keep him apprised of any mention of the beast.

Just last night, Norm had read an online article from a mid-Jersey paper about several campers hearing something unnatural in the woods. One of them was brave enough to leave the tent, looking up at the night sky just in time to catch the fleeting form of a winged creature that shouldn't be.

It was the second Jersey Devil sighting in as many weeks.

Maybe, Norm thought as he typed, *we have the start of something we can both sink our teeth into.*

Chapter Five

"This is not one of your better ideas," Joanne whispered, sitting upright, still zipped in her sleeping bag.

A chilling, distant cry of an animal had woken her from a light sleep. Her heart felt as if it were pounding out of her chest.

Noah rolled over to face her.

"What?" he said.

"Didn't you hear that?"

"You mean that owl?"

She slapped his sleeping bag, hoping she got his chest underneath. "That wasn't an owl. It sounded like . . . I don't know . . . like a kid that's been hurt really bad."

Joanne's father had been an avid camper. She'd grown up in the woods of Maine and New Hampshire. The cry of an owl or frightened fox was nothing new to her. What she'd just heard out there, beyond the flimsy safety of their tent, came from no animal she'd ever heard before.

Noah tried to put an arm around her. "Why are you freaking out so much?" His voice was thick from the six-pack of beer he'd had before they turned in. Joanne wished they'd kept the little fire going.

"I don't know. Maybe it's because you have me in the middle of nowhere scouting out places where a monster has been said to live for a couple of hundred years," Joanne said, pulling the top of her sleeping bag up to her chin. She knew she sounded ridiculous, but it's how she felt.

"Oh, come on, honey, you know all those stories of the Jersey Devil aren't real. Unless you're talking about the hockey team." He laughed, but she wasn't amused.

"I don't know. All the locals we talked to seemed pretty sure it's real," she said.

"They were messing with us. We're outsiders. The moment I said I was starting a Jersey Devil camping tour, they went into their 'fuck with the interlopers' bit."

"But there wasn't a single person who didn't believe in it. I was cornered by a woman in the restroom who practically begged me to stop what we were doing. She looked pretty sincere. I think if I stayed any longer, she would have started crying."

Noah shifted so he was on his back, hands behind his head.

"There's something else about the Pinelands I should have warned you about that may change your mind about all the local yokel tales of the devil flying through the night searching for victims."

She shot him a cutting glance, but in the dark, she knew there was no way for him to see it.

"Oh, so you wait until we're all the way out here to tell me the truth?"

"It's not as if I lied to you, Jo. There's just a teeny part I left out. The Wharton State Forest isn't just the center of most modern-day Jersey Devil sightings. There may also be some pot farms here and there."

"Are you kidding me?" Now Joanne was fuming. Illegal pot farms were dangerous places to stumble upon. They were always guarded by armed men who wouldn't give a second thought to shooting you the moment you crossed their invisible line. When she lived in Maine, she'd heard stories about backpackers taking a wrong turn, stepping into dangerous situations. When people went in the woods and never came out, most people assumed they'd stumbled into a pot farm and were now fertilizer. It was a growing problem in the United States as demand increased. Naturalists were pro-legalization of pot more for their safety than for getting high.

Noah said, "Look, it's just something I've heard. No one has any proof."

Joanne thought back to their long drive through the endless, pitted roads of the Pinelands. They were literally in the ass end of God's country. Yet, she'd spied a lot of nice houses, some of them brand-new estates surrounded by thick gates. What kind of work out here could net a person the money needed to build places like that? She'd bet her life that at least half of those amazing houses were owned by pot farmers.

Noah had camped about five times in his entire life. The Jersey Devil camping tour was a cool idea. There were other tours taking people to places the monster had been sighted since the 1700s, but none of them promised an entire weekend experience, sleeping in the very spots it called home. Thanks to all those cable shows, interest in creatures like the Jersey Devil was rising. Noah said that if Jersey Devil enthusiasm died down, they could always change it to a tour of haunted ghost towns in the Pinelands.

He needed her camping expertise, and she was glad to help.

But now his stupidity could get them killed.

"You have no idea how dangerous it is," she said. "People die all the time hiking blindly."

"But if we stayed on the trails, we wouldn't get to the good spots." He reached out to turn on the lantern. Joanne grabbed his hand.

"Don't!"

"Why?"

"You'll give us away, idiot."

"Afraid the Jersey Devil will see us as he's flying around?"

It took all of her strength not to scream in frustration. She loved Noah. She really did. But his whole man-child act was wearing thin now that they were both approaching thirty.

Joanne said, "If we're on the outskirts of a pot farm, we don't need a beacon drawing them to us. They might even know we're out here now, making those noises to scare us off. They could have seen our fire earlier."

"I think you're being a tad paranoid. You sure you didn't sneak off to one of those farms by yourself and take a few samples?"

She lay down and turned her back to him.

"I really wanna punch you right now." Grinding her molars, Joanne contemplated socking him in the jaw if he said one more stupid thing.

She heard him rustling in his sleeping bag. "Look, I'm sorry I didn't tell you about it before. I realize now I should have, considering you're the expert out here. But this is a pretty famous location. An old glassworks used to be here, along with a little town. That town was plagued by the Jersey Devil for a whole month in the summer of 1823. They say it killed their dogs, chased kids and would scamper on the rooftops, clawing to get in at night. After the factory closed, the town was abandoned. A fire eventually wiped out all the structures. We have five more nights and campsites to scout. Please don't be mad. If you want, we can pack up and leave right now."

Her anger softened. He was really into this whole venture and could make it work—if his own stupidity didn't get in the way.

"Is there anything else I should know?" she asked.

"That's it. I promise. So, do you want to pull up stakes?"

Joanne sighed. "No, it won't do us any good to go stumbling in the dark." She got out of her sleeping bag and rummaged through her pack. She took the bowie knife from a side pocket and placed it, in its leather sheath, next to her inflatable pillow.

"Jo, I really am sorry." Noah caressed her shoulders, kissing the back of her neck. Staying mad at him was difficult. It was like being upset with a toddler for drawing on the walls. He didn't know any better. At least that's what she always told herself.

"It's okay. In the morning, we're going to *carefully* scout the area. If you plan to make this one of the campsites, we have to make sure it's safe."

He showed his appreciation of her forgiveness in one of her favorite ways, and when he finished, she drifted off to sleep.

The next morning, Noah shouted for her to wake up.

"Babe, come out here. You have to see this!"

Groggy, Joanne extricated herself from her sleeping bag, stumbling to get her boots on. The sun was out and there was a slight chill in the air. Noah stood by the fire pit they'd made, shirtless, hands on hips, looking down.

"Good morning to you, too," Joanne said, wiping sleep crud from her eyes.

"Come here," he urged, motioning for her to stand beside him. "Look at that!"

He pointed at two hoofprints by the circle of stones. They were too small to be those of a horse, but too big to be something like a goat.

"What do you make of that?" he said.

"I'd say some stray animal walked through here last night."

He smiled, and it made her nervous.

"All right, now look up."

She craned her neck back, staring at the branches of a pine tree.

"What do you see?" he asked.

"Nothing."

"What should you see?"

Her breath instantly left her lungs.

"Holy crap, where's our pack?"

They'd tied their pack with food on a very high branch last night. It was gone.

"Look a little higher," Noah said.

She looked up and up until she got dizzy. There, at the very top of the one-hundred-foot tree, were the fragmented remains of their pack. Before she realized it, she was gripping his hand.

"I don't think those were pot farmers last night," he said.

Chapter Six

April Willet, tall as a model, her mousy brown hair trailing behind her, ran up to the tractor holding her cell phone out. The sun caught her wide, green eyes, sparkling like emeralds. "Ben, did you see this?"

Her big brother slipped his Beats headphones off and shut the tractor down. Just like his grandfather, he'd been listening to Dean Martin while he worked the cornfield this morning. He'd picked up the expensive headphones to save his ears from all the damage the farm machinery could do to him. And it was a good way to shut out the rest of the world.

"April, I got a lot to do today. Why aren't you at the store?"

Willet Farms comprised three farms in Pine Bush. Old Boompa had built himself quite the little empire. They even had a combo farmer's market and general store that April had been put in charge of when she turned twenty-one. They sold fresh produce, apple juice and ciders, honey, pies, jams, you name it. April preferred being in the store to working the farms, and she was good at it. In the fall, she organized hayrides, pumpkin and apple picking, and even did a little haunted maze come October.

"Brenda's covering," she said, handing him the phone.

"What is it?" he said, shielding the sun from the screen. It was almost impossible to see what she'd pulled up.

"It's another Jersey Devil sighting," she said as matter-of-factly as she would note a rabbit hopping out of a row of corn. "That makes three this month."

Because she spent a lot of her time outside the store, tending to the produce they kept in wooden bins, her skin was bronze and smooth. Ben had caught his best friend, Steven, staring hard at her a few days earlier. He hadn't liked the look in his friend's eyes, so he grabbed him by the collar and showed him the door a little rougher than he'd had to. They hadn't spoken since. Sure, April was twenty-five, but he was still her older brother by five years and insanely protective of her. It was a miracle he'd let Alan marry her, not that April could be stopped once she set her mind to something—even marrying a dillwad.

Ben (his parents liked to joke that they'd named him after that movie with the rats) may have been the shortest in the family of giants and Amazons at five-seven, but he was also possibly the strongest. He definitely had the worst temper, even more so lately, which was why he liked to work out here alone with his headphones on. Well, he was never entirely alone. A pint of Johnnie Walker kept his pocket company most days.

Ben cracked his neck and took a swig from his bottle of water that had some splashes of whiskey. Everyone thought he drank iced tea—a lot.

"You stopped me for that?" he said, unable to hide the irritation in his voice. April looked as if he'd lashed out and smacked her.

"I thought you'd be interested," she said. "Three is a lot, you know."

He let out a deep breath and handed the phone back to her. "I'm sorry. It is?"

April grinned. "Big-time. If this keeps up, we'll have another 1909 on our hands."

Looking across the cornfield, feeling the weight of the work to be done, he said, "Okay, why don't we all talk about it later at dinner?" He went to put his headphones back on, but she grabbed his arm.

"Boompa's gonna fucking freak."

"He just might, if three is as big a deal as you say it is."

"Trust me. All right, go back to your plowing, young man. I'll go tell Mom and Dad."

"Ape, save it for dinner. They had to go out to do some stuff. They'll be back later."

For a moment she looked crestfallen, then she brightened. "I can't wait to see Boompa's face."

She ran back toward the store, which was a considerable distance from the tractor.

Ben brought the big machine back to life.

The whole town looked to the Willets as the models for the simple, honest American family. If only they knew the glue that held them all together.

Bill Willet met his wife, Carol, for lunch at their favorite diner. Carol had an appointment at the bank and Bill said he had to talk to their insurance agent about making some changes to their homeowner's policy.

He'd stopped at the barber, greasing Phil's palm with a ten-spot to bump him up so he could get to the diner in time. A couple of the men waiting griped, all older with less hair on their head than Bill had on his nuts.

Phil told them to pipe down. They were retired and had no plans, while Bill had to break his back so they could buy local and feel better about themselves.

Carol reached across the table and ran her hands over Bill's freshly shorn head. "I love it when it's fuzzy," she said.

"There seems to be a little less fuzz every time I come here," he said, spooning out a chunk of ice cream.

Bill smiled, giving the acting performance of a lifetime. If Carol only knew where he'd actually gone before the barber.

The weird circular movement his hand had been making off and on had been easy to conceal and explain away, to himself at least. It must have been a pinched nerve or pulled muscle. Hell, he'd been pulling and pinching things every day on the farm.

But when he began to lose his train of thought, forget simple words and names, and found it hard to follow a simple story in a newspaper, he got concerned. Not wanting to alarm Carol or the kids, he'd made an appointment to see Doc Stasolla. The man took enough blood to feed a nest of vampires. He brought up two words Bill had never heard of before—Huntington's disease. He explained how it was a degenerative disorder of the brain, how it affected motor and mental skills, and even though it sounded dire, he could be wrong. If he was right, they were making great strides in treating the disease.

Walking to the barber, Bill looked up Huntington's disease on his iPhone.

It was bad. Suddenly, he had the immediate urge to take a shit, but there was nowhere to go. He jammed the phone in his pocket, trying to put everything out of his mind.

He said he could be wrong.

But if he was right . . . Shit. Bill would end up a twitching, mush-brained vegetable.

Jesus H. Christ.

His father liked to say he was as tall as he was wide, though that was a bit of an exaggeration. He was all muscle from a lifetime working on the farm. People who didn't know him veered away from him because he looked meaner than a rabid raccoon. A lot of that was due to the harelip that gave his face a dastardly turn. Those close to him knew that he was just a big softy. His daughter, April, was the one they should watch out for.

It was all going to be taken away by diseased cells as they ate away his brain.

No. Stop thinking the worst. Doc's been wrong before. Remember when he told us Ben just had a bad case of the flu when he was ten? He never once thought it was Lyme disease until we took him to that specialist in Westchester. Doc's not infallible, and he is getting older.

Ben. Now there was a worry they'd been gnawing on a lot. The son who returned from Afghanistan wasn't the same man they'd watch leave when Obama swore to end the war. Fucking liar, just like all the others. Ben had always kept to himself, but even more so since he came back. There were things he wasn't telling them. It was tempting to try to force them out, but Bill knew they had to wait until he was good and ready.

And now there was this.

No point telling Carol. Not yet. Wait until the tests come back.

"Will you take that gum out of your mouth?" Carol said.

Bill chuckled. "I didn't even know it was in there." He wrapped it in his napkin. He went through two packs of Big Red a day. It beat smoking and was a hell of a lot cheaper. Hey, at least he didn't have cancer, right?

Carol's phone vibrated. She swiped her thumb across the screen, read for a bit and frowned.

"Bad news?" Bill asked, dipping a French fry in brown gravy.

"No. April sent me a link to a report on a Jersey Devil sighting."

That made Bill sit up straighter in the booth. "That makes three in just the past few weeks."

Carol nodded. "She said she'll tell your father and Daryl at dinner. You think it's time?"

Bill got quiet, thinking things over. Old Boompa was definitely going to take notice, but he'd be cautious. He'd waited almost sixty years. He wouldn't go crashing headlong now. But he didn't have another sixty years ahead of him.

"Let's just hope it's getting real close," he said, scratching at his side, wondering how long it would be until he could no longer control his hand.

Just focus. Even if you do have it, this Huntington's disease (should I ask if it's something linked to people who hunt?), you're okay now. Maybe things are happening now for a reason.

They finished their meal in silence, each running through mental checklists. Three was a lot in such a short time span. Of course, it could be three hoaxes, one inspired by the other.

Or could it be what they were waiting for? The dark cloud was on the horizon, and they'd been preparing to do some serious storm chasing.

Chapter Seven

"I'm all B-B-Bigfooted out at the moment," Norm Cranston said to Terry, his agent, over lunch at Villa Italia. Terry lived and worked in Brooklyn. He flew down to meet Norm in North Carolina once every few months. They'd been seated at one of the few outside tables. A slight breeze kept blowing Norm's napkin off his lap.

"It's a quick in and out," Terry said before shoveling garlic and cream coated gnocchi in his mouth. "You fly to Washington on a Thursday, you're home by Saturday."

Norm sighed. "I haven't even been back from Ohio for a week yet. I'm not getting any y-younger. Seven days in the wild takes me twice as long to recover. I missed my bed. I missed my toilet. I'm just tired. The last thing I want to do is h-h-hop on a plane across the country just to look at nothing so the Vacation Channel can edit it to make it seem like it's the place to go for amateur m-monster hunters."

Terry pointed at him with his fork. "You're getting jaded."

"And you want to get paid, no matter h-h-how I feel.

Look, I'll take the next gig after this one. Just let it s-slide, okay?"

A pretty girl walked by their table, hips swaying seductively in a very tight skirt. Her eyes lingered on Norm's straw hat. He thought he saw a flicker of recognition in her eyes, but she was gone before she made the connection. He was king of the nerds thanks to his public appearances talking about mythical animals, but every now and then a woman totally out of his league would come his way, wanting to know what it was like to be on TV.

"Because you look like shit, I'll give you a break this time," Terry said, emptying his wineglass and signaling the waiter for a refill.

Norm pushed a meatball around his plate. The pasta smothered in Bolognese sauce seemed to have expanded exponentially in his gut.

"Ah, Terry, you're a p-p-prince," Norm said. "And thanks for the compliment."

"You look like you haven't slept in days."

"Funny thing is, that's all I've been doing. I didn't sleep out in the woods. My back was killing me the w-w-whole time. Plus, I forgot to bring my acid reflux meds, so my insides were burning. I told you, I need time to get back to s-stasis."

"The History Channel is thinking of sending a crew to you in a couple of weeks. They want to do a segment with you on that fish."

"What fish?"

Terry gesticulated with his hands as if he could mold the fish in question from thin air. "You know, the big one that was dead for like a million years."

"The coelacanth?"

"Yeah, that's the one. It's some special about animals

that people thought were extinct but weren't. You know the routine. They shoot for a whole day, you get a few minutes airtime. The usual pay, which isn't bad for sitting in your living room looking respectable."

Norm ran his hands down his long goatee. It was a reassuring tic he'd developed over the years. He knew he did it, but didn't feel the need to stop. What was the sense of growing facial hair if you couldn't stroke it while looking thoughtful or, in this case, intrigued?

"Sounds good to me. Book it if th-they confirm."

Terry clapped his hands, his way of signaling that subject was done and moving on to the next order of business. "Okay, now let's talk about your book. Crypto Press is hot nuts to hear what you have up your sleeve. That last book on the skunk apes sold really well for them. If they can get two books from you a year, everyone will be happy."

Norm wished the book contracts paid well, but they were really labors of love. In this day and age, the value of the writer seemed to shrink with each passing year, while idiots who starred on reality TV shows were thrown cartloads of cash to have some poor slob ghostwrite their salacious autobiography or cookbook. He was in a strange position, being a person on reality-based programs, but no one wanted to hear about his sex life or his recipe for lasagna. The only thing juicy about his story was the anti-anxiety pills he took before appearing on camera to stifle his stutter. And considering he went through about one prescription, thirty pills in all, a year, that hardly qualified as a drug scandal.

He replied, "I h-h-have something I need to look into a little more. In fact, I may be going up your way soon.

There are some Jersey D-D-Devil reports that sound interesting."

"You're going to the Pine Barrens?"

As aloof as Terry seemed, Norm knew the man was fascinated by the things he studied and investigated. He beta read all of Norm's books and had pretty good recall.

"Yep. Never been there b-before. Never really had to. The Devil has been keeping a low profile for a long while."

"You think you live in the sticks? This place is like Manhattan compared to the Barrens. I went there a couple of times when I was in high school. You could drink and bang all night and there wasn't anyone for miles to bother you. But at night, it's creepy as hell."

"So you know all about the state pet monster?"

Terry thought for a moment and said, "Just the basics. It was supposed to be the thirteenth child of old Momma Leeds back in the 1700s. When she finally pushed it out, it wasn't human at all. It ate the family, flew off and has been terrorizing people ever since."

Norm bobbed his head. "Not b-bad. You're just missing a few points. You see, when Leeds was in the worst of her l-l-labor with the child, she cursed it to God or the devil. The story goes either way. So does the b-birth. Some say the baby boy came out normal, then transformed into a creature that was part g-goat, bat and dragon. Others, like you, say it came out tainted by her curse, a living d-demon. It burst through the lone window in the Leeds home and plagued the f-family for many years. It feeds on livestock, stray animals, and takes delight in scaring people half to death, like a true devil."

"You don't believe it's alive, do you? It would be over two hundred years old."

"It could be a flesh-and-blood a-animal, one that had interbred with others, passing down its genetics. Or the whole thing could have been a c-c-c-over story concocted by the L-Leedses, who may have seen their child was deformed, killed it quickly and needed to explain why kid number thirteen wasn't a-around. Or, maybe the kid did survive, someone with such unsightly physical traits that he's lived a feral kind of life, maybe snatching a stray woman here and there to spread his seed. Either of those e-e-explanations seem more likely to me than a cursed child that transforms into a b-beast that seemingly never dies."

Terry sat back in his seat and looked up at the passing clouds. "You ever in your wildest imaginings thought you'd make a living off this kind of stuff?"

Norm chuckled. "As a kid, I hoped, but figured I was doomed to work like my father and all the f-fathers around me. Trust me, I don't take this for granted. Plus, there's always the chance I'll not only get to debunk a myth, but discover a new species. That wouldn't be too sh-shabby."

"Well, better you than me on this little foray. Those forests are not for the faint of heart."

Norm sipped at his beer. "You're just a city boy."

Terry waved him off. "That wasn't it. I've been to a lot of places in my life, some of them remote and weird, but the Pine Barrens take the cake. If anyplace is going to have a strange creature living in it, that's the joint. You'll see. Fucking Spooky City."

His agent looked truly uneasy. That gave Norm a good laugh. "I'll remember to b-bring my flashlight."

Terry waved for the check. "Do yourself a favor. Remember to bring your gun. If the Jersey Devil doesn't get you, something, or someone, else will."

* * *

When Wyatt pulled his father's handgun from his pocket, Jackson and Alex took a step back, eyes glued to the steel death dealer.

"Whoa," Alex said. "Where did you get that?"

"I know the combination to my father's gun safe," Wyatt replied, somehow feeling older than his twelve years holding the gun.

"He's gonna kill you," Jackson said, reaching out to touch it. Wyatt swept it away, stowing it back in his pocket.

"Only if he finds out," he said. "And the only way he'll find out is if you blab to your fat mother."

"I'm not saying anything," Jackson said. He'd long since given up defending his mother. She *was* kind of heavy. She'd even started using those scooter carts at the supermarket this past year. She was also the town gossip, oblivious to the fact that most of the gossip floating around centered on her growing girth and how she was probably an unfit mother.

Her son was, after all, in his friend's yard wondering what to do with a pilfered gun.

"Hey, I can go through the recycling bin outside my house and get some bottles we can shoot at. My father had some friends over the other night and there are a ton of beer bottles in there," Alex offered. He had a couple of BB guns that they all shared from time to time, taking potshots at trees, the occasional squirrel and, if they really wanted to prove they were deadeyes, birds in flight. So far, the wildlife had emerged from their BB gun afternoons unscathed, though Wyatt swore he winged the hind end of a black squirrel.

Wyatt nodded. "Yeah, that'll be cool. Go fill a bag with them."

Alex sprinted out of Wyatt's yard. His house was three lots over.

There was no question as to where they were going to try out the gun. Wyatt's backyard abutted the southwest demarcation for the Brendan Byrne State Forest. In fact, once you walked the fifty feet in his yard, you were met by tightly packed trunks of pine trees that seemed to stretch on forever.

Last summer, the three of them had set out to see how far they could go while walking a straight line until they found another human being. Armed with a compass, full canteens, beef jerky and one of Alex's BB guns, they'd marched until their legs were sore, falling far short of civilization. Exhausted, they drank their water, ate their jerky and shot all of their BBs straight up into the air for no discernible reason other than to see if any would hit them on the return to terra firma. The walk home seemed to take forever.

It did teach them that the forest of the state park was like stepping into another world, one that was hidden from their own. They could have built a hundred-foot bonfire out there and no one would have known.

Alex came back, the bottles clinking in the plastic shopping bag. A lock of his blond hair escaped from under his Nets cap. "Got 'em!"

"Good." Wyatt, who was taller and bigger than his friends, took the bag and headed for the woods.

"How many bullets you got?" Jackson asked, hopping over a fallen tree.

"There are six in the chamber and I grabbed four more," Wyatt said. He knew he sounded cool as hell.

Six in the chamber. He'd heard someone say that in an action movie once. It felt awesome to actually mean it.

"Won't your father notice they're missing?" Jackson said.

Alex backhanded his arm. "Jesus, do you have to worry about everything? Stop being such a lame ass."

Jackson had always been the jittery conscience of their trio. Sometimes he annoyed the hell out of Wyatt. But today, even Jackson couldn't bring him down.

He helped ease his fears by saying, "Nah, my dad's got like hundreds of bullets in the safe. Most are in boxes, but he's got a few just sitting there. No way he knows how many are in there and even if he did, I can't see him counting them."

Wyatt's mother had been cleaning the house, some '80s hair band blasting out of the Bose speakers in the living room. With the windows open, the music invaded the entire neighborhood. Wyatt knew they were getting to a good spot to shoot when he could no longer hear her old-people music. She even still wore faded black concert shirts she'd gotten back in the day. He thanked God she'd ditched the high, heavily hair-sprayed metal hair. But she was still embarrassing.

They trudged along wordlessly for another ten minutes. Each was lost in the excitement and feeling of danger.

"How about here?" Alex said when they came upon the rotted foundation of a house. All that was left were crumbling stones at four corners. The wood had rotted and returned to the earth long ago. There were lots of places like that out here. Wyatt's father told him that the Pinelands were once filled with all kinds of factories and towns and even resorts. Things changed and the places were abandoned. He admonished him to never,

ever, go into a structure that was still standing. They were dangerous places and could get him and his friends killed.

"This is good. We could set the bottles up over there." He pointed to a tree that had grown at a sharp angle. Must have been damaged by a windstorm decades ago. Now it looked like an old man's crooked spine. A thick, wide limb was the perfect shelf for the bottles.

"Come on, help me set them up," Alex said to Jackson.

Wyatt took the gun back out, unable to get over how heavy it was. For something so small, it felt as if gravity had a special affection for the gun.

This was going to be epic.

He looked over at the sound of breaking glass.

"Sorry," Jackson said, pushing leaves over the dead soldier with his sneaker. "It slipped."

"It doesn't matter," Wyatt said. "They're all going to be broken soon."

Alex chuckled, taking great care to make sure each bottle was perfectly balanced. It was a calm, clear day, but here, under the dim canopy of the trees, sudden gusts of wind trapped and fleeting between the rows of mighty pines were no stranger to them.

"Can I go first?" Alex asked, eyeing one of the bottles.

"No way," Wyatt said.

"Come on. How many times have I let you use my BB gun? Like a hundred?"

"I don't mind going last," Jackson said. Wyatt knew why. He was hoping there'd be no more bullets by the time it was his turn. Sure, he was intrigued that Wyatt had swiped the gun, but he could tell his friend was kind of scared.

"How about this," Wyatt replied, a compromise

popping into his head. "I'll take the first shot, but then you take the next three."

"Shit, yeah," Alex said with a big grin.

There were seven bottles on the branch, crying out to be shattered. "I think that's enough," Wyatt said.

"Just one more," Jackson said, balancing a Coors bottle with the tip of his finger. Alex ran up beside Wyatt.

"You think it has a huge kick?"

"I doubt it. It's just a small handgun."

"Yeah, well, you better be ready, just in case. I think you're supposed to keep your arm stiff, like with your elbow locked," Alex said.

"Don't do that," Jackson said, still working at the bottles. "You have to keep it loose. I watched a bunch of videos on YouTube about it."

Wyatt knew enough to listen to Jackson. Of the three of them, he was the one with the good grades. When he wasn't studying, he was looking up how to do all kinds of stuff on the Web.

Wyatt opened the chamber so he and Alex could see the bullets nestled in their chambers.

"This is crazy," Alex said. "Can I hold the spare bullets?"

"Sure." Wyatt fumbled for them in his pocket, handing them over. "Come on, Jackson, I'm dying of old age out here."

When he looked over to his friend, he almost dropped the gun.

Alex let out a short, incomprehensible grunt, taking an involuntary step back.

Jackson saw their faces and said, "What's the matter?"

He didn't see the creature standing right behind him.

Chapter Eight

Jackson screamed as Wyatt pulled the trigger.

He's trying to kill me!

Diving to his right, he covered his ears as his friend fired off all six rounds. He thought for sure he'd been hit.

Is this what it feels like to be shot? Numb? Did he hit a main nerve? Oh, my God, how will I stop the bleeding?

"Stay down!" Alex screamed.

Stay down? Why did he want him to stay down? Was Wyatt reloading to finish him off? If he was shot way out here, he was as good as dead.

Rolling onto his back, Jackson felt dizzy, he assumed from blood loss.

A fetid gust of wind blanketed his upturned face. He had to fight to keep his lunch down. Before he could take a clear breath, another blast of oxygen left to rot burrowed down his nose and throat.

Looking up, he screamed.

A creature that shouldn't be possible in nature flapped its wings ten feet over him. Thick green fluid leaked from a spot on its rib cage.

Wyatt shouted, "Get the fuck away from him!"

He must have reloaded, because two more cracks split the air, deafening Jackson.

The creature bleated like a wounded goat, which is kind of what its face looked like, turned and pushed its way through the air currents to the top of the trees. Jackson watched it circle once before heading what he assumed was south. His mind was in such a fog, he wasn't sure he could even spell his own name at this point.

There was a mad crunching of leaves, and Wyatt and Alex were on their knees beside him.

"Are you okay?" Wyatt asked. Sweat poured down the sides of his head. His face was pale and Jackson detected a slight tremor in his grip as he helped him into a sitting position. "I didn't hit you, did I?"

Jackson took several breaths, running his hands over his body, looking for wounds or blood. He almost wept with relief when he realized he was unscathed.

"I'm fine. I'm fine."

Alex urged them, "Come on, we gotta get outta here. What do we do if that thing comes back? We only have two bullets left."

Wyatt agreed with rapid nods. "He's right. Come on, Jack."

The world spun when he stood, but he didn't fall. Alex was already twenty feet ahead of them, his legs picking up speed. Wyatt held on to Jackson's elbow as they ran to catch up.

"What was that thing?" Jackson asked, constantly checking what sky he could see through the gaps in the trees.

"Dude, I think it was the Jersey Devil."

As much as Jackson wanted to deny it, he was afraid Wyatt was right. Everyone who lived in the Pinelands knew about the Jersey Devil. They were taught the legend over and over by older family members and friends. You could throw a stone in any direction in the Pinelands and hit someone who had either had an encounter with the horrifying beast or knew someone who had.

The thing that flapped its leathery wings over him had to be the Devil. It was almost as large as a man with a head bordering on a goat and a horse, with a long neck, compact body and long, whipping tail.

The boys ran, not slowing down even when painful stitches stabbed their sides. When they finally burst from the tree line into Wyatt's yard, they collapsed onto the freshly mowed grass, lying on their backs, gasping.

After a while, Alex said, "Holy shit, Wyatt, you shot the fucking Jersey Devil!"

Wyatt ran his hand over his sweaty forehead.

"I did, didn't I?"

Jackson added, "I don't think anyone's ever done that before. I'm pretty sure you hit it, too. It looked like it was bleeding, but not regular blood."

They lay in silence, cautiously scanning the sky.

There was no sense swearing one another to an oath of silence. One, or all three of them, was going to tell. Some secrets were just too big to fit inside a person.

Sam Willet spent a hot afternoon in the henhouse collecting eggs and making minor repairs. In this kind of cloying heat, the stench could burn the nose hairs from a man, but Sam had developed an immunity to it long ago. A farmer with a strong olfactory sense was in for a long, tough haul.

The rest of the family was scattered about the three

farms, with April happy in the air-conditioned store. He grabbed a green bandana from his pocket and wiped his brow. The hens clucked nonstop, chattering on about whatever birds with a brain the size of a pea concerned themselves with.

There was a time when he used to talk back, light-heartedly discussing his day and the chores he had to do while they got to sit around and yammer all day. His wife had caught him a couple of times, and the ribbing he'd endured was enough to shut his yap for good. Lauren was probably watching him right now, waiting for him to slip into chicken whisperer mode. Sam smiled at the thought.

He eyed the large eyebolt in the floor of the coop. Before he'd put a spit shine to the coop, he hadn't been able to see it through the feathers and straw and shit.

"Can't hurt to check on things," he said aloud to himself, not the hens.

Bending down to grab the ring wasn't as easy as it used to be, but he also wasn't grumbling in pain. The old back still had some life left in it, despite decades of doing his best to wear it out.

As he pulled, a doorway in the floor opened. One of the more curious hens hopped down to inspect it and fell into the darkness.

"Damn stupid bird," he chuffed, pulling the door all the way back until it rested at a ninety-degree angle.

He walked down a narrow set of wooden steps, reached out, found the chain and pulled. A sixty-watt bulb gave light to the tightly packed room. Sam grabbed the hen with both hands and brought it back up to the coop. He then closed the door behind him. It didn't even so much as creak. Sam always carried a can of three-in-one oil in his back pocket. He had a thing about rusty hinges.

Sam ran his hands over the mounted .308 caliber Russian SKS rifles. There were six in all, purchased over the years at various gun shows. Metal cases containing all the ammo needed to hold back an army were stacked beneath the rifles. The SKS was a workhorse of a rifle, able to shoot even when banged around or covered in muck. They'd always been his personal favorite. Opposite them were Ben's AR-15s, polished to a high gloss.

There were plenty of handguns, so many he'd lost count years ago, as well as tasers, utility knives, daggers and even bayonets. April's first pink pepper spray was on a shelf, the contents empty. She'd emptied it in her ex's face one night when he wasn't taking to the notion of divorce. The next day, she'd come down here and placed it on that shelf as a reminder that all those years of preparation had been worth it.

Having lived through several wars, including the scariest of all, the Cold War, Sam swore that he'd never be caught with his pants around his ankles. He wasn't one of those doomsday preppers, and truth be told, if a nuclear bomb hit, his biggest hope was that the farm was far enough from any major targets to keep them safe from the initial fallout. He'd meant to build a proper shelter in the seventies, but the demands of the farm took up all his time. No, if a bomb ever hit, the family would have to stick to the basement of the house or the storm cellar.

Or the weapons cache, though that wouldn't hold a person for long. He'd stocked some jugs of water and K-rations just in case, but it wouldn't see anyone trapped down here through to the end of Armageddon.

That really wasn't what this room was for.

If he wanted to do what no one else had ever done, he needed to be ready. No bringing a knife to a gunfight. Better to bring an atom bomb to a fistfight.

Boompa settled into the lone chair, took down a rifle and began the calming process of cleaning it. He whistled an old Mel Tormé tune, happy to be out of the heat and away from the nattering chickens for a spell.

Daryl Willet lay sprawled on the couch, a bowl of chocolate ice cream on his stomach, his Mets hat pulled down low over his brow. He watched a rerun of *The King of Queens*, his laughter making the bowl teeter on his belly. It'd been a long hot day and he was bone tired.

"That's where I want to live," he said. "Right there in Queens. I want neighbors I can touch just by reaching out my window, restaurants and clubs down the block and easy access to the city."

April was in a rocker tapping away on her laptop. Since her divorce, she'd moved into the farmhouse at the Willet Farms vineyard. The vineyard provided the grapes for a thriving winery over in New Paltz. *Drink Local, Taste International* was the slogan. The vineyard was another example of Boompa's taking a gamble and winning. She loved the cozy house, especially the part about not having Alan anywhere near it, but she also liked to be around her family. She ate dinner with them most nights and hung around for a couple of hours later. It was comforting, and Lord knew she needed comfort.

"You also want to deliver packages and be married to a wife who scares the crap out of you?" she said.

Daryl tipped his cap up. "I'd work in Manhattan or Brooklyn, get a nice desk job making six figures. My wife would be a Puerto Rican honey who owned a hair salon and left smoke in her tracks because she's so hot."

April laughed. "That's a pretty nice fantasy life you have there, you sad, sad schmuck."

He cringed. "Hag. It could happen. I'm not old like you and Ben. I have my whole life ahead of me."

"Oh, please, you're not that much younger than me."

"Five years buys me a lot of time," he said, spooning the rest of the ice cream in his mouth. "All I know is that I don't want to spend my life on the farm. A whole different world is just an hour car ride away."

"Well, then you should look at going back to college. Not many six-figure jobs out there for a guy with one year of community college under his belt."

April winced when she said it. School was a sore spot with Daryl. The kid had always had his head in the clouds. He could never stick to anything beyond the honeymoon phase. It was a miracle he'd made it through high school. He'd kept threatening to leave Pine Bush and head out to Alaska to work the pipeline at the start of his senior year. He'd even gone so far as to buy a plane ticket. The plan was to head out west with his partner in crime, Brant Halpert, but Brant got cold feet and Daryl never made it to the airport. Brant was now a baby daddy, working as a waiter at an Olive Garden in Newburgh.

"I've been looking into it," he replied, surprising her.

"Really? Where?"

"I was thinking of going to the Culinary Institute in Manhattan. Who knows? I downloaded the fall course booklet last week."

April leaned over the arm of the rocker and gave him a pat on the shoulder. His muscles, even in repose, were rock hard. "Way to go, little bro. I'm proud of you."

"I'm only worried about one thing," he said.

"You know Mom and Dad will pay for you. You'd be the first one in the family to get a bona fide degree."

"It's not that." He sat up, settling the bowl on the table. "I'm worried about what it would do to Boompa."

April sighed. "You know he wants what's best for you. And he knows you're not cut out for this. Cooking, yes. Heavy-duty working year in and year out, no. You bitch and whine too much to be a full-time farmer. For a big gorilla, you're soft as fresh shit."

He swiped at her with a pillow and missed.

She knew their grandfather loved Daryl in a very special way. She didn't begrudge them their close relationship. Boompa had always been a fan of underdogs and lost causes. Daryl was a true dark horse. They all knew he just needed to find his thing and he'd ride it to the top.

"I think it might upset him too much, my being away," Daryl said. "He's not getting any younger. What if something happened to him while I was away?"

You're afraid of losing him, she thought.

"It's only New York. You'd be home weekends if you wanted and could even drive home for dinner a couple times a week, if you didn't have too much homework— or partying. He'll be fine. I'll take extra care of him."

Daryl chuckled. "He'll starve if you take over the cooking."

"I'll practice," April said.

Her computer chimed an alert. There was a new message in her in-box. April clicked it open. After scanning the first few lines, she covered her open mouth with her hand.

"What is it?" Daryl asked. He turned his Mets cap around on his head.

April clicked the link in the e-mail, opening up a page from a New Jersey paper.

"Some kid shot the Jersey Devil," she said. It felt as if her heart had paused, refusing to beat until she read the entire article. Her fingertips suddenly felt ice cold.

"You're kidding, right?" Daryl said.

"I'm not, but there's always a chance the kid in the story is."

Daryl read the story over her shoulder. "That seems like a pretty wild story to make up to cover for the fact that he stole his father's gun. I'm thinking everything that's been going on down there is adding up to more than coincidence."

He and April both absentmindedly scratched at their hips.

"You think we should call a Brady family meeting?" April said.

Daryl's mouth grinned, but his eyes looked nervous. "I think we have to."

Chapter Nine

Rafael Santiago read the same story as April and Daryl Willet. He had the benefit of living in Egg Harbor City, a very close drive to the Wharton State Forest, the area that had been called the epicenter of Jersey Devil sightings. He'd loaded up his Yaris and headed straight for the Batona hiking trail that cut through the center of the forest.

The kids in the story hadn't been very far from the south entrance to the trail. Rafael figured to spend the night, armed with his camera and phone, ready to record some sweet footage for his blog.

"This'll get so many views," he said to himself, veering from the trail. "Maybe I'll use this to start my podcast."

Rafael had been blogging about strange monsters in America for two years now. He'd garnered a group of hardcore followers who supported him with page likes and sharing, but the numbers he'd hoped to have just never materialized. He took time to research every post, double-checking to make sure he had his facts straight and citing his source material. He liked to consider himself a bit of an academic. That alone should have made him the lone voice of reason in the world of the paranormal, monsters and cryptozoology.

By comparison, there were people posting outright hoaxes, and writing them poorly, who had twenty times more followers. It burned his ass, seeing such sophomoric work getting all the attention. But then he realized a few of them were doing something he hadn't considered. They would go to certain "hot spots" and film on-location pieces, like the two guys who gave a video tour of Fouke, Arkansas, where the legend of the Bigfoot of Boggy Creek was born. And there had been the kid who interviewed people in his hometown in Puerto Rico who believed they'd had encounters with the infamous Chupacabra—the goat sucker.

It amazed him that he hadn't thought of it sooner. Of course, short videos were the way to go. Hook them with a video to match their attention span, and keep them coming back for the detailed information he would link to each video.

Since his accident at the casino where he'd worked in Atlantic City—he'd taken a fall down stairs that didn't have a Caution/Wet sign—there had been plenty of time to devote to his little passion. His back was feeling better, but there were still days he could barely get out of bed. His mother was only too happy to have him back home. He was never sure if his father shared her enthusiasm. Pop was a man of few words.

The sun was starting to set, casting long, crooked shadows over the forest floor. Pretty soon it would be pitch black. Rafael had been filming his hike, giving background on the Jersey Devil, stressing that he was walking in the Devil's footsteps. He had to stop himself a couple of times. "You're being overdramatic."

Then he'd shake it off and resume, knowing that more drama equaled more views. And more views meant . . . well, it justified all of his efforts and gave him a little ego boost.

He'd ventured off the trail so he could find a spot he could claim was where the kids shot the Devil. The forests out here all looked the same. No one would know, even those kids. Filming in night vision to make it creepier, he'd tell the kids' story and hunker down to see if the beast made its return. There'd be a lot of editing that would need to be done, but he had the time. Maybe he'd make several versions. He could have a one- or two-minute teaser, a more robust five-minute video that gave all the nuts and bolts, and a full, half-hour video with music and everything.

Rafael took a swig of water, set his backpack down and took out his tripod. He wanted some nice steady shots. That *Blair Witch* shaky cam stuff made him nauseous as a viewer. He didn't want to subject his own viewers to the same fate.

After he secured the camera to the tripod, he checked his phone.

"No bars. No shock."

Not that he had anyone to call. He wore his loner badge with pride. Making friends had never been easy. It was why he enjoyed his blog and social media interaction. That was easy. He had hundreds of online "friends." What else did he need?

Setting the camera to night-vision mode, he sat still and panned around the area.

Need some good scenic shots for filler, he thought.

The wind scattered the leaves on the ground, flitting around him.

It was quiet out here. He'd never been big on the outdoors. The closest he'd gotten to camping was sleeping in his sleeping bag on the back porch once when he was ten.

There wouldn't be any sleep tonight. He didn't have camping gear. This was all about capturing something that rang of authenticity.

"Come on, critters, isn't anyone curious?" he whispered. "Give me some eye shine so I can make people wonder if the Devil is near."

Any sound or image he captured tonight could be edited and presented in a way to make his viewers believe he'd had a close encounter with the Jersey Devil.

He stiffened at the sound of scurrying behind him. Swinging the camera around, he searched for the source of the noise.

"Too late for squirrels. Any raccoons out there?"

Even with night vision, he couldn't see any sign of life. Whatever it was must have been small and fast, like a chipmunk or something. Chipmunks were too tiny for even him to make seem larger and threatening in a video.

Rafael's stomach grumbled. He went to his backpack, searching for the energy bars he'd stashed in a side pocket. They were mixed among warm cans of Red Bull. He found a bar, threw the wrapper on the ground and ate it in two bites. It was dense and sticky and tasted like peanut butter-flavored straw, but it would kill his hunger pangs.

I should get onscreen and talk about the shooting. Maybe I should read the article again so I don't have to do a million takes.

Using his phone as a flashlight, he plucked the folded

newspaper article from his jeans pocket, reading it over a couple of times, memorizing key parts in the story.

The frenetic sound of flapping wings overhead had him ducking faster than a frightened deer mouse, even though he could tell the flyby was nowhere near his head.

"Bats. Nice."

Now that was atmosphere!

"I should have gone to film school." He downed a Red Bull, crushed the can and chucked it into the darkness.

He liked the way the pine trees were bunched together to his right. They looked ominous, like a haunted wood that swallowed up curious little children. Swiveling the camera, he paused when he heard something move. It was quick, seeming to stop the moment he became aware of its presence.

The forest suddenly felt darker, the realization that he had no outdoor skills holding a more dire weight.

Rafael stayed perfectly still, taking slow, deep breaths.

What if it was a bear? New Jersey had seen an increase in bears over the past few years. A few of them had been tracked and shot recently for venturing into people's yards, one of them mortally wounding someone's dog that had been chained up.

The feeling of being watched, even stalked, twisted an icy knot in his stomach.

But wouldn't a bear be louder? Did they take their time with their prey, feeling them out? He had no idea.

There was that sound again! Only this time, it came from somewhere on his left.

A rancid smell rose from the forest floor. His nose crinkled. What was that?

You're being a baby, he thought. *It's only been dark for less than an hour and you're already freaking yourself out.*

Those sounds were real. And so was that smell.

Wait. Just look through the camera. If anything's there, you'll be able to see.

He almost smacked his forehead at his cowardice.

Tilting the viewfinder up, he peered at the screen, the brightness hurting his eyes for a moment so he couldn't make anything out. He rubbed them hard, blinking away the pain.

Rafael looked again.

He felt the warmth on his thighs before he realized he was pissing himself.

"This can't be real," he muttered, stepping away from the camera.

The image of three creatures less than ten feet ahead of him caused every hair on his body to stand on end. They were no more than a few feet tall—a trio of what looked like upright horses with wings and flicking tails. One of them looked straight at him—into him—and hissed.

"What the fuck?"

Rafael stumbled over his own feet, landing hard on his ass. He could no longer see them, but he heard their shuffling feet coming closer. Closer.

Razor-sharp teeth clamped down on his right knee-cap. Rafael wailed, trying to kick it off while protecting his face with his arms. One of the creatures snatched under his armpit, tearing through his shirt and pulling a wet chunk of flesh away. The pain was excruciating.

He cried out, the dense trees absorbing his wails.

When the third creature dove between his legs, he went from praying to be left alone to hoping he would die quickly. It must have severed an artery, because he heard a whoosh of wind, like when he and his father bled the radiators in the fall, followed by the unmistakable sluicing of his blood from the ragged wound.

They were all over him, snatching away pieces from head to toe. When he opened his mouth to scream for mercy, teeth clamped around his tongue and tore it out.

Rafael twitched as his life bled away.

The beasts danced over his body, feasting.

Chapter Ten

Norm Cranston had meant to work on his book, but he'd gotten sidetracked during some online research, casually checking for new videos on YouPorn. After clicking through several, including a playlist on big-breasted threesomes, his pants had tightened considerably. He was about to remedy the situation when his phone rang. The workout routine of the single male interrupted before it could begin.

He looked at the call display. It was Sam Willet.

Good old Boompa. Not that he'd call him that. He'd tried once and it felt strange.

"Looks like this'll have to wait," he said, closing the browser window. His cat Salem jumped onto his lap, bumping into his hard-on. He turned crimson, shooing him away. "Hey, Sam, how have you been?"

The old man sounded thirty years younger than his age. "Keeping busy as always. Got a lot of mouths to feed."

Norm thought about the man's responsibility. His farm employed not only his family, but probably a quarter of the town. And here Norm often bitched about taking care of his cat.

"You have any more UFOs up y-y-your way?" Norm asked. For a spell in the eighties and nineties, Pine Bush had been a mecca for UFO enthusiasts. On the heels of the flap of Hudson Valley sightings, the rural town had been host to unexplainable lights in the sky for over a decade. Things got so bad, they had to pass a town law forbidding stargazing on the side of the roads. UFOs had never been Norm's thing, but he did find places like Pine Bush fascinating. Aside from the aerial phenomena, there had been dozens of ghost sightings and even one case of someone claiming to have seen a Bigfoot. Norm chalked the lights up to experimental planes from the nearby military base and the rest to general excitability.

"Nah, it's been real quiet. Just the way we like it. But there is something going on not far from here that's caught our attention."

"Really? What's up?"

Norm knew what it had to be. The Willets were a lovely family, real salt of the earth people, but far from average. The realization had smacked him in the face the moment he'd walked into Sam's house and saw all of the Jersey Devil material and memorabilia scattered on the shelves and walls.

"I think you know what has somehow woken up," Sam said.

"If I didn't know better, I'd swear you sound excited."

Sam took a deep breath. "If I'm right, I have some reason to be."

"You never did tell me the whole story."

"I'm thinking that it's getting to that time to do just that. But before I do, I have to be sure. You back home or are you out in some pueblo blabbing about the Chupacabra?"

"I'm home. Just taking a break between g-gigs, trying to make some headway on this book I've been contracted to write." Salem purred at his feet. Norm scratched behind his ears. The cat flopped on the floor, rolling onto his back, wanting his belly rubbed.

"You interested in taking a trip north?" Sam asked.

"I've seen a couple of interesting reports out of the Barrens lately. Is there something else I've missed?"

"I'll send you a link to a story that came out today. No one's saying it's the Devil, but I'm not about to discount it."

Norm's e-mail bleeped. He opened the link Sam sent. His mouth went dry.

"Sam, you d-don't think . . ."

"I do, buddy, I do."

"But the Jersey Devil doesn't k-k-kill people. Maybe a dog or chicken has been attributed to it, but never a person. This just doesn't fit the history, unless you subscribe to the sensationalist crap that says it killed its family when it popped out of the womb—which I know you don't."

Sam Willet said, "You're right, I don't. For more years than I can count, I thought it was dead. I'd hoped it was alive, just keeping low, but I was starting to give up hope. Maybe it went somewhere else for a while, or hibernated, I don't know. Whatever woke it up changed it. This isn't like 1909. It's brazen now. I have to find out. For the sake of my family."

For the sake of his family? Norm couldn't imagine how the return of the Jersey Devil could have any real significance for the Willet family. Of course, it couldn't just be morbid curiosity. Not the way their fascination had been focused on the cryptid.

"Are you serious, Sam?" he asked.

"As a heart attack. And at my age, you don't joke about that." Norm grinned when he heard the old man chuckle. "Think of this as research for your next book."

He had to admit, his curiosity was piqued. Depending on where things led, this could be the book that would pad his bank account. He wondered if Sam would let him print his story, even with an assumed name. Three generations of a family gripped by tales of a monster born into legend when the country was young. What could it be that connected all those dots? At its core, the book would be about the people more than the monster, and that, in essence, was what sold.

"When are you planning to go there?" Norm asked.

"Saturday. We're all heading down."

Norm took off his straw hat, looked at the sweat-stained band, and secured it back on his head. He said, "I'll b-book a flight out of Charlotte to Newark. Tell me where to meet you."

Ben Willet sat on the back porch, nursing a beer after sneaking a few nips of Johnnie Walker from the flask he kept under the porch steps. The sun was setting in a violent display of pinks and purples, making the ribbons of clouds in the distance look like cotton candy. The screen door opened and his brother, Daryl, came out holding two beers by their longnecks.

"Figured you'd be ready for another," Daryl said.

Ben wondered if his brother knew more than he was letting on.

He drained the Rolling Rock and took the proffered Budweiser.

"Where's April?" Ben asked.

"She's coming. She's just drying the rest of the dishes."

"Mom and Dad know?"

"Nope."

"Good."

They took long pulls from their beers, staring off at the horizon. Boompa had been excited as hell all day and through dinner. He was upstairs in his room right now, packing. Their mother and father had been more subdued, warning Boompa he'd bust a heart valve if he didn't take a breath.

Ben wasn't as sold on the story as Boompa, but that didn't matter. Their grandfather was heading down to the Pine Barrens with or without them. The latter wasn't an option. They'd need him out there, especially if the old man's hunch was right.

April came out with a full glass of wine. The hem of her shirt was wet from standing close to the sink.

"Thanks for abandoning me," she said to Daryl.

"What? There was hardly anything left. This beer was calling out to me."

"You're not even legal to drink," April said, tapping the bottom of his beer with the tip of her boot.

"If I was in college, I'd be drinking a hundred times more than I do now and that would be acceptable," Daryl said.

"He's old enough to serve if he wanted, he's old enough to drink," Ben said. That closed the case. He knew they didn't defer to him because he was the oldest. No, they danced around him on eggshells because they

didn't want to upset him. Most times, it pissed him off.
Not tonight.

"Come on," Ben said, pushing off the step, headed
toward the cornfield. His brother and sister followed close
behind. When they were a few rows in, he stopped and
inspected one of the ears. It wasn't ready just yet. Ben
loved early August corn. Nothing in the world was
sweeter. He'd eat it straight off the stalk. When he was
in the Middle East, he fell asleep many a night dream-
ing about eating corn while he walked the fields.

"Okay, brother, why the secrecy?" April asked, twirling
the wine in her glass.

As kids, he and April used to pretend the cornfield
was another world, teeming with monsters and heroes,
booby traps and secret lairs. Somehow, even if they'd
been fighting like cats and dogs all day, the moment
they entered the cornfield, they were best buds. To
them, there was magic in the endless rows of tall
stalks. And in the face of such magic, they had to band
together, both to thwart the black forces and revel in
the white.

By the time Daryl was old enough to play with them,
Ben was driving and had long since lost that tether to
the mystery of the fields.

"I want to ask you both something," Ben said.

"Shoot," Daryl said, finishing off his beer and tucking the bottle in his back pocket.

"What do you really think of the story about the guy
they found mauled to death in the state park?"

April sucked on her teeth for a bit, then said, "I mean,
it could be it. I looked on a map and it wasn't far from
where that kid took potshots at the Devil."

Ben shook his head. "That could have been done by
any number of animals out there. For all we know, he

fell, broke his neck and lay there like an all-night buffet. They have coyotes down there, not to mention black bear and bobcats. Even some wild dogs could have done that to him."

"You saying you think Boompa's jumping the gun?" Daryl asked.

"I'm saying we have to be prepared for anything. A Jersey Devil is one thing. A black bear is a whole other can of worms."

April patted him on the back. "That's why we have you, Mr. Munitions. It's not like we're going in unarmed."

They paused when a flock of geese honked overhead in a loose arrowhead formation. It seemed as if they brought a cooling breeze with them.

"Here's the other thing," Ben said. "What if Boompa is right? The Jersey Devil doesn't kill people. Hell, for centuries, all the damn thing does is run or fly *away from* people. That kid who shot it said it stuck around long enough for him to empty his gun. It wasn't the least bit afraid until it'd been hit. Those campers said it took their food bag and pegged it on top of a tree. And now this. I don't like the way any of it sounds. This could be dangerous."

"But we have to find out," Daryl said. "You ever get the feeling Boompa's been hanging around just to get this chance? Like he refuses to die with this big question hanging over him."

April rubbed her brow, looking up at a moon that was getting brighter by the minute. "I can't say it hasn't crossed my mind. And I would like to see him get some peace before he joins Grams. We're going to have to be extra careful then," she said. Her face pulled tight when she mentioned their grandmother. They all missed her fiercely.

"I'll need you all to listen to me then," Ben said. He felt a tight tension in his chest. It was the same feeling he got whenever his platoon had been asked to check out an abandoned village. You never knew what the hell you were walking into. Guys died or were maimed in the blink of an eye.

"We will, big bro, trust us," Daryl said.

Ben knew there was no sense asking them both to stay behind. If he could have his way, he'd leave them all at the farm while he sought out the Jersey Devil himself. He was the only one with combat experience, and if the creature's actions were any indication of what was to come, blood would be spilled. He didn't want to see any of them hurt. What happened to him was never a concern.

"Even if we do find it, do you think it'll change anything?" Ben said.

April sidled next to him, lifting his shirt to expose his side. A bright red birthmark marred his pale flesh. The mark was in the shape of a cloven hoof. "You mean like make this go away?"

She dropped his shirt, lifting her own, revealing an identical birthmark. Daryl did the same.

"I don't know," Ben said. "At least we can find out what it means."

Their father also bore the same mark. They hadn't seen it since they were kids, but they knew it was there—a brand that had haunted them all their lives. Ben knew it was more than that. Much more. They all knew Boompa's story by heart, how their grandmother was the first to bear it. He'd suspected there had to be more, but if the old man hadn't seen fit to tell them, he must have had a damn good reason.

Maybe the answer was somewhere out there in the Pine Barrens. And maybe the only way to find it was through the barrel of a gun.

Chapter Eleven

Sam helped Bill and Ben load the guns and other weapons into a secret compartment in the old Ford van they'd begged him to junk or sell for years. It was a hot morning. The sun felt like it was sitting right on their shoulders. Sam was ordered to sit in the shade for a minute.

"Who do you think you're talking to?" he asked his son.

Bill licked beads of sweat from his upper lip. "A man old enough to know not to give himself heatstroke."

Bill's jaws worked furiously on a wad of gum. He'd seemed out of sorts the past few days, lost in his own world. Sam wondered if he was thinking of his mother, and how things may be coming full circle. Lord knows, his own brain had been burning night and day with the same thoughts.

There was no sense arguing with his pigheaded son. "I'll do that if you take this," he said, holding out a rosary, the beads worn from years of handling.

"Thanks, but no. Mom's rosary belongs in your pocket." Bill slung a vinyl rifle tote off his shoulder and put it in the van for Ben to stow away.

"Will you at least put on my music?"

His son stood with his hands on his hips, watching Carol, April and Daryl stow camping gear into the new minivan the family had bought last year.

"Fine," he said. He went into the old van, took a cassette from the box under the passenger's seat and popped a Dean Martin tape into the van's radio. He cranked it up as far as the blown-out speakers would allow. Dino warbled about what would be a kick in the head.

Sam smiled at Bill's eye roll. The apple fell far from the tree as far as musical taste was concerned. "You just made an old man happy."

Bill almost dropped the box of old cassettes and smiled. They clattered like windup teeth. "Well, at least I can scratch that off my bucket list."

They both chuckled while Ben latched the compartment door in place. "All set," he called out.

They were doing their best to make light of the day, but Sam knew what lay ahead weighed heavily on all of them. They would either return from this trip empty-handed and dejected, or with the very thing the whole Willet family had been hoping for since the day Bill was born. The moment Sam saw his boy emerge from his wife screaming his lungs out, Lauren weeping with happiness and exhaustion from a labor that would have killed a lesser woman, he knew this day would have to come. He only wished he was a few years younger. Hell, make that a few decades.

Regardless, he still had enough left in him to do what had to be done.

"You ladies need help with the food and coolers?" he asked his daughter-in-law.

Carol waved him off, "We've got it. You need a cold drink?"

Truth be told, he did, but he wanted to hold out a while. "I'm all right. I'll have an iced tea when we're on the road. It'll go perfect with my jerky."

Ben turned out to be quite the hunter, what with all that marksmanship training in the military. He'd bagged two deer this past fall. Sam made a hell of a jerky with the meat they didn't use for steaks, burgers and chili.

Daryl lugged a blue cooler into the minivan. "How are we gonna sneak all those guns around when we get there?" he asked.

"Son, you have no idea how remote the Pinelands are. It makes this place look like Times Square. Your grandma and I had a few special places we'd sneak off to back when we were keeping company. With any luck, I'll still be able to find them."

Daryl's brows rose. "And what exactly were you and Grams doing in the woods?"

"Don't you worry yourself about it."

"Does 'keeping company' mean you were married or dating?"

"She was my steady. We weren't married just yet. But it wasn't long before we were."

His grandson gave him a light punch on the shoulder. "You sly dog."

"Don't go getting any lewd ideas in your pointy head," Sam said, shooing him off. "Go finish helping your sister."

Watching Daryl walk to the house with his patented saunter, Sam had to smile. Those woods were better than a hotel back then. It was where they'd lost their virginity—to each other, of course. The old ironworks factory had been their secret spot. They'd escaped to it as often as they could. They used to figure the last folks to walk the factory had been dead and gone a hundred years or more. Sometimes, after they made love, they talked about building a home there, far away from everyone, just the two of them.

If only they hadn't gone back that last time. Everything would be different.

Would Lauren still be here? he wondered. She'd passed on just a year shy of seventy. It was her heart. He couldn't help wondering every day since she'd left them if the stress was what wore her out.

I'll have a chance to ask her soon enough.

"Bill," he called to his son. "How about me, you and April ride in the Ford? If we get pulled over for any reason, it'll help to have a pretty face to distract the police from looking too deep into the van."

"And what if the cop is a woman?"

"Well, that's why you'll have me in the van," Sam said with a wink.

Joanne set the timer for her meatloaf and settled onto the couch. She had forty-five minutes all to herself. It felt great to get off her feet. She heard the water in the shower pelting the vinyl curtain, Noah trying in vain to lay down some old-school rap. She hoped to God the neighbors couldn't hear.

She took a sip of wine and picked up her cell phone. There was one voice mail waiting for her.

"Funny, I didn't hear it ring."

Of course, she'd had her earbuds in, listening to music while she was preparing dinner.

She listened to the message, then replayed it.

"Noah!" she shouted, running to the bathroom.

"You can go to the bathroom if you need to," he said from the shower.

"You know that guy on TV who's on all those monster shows?" she said, still looking at the phone.

"Who?"

"The dude with the hat. He's the what do you call it? Crypto something. He's got that long goatee."

The faucets squeaked when Noah turned the water off. "Oh, yeah, Norm something. What about him?"

When he stepped out of the shower, the water beading off his hard body, Joanne had to resist the impulse to ravish him. She'd wanted to save it for after dinner.

"He just left me a message," she said.

"Are you kidding?"

"No. He said he saw your post about that thing that happened to us at the camp location for the tour. He wants to meet with us tomorrow to talk about it."

Noah dropped the towel, smiling like it was his birthday. It was impossible not to notice that he was actually getting hard. He picked her up, crushing her to his chest. His cock pressed against her belly.

"Holy crap, that's awesome! We haven't even started the tours yet and we already have the most famous cryptozoologist in the world interested in meeting us! Oh, my God, this is gonna be huge right out of the gate."

Despite his excitement, and her growing arousal, they'd both forgotten that the Jersey Devil Camping Tour had been put on the back burner because they were both leery of going back in those woods. First, there was that kid claiming he shot the Jersey Devil. He was probably full of shit, but he did shoot at something. Kids with guns in the woods worried her. And then there was that guy who was literally chewed up around the area that was close to one of the selected campsites. Things were getting too freaky. Plus, Noah still hadn't been able to find someone who could lead the actual tours while they ran the business side of things. Interest from Norm Cranston would give them the cachet they needed to amass applicants for the job and people eager to do some monster hunting.

"So that means I should call him back and tell him yes?" Joanne asked once he put her down.

"Hell, yes, it does!" He reached around, squeezing her ass. "And when you're done, meet me right back here."

Joanne's heart fluttered and she blushed, even though they'd been together for three years. He had that effect on her. And this was a moment to celebrate.

Rushing to the living room so there were no distractions, she hit redial and took a few deep breaths.

Norm Cranston paced in his bedroom. His open suitcase was on the bed, clothes packed tightly as only a professional traveler could cram a wardrobe into a tiny box. He tapped his cellphone against his forehead.

He had every reason to doubt the little camping tale told by the couple from the fledgling Jersey Devil tour. It seemed like the simplest, most transparent publicity stunt possible. Only a sucker would believe them.

But there was something in Joanne's voice that made little bells go off in the back of his be-hatted head. She sounded sincere. He'd know for sure when he met her and her partner, Noah. Norm's bullshit detector had become a finely tuned instrument over the years. It was an absolute necessity if you were going to spend your life chasing down monster stories. Sure, he'd been fooled a number of times, but as he got older, a healthy dash of aged cynicism helped refine his filter.

The call he'd just had with that Wyatt kid who'd stolen his father's gun and did what no one else has ever done, that had him thinking hard. His father was none too pleased with the story and Norm had to work hard to get him to talk, much less agree to meet with him for a bit when he got into Jersey.

"That kid will be the death of me," his father moaned once he'd let his guard down. It was funny how people opened up to him as if he were an old friend when they realized he was *that guy on TV.* "First he does the one thing I've told him time and time again to stay the hell away from. If he wasn't so scared when he came home, I would have kicked him square in the ass. I tell him to keep the story to himself. We've been living here since he was born and we're still considered outsiders. I don't need my neighbors thinking he made something up just to show we're down with the local folklore. So what do he and his friends do? They blab to all their friends, including one whose mother is a reporter for the local rag. You have any kids, Mr. Cranston?"

"None that I know of, no."

"Don't get me wrong. Wyatt is the best thing that ever happened to us. But, man, the worry kids bring out in you ages a man."

Again, Norm's BS detector remained silent during their entire conversation. This family wanted nothing to do with the story. The only question now was what did Wyatt and his friends see? He'd definitely shot at something, but what?

Salem jumped onto the suitcase. Norm stroked his head.

"Well, we'll see when I get there. And then it's on to the Willets'."

The cat purred a long, wistful *meow*.

"I wish you could come, t-too."

Sam had said the whole family was heading for the Pine Barrens. What on earth were they planning to do?

"Come on, big guy, let's get you to your vacation home," he said, carrying Salem to his pet carrier. The cat put up a fuss, raking its claws on Norm's arm. He held steady, and soon Salem was safe inside, hissing, his tail puffed out to three times its size.

Staring at his cat through the wire mesh, Norm wondered.

Were the Willets planning to catch the Jersey Devil?

If any family could do the impossible, it would be them.

Chapter Twelve

Heather Davids used a battery-powered blower to inflate the queen-size air mattress. The reedy whine of the machine seemed sacrilegious out here in the peaceful woods.

Too bad, she thought. *I'm not sleeping on the ground.*

Her boyfriend, Tony, and his idiot pal Justin took over an hour to get the two tents up. They were more comfortable strutting on the boardwalk at Seaside Heights than roughing it in the forest.

Ever since Tony lost his job and had to move back home, their sex life had taken a downward turn. Hotels were expensive, unless they went to one of those fleabag roach motels where you paid by the hour. Heather was very clear that she wasn't going to get bedbugs just so he could see her naked.

So now here they were, camping in the middle of nowhere just so they could spend some time together.

She should feel more sorry for her best friend, Daniela. It was Tony's idea to bring Justin along and play matchmaker. He thought Daniela took too much of Heather's time, so why not hook her up with Justin?

If only he knew Daniela was a lesbian.

If only *anyone* knew.

They'd been friends since first grade at Holy Assumption grammar school. Heather knew Daniela was different from her back in fourth grade, when her friend stared at the pages of the *Sports Illustrated* swimsuit issue with the same glazed-over look as the boys.

But being a good Catholic girl in a strong Italian family precluded her from even considering making her sexuality a topic for discussion. Heather would hold her secret to the grave, though she did encourage her often to just come out with it and shed the heavy weight that she'd been shackled to whenever she was around her family.

"Times have changed," Heather would say. "Shit, my niece in middle school says that it's cool to be gay or bi now. They bully the *straight* kids!"

Daniela would shake her head. "Yeah, but my family hasn't changed."

Being a good sport, she'd agreed to come along, prepared to use the usual excuse to stop Justin, and any man, in his tracks—she had her period and her cramps were killing her. Heather giggled to herself, thinking about all the guys who had gone home balled up after a date with Daniela. She was gorgeous, with long black hair, full lips, green eyes and the kind of body women paid a plastic surgeon for. That body just wasn't put here for Jersey boys.

"I'm getting hungry," Heather said, topping off the mattress and dropping two thin pillows on it. "I hope you guys brought something good."

Tony and Justin opened the cooler, diving through the ice for cans of Coors Light. They popped the tabs open, being gentlemen enough to hand them to her and Daniela.

"I picked up a bunch of camping food packs from the Sports Authority," Justin said, emptying a bag of foil pouches. "It was either that or heating up cans of beans."

Heather pawed through the packets of food. "Let's see, we have macaroni and cheese, Southwest chili with beans *and* meat—that should be lovely. I can't imagine what kind of meat they used here. I'm sure it's not from the Pork Store. Beef stew with vegetables." She crinkled her nose in disgust, squeezing the packet. "Ugh, I can feel the meat crumbling like wet charcoal. I think I'll pass."

She took a long drink, savoring the icy sensation as it settled in her empty stomach.

"I knew you guys would screw it up," Daniela said with a wry smile. She reached into the bottom of the cooler. "Which is why I brought this!"

She pulled out a package of Sabrett hot dogs. "Aaaaand, this!"

From her backpack, she extracted a collapsible hot dog roasting fork, long enough to hold three hot dogs over a fire without burning your hand. Tony and Heather gave her a round of applause. Justin sat on the cooler, looking dejected.

"I was just trying to be authentic," he said.

"Dude, you know me and you are eating what's in those freeze dried packs, too," Tony said, inspecting the label for the mac and cheese. "I'm so hungry, I could eat deer shit."

Heather motioned to the woods around them. "I'm sure you'll find plenty to eat if that's your thing." She laughed when he threw her over his shoulder, beer sloshing down his back. He spun around until her head was swimming, his hand firmly on her ass. When he put her down, she collapsed into Daniela, who did an admirable job holding her up.

"Why don't you guys get some wood and rocks to make a decent fire pit," Daniela said. "We'll watch and give you direction when needed."

Justin jumped up, chugging his beer. "Come on T, let's get manly."

Tony gave Heather a long kiss. "It'll be nice to have a fire," he said, staring into her eyes. "Kinda romantic."

Heather leaned close to his ear. "The more romantic you make it, the more treats you'll get later."

She swore she could feel actual heat build between their close bodies. He kissed her again. "That a promise?"

She nodded.

"Let's go, Justin. I'll get the rocks, you look for good, dry wood." He handed his friend the mini axe he'd borrowed from his uncle. They set off searching the leaf-littered floor within sight of their little camp.

Daniela handed Heather a fresh can of beer. She ran the cool surface over her forehead and neck before opening it.

"I'm glad I brought my noise-canceling headphones," Daniela said, swatting her thigh. "I think it's going to get pretty loud out here tonight."

"You know what they say, if the tent is rocking . . ."

Daniela emptied a handful of mustard packets from her pocket.

"You sure you're okay sharing a tent with Justin?" Heather asked.

Daniela nodded. "He's harmless. Now, if Tony brought his brother Jimmy along, I'd be sleeping in the car."

They laughed, tapping their beer cans together. Jimmy was a year younger than Tony and the quintessential guido. The smell of his heavy cologne would have been enough to chase the wildlife away for miles.

Tony came back and laid an armful of rocks near them. "Got more to go," he said, taking a swig from Heather's beer.

Justin was hacking away at a fallen branch as thick as his forearm twenty feet to their left. Tony walked with an exaggerated swish to his hips in his direction, plucking a jagged rock from the ground. "Now no looking at my ass, no matter how hard it is to resist," he said.

"Boys," Daniela said with a shake of her head.

"Meanwhile, you know him and Justin check out our asses every chance they get. I hope they get a fire going soon because I really am starving," Heather said.

When Daniela didn't reply, she nudged her. "You have to be as hungry as I am."

Daniela was looking up somewhere over the heads of Tony and Justin. "Hey, I thought bats only came out at night," she said. "I wish I brought a hat now."

Heather looked at the bits of darkening sky between the swaying cones of the pine trees. She didn't see anything. But she thought she heard something, like a high chittering that could very well be a bat.

"I won't be sitting out here long if there are going to be bats everywhere," she said.

"Hey, guys," Daniela called out. "Watch out for bats!"

Tony and Justin froze, eyes furtively looking for the winged rats. "What bats?" Tony bellowed.

"I think I saw something flying above you."

Justin held the axe over his head. "They better not even try to mess with me. I'll smite them with my Paul Bunyan peacekeeper."

Heather snorted beer from her nose. "Ow, that burns."

She broke into a fit of laughter. Daniela wiped beer from her upper arm.

"Gross," she said, cringing.

"Sorry," Heather said with her hand over her mouth.

There were several heavy thumps as the rocks fell from Tony's arms.

"Bro, do bats have tails?"

Justin let out a nervous laugh. "What? No, they don't have tails. Not even in the comics."

Tony said, "I swear, I just saw something that looks a lot like a bat circling over there." He pointed to a spot over Justin's shoulder. "And it had a freaking tail."

Heather wasn't falling for it. Tony had played enough pranks on her over their two-year relationship to the point where she'd grown a thick prank callus. But Daniela looked like she was starting to tense up. So was Justin, but she assumed he was just playing along to "scare the girls."

"Ha-ha, butthole," Heather said. "Get cracking so we can make a fire."

Something shook a branch overhead. It sounded as if the world's heaviest squirrel had leapt onto a heavy limb. Heather jolted.

"Great, now you have me all tense," she said, glaring at Tony. He didn't even look her way.

"It could be a bird," Justin said. "There's all kinds of swamps and ponds and stuff around. Those long skinny birds are everywhere. You know, cranes and shit like that."

Tony bent down and gripped a heavy rock.

"I don't think that was a crane," he said.

"Come on, guys, cut it out!" Heather shouted.

Tony glared at her. "I'm not messing around, Heath!"

Daniela said, "I'm going in the tent. Come with me."

Heather's stomach bunched into a knot the moment she met Tony's eyes. He wasn't kidding around. He saw something, and it was freaking him out.

"Why don't we all go in the tents until whatever it is passes through?" Heather said.

The boys shook her idea off. Even outside their element, they still had to show they were alpha males. "I wanna see it for myself," Justin said.

Heather shot back, "Suit yourself. We're bringing all the beer into the tent and—"

Daniela's scream cut her off.

Three dark brown shapes swooped down with horrifying screeches. Before Tony and Justin could react, the shadowy blurs were on them. Heather cried out the same moment Tony yelped in agony.

"Tony!"

Hearing her voice, the creatures retreated back to the sky.

"Oh, my God!" Daniela wept, collapsing into Heather.

The winged creatures were gone, but so were most of Tony and Justin. All that remained of them were their legs, all four standing upright, everything from their kneecaps up missing. Blood ran down what remained of their legs, until one by one, they collapsed with wet thuds.

Heather screamed so hard and long, she was sure she'd never be able to stop.

Chapter Thirteen

Bill Willet drove the old van down the Jersey Turnpike. They'd just crossed the George Washington Bridge, having endured a traffic snarl that set them at a snail's pace for two miles. He kept glancing at the temperature gauge, sure the old rust bucket would overheat. The last thing they needed was a trip to a mechanic. And if the heat they were packing were to be accidentally discovered, well, they'd be up shit creek without a paddle, boat or arms to swim.

April sat next to him, her window wide open, enjoying the light summer breeze. Bill caught quite a few men checking her out back when they were inching along. It was hard to resist his fatherly instinct to tell them to keep their eyes in their heads, even though April was in her mid-twenties and already divorced. Instead, he settled for one of his world-class sneers, which looked to have given at least one fella a case of whiplash as he jerked his gaze back to the road. Bill only had one baby girl and that she would remain until his dying day.

Which may be sooner than you think.

His left hand shivered and he dropped it to his side so no one could see. His test results would be there when they returned from Jersey, but he already knew. Something was wrong, had been wrong for some time now. Huntington's disease. He'd had to sneak peeks in the computer, reading up on what was possibly killing him. What he read was far from encouraging.

"So tell me, Boompa, how long did Grams live in Jersey?" April asked.

The old man had taken a nap in the back when traffic was tied up, but he was up and fresh now.

"Oh, it wasn't long. Maybe a couple of years, though it felt like an eternity at the time. Her father moved the family to the Pinelands right after she graduated high school in the Bronx. He was a foreman of a construction crew and went wherever the work took him. Your grams and I had been seeing each other for about a year when her father broke the news. We were in love by then, so I moved not long after."

"That's so sweet," April gushed. "What were you, like nineteen at the time?"

"Just turned twenty. I wanted to marry her right then so she could stay in New York with me, but my parents advised me to wait. It was good advice. I moved close to her and spent the next two years building up my savings so we could have a good start."

April curled the ends of her hair in her fingers. "I wish I had waited before marrying Alan. If I was smart, he'd still be waiting and I'd have forgotten all about him by now."

Bill pulled into the left lane to get around a slow moving SUV. "Look on the bright side. You got out the moment you realized what an absolute waste of space he was and you're not tethered to him through a child," he said. He couldn't count the days and nights he and Carol had fretted, waiting for April to gush that she was pregnant, both of them knowing the marriage was destined to crash and burn.

Instead of defending her choices, April smiled. "Amen to that, Dad. Testify!"

She whooped and gave them both a high-five. He admired his daughter from the corner of his eye. April had been as spirited as a wild horse since the moment she'd learned to walk. Alan never stood a chance. Bill wasn't sure any man did.

Even though she'd heard Boompa's story a hundred times, she prodded, "So, was the plan to get married and stay in, what was that town?"

"Tabernacle," her grandfather said. Bill thought he saw the man's face turn wistful. "It was nothing but farms out there. Your grandmother's father rented a house on a small plot of land on the outskirts of one of those farms, though he didn't do any farming himself. It was cheap and actually pretty cozy, if I remember correctly. Much better than the room I rented at a boardinghouse. I'd been working in a cranberry field while we kept company and was sick to death with the smell of them. Couldn't get the scent out of my clothes or the room." He scratched his beard, sighing.

April said, "And you both left Tabernacle after . . ." she paused. There was no need to say it. Everyone in the family knew what happened next.

"Yep. She couldn't stay there. It was too much for her nerves. Oh, I put on a good face, but truth be told, I was getting kind of skittish out there. The nights were so dark and quiet, but after what happened, I imagined all sorts of things. What made it worse was knowing that my imagination was less terrifying than the truth."

The vibe in the van grew dark, bordering on melancholy.

Three generations of Willets had been haunted by what had happened down in Tabernacle, smack dab between two forests that were the perfect hiding places for the unspeakable.

All Bill wanted now was a way to put an end to it all while he still could, much like his father. An end to the worry, the speculation, the doubt of what the future held for him and his children. What had plagued them couldn't be found in any of the Jersey Devil stories over the centuries. Their tie to the legendary creature was uniquely their own.

And it was high time they severed it.

"Holy shit Mark, you have to see this!"

Kelvin Anders fumbled with his cell phone, taking picture after picture of his grisly find. He and his neighbor Mark Oberman made monthly trips all around the Pinelands, searching for the remains of the unbelievable number of ghost towns that lay hidden in its depths. He'd once read that there were more ghost towns in the Jersey Pinelands than the American West.

So much of the sandy soil in the Pinelands, called sugar sand, acted like a kind of quicksand for old mills, factories and homes. Over time, whatever was still standing was eventually sucked into what became a sandy grave. Kelvin and Mark liked to locate and document those towns, taking pictures for themselves only, even if it was just a few foundations or scraps of weathered timber. It was a harmless hobby that got them out of the house. Every foray into forgotten history was capped by a trip to the Cornerstone Bar a few blocks from their house, where they'd alternate buying rounds and look at the pictures they'd taken.

Kelvin was pretty sure they wouldn't be ogling these snapshots.

Mark jogged over with heavy footsteps. He'd only gone twenty or so feet and he was already winded. Neither of them were getting any younger, these trips in the woods pretty much the extent of their exercise. Too much time on their asses in office cubicles had made them soft.

He recoiled when he looked at what Kelvin was photographing. "What the hell?"

"You think some illegal hunter is dumping carcasses here?" Kelvin asked, holding a hand over his nose. The sound of buzzing flies was deafening.

"Not with a pile like that," Mark said, stepping back but still enveloped in a dome of putrescence. "If I didn't know better I'd swear that was a bear stockpile, but I don't think they gather up that many kills in one place. And I'm not even sure there are any bears out here anyway."

Out here anyway was near Speedwell, on the edge of the Wharton State Forest. They'd been looking for the remains of a town called Friendship, which used to be one of the biggest cranberry operations before the turn of the twentieth century. They never expected to find this.

Kelvin bent closer to the small pit. Inside was a circle of skinned animal carcasses. Chunks of meat had been torn from hides, organs left to spill out of split cavities. Bones protruding through denuded flesh appeared to have been snapped—soft tissue like eyes and tongues either devoured or liquefied.

"It looks like there are at least three deer, a couple of dogs, maybe a coyote, definitely some cats. And I don't know what the hell that is," he said, pointing to a large pile of random meat and bone.

"I'm gonna be sick," Mark said. He stumbled off to puke against a tree.

Kelvin was as fascinated as he was repulsed. Who or what would do something like this? Could it have been one of those Satanic cults? Maybe they'd had a mass sacrifice. But did Satanic cults still exist? He couldn't remember the last time he'd read a reputable report about one. That was all sensationalist stuff from the '70s and urban legends told to scare kids from going out into the woods or abandoned homes.

More likely it was the work of a crazy person, someone who had checked out of society and was living out here like a wild man. Which meant he and Mark had just stumbled into his special place.

There had always been that fear, traipsing in the middle of nowhere. The Barrens were notorious for being home to strange and outright aggressive people who didn't want to be found. If what was in this pit was any indication, someone a tad on the violent side could be very close.

"I think it's best we get out of here, now," Kelvin said. He was done taking pictures. He couldn't shake the sudden feeling they were being watched. Normally, he'd say it was his own mind messing with him, but not today. Not with a ring of flayed animals in front of him.

"You read my mind," Mark said. He'd locked one arm to support himself against a tree. He looked as green as spring grass. "Maybe we should call the cops."

"We're definitely calling the cops," Kelvin said as he hustled past his friend. "Come on."

He heard Mark culling wads of spit deep in his throat. "Just let me get everything out," he said.

Their car was parked on the side of the road, maybe a hundred yards away. Kelvin wished he could teleport right into the driver's seat. Every noisy step they made was a beacon, a dinner bell ringing for the maniac who had left the gory tableau for them to find. Absent any weapons, he grabbed his keys, three of them poking from between his fingers as a makeshift brass knuckles with bite.

He waited for Mark, staring ahead, looking for signs of anyone that could pop out on their way to the car. Sometimes on their excursions, they would bring Mark's metal detector. It would be as good as a steel bat right about now. Too bad it was in his buddy's garage at the moment.

"What the hell is taking you so long?" Kelvin said, turning.

Mark was nowhere to be seen.

"Mark? Mark?"

His heart went into an instant gallop. Kelvin walked slowly back to where Mark had been standing.

Where the hell could he have gone? He's about as nimble as a hobbled bull.

"Hey, Mark! Quit fucking around."

His heart raced. Mark wanted to get out of Dodge as much as he did.

Had the person who filled that pit found him chucking up the last of his lunch?

But if there'd been a struggle, he would have heard. It was as if Mark had been sucked though a sinkhole.

With the soil the way it was out here and all kinds of underground waterways, that was a distinct possibility.

Kelvin cupped his hands around his mouth, no longer worrying about alerting a madman in the woods. "Maark! Mark, where are you?"

He stopped short when he got to the tree Mark had puked on. His slick, brown vomit was still there, running slowly down the jagged bark.

There was no sinkhole.

For a moment, darkness crept into his periphery and he felt the ground pull out from under him.

Mark's severed head lay in the leaves, the flesh of one cheek flecked with dirt, his eyes wide open and terrified. As Kelvin stood transfixed by the mind-numbing sight, he thought he saw his friend's mouth open slightly, as if he wanted to say some last words before the final vestige of life bled from his soul.

Kelvin turned and ran, spitting up bile as he navigated between the trees faster than he'd moved since high school.

Chapter Fourteen

Norm had timed it so he'd arrive at the agreed-to spot in the Pinelands at the same time as the Willets. After he'd landed at Newark, he rented a small SUV with four-wheel drive, just in case. He'd heard a lot of the more remote roads in the Barrens were barely roads at all, eager to grab hold of unprepared cars and never let go.

He'd come early so he could make a couple of stops and interview a few of the Jersey Devil witnesses. Again, they all passed his BS detector. He'd been most skeptical of the couple, Joanne and Noah, simply because they had a vested interest in having their own encounter with the creature. What could be better for a Jersey Devil tour business?

When he saw the look of genuine fear in Joanne's eyes and heard Noah talk about how they'd delayed starting the business because the whole thing had made them nervous, he knew they were telling the truth.

So was the kid, Wyatt, who was more excited than afraid now that he was in the safety of his home and could brag a little that he'd faced the Jersey Devil and won.

His father shot him a warning glance when it looked like he was getting too enthusiastic.

"Don't forget," Wyatt's father had said, "none of this would have happened if you hadn't stolen my gun. None of this *should have* happened." His father was a big man with a neat, black beard and forearms that looked like they could cleave a steel girder in two. Norm wouldn't want to mess with him. And by the look on the kid's face, neither did Wyatt.

The plan was to meet the Willet clan in the small town of Chatsworth, simply because it was known as the Gateway to the Pine Barrens. Norm loved the small American town look and feel of the place. He took a few dozen pictures and some video with his phone, which was better than the old video cameras he used to lug around in the early nineties. Chatsworth was famous in the area for their annual cranberry festival, cranberries having supported countless businesses and families in the region over the past couple of centuries. He was kind of disappointed that the festival was months away. Being from the Carolinas, Norm loved a good country fair. He remembered working the ox pull matches at the Beaufort Days Fair when he was a teen. Just thinking about it brought back the smell of fried dough and barbecued meat, the laughter of kids on rides the local fire department had erected, and most of all, the beautiful girls all dolled up for a night on the midway.

He had to remind himself he wasn't here for livestock contests and corn dogs.

The state trooper that blew through the red light on Main Street, lights flashing frenetically, brought Norm back to earth.

It was a hot day, especially standing out under the sun, watching the car spit dust up in its wake. His hat did yeoman's work keeping the rays off his head, but the humidity had made his clothes feel as if he'd just pulled them from the washing machine.

There was a general store, yes, an actual general store, right across the street. Norm couldn't believe it. There were even two rocking chairs on the covered porch. A tiny bell clanged when he walked in the door. He was greeted by an icy blast of air-conditioning.

Enjoy it while you can, he thought. The days ahead would be spent outdoors.

"Hi, how can I help you?" an older woman sitting behind the counter asked. She had long gray hair tied up in a tight braid, kind eyes set within wrinkles that could only come from a lifetime of smiling.

Norm smiled, doffing his hat for a moment. "I'm just grateful it's nice and c-cool in here. Do you have anything cold to drink?"

"Right behind you," she said.

There was a cooler filled with an assortment of old-time soda. He found a bottle of birch beer, popped the cap with the bottle opener on the side of the industrial cooler and pocketed the cap.

Did I just stumble into a time machine?

"That'll be a dollar," she said. He passed her a buck and she rang the sale in a cash register that had to be older than the Empire State Building.

"Is it all right if I drink it in here?" he asked.

"Suit yourself. If you get hungry, we make some of the best fudge in the state."

He perused the trays of different flavored fudge in the display case. His stomach rumbled.

They both looked out the window when another state trooper car wailed down the street.

"I wish they'd slow down," she said. "It's not like they can help the person they're rushing off to."

Norm leaned on the counter.

"You know w-w-where they're going?"

"I do. I like to listen to the police scanner. It helps kill the time. Plus, I get to know what's going to be on the police blotter section of the paper before everyone else." She patted a small black box on a shelf behind the register.

"I'm curious, what exactly are they rushing off to?" Norm asked. "Was th-there an accident?"

The woman opened her mouth and stopped. Norm worried that he'd said something wrong and was going to be ejected into the heat.

"Say, aren't you that monster guy on TV?" She cocked her head, staring at him, trying to tie the hat and goatee to his image on the television.

"I'm afraid I am," he said with genuine humility. It was still strange, being known as the monster guy who did all those weird cable shows. He waited for her to ask him why he didn't stutter on TV. Then again, he was doing pretty well today. Maybe she didn't even detect it.

She pointed an arthritic finger at him. "Weren't you scared when you went out looking for the Lizard Man down in Bishopville? I remember when it happened. I was living in South Carolina at the time, just fifty miles south. If you ask me, I think what they saw was a Bigfoot, not some lizard that walked on two feet."

Norm had to restrain himself from laughing. He could remember a day when only kids and crackpots knew about these kinds of things, especially a legend like the Lizard Man. Television was good for something.

"There really wasn't anything to be afraid of except

the bugs. The Lizard Man hasn't been seen there in a long, l-long time. The people of the town were wonderful to me, though. That's not always the case when I waltz in with a camera crew."

"Are you here to film something about the Jersey Devil?" she asked.

Norm tugged on the end of his goatee. "Not yet. Just doing some scouting, I guess you could say. You ever see it for yourself?"

She shook her head sadly. "I didn't, but my mother did when she was around twenty. It just popped up in the woods behind our house and nearly scared her to death. Before she could even scream, it flew off and she never saw it again."

Finishing his birch beer, he asked, "Do a lot of people believe in the Jersey Devil around here, or is it just fun to have it as kind of the state mascot?"

She went to the display case and cut him off a piece of fudge. "On the house," she said. "You won't find any shortage of people that not only believe it, but have seen it, heard it or know someone who has. The thing is, we keep these things to ourselves, mostly. You could almost say that folks feel if you talk about it too much, it'll find you to, in its own way, get you to zip your lip."

There was a sparkle in her eye that Norm interpreted as either she was delighted in letting him in on a local secret or pulling his leg, just a little. The fudge, raspberry cheesecake, was unbelievably good. He asked her if he could get two pounds to go.

As she was wrapping it in a brown paper bag, he said, "Oh, about the police. What exactly h-has them in such a hurry"

"They found another dead man in the woods." The register clanged again as he paid for the fudge. "Well, *they* didn't exactly find him. From what I can tell, two men were out in the woods and one of them found the other dead."

"That's horrible," Norm said. Suddenly, going into the endless forest of the Pinelands had lost its appeal.

"That's not the worst of it." She bent closer as if to whisper a secret, which was odd because they were the only ones in the store. "I thought I heard one of the staties say all that was left was the man's head."

Norm listened to the police scanner with the woman for another few minutes, until he spotted an old van and a bright red new minivan park across the street.

"I think my friends are here," he said. "Thank you for the fu-fudge and the company."

Before he could leave, she tapped his arm. "You think you could do an old lady a favor?"

There was no way he could resist. "I sure can."

"Be very careful out there. And I'm not talking about the Jersey Devil. There's something strange going on around these parts. I'd like to know that you're safe."

He put his hand over hers. "How about this? When we're all done, I'll come back and show you I'm okay. I know I'll need more of this delicious fudge by then."

She smiled sweetly. "I'd like that."

The second he opened the door, he regretted it. His body had acclimated to the cool store, and now it felt even hotter than before.

The Willets emerged from their vehicles, Sam waving when he saw him.

"Hey there, stranger," Sam Willet said. He was wearing a stained baseball cap, the bill's fabric frayed.

"We picked a wonderful day for hunting," Norm said, already feeling sweat pop out around his neck.

"Aw, it'll be much cooler once we get under the trees." Norm took in the Willet family.

Good Lord, if I were the Jersey Devil, I'd run for the hills knowing they were coming for me.

They were all tall, with the exception of Ben, though he looked as solid as a brick shithouse. Norm knew he'd spent time overseas in the military. The guy looked like a man who had seen things he couldn't un-see. There was a brooding silence about him that separated him from the rest of the family. As mean as Ben's father looked, Norm was pretty sure Ben was the true one to fear.

April looked like a model from a country music video, tall and lean and tan with denim shorts and a very tight T-shirt. Her brother Daryl, still wearing that dirty Mets cap, wore a smile like a sheriff wore his badge. He was the tallest in the family and Norm wouldn't be surprised if he scaled skyscrapers in his spare time.

Then there was Bill, with his buzz cut and Halloween mask for a face, hands like Easter hams and a jaw cut from some kind of Disney hero. His wife, Carol, was long and slender, but with a chest that defied gravity. *Good old country genetics*, he thought. She looked ten years younger than her age. He talked to her and Sam often. Carol was the family cryptozoologist, interested in things beyond the Jersey Devil. They once spent an entire night talking about Long Island's Montauk Monster over Skype. They both agreed whatever it was that washed up on the shore was some poor animal that had been experimented on at the Plum Island facility. Nothing to gather the villagers over.

Sam shook Norm's hand. "I'm so glad you could

come. We seem a bit obsessed about this, but we have our reasons."

"I just can't believe I hadn't done this m-myself years ago. I guess I've had too much Sasquatch on the brain," Norm said.

And I can't wait to find out what secret you've all been holding on to.

Norm got knuckle-breaking handshakes from the men and back-cracking hugs from the women. It made him realize how soft he'd become. Everyone looked happy to see him, but he could feel an undercurrent of tension.

He told them about the man's head that had been found less than an hour ago and generally where it had occurred.

"It sounds awful, but I don't think it bears the MO of the Jersey Devil," Norm said.

Sam Willet scratched at the gray stubble on his neck. "I'm not so sure, Norm. I'm not so sure. It would be easy to dismiss it, but I think everything that's been going on can lead back to that damned thing."

"That's a pretty big stretch. I mean, this is well beyond the scope of any animal, real or un-undiscovered. If people are d-dying from animal attacks, I'm more inclined to think of a rogue bear."

"Not many out this way, believe it or not. Just call it a feeling, mixed with some history that's not been talked about before."

There were so many things Norm wanted to ask the family on this trip, and he planned to make good use of their time together.

"Well, if you were planning to go anywhere near where that man was killed, I'm pretty sure the cops have cordoned off the area," Norm said.

"Not today," Bill said. "My father wants to visit the highest point in the Pinelands first." The big man dropped his keys, swiping them off the ground quickly.

"You'll never get a truer lay of the land," Sam said. "You brought your cameras and other gear?"

Norm nodded. "All in my fine little rented truck over there." He pointed towards the white Honda CRV.

Daryl and April broke into laughter. "I wouldn't exactly call that a truck," Daryl said. Even Bill had a crooked grin on his face.

Here Norm was, a man born and raised in the South, and he was getting out-rednecked by these New York farmers.

He looked at the pristine Japanese car, and smiled himself.

Ben walked back to the minivan. "Come on, you can follow us," he said in a clipped tone, not waiting for a reply.

Bill added, "Stay close, because GPS is pretty sketchy out here. Cell service, too. We've had one bar at most for the past half hour."

Carol handed him a manila folder. "Some notes on the Jersey Devil, including a few things you're not going to find other places. I can go over it with you tonight, once we set up camp."

"Th-thanks," he said. He dropped the folder onto the passenger seat and turned up the air-conditioning in the car.

"Why does this feel like a military operation?" he said into his audio recorder, staying two car lengths behind the minivan. "I don't think the Willets are here to swap stories and bang the brush for the Jersey Devil."

He wasn't aware how close he was to the truth.

Chapter Fifteen

You couldn't get any higher than Apple Pie Hill. Ben had worried that there would be a steep ascent to the hill and they'd have to turn around. The old van in the lead wasn't cut out for that kind of driving anymore.

To his surprise, getting there was easy. He watched April's arm sway up and down with the wind current the entire drive. It was a beautiful day out. Some would say it was hot, but after a tour in Afghanistan, Ben had promised never to complain about the heat again. They parked in a lot next to a wood sign for the Batona Trail.

Getting out of their vehicles, he heard Daryl ask, "How far is it from here to the fire tower?"

"Just a little hike," Boompa said.

The famous fire tower would be a great recon vantage point. If they were going to search for the Devil in the surrounding forest, he wanted to see what they were up against.

"April, you need to put on some jeans," Ben said, eyeing his sister's too-short shorts.

She flipped him off, though with a smile.

He slung a backpack filled with water, energy bars

and other essentials out of the van and onto his shoulder. It was heavy, but manageable.

"All right, I guess you don't mind ticks burrowing under your skin."

She looked to their mother to confirm.

"He's right. They're all over the place out here. You don't want Lyme disease."

April rolled her eyes, grabbed her pack from the minivan and went back to the van. "I'll be out in a second."

The heat bugs were belting out a chorus. Ben almost couldn't hear himself think. He took a quick hit from his flask, careful to make sure no one saw him. There was no pleasure in the whiskey burn.

Can't go down this road. Not now. Pull your shit together.

Stepping casually away from the family, he tossed the flask into a thick tangle of bushes. That was it. There was no retrieving that silver little fucker. Ben wouldn't say he had a drinking problem, but he knew he was skirting awfully close. The drinking made it easier to be with people, even his family. Sometimes, he felt so clenched up inside, he was afraid to open up, lest everything come exploding out.

And there's no telling what'll come out, is there, Benny Boy?

He saw that Norm Cranston's face was already as red as a baboon's ass. He went to his grandfather. "You can stay here if you want. I have a map and can take everyone."

Boompa patted his shoulder. "Don't worry about me. I still know how to walk."

Ben opened his mouth to protest, then shut it. There was no arguing with the man.

He unzipped his pack, making sure the Beretta was

exactly where he'd put it. He wasn't going anywhere without it.

"Everyone ready?" he said, noting his sister's jeans.

"Lead the way, young grasshopper," his father said. He'd found a gnarled branch and was holding it like a walking stick.

The path was obvious to follow, but choked with overgrown vegetation. Twenty yards in and they were swallowed by clouds of mosquitos. Ben took out a bottle of insect repellent and passed it along.

"Some of these look like they could be the Jersey Devil," Norm said, walking in the middle of the pack. He swatted them with his hat.

"No shit. This is nuts," Daryl said.

"Watch your mouth," his mother snapped.

"Really?" Daryl said, walking heavily, as he always did. You could hear Daryl coming from another county away.

"You and your fucking mouth," April scolded him. Ben turned to see the sly grin on his sister's face. "Not in front of company, little brother." She looked to Norm, who blushed.

"Welcome to the family," Boompa said. He was keeping a good pace and not winded at all. Ben was impressed. "We work like mules and cuss like sailors."

Ben veered to the left, pointing at the ground. "Watch out, broken glass." Someone who most likely didn't celebrate Earth Day had smashed a twelve pack of Bud Light bottles on a rock protruding from the weed-choked path. He was surprised at the amount of litter thrown about. Water bottles had been jammed in bushes, cigarette packs squashed underfoot.

When they came to a clearing, they stopped to admire

the view. A whole green and blue world had suddenly opened up before them.

"This is it," Boompa said.

A sixty-foot fire tower rose ahead of them. Stairs zig-zagged in the center of the structure, leading to the viewing platform. The red and white paint was worn and flecked. Some idiots had even taken the time to spray paint illegible graffiti.

"You know, your grandma and I lived not too far from here way back before there were things like cars and flying machines."

Ben offered bottles of water. "You want to rest for a second before we climb up the tower?"

Boompa was already stomping towards the tower. "Gotta make the best of the daylight while we have it," he said over his shoulder.

Ben said to his father, "We have to keep an eye on him."

His father gripped the walking stick, his knuckles white. He was looking just a shade better than Norm. It couldn't be the heat or physical exertion. The man was up before the crack of dawn every day, working his ass off. He may have just been worried about what they'd find. Anything that could put its mark on three generations had power that was wise to respect. "I think we're going to have our jobs cut out for us."

He offered some Big Red to Norm, who happily took a stick, tucking the foil wrapper in his pocket. "A little cinnamon boost never hurts."

Their footsteps chuffed up the tower's steps, every-one following the octogenarian, trying to keep up with him. The view from the top was breathtaking.

Norm's labored breathing caught Ben's attention. The TV cryptozoologist leaned heavily against a rail. He caught his eye and said, "I'll be all right. This is what happens when you spend most days sitting on your ass being entertained by your cat. Even when I'm out in the field, I tend to take the road most traveled . . . and level."

They could see countless miles of dense pine trees, with breaks here and there revealing fast-moving rivers.

Boompa said in voice fit for a tenured docent, "The Pine Barrens make up over one million acres of pre-served forest land. Down there are towns lost to the ages, wetlands that may have never been seen by human eyes up close, more cranberries and blueberries than the world could eat in a year, farms, industry, modern homes, old homes, and somewhere in all that covered darkness, the Jersey Devil. If you look way over there, you can kinda see Atlantic City and Philadelphia through the haze."

Ben knew logically how large the Pine Barrens were, but seeing it laid out like this was overwhelming. They could spend lifetimes exploring it and still not cover every square inch. The sheer vastness of the area worried him.

At least we'll always have cover, he thought. Cover, to his way of thinking, was the perfect fallback position. But just as they would have places to hide, so would the creature.

"So where are we going tonight?" April asked.

Boompa pointed to the east. "I know a place we can basically disappear into the forest. There are plenty of areas between the Batsto and Wading rivers where we can set up. Once we're in that deep, we're officially in no-man's-land. We'll have to be extra careful."

"Because of the Devil?" Daryl asked. He leaned over the rail, gazing at the distant ground.

"Well, that, yes, but there are lots of people who live

out there that don't take kindly to strangers. There are whole generations of hermits who see things a different way. Not to mention some of the wildlife is a smidge on the untamed side."

Ben watched Norm stroke his long goatee, looking slightly nervous.

"Okay, so we have the Jersey Devil, animals and crazy people to look out for," Ben said. "Anything else?"

"The locals call themselves Pineys," his mother added.

His father chuckled. "Well, there are also brown recluse and black widow spiders, usually tucked away under crumbling foundations and abandoned homes. Believe it or not, there are rattlesnakes out here and bobcats, too."

April shivered. "I don't care about snakes and big cats, but spiders creep me the hell out." She bent down to tuck the cuffs of her jeans into her socks.

"I thought witches dug spiders and creepy crawlies?" Daryl said, nudging her with his knee, almost knocking her over.

"Schmuck," she said, punching his shin. Daryl pretended to be hurt, hopping on one leg.

His grandfather said, "We won't make it all the way to where I'd like us to be today, but we should get started. We'll at least be able to stow our trucks where they won't be stumbled upon."

Norm Cranston's hi-tech digital camera clicked repeatedly as he took panoramic shots of the Pinelands. The cloudless sky revealed as much of the forest as one could ever see from this vantage point. Ben stayed with him while the rest of the family noisily walked down the tower stairs.

Ben saw a dark shape quickly rise above the pointed

tops of a clump of pine trees several hundred yards to the west. He pointed it out to Norm.

"See if you can get a picture!" he said.

The blurred shape had a large wingspan and long body. It could have been a heron or even an eagle. And that's exactly what a rational person would think.

Norm snapped some shots before it dove back into the trees. They waited for a minute, but it didn't return.

"Let's see what w-we got here," Norm said, pressing a button to review the series of pictures.

In all, he'd captured four frames of the winged shape. Even enlarging it on the small display screen didn't help bring out any definition.

"Is that a tail?" Ben asked.

Norm exhaled loudly. "Or it could be long legs trailing behind it. I'll get a better look when I download it onto my laptop. I'll bet my house and cat that it's just a regular bird. I mean, what are the odds we'd catch the Jersey Devil right off the bat, in the middle of the day?"

Ben stared across the green pines. His hand automatically went to his side.

"Better than you think," he said.

Chapter Sixteen

The woman woke up to screaming. Wiping the dirt from her face, she stood, her back against the bare wall.

They'd come home. And they were hungry.

She looked up at them, saw the ravenous look in their eyes. Bumping and snipping at one another, playfulness bordering on something much darker.

When it was like this, it was best not to move. Holding her breath for as long as she could, she exhaled slowly, her stomach muscles moving outward oh-so slightly.

Become one with the wall. Sink as far into the earth as possible. But don't break eye contact. Never do that. No. That would be the sign. Weakness. They didn't like that. Especially not from her.

The change in them had been sudden, stark, terrifying. Seemingly overnight, everything had gone mad. The bad stuff had . . . altered them. Done something to their minds. If only she had been able to keep them here, safe, close, away from the bad stuff.

You could only hold on to them so long.

When the others had tried to stop them, it hadn't gone

well. No, that was an understatement. It had gotten them killed. Then eaten. Their bones were right over there. Not a scrap of meat left on them.

She didn't want that to happen to her. So she quickly learned to fade into the background. They sniffed the air, wet snorts of dissatisfaction daring her to cringe.

Eventually, they turned and left her in the gathering gloom. Looking for more.

Her joints ached when she finally moved, padding silently across the floor in bare feet. She squeezed her breasts until it hurt. The pain centered her. Made her forget the fear.

She snatched a beetle skittering along an exposed root, crunching it between her teeth, tiny sharp bits stabbing her gums, her tongue. Before there was no more sun, she went to her hands and knees, pulling fat worms from the ground.

Eat, then sleep.

They drove for miles down a two-lane road that went from paved to simply carved into the forest. The whole trip, they only saw one car, and it was going the other way.

Carol sipped a Diet Coke in the middle seat of the minivan and worried. Yes, this area of the Barrens was on the remote side, but there should be people about, from locals to nature lovers out to hike the trails or canoe the rivers.

The murders have everyone spooked, she thought. But she knew it went far deeper than that for many of the locals. They were afraid, and for a very good reason.

She wondered how Norm would react later when he saw the arsenal they'd brought. Maybe he'd be thankful once they told him the full story—the real story. He didn't know that she'd once been a Piney herself, though she'd left right out of high school to become a legal secretary for a law firm in Manhattan. All her childhood, she'd dreamed of getting off the family's cranberry farm and living in the city. And she did just that.

Until she'd met Bill when he was on leave. He'd caught her eye in a piano bar on East Fifteenth Street. Her friend remarked how he looked like a maniac, and he did look rather imposing, but Carol couldn't help her attraction. When he bought her a drink later in the night, and his scowl was lightened to a sideways smile thanks to a mix of whiskey and beer, she surrendered to his rough charms. Here was a man in the truest sense of the word. Carol had always been taller than all the girls in her class, and most of the boys. The handful of boyfriends she'd had looked like kids she was babysitting when they went out.

Not with Bill. They spent every waking moment of that weekend together. When he left, he did as he promised and wrote and called her constantly. Two months after that weekend, she told him she was pregnant.

Then came Ben, a wedding her parents didn't approve of, and she was back on a farm once again. Except this time around, she wanted to be there, and loved every minute with Bill and his parents, Sam and Lauren. They treated her like a daughter the moment they met her.

She was no longer a Piney, and that suited her just fine.

But the Pines weren't done with her. Not by a long shot. She couldn't deny it when Ben was born. Then came April and Daryl and the certainty that she would be back here one day.

Carol had long ago accepted that fate was always at

work in everyone's lives. What were the odds that Bill would meet a girl from the Pines when he came to a city of millions of people? No, they were meant to be, just like what was happening now was meant to transpire.

As a Piney, she knew more about the Jersey Devil than what was in books and TV specials. Everything except the marks and what they meant. It couldn't be good. She'd gladly give up her life to know, if it meant sparing her children from the lifetime of worrying and confusion Lauren had suffered. Bill was able to compartmentalize it, bringing the question to light only when he felt the need. Carol, she fretted about it night and day, searching for anything, even among other legends, that could explain it. The few parallels she did find scared her.

Sliding in her seat when Daryl took a hard right into a cut in the trees just wide enough for the trio of cars, she said to her sons in the front seat, "You know I love you both, right?"

"Of course, we do," Daryl replied. "We love you, too."

Ben gave her a thumbs-up. He wasn't one for outward signs of affection, and she was fine with that. It was just a part of him and she loved all the parts, even the ones that came back from the military altered.

The minivan rocked from side to side. Branches scraped against the roof like nails on clay pots. The suspension cried out for its life as Daryl seemed to hit every pit in the so-called road.

"The van's going to need a paint job and new undercarriage when this is done," Carol said. Some of her Diet Coke had spilled onto her lap.

"It's the best I can do, Mom," Daryl said. "When Boompa said he was going to lead us off the beaten path, he wasn't kidding."

They had to take it slow or else they'd wreck the minivan. "How in the hell is that old van not falling to pieces?" she said.

"It's old but it's solid, like Boompa," Daryl said with a quick laugh. Ben kept his eyes on the road ahead, even though he wasn't the one driving, as if he could will his little brother to find the less rugged parts of the path.

They drove that way for miles. Carol watched the bright blue sky between the lush tree limbs take on a darker cast. "We better stop soon."

No sooner had she said that than the rickety van's brake lights flashed. There was a white, sandy clearing ahead. Carol got out of the minivan. The sharp edge of the heat was dulled here, but the humidity seemed worse.

They stopped in the middle of a square of disintegrating structures. Partial stone walls remained here and there. A hulking iron tub, filled with old leaves and forest detritus, was the only solid object around. Carol spotted three crumbling steps leading to nowhere. A tree had grown around a metal pole, absorbing most of it.

Her father-in-law practically jumped out of the van.

"This'll be good for tonight," he said. "There's a pond over that way if anyone wants to take a swim."

"I think I'll pass," April said.

"What is this place?" Carol said, her feet crunching on a small shard of glass stained brown.

Boompa looked around and sighed. "This was where Lauren and I used to come when we needed some alone time." She thought she saw the shine of a tear at the corner of his eyes. "It was some kind of factory long before we found it. We never bothered to ask. Thought by doing that, we'd be giving away our private spot.

There were a few more walls back then. Another fifty or so years and the whole thing will probably disappear."

Wildflowers grew in bunches everywhere the sunlight could pierce the pine tree canopy. The air smelled of wild onions.

Carol looped her arm around his. "You know, I can picture you and Lauren sneaking out here, two young lovebirds making big plans."

He patted her hand. "That we did, honey. That we did."

"I'll get some things from the van," Ben said with no interest in what this place meant for his grandfather.

She knew what *things* he meant.

"You going to be okay?" she said to her father-in-law.

He nodded. "It was my decision to come here. I'll be fine. I like to think Lauren's right here with us, even though it's . . ."

Walking away before he could finish, Bill clomped over and kissed the top of Carol's head. "It's kind of strange, being here. Dad used to tell me about this place. I had a totally different picture in my head, especially when I was a kid. Kind of thought there'd be a castle or something." He watched his father gather some stuff from the van. "I like what he said."

"Oh?"

"About Mom being here. With all the bad stuff to think about, that's the silver lining."

She smiled. "I like to think he's right. I miss her, Bill."

Her husband cradled her face in his hands. "I do, too. We're doing this as much for her as ourselves. If she's watching, and if we're lucky, she'll finally be at peace."

Carol watched her children and Norm Cranston work on getting the tents erected. Ben, April and Daryl were all adults, but they would always be her babies. She was positive Lauren was watching them as well, proud as any grandma could be, and just like Carol, probably a little scared for them. They'd waited all their lives for this moment, and now that it was here, she was frightened.

"I just want us all to be safe," she said. Then, gathering herself, she said, "Help me get this cooler out. I'm sure everyone is hungry and thirsty. What's that you used to say? 'Smoke 'em if you got 'em'?"

Night came fast. They had a good fire going and full stomachs, thanks to Daryl's chuck wagon cuisine expertise. The family, usually as spirited as wild horses, was pretty quiet. No bickering between April and Daryl, which was rare. They were thick as thieves and bothersome as cats living in a sealed room.

At least the smoke from the fire kept the flies at bay. As the day wore on and they worked up a sweat, the flies and gnats descended on them as if they were fresh road apples.

Sam knew he had to fill Norm in on the reason they were all here. For some reason, he couldn't find the right words to start.

You're too old to stall for time, he admonished himself. *Better to just spit it out.*

He was about to start from the beginning when Norm jumped up. "I almost forgot to check those pictures." He ran over to his SUV, opening the trunk.

"What pictures?" Sam said.

Ben said, "I saw something flying over the trees for a second while we were on the fire tower. Norm got a few pictures but we couldn't tell what it was on the camera."

April was roasting marshmallows, three to a stick.

They'd been burned black, just the way only she liked them. "It was probably just an egret," she said.

Norm came back to the fire pit with a huge black laptop. He plugged a USB cord between it and his camera. It took some time to download.

"You know you won't have any place to charge that," Bill said. His words sounded a little slurred. He'd only had two beers. Sam wondered how he'd missed his son becoming a lightweight.

"No worries," Norm replied. "I have multiple battery charges. I use them all the time in the field. I like to write all my notes at night, while things are still fresh in my head. It's also good to load up any pictures I took as a backup." He pushed his straw hat higher up on his head while he waited.

"Okay, let's find them," he said, moving his finger around the pad on the laptop. Sam moved closer, as did the rest of the family.

It can't find us that fast, can it? Sam thought.

Norm clicked on the first picture. A fuzzy shape looked to have burst from the top of the tree line, screaming towards the sun like a modern-day Icarus.

"Let's just enlarge this and do a little enhancement," Norm muttered. Sam saw that April had let charred marshmallow flakes fall on Norm's shoulders. He was too busy fiddling to notice.

The blown-up picture didn't clear things up much.

"Whatever it was is brown all over," Carol said. "Could be a hawk."

"That's what I thought," Ben said.

"Let me try another," Norm said. The next two were even less defined. "It was moving really fast. It took off into the trees like it had sp-spotted prey."

"One more to go," Ben said.

Norm clicked to the next picture. He must have caught it in a moment when it paused before making its speedy descent.

Sam's stomach tightened.

"Hold on," Norm said, fingers fidgeting with the control panel to sharpen the image. He clicked the enlarge button once, twice, three, four, five times, until the whole screen was filled with the creature.

"That's no fucking hawk," April said.

"Jesus," Ben said, dashing for the bag of guns.

Sam stared at the image of the beast from his nightmares. The creature had a long neck with wide, leathery wings. Its head was turned away from them, but he knew it would look like a hideous amalgam of horse and goat. And that was indeed a tail, long and thin, like a whip.

It knew they were here. From the moment they'd stepped into the Pine Barrens, it was stalking them.

"You son of a bitch," Sam said to the still image of the Jersey Devil. "I'm not going to make it easy this time around."

Norm looked at him. "You b-better tell me about the f-f-first time, now."

Chapter Seventeen

The forest went eerily silent around them. Every flutter of the leaves overhead made April jump. Ben unzipped the big bag. She watched the cryptozoologist draw a silent breath when he looked into the bag.

"We have plenty for you, too, Norm," Ben said, grabbing an AR-15 for himself.

"What the h-hell's going on?" Norm asked.

The moment April saw the picture of the Devil, her senses had sharpened to a fine point. She knew they weren't out here to sing campfire songs and eat marshmallows. But seeing the creature, and knowing that it showed itself to them on purpose, to let them know it was aware they were coming for it, made everything all too real.

Her grandfather put an arm around Norm. "This is all just for our protection," he said.

Yeah, right, April thought. They'd been planning for this for as long as she could remember. They weren't walking out of here without a dead Jersey Devil in the rubber body bag Ben kept in the van's hidden compartment.

To his credit, Norm said, "Don't b-bullshit me, Sam.

You have enough weapons here to take down an entire town. You want me to d-document your family killing what may be an undiscovered species of animal?"

"It's not an animal," her father said.

"How could you know that? The legend of th-this thing has been around for centuries and not a s-s-s-ingle person has an answer," Norm said, pacing around the fire.

Bill rose to his full height. Norm had to look up to meet his steely gaze. Her dad looked pretty pissed, but April knew his anger wasn't directed at Norm.

He pulled up his shirt, turning his side toward Norm. "I know because of this!"

Norm looked at him as if he'd lost his tether with reality.

"What are you talking about?"

"Look closer."

In the orange flicker of firelight, Norm bent to inspect Bill's side. The red birthmark in the shape of a cloven hoof was a throbbing redness that looked like an infected wound. Norm's eyebrows went to the top of his head.

"What is that?" he asked.

"It's a mark. I've had it since I was born," her father said. She watched her mother pull her lips into a tight line.

April lifted up a corner of her shirt. "I have it, too. So do my brothers."

Daryl and Ben showed their marks to Norm. His eyes nearly popped out of his head.

"I, I don't u-understand," he said.

Boompa said, "My wife, Lauren, was the first to

have one. Except she wasn't born with it. It came to her later, not far from here."

A bird screeched somewhere in the distance. Everyone paused. Hands clung tighter to weapons.

Boompa continued. "It was given to her, by that thing. And she passed it on. Norm, my family's been marked by the Devil, but we don't know what for. I aim to put an end to it now."

Ben said, "When we kill it, we want you to show it to the world. You decide who gets the body, or samples, or whatever. You can even leave us out of the story, say you bagged it. We may be here for different reasons, but they're pretty sympathetic to one another."

Norm threw up his hands. "Do you all know how crazy this sounds?"

April was quick to reply. "Yes, we do! If we didn't have these reminders branded on our flesh, it would have been easy to forget all about it. But they're there. It has to be this way. You can study the damn thing all you like, but not while it's alive."

With her emotions riding so close to the surface, she almost let slip a secret she was too terrified to tell even her best friends. Once she had been told the family secret about the mark on her sixteenth birthday, it scared the living hell out of her. She'd always wondered why her brothers wore shirts on sweltering hot days, even in the pool. The thought of passing it on and the unknowable consequences gnawed at her from the very first time she'd had sex with Frank Lommer the day *before* prom. She'd been a virgin. As much as he wanted to see her in all her birthday suit glory, she'd refused to let him turn on the light so he couldn't see her strange birthmark. Despite his protests to go bareback, she insisted he wore a condom. Getting pregnant was not an option—not knowing she could pass this weird mark onto her child.

It was why she'd had her tubes tied before she married Alan. There was no way she was bringing a cursed child into this world.

The most frightening thing in all of this was not knowing what the mark meant. It pained Boompa, losing Grams before they could find an answer. He worried about her soul day and night. She'd overheard him praying to protect her and guide her to heaven one night. The desperation in his voice brought her to tears.

"So, this is a monster hunt in every sense of the word," Norm said. He stared into the fire, the shimmering light casting his face into alien patterns.

Boompa replied, "Yes, and I'm sorry I didn't tell you before you came. But I got the sense that once you'd recovered from my divulging our true intentions, you would have been here anyway. Something has it riled up. It's killing people. Someone has to stop it, and I'm pretty sure no one else would even think to do what needs to be done."

Norm's shoulders shook as he laughed. "You're right about that, Sam. I doubt the cops would s-s-send a SWAT team out here to take down the Jersey Devil, even if a hundred people were k-killed."

"They'd be too busy looking down when they should be looking up," Daryl said, tossing a plastic bottle into the fire. He'd kept the cap on so it burst with a loud pop.

April's father put a beefy hand on Norm's shoulder. "We're not going to force you to do anything you don't want to do. If you want out, I'll lead you to the main road first thing in the morning."

She knew what the answer would be. Sure, the man was put off by the guns and the thought of killing a legendary creature, but she also knew he'd never come this close to proving the existence of *any* cryptid, living or dead.

"If you're all going to run around shooting everything that m-moves, I can't be a part of that."

"We know our way around firearms, Norm," Boompa said. "We're no dummies. The only thing we're gunning for is the Devil." He held out a can of cold Schaefer. "Care to drink on it?"

Norm stood there, shaking his head, taking a moment to look at everyone. April smiled when he caught her eye. She wasn't sure whether it was comforting or just made her look plain insane.

Finally, he took the beer and said, "I must have lost my mind from the heat, but I'm in."

The family tilted their drinks toward him and gave a "Cheers," in unison.

Daryl's soda stopped halfway to his lips. He motioned for them to be quiet.

"Anyone else hear that?"

Ben looked above them. "What'd you hear?"

April, preferring her .38 special because they never jammed, cocked the hammer back. Norm got real jittery, seeing how fast they all went into defense mode.

Daryl pointed behind Norm. "I thought I heard a branch snap, but I could swear it was overhead."

"Everyone take it down a notch," Bill said, his head swiveling from side to side, jaws chomping on a thick wad of gum. "Relax those trigger fingers."

April noted how her mother had put her rifle down in exchange for her phone. She was actually recording!

"Mom, what are you doing?" April whispered. "It's too dark to see anything anyway."

"There's enough firelight right now. Just watch my back."

Crack.

This time they all heard it, and it was indeed coming from somewhere in the trees. Everyone's attention was drawn to the area behind Daryl.

"Raccoon?" Norm asked.

"Maybe," Boompa said.

No one moved. They waited patiently for even the slightest sound, eyes scanning the pitch for anything creeping into the circle of light.

"You catch that?" Ben said.

"What?" April said.

"Nothing. Absolutely nothing. Something's there and it scared everything else away."

April didn't realize she'd been grinding her teeth until pain shot through her skull.

Dad's right. Just chill out. It could be a squirrel jumping around.

A log popped in the fire and everyone but Ben flinched, heads twisting toward the sound.

That must have been the moment it was waiting for.

A soul-quaking screech rent the night in two. They didn't see it so much as feel it as it flew just over their heads, leaving a foul animal stench in its wake.

"What the fuck was that?" April screamed. The fast-moving shadow had been larger than a bat, but nothing like the purported size of the Jersey Devil.

The flying creature swooped again, this time lifting the straw hat off Norm's head.

"Crap!" Norm cried out. April saw a flash of blood ooze down his forehead.

Daryl took a shot at the retreating creature, but it was too fast. The sharp crack of his rifle sounded ten times louder than normal in the still night air. "Dammit!" he cursed.

"Get the floodlight," Ben shouted.

April darted to the old van. Boompa had installed floodlights that pointed in each direction of the compass on the roof. They were connected to a separate battery he'd mounted inside the van. She flicked the switch. Night outside the van's windows instantly turned to day.

Her blood froze when she heard her father mutter, "This can't be possible."

Chapter Eighteen

Sam Willet had played out this scenario in his head a million times over the past sixty years. None of them had prepared him for this.

"Everyone just hold your fire," he said. April emerged from the van with a look of pure terror on her face. She aimed her pistol into the trees.

The problem was, they had been preparing all this time to track down and kill the Jersey Devil.

Singular.

He took a moment to count. There were ten of the creatures perched on thick tree branches above them.

Ten that they could see in the harsh glare of the floodlights. The sudden, searing brilliance didn't even make the bastards flinch.

That they were descended from the monster of the Pine Barrens, there was no doubt. They looked to range in size from two to four feet high, each with a wingspan twice that.

"They look like baby dragons," Norm whispered.

"That they do," Sam said.

Norm was right. Their smallish, equine faces stared

at them, black, impenetrable eyes reflecting the bright lights like a jeweler's lamp glinting off a handful of onyx stones. Brown flesh was pulled taut over lean bodies, rib cages showing through on most of them. Their hind legs ended in hooves, so they had to use the sharp claws at the end of their thin but muscular arms to balance on the branches. Fleshy tails whisked back and forth, the way a cat's would before it pounced.

Sam kept one of them in his rifle's crosshairs. It would be so easy to blow it to pieces right now. But if he did, what would the rest do in retaliation? The creatures outnumbered them and had the advantage of flight.

"I never heard of more than one Jersey Devil before," he said.

"Well, we have more than one now," Daryl said.

Carol tilted her camera over her head to get a clearer shot, while Norm simply stared with a mouth wide enough to catch a thousand flies.

Ben said, "You all need to get in the van. We're too exposed out here. I have this thing on automatic. I'll spray the trees with cover fire. The moment I do, all of you run for the van."

His modified and illegal AR-15 would probably take a few of the creatures out of the game. Sam knew his grandson was right. Even with all of their guns, they wouldn't stand a chance against animals that knew the territory and could zip around them like hummingbirds.

"If these are the kids, Mom and Dad might not be far behind," Sam said. What he didn't voice was his concern that if they were, the van would be a flimsy shelter. He'd come across the Jersey Devil before, and he knew what it was capable of. Now there were ten surrounding them. Thin steel and glass would be no match.

Daryl said, "I'll help you, bro."

"No you won't," Ben snapped. "Make sure Mom and April get inside safe."

The devil children remained perfectly still. Sam could sense they wouldn't wait much longer.

Bill said, "Okay, son, now!"

Ben's rifle blurted molten fire. The Jersey Devils leapt from their perches, howling like wounded owls. The trees exploded into a rain of sawdust.

"Go, go, go!" Sam shouted, ushering April and Carol in ahead of him while Ben emptied the magazine in a 360-degree arc. Daryl took a few shots before clambering inside. Sam had to practically drag Norm into the van. The man's legs had locked the instant the shooting began. Bill crashed into them both as he and Ben slammed the door shut behind them.

It sounded like the van was being pelted by heavy stones as the winged oddities hurled themselves against it, oblivious to their own safety. April yelped when one of them went face-first into the rear window, the thin glass all that separated her head from its own. Tiny spiderweb cracks etched outward from the impact.

"Did you hit any?" Sam asked his grandsons.

"I think I got a couple of them," Ben said. He looked like he desperately wanted to go back outside and finish the job.

"I definitely saw one literally explode," Bill said. He had an arm draped over Carol, his hand on April's shoulder.

"I can't b-believe what I just saw," Norm said, regaining his wits. "That's a small army out there. And they're not a-a-afraid at all."

The side door thumped when a body smashed into it. Daryl jumped, aiming his rifle at the door.

"Don't shoot in here!" his father yelled.

"I won't, I won't."

The kid was breathing hard, but he didn't look afraid. Knocked on his heels a bit, but ready to face the madness outside if need be.

Sam was damn proud of his family—and angry that he'd led them here. How was he to know it would be like this?

Something sharp raked across the van's roof.

"Somebody has to have heard all that shooting," Norm said. "What do we say when the cops come here and those things fly off?"

"No one's coming," Sam said. "When I tell you we're in the middle of nowhere, I mean it. Any locals that live out here aren't going to give a damn about someone shooting. It happens all the time. For some, the reason to live here is just so they can fire their weapons whenever they want."

The small Devils flew in and out of the floodlight's beams, vicious blurs of pure animus. One of them made a sharp right turn in midair, heading straight for the front windshield. At the last second, it pulled into a skid, bringing its hooves to bear on the glass. Sam winced when it hit, but the windshield held.

"This old rust bucket can't take many more of those," he said.

Bill angled toward the side door, moving Daryl out of the way. "Ben, hand me your rifle."

Ben had been in the process of reloading.

"No way, Dad. I'll go out there. You know I'm the better shot."

"I don't need to be a good shot with that. I just need to pull the trigger and hang on."

Ben moved to block his father.

"Look, you're my son and I'm not sending you out there. I don't care if you're Wild damn Bill Hickok."

"I'll go with you," Sam said.

Bill shook his head. "No, you stay in here, too. They just need someone to put the fear of God into them. Hopefully, they'll go back to wherever they came from."

Everyone knew there was no arguing with the man. Ben reluctantly shifted away from the door, passing his AR-15 to him.

"If I see you're having trouble, I'm coming out," he told his father.

If he gets into any trouble, we're all going out, Sam thought.

Bill threw the door open. One of the flying devils careened into the rifle, almost knocking it from his hands. It must have been a hell of a strong little beast, because Bill used to tear phone books in half for fun. His grip was deadly.

He went into an immediate crouch, strafing the trees with gunfire.

"Go on, get the hell outta here!" he shouted. The devils released a chorus of screeching that made Sam's heart throb in his chest. It sounded like they were calling for help.

Dear God, don't let there be more of them.

But deep down, he knew there had to be. These things were young, and where there were young ones, the adults were never far behind.

"Close the door!" Bill shouted.

Ben dragged it shut. He, Daryl and April hustled to the front of the van so they could see what was happening. The sound of the AR-15 was deafening.

The van rocked to the side, and they heard Bill cry out. Sam held his breath. He exhaled once he heard return fire. That meant Bill was still up and doing what he had to do.

"I think they're leaving," Daryl said. His face was pressed to the windshield. A smear of some sort of bodily fluid ran down the center of the window.

Sam nudged his grandchildren aside to get a better look. He didn't see any more flying demons. His son took a few more shots, and things went quiet.

Carol opened the door a few inches.

"Is it okay to come out, honey?"

"Give it a minute, but I think so." Bill's voice was strained, as if he were in pain. Carol must have heard it, too, because she didn't wait that minute.

They piled out of the van while Norm maintained his spot on the floor behind the driver's seat.

Bill stood scanning the trees. Blood ran down his head and neck. One of his forearms had been torn open, a flap of flesh dangling in the cool night breeze.

"Oh, my God!" Carol said. "Daryl, get the first-aid kit from the minivan."

"On it," Daryl said, running to the other car with his rifle at the ready.

"It's not so bad," Bill said.

"Bill, you have blood everywhere! And that wound is going to need stitches," Carol said, holding his arm tenderly. He winced when she touched the gash with the pad of her index finger.

"April was always better at sewing," he said, trying to smile.

Sam took in the condition of his son, feeling his belly ignite. He wanted to get his bare hands on the ugly sons of bitches and twist their heads off.

"The good news is, there are fewer of them now,"

Ben said. He was staring down at the forest floor. "The bizarre news is this."

He pointed at a carcass in the leaves. A big hole had been punched in its belly, spilling guts and blood everywhere. Its wings were spread out, as if it had died by crucifixion. Sam, who always carried a pocket flashlight, shined the beam on the body.

"Jesus Christopher Columbus," he muttered. "That can't be."

One of the consistent traits of the Jersey Devil over the centuries was its horse or goatlike face, or as Norm called them before, dragons. The Devil was, by all accounts, a hellish mix of several types of creatures, all damned into one.

This one was different.

The openmouthed face that stared up at them with filmy eyes looked almost . . . human.

Chapter Nineteen

Carol Willet leaned as close as she could to the dead creature without touching it. The smell coming off the shredded thing was incredible. Norm Cranston was crouched opposite her, snapping pictures with his phone.

"What about the others?" she asked.

Her husband and sons had been searching the ground for the remains of the other winged creatures while April and Boompa kept a watch out for another wave of attacks.

"They're too messed up to tell," Ben said. "Though there is one with half a face and it sure doesn't look like that."

"From what I can tell, we nailed four altogether," Bill said. His heavy footfalls stomped beside Carol. "At least that's four less we have to deal with."

Norm shook his head in dismay. "Yes, but that's four out of how many? I've never even imagined anything like it—and I've spent my life looking for shit like this! Do you realize the implications of what we're f-facing?"

April took a moment to refill the empty chambers of her pistol. She'd been unnerved when everything started, but she was in control now. Of all her children, Carol worried about April the least. She was stronger than even her own father suspected.

The Jersey Devil in front of Carol was every bit the legendary creature, only in miniature form. Yes, the face bore more of a resemblance to a small child than a horse, but everything else was just as people had been describing the beast since Mother Leeds had cried out and given birth to the monster in the 1700s. This thing was so bizarre, she wouldn't be surprised to find it shared traits with a fish or mountain lion. It was a mishmash of so many different animals, maybe it shared some sort of DNA with monkeys, which would explain that pale, hairless face.

Thinking about flying monkeys veered her mind toward Oz. She shook it away. This was no child's fantasy.

"It does make sense that there are offspring," Boompa said. He held the barrel of his rifle over his left forearm. "Nothing on earth is immortal, not even something that we'd consider a resident from hell. To be around this long, it would have to procreate. I guess it's just been slightly busier than normal."

Norm jogged to his car, returning with a clear plastic bag.

Carol reached out to see what the wrinkled flesh of the creature felt like. Norm stopped her with a light tap on the wrist.

"Sorry," he said, catching Bill's hard stare. "There are short, coarse hairs all over its body. There's no telling what infection you'll get if one of those hairs gets under your skin. I also don't want you to contaminate the sample."

"Thanks for stopping me," Carol said. "I'm not too

crazy about the idea of catching some Jersey Devil disease."

"From what I can see, these things are breathing diseases," Daryl said. He chugged down a bottle of water, pouring some on top of his Mets cap.

Norm laid the bag over the creature, then plucked the limp body up through the bag, turning it inside out so the remains were now inside. It was a struggle, droplets of his sweat pattering against the plastic. Grunting, he tied the end with a triple knot. "I need to get this thing on ice."

Everyone looked to the two coolers. Ben said, "I'll empty the smaller one into the big Coleman." Sticking his rifle butt into the ground, he flipped the tops off of each cooler and started transferring drinks and food.

Norm held the full bag in front of him. "You're right, Sam. In order for the species to survive, whatever species this belongs to, it's had to mate. Seeing this, I don't believe its ancestor ever came from a woman, no matter how loudly she cursed its existence. This . . . this is j-just incredible. I never thought something could live undiscovered in New Jersey until you took us to the lookout tower. After that and seeing these things, if you t-t-told me dinosaurs were roaming around I might believe you."

Boompa eyed him curiously. "You're not upset that we had to break a few eggs to get your specimen, are you?"

Norm's eyes were glazed. "With the way they were dive-bombing us, I wouldn't have stopped you for all the money in Vegas." He placed the body in the cooler. Ben shut the lid with his boot.

"So, what do we do now?" Carol said. While every-one was concentrating on the body or looking out for more living Devils, she'd noticed that their tents had been shredded to ribbons.

Bill followed her gaze and said, "We sleep in the vans. I'll bring them closer together. We'll take turns on watch, two people to a shift, one in each car. Ben and I can take the first shift."

Carol caressed his cheek. "Oh, no, you're taking it easy. That's no small amount of blood you lost, and you're going to feel pretty weak once April gets done sewing you up."

She looked over to Norm, making a note to clean the bloody scratch on his head.

"Yeah, Dad," April said, tucking the gun into her back pocket. "We should do that now. Boompa, you want to pass me that bottle of Maker's Mark you keep in the Ford?"

"What bottle of Maker's Mark?" he said. April narrowed her gaze at him, her hands on her hips. He was the first to break their staring contest. "Yes, I'll get it."

Carol suspected the old coot was having a snort every now and then. The question had always been where he stashed his booze. She should have known it was in his beloved van.

"Hey, Daryl, take some bottles of water for the minivan, in case anyone gets thirsty," Ben said, tossing a plastic bottle at his brother. Daryl snagged it in midair.

The boys went about preparing their sleeping quarters, bringing small inflatable pillows and blankets into the vans. Ben said, "I'll stay in the Ford with Boompa and Norm. You guys take the minivan. April, you want to take first watch?"

"I'm on it," she said, breaking out the sewing kit they kept with the box of first-aid supplies. Boompa gave her the half-empty bottle of Maker's Mark. She poured most of it on the ragged wound on her father's arm. Bill hissed. His hand jerked away, the wrist turning as if someone were twisting it. "You can drink the rest, Dad. You'll need it."

He flashed a grin that would make trick-or-treaters head for the hills. "Just make it fast. It doesn't have to be pretty."

April raised an eyebrow. "Oh, I know Mom likes a rugged man. The more scars the better, right, Mom?"

"I've always dreamt of being married to Frankenstein," Carol replied. Looking at the flayed flesh on Bill's arm gave her sympathetic pain. She held a flashlight over his arm so April could see better. To her credit, her daughter was fast with the needle. When she was done, he did indeed knock back the two shots that were left in the bottle.

"Thanks, hon," he said, inspecting her work. Tiny bubbles of flesh protruded between the knots. "We should all get inside now, before those things come back. Maybe they won't bother with their kamikaze routine if they can't see us."

No one argued with him. Despite their being jazzed by the attack, they were also tired as hell. Carol could already feel her eyelids starting to droop. She helped her sons put the fire out, pouring ice water on the embers. The less they stood out in the forest, the better. Unless those things could see in the dark, or possessed echolocation like bats. She shivered at the thought.

She said good night to Ben, patting Boompa on the shoulder. She hated them being apart, but they would have been too cramped up in one vehicle. "You watch out for our boy," she whispered to the old man.

He winked at her. "Hell, Carol, he'll be watching out for all of us."

Ben sat straight in the driver's seat, eyes peeled on the trees. There was a hardness to his look that hadn't been there before he'd joined the service. Sometimes, when she caught him staring off, unaware that she was near, it scared her. What had he seen? Worse yet, what had he done? He hadn't said a word to anyone.

But Boompa was right. Her son would be the one protecting them. It made her proud as much as it broke her heart, not knowing or being able to heal the hidden wounds he carried with him day after day. Though, as odd as it seemed, he looked more in control right now, more himself, than he'd been in months.

Chapter Twenty

Daryl and Norm had the last watch. They were the lucky ones who got to view the sun as it came up, chasing the darkness away. Being able to actually see made their shift much easier. The youngest Willet watched Norm rub his eyes in the Ford, his mouth open in a wide yawn.

Daryl's family slept behind him, his mother and father leaning against one another in the center row and April laid out in the third. She snored like a jackhammer.

His bladder demanded release. He quietly got out of the minivan, slowly closing the door. Tapping on the Ford's window, he said to Norm, "Come out for a sec and watch my back. I gotta pee."

Norm clambered out, smartly keeping the rifle Ben had given him pointed at the ground. "Me, too," he whispered. "I've been holding it in so long, it hurts."

"I'll just go behind the van," Daryl said. "Keep an eye out, okay? Hopefully, those things don't come out in the day so I can make a decent breakfast for everyone."

"You're the family cook, huh?" Norm said, stroking his long goatee. There were heavy bags under his eyes.

"I prefer to be called the family chef. Cooks work at diners."

Daryl chuckled as he disappeared behind the van. He unzipped and a river immediately poured out of him. It felt so good, his body tingled all over.

The air still clung to the night's coolness, but he could tell it was going to be another scorcher. When he was done, he motioned to Norm. "Batter up."

"You mind holding on to my rifle?"

Daryl held his hand out.

He heard the heavy splash of Norm's stream while he looked around. It would be easy to find the other Devil bodies now. He was tempted to look, but thought it might be best done *after* he'd eaten. Seeing those dead critters might send his appetite for the hills.

Twirling around when he heard a branch snap, he said, "That you, Norm?"

The cryptozoologist's peeing cut short.

"Norm?"

Daryl's heart raced. He should wake his brother up now. Shit, he should wake everyone up now.

"Norm, is that you?"

He held his rifle level with his chest.

Stay cool. You don't want to shoot Norm if he peeks out from behind the van.

A woodpecker knocked furiously at a tree in the distance. He inched toward the back of the van. How could one of those things have gotten to him so fast, without him hearing it? Unless it was the head of the Jersey Devil family. No telling how big and stealthy it was.

Daryl tensed, nearly pulling the trigger when Norm popped into view. His arms were high up over his head.

"I'm not going to shoot you," Daryl said, relaxing.

"Though it would have helped if you'd answered me when I called out to you."

The man's mouth opened but nothing came out.

"You okay?" Daryl asked.

Norm stumbled forward, nearly crashing into him.

Three men stepped out from behind the van, each leveling double-barreled shotguns at him. They wore dirty jeans and T-shirts, each with an olive vest, the pockets bulging with what Daryl could only guess. They looked to be his father's age, with faces weathered by time and toil.

"Put the gun down, son," the man with the dirty Mobil Gas cap said. "I won't ask again."

Daryl reluctantly did as he was told.

"Get everyone else out."

Daryl shrugged his shoulders. "There aren't any others."

The man with wiry shoulder-length hair and a week's worth of stubble shook his head. "Do you think we're idiots? There are three cars and two of you. Hurry up!"

His voice echoed and Daryl saw his father's face appear in the minivan's front window.

"Norm, you get my mother and father," he said, knowing he had to warn Ben not to do anything rash. While Norm stumbled to the minivan, Daryl opened up the side door of the Ford. Ben must have heard the man's voice because he was wide awake, cradling the AR-15 in his arms.

"Not now," Daryl mouthed. Ben took a moment to read his face, and seemed to understand. He laid the big gun down.

"Boompa, get up, we have company," Daryl said, shaking his grandfather awake.

"What?" he grumbled. Then he turned and saw everyone else gathered outside. He bolted upright. "What's going on?"

"Some guys with guns just walked into our camp," Daryl said. "Maybe they want to invite us to a potluck dinner."

The men kept their shotguns pointed at everyone. Daryl knew those things were powerful. One blast could take two of them out. He thought he saw a wet stain on Norm's pants.

"You the ones doing all the shooting out here last night?" the one with the Mobil cap said.

No one answered.

The one that hadn't spoken yet, he wore a red bandana over his head, broke away, looking around. He used the barrel of his shotgun to poke through the leaves.

Daryl cast a quick glance at his father and Boompa, wondering which would be the first to talk. His father glowered at the men as if he hadn't a care that they could blow him away in the time it takes a fly to evade a swatter.

"I'm trying to be nice here," Mobil cap said. "What I could have done is stormed out here last night and started shooting back at the people who were tearing up the place. None of you would be standing here now."

It was Boompa who broke their silence. "I apologize for disturbing your peace. But we had a very good reason for it."

"What reason was that, old-timer?"

"Ho!" the one with the bandana cried out. "They got one. Looks like more than one."

Mobil cap said, "Everyone get against the van over there. I want you all standing nice and tight together. Ernie, you keep an eye on them."

Ernie motioned to them with his shotgun to shuffle beside the Ford. Daryl wondered if his brother would use this moment to make a move, now that they only had one gun trained on them. He hoped to hell he wouldn't. Surely, someone would get shot or worse. But Ben had always been a little unpredictable. He was the one who carjacked his own limo in the middle of the prom so he could give his date, Kaitlin DelMonte, a two-hour joyride that ended with his father paying twice the rental fee to settle things down.

Don't be reckless now, not with the whole family's lives at stake.

"Jesus Christ, there's parts of them all over the place." Mobil cap exhaled. He looked at Daryl and his family with pure menace. "You brought them here! Because of you, I, I . . ."

The one with the bandana put a hand on Mobil cap's shoulder to settle him down. For a moment, Daryl thought the man was going to open fire on them. His father must have thought so, too, because he had positioned his body in front of them.

Mobil cap paced around their camp, muttering to himself. Daryl couldn't make out what he was saying, but judging by his tone, none of it was good. This was turning out to be a horror novel come to life—family goes camping, comes across backwoods Pineys and ends up in pieces in mason jars.

His only comfort was the strength of his family. They hadn't spent their lives prepping for worst-case scenarios for nothing.

"I want you all to see what you've done," Mobil cap spat, pointing at them. "For every action, there's a reaction. You need to know the consequences of your actions. Ernie, Chris, line them up so we can show them."

Daryl felt a heavy push at his back and was shoved into April. "Ow, Christ!" she yelped.

Chris, Mr. Red Bandana, pushed his shotgun into the small of his back. Daryl had to stop himself from spinning around and beating his face with his own weapon. It would be easy to execute and would certainly take the man by surprise.

But there were Ernie and Mobil cap, too, and Daryl didn't want anyone getting hurt.

Just make them think they have you beat. We'll find our moment.

They marched them into the brush, down what appeared to be an old game trail, headed to someplace Daryl was sure they'd rather not be.

The sun had burned away the last vestiges of the night's chill, already hanging low in the sky. Bill swatted a moth that buzzed around his head. He walked behind the man who looked like he wanted to shoot them. When he reached back to hold Carol's hand, the one called Chris shouted, "Hands to yourselves!"

How the hell did we end up in the middle of Deliverance? Bill wondered. He knew all about the Pineys, thanks to Carol, especially the ones who had made it a point to stay off the grid. They must have strayed onto their land. Pineys didn't appreciate people setting up camp on their land, especially people who charged the night with gunshots.

They know exactly what we were shooting at. That guy Chris wasn't even surprised when he saw those bodies.

"Where are you taking us?" Bill said, dropping his voice a couple of octaves lower than usual to maybe put a little bit of fear into them. Sure, they had the advantage now, but he wanted them to be clear that without those guns, he was not to be trifled with.

He looked at his watch. They'd been on the move for close to thirty minutes.

"You'll see soon enough," their leader said.

"You got a name?"

The man didn't turn around when he surprisingly replied, "Joshua. And no, I don't give a rat's ass what your name is. Keep moving."

Bill looked back to his father and kids. They all seemed to be holding up pretty well. April and Ben wore dark scowls. He could see they were planning something. Hell, they all were. Well, maybe not Norm, who looked about ready to shit himself.

They came to a break in the trees, giving way to an enormous green meadow. He thought he saw a house way in the distance. They had to crawl through the gaps of an old wooden fence to get to the meadow. Joshua leered as they made their way through the fence, Bill having an especially hard time because of his size.

"Almost there," Joshua said.

The grass was especially tall by the fenced perimeter. Tiny white bugs leapt like rice on a hot skillet as they trudged along, lighting on their clothes before flicking back into the grass.

When they caught a stiff breeze blowing towards them, Bill's nostrils flared. The pungent odor that cascaded over them wasn't unfamiliar.

It was the smell of death, and it got worse the farther they walked into the meadow.

"You like that?" Joshua said. "You smell a dead animal, I smell something much more important. That's my livelihood rotting out there. You did that."

"How could we do whatever you're accusing us of when we weren't even here?" Bill asked.

"You look like a smart man. I think you'll figure it out."

They came upon the first carcass, a lone black-and-white cow on its side, its abdomen ripped open. The steady hum of feasting flies set his nerves on edge.

"Oh, my God," Carol said, covering her mouth and nose with her hand.

The flesh of the cow's face had been peeled back. Its eye was missing, along with its tongue. The poor thing's hide looked as if it had served as a scratching post for a pride of lions. It had been utterly destroyed.

They stood around the cow, shotguns at their backs.

"It isn't pretty, is it?" Joshua said.

"I still don't see how you can blame us for this," Bill said, though he was starting to put the pieces together and it was making his stomach clench awful fierce.

"Take a look around," Ernie said.

When they looked up and past the disemboweled cow, they saw similar lumps of decaying flesh everywhere.

"No," Boompa said. He sounded like the wind had been knocked out of him.

"I think I'm going to be sick," Norm said. He bent over, clasping his hands on his knees, breathing heavily through his mouth.

Bill tried to count the dead cows. He lost track after twenty-five. There were probably others in areas they couldn't see.

"They got all of them," Joshua lamented. "In just a few hours, I lost every head I owned."

"Then you know what *they* are, right?" April asked.

Joshua's hand clenched and unclenched the shotgun. He said, "What I do know is that they've left us alone, until you all came along and brought them to us. I don't know how or why you did it, but those damn things took it out on my livestock."

Bill held up his hands. "Look, we never intended anything like this to happen."

Ernie barked, "I saw all those guns you have and it sure as shit seems to me you didn't come here with good intentions."

"That's not what I mean. We came out here to find the Jersey Devil. We have our reasons. We didn't expect what happened last night, and despite what you saw, we weren't really prepared. I'm sorry that those things came here and murdered your cows. We're farmers ourselves, in upstate New York. I'll personally replace your cows."

Joshua slowly shook his head, spitting at Big Bill's feet. "What's the point? They'll just come back and do it again. You cursed this place. We never gave the Devil any reason to sniff around here. Now that it and its offspring know we're easy pickings, we'll have to leave this place. My family's been here for seven generations. You gonna find us a new place to live, too?"

The man's face turned dangerously red. He was mad and scared and looking for someone to take his fury out on.

He let loose with a screeching whistle. A dozen heads popped up from hiding places in the field. Bill cringed when he realized they'd been ducking behind the foul-smelling cow carcasses. Four more men, a few women and children that could be no older than ten or twelve approached them. The adults held rifles. The children carried great cords of rope.

Joshua said, "I figure we have one chance. For some reason, the Devil and its kin wants you folks just as much as you seem to want it. So, we're going to give them a chance to meet your acquaintance. Maybe when they see what we've done, they'll be of a mind to let us be."

"You can't be serious!" Bill said. He moved to get closer to Joshua and was jabbed in the side by the butt of Ernie's shotgun. He dropped to a knee.

Shit, that hurt! His kidney felt as if it had ruptured.

"You'll make fine scarecrows. Except instead of keeping the scavengers away, you're gonna bring them right to where they want to be." Joshua motioned to the others. "Go on, tie 'em all up."

Chapter Twenty-one

The moment they started to protest, Joshua fired a shot over their heads.

"Anyone wants to put up a fight, I'm happy to convince you otherwise," he said.

Sam Willet couldn't believe this was happening. Ever since they'd stepped into the Barrens, it was like waking up in the middle of a nightmare. A pair of teens, a boy and a girl, roughly grabbed his arms, pinning them at his back while they worked the rope around his wrists. They tugged it so hard it hurt.

"This is what you're teaching your family?" Sam said. He watched his own family and Norm succumb to the heavily armed group. His blood boiled. "How to murder innocent people?"

Chris removed his sweaty bandana, wiping his face with it. "Come on now, you're all human, and we know there isn't a man or woman alive that's innocent."

He heard the heavy knocking of wood. Sam turned to his left to see another contingent of Joshua's family pounding what looked like six-foot stakes into the ground. How many of them were out here?

They're going to crucify us!

"We didn't know the Jersey Devil had spawned so many of those things and we had no way of knowing they would kill your livestock!" Sam grumbled. "We were just defending ourselves."

Joshua shook his head. "But you came out here to stir things up. It's not my fault you're too stupid to know when to stay away."

"You can't do this!" Carol said.

"But yet we are," Ernie replied, tying her ankles together.

Ben had kept silent, giving no resistance until he threw an elbow at the older man who was busy cinching a knot around his waist. The man clasped his nose and went down, blood gushing between his fingers.

With all eyes on Ben, April lashed a kick at the kids by her feet, sending one sprawling into the grass. With her hands tied behind her back, she ran into the woman working on Daryl, driving her head like a charging bull into the woman's stomach.

Daryl and Bill reared back, trying to smash their heads into the people behind them. Daryl slipped, missing his mark and falling on his back.

Bill made the connection, but it was a glancing blow off Chris's shoulder.

Joshua stormed over to Carol, jamming the shotgun under her chin. "Enough!" he commanded. Carol yelped, the barrels still hot from the warning shot he'd fired before. "One more person tries to show they got balls and I'll take her goddamn face off. You all hear me?"

Sam's legs quivered. The fight was immediately taken out of all of them.

"All right. This shows you're not entirely stupid," Joshua said.

The rest of the work was done silently and with frightening efficiency. Sam would swear they'd lashed people to stakes before.

He had to try to appeal to their humanity. The man was scared, worried about his family, his land, their legacy. He could understand that.

But to be so terrified that you would sacrifice seven people to beasts like the Jersey Devil? For all the silence that had shrouded the myth in recent years, something far more sinister had been brewing under the surface.

"What makes you think leaving us out here for those Devils will get them to leave your family be?" Sam said.

An older woman with oily salt-and-pepper hair, wearing overalls and heavy work boots, looked up at him and replied, "We know that offerings have worked in the past. Give the Devil its due, and it moves on."

Sam sucked in a deep breath as Joshua and another man roughly dragged him to the stake. Three children, all of them towheaded with cheeks stained green from being in the grass, began the work of lashing him to the stake.

"I know exactly what you're talking about," Sam said. "But that was in the past. What's happening now is different."

"And how would you know that?" Chris said. He had April's arm in his dirty hand, leading her to the stake next to Sam.

"I used to live here, over in Tabernacle, back long before you were born." He looked to the couple that was maybe a decade younger than him. They stopped what they were doing. "I saw the Devil with my fiancée, pretty close to where you found us. I know what it's like. It took my woman from me, ripped her right off the blanket where we were having our picnic. We didn't find her until the next day."

Sam noticed his family staring at him. He'd hinted at what had happened over the years, but never divulged the entire story.

This is probably your last chance, he thought.

"We formed a search party that night, but couldn't find a trace of her. I thought for sure I'd never see her again. Once you've seen the Devil up close, you can't imagine anyone surviving direct contact with it. The look in its eyes alone is enough to kill a man. It wasn't evil, so much as it was the absence of anything decent or natural. My Lauren spent twelve hours with that beast from hell, and she was never the same again. Spent her whole life wishing she could remember what happened, but maybe not knowing was a blessing. She tried to get past it, move on with her life, but I lost the best parts of her that night. I think I pretty much lost the same parts of myself, too."

He was looking down at his feet, picturing that night, the way the Devil swooped from nowhere, the size of a man with the wings of something prehistoric, that awful goat's face and whipping tail. How Lauren had screamed, him frozen with fear, only moving when it was too late, as the Devil wrapped its arms around her waist and carried her off, her screeches fading and fading until she was gone.

He wept for Lauren as openly as he had the day she passed.

When he looked up, everyone had stopped what they were doing.

"When we took her home," he continued, "her family's neighbor told us what to do. We tethered a lamb in the field outside her house, cutting it so it would make enough noise to attract the Devil. I listened to that animal bleat for hours, until my mind just shut down. When I woke up in the morning, it was gone."

Joshua approached him, studying his face.

He said, "And did the Devil ever return?"

Sam shook his head. "No. That was the last we saw of it. Lauren and I left not long after, but her family stayed. They never heard or saw it again."

There was more to tell, but not here, not to these people. It wasn't going to be necessary. For the first time since the Pineys had grabbed hold of them, they were listening.

Joshua said, "Well, then you more than anyone can appreciate why we're doing this."

"Son, what's out there right now is nothing like what happened to me and my wife. That's not just the Jersey Devil. It's a legion of death. Something's not right about them. How long have they been prowling around?"

Ernie said sharply, "Don't tell him, Josh. What's the point?"

Joshua considered it, scratching under his cap. April looked ready to open her mouth but Sam shut her down with a quick look.

"It's been a couple years," Joshua said, flexing his shoulders. "We've all heard them passing by, but we hadn't seen any until today. Other folks have, though. We may look like we're in the ass end of nowhere, but word still travels. When they come, they're like locusts. Sound like 'em, too. I've heard tales of Devils that look . . . different. Some people think they've multiplied to equal the sins we commit to one another and the earth. That's a lot of holy roller preacher crap that I don't buy into."

Sam said, "I don't know what's changed, but I get a

very strong feeling that the old stories and rules don't apply anymore. If we hadn't fought back last night, we'd have ended up like your cows. Like my son said, we can replace your livestock. Hell, if you let us go, I'll take you to my farms and let you take your pick, plus ten more."

"We set you free, and you'll just run off, leaving us here with nothing and no place to go," the greasy-haired woman said.

"No, I promise you we won't. In fact, if you agree to watch over my grandson over there, he'll stay with you until we hunt these things down. You want to be truly free out here? Then let us take care of the problem."

"I am not staying here with these people," Daryl shouted, struggling to get his hands free. Chris and another man each grabbed an arm and pulled until he grunted with pain.

"You'll do what I ask you to do," Sam said. He didn't want to be harsh to the kid, but he had to show Joshua he was strong in his convictions.

"I'll stay in his place," Norm said.

Sam ignored him. He knew that Norm wouldn't be the proper bargaining chip. "What do you say? I leave my kin with you, trusting you'll keep him safe. When this is all done, you'll get everything you lost and more."

Joshua put his hand on his hips, looking up at the sky. No one spoke. Surely the man heard the raw honesty in Sam's words. What he was offering was incomparable to having the blood of seven people on their hands, without knowing for sure it would even change a thing.

"And what if you fail? What if those Devils get you like they got my cows?" Joshua said.

"They took us by surprise once," Ben said. "It won't happen again. I packed for every eventuality."

There was a cold reassurance in his grandson's voice that even gave him pause.

"We won't stop until we're done," Sam added. "There's a very good reason why, but it's something I don't feel needs to be shared. You believe your land is tainted. My bloodline has been affected just the same, if not more. I have to end it, now."

To his surprise, the greasy old woman barked, "Cut them loose. It's a square offer. We'll hunker down until they come back for their kid."

Daryl came to him rubbing his wrists. "Boompa, you can't do this to me. You guys need me out there."

He smiled at his grandson. "I'll feel better knowing you're safe. Someone has to do it, and you're better with people than anyone else in the family."

Daryl narrowed his gaze at him. "So you want me to stay because I'm a people person?" He lowered his voice to a whisper. "You think I'm the yokel whisperer or something?"

Sam saw the sarcastic glint in Daryl's eye and wrapped his arms around him. "I think you're the one who can put a bright spin on just about anything. Plus, you get first crack at these things if they come back this way."

"You're gonna realize you need me out there, old man. Who else will carry your sorry butt around when your bunions act up?"

"I'll leave that for Norm," he said with a wink.

A fluttering shadow tearing across the field caught his eye. Sam looked up, searching the blue sky.

"Anyone else see that?" he said.

The two families looked around, scanning every square inch of their surroundings. The nearest trees were hundreds of feet away, so they weren't in imminent danger of something swooping down on them from above.

Still, there was something about the bulk and speed of that shadow that didn't seem right.

"I thought I saw something going from east to west, but I didn't get a good look at it," April said.

"Same here," Chris said, his shotgun pointed at the sky.

It was strange, Sam thought. Just a few minutes ago, these Pineys were going to string them up for Jersey Devil food. Now here they were united against a common enemy, but only because he had promised them something in return for their freedom.

"Why don't we get the kids to the house," Joshua said. "And you, too."

"Daryl."

"Right, Daryl."

It hurt Sam's heart to leave Daryl behind, but he knew it was the right thing to do. Carol lost her battle to hold back tears, pulling him into a tight embrace. She whispered something in his ear, but he couldn't hear what she'd said.

The Piney family headed back to the house in the distance. Joshua and Chris waited for Daryl. "Come on, I don't want to be out here any longer than I have to," Chris said.

"You have to at least let us say good-bye to him," April said, wrapping her arms around her brother's neck. She gave them a defiant look that made them quickly look away. "Don't be your usual smartass self," she said. "Just stay safe."

"Yeah, whatever," he said, though with a smile.

It was Ben who cut their farewells short.

"Something's moving in the grass," he shouted,

pointing to a spot ahead of the departing family. "It's coming right at them."

Sam squinted to see the undulating, knee-high grass. It looked like rippling waves fanning out before an approaching shark. His spine stiffened, his hands gone cold.

"Ernie, in front of you!" Joshua screamed.

Before anyone could react, one of the women hollered as if she'd been burned by a blue flame.

It was the woman with the greasy hair.

"Mom!" Joshua shouted, running toward her.

The woman slipped out of sight for a moment and the squeal of the children was enough to jangle even the hardest nerves.

When she came back into sight, she was in the clutches of a creature straight from the bowels of hell.

Chapter Twenty-two

Ben reached for a gun that wasn't there.

Goddammit!

He couldn't believe what he was seeing.

The old woman dangled upside down, blood trickling from a wound around her neck. Her wails degraded to desperate gurgles. The bass boom of shotguns rattled his rib cage.

One of her ankles was lodged in the mouth of the mother of all Jersey Devils. It was everything people, and Boompa, had described. The tan goat head, though as large as a horse's, looked down at them with eyes black as the empty pit of a haunted mine. It didn't make a sound, other than the steady whoosh of its wings as they beat at the still, humid air. It pulled its cloven-footed legs up to avoid the devastating shotgun pellets, scaling twenty feet higher in a second.

The Piney family opened fire on the creature. It moved so swiftly, they may as well have been throwing rocks at it.

"We have to get out of here, now," Ben said. "While they're distracted."

His mother snapped, "We have to help them!"

"With what?" he said. "Our fists? We can't fight that thing, and once it leaves, they'll tie us up for sure. We need to get back to our vans and get our gear."

"We should at least try," April said.

"Dad?" Ben said, looking for an ally.

The Devil flew around the family as if it were taunting them. The woman had stopped trying to scream. She must have passed out. Or worse. More shots were fired and Ben was pretty sure he saw her take one to the gut. Whether it was a mercy kill or an errant shot, he didn't want to stick around to find out.

Ben's father looked to the family, then the way they'd come in to the field. "He's right, we have to get the hell out of here. At least they have weapons."

"Of course, he's r-r-right," Norm said, already heading opposite the action. "Protect your family."

Daryl grabbed April by the hand, pulling her away.

"I'll take the rear," Ben said, not that there was anything he could do to protect them should the Devil veer their way.

His mother, father and grandfather swept past him. He worried about Boompa, hoping his heart could hold out. What they'd been through was difficult for anyone even half his age.

"Catch her!" Ben heard someone shout.

The Jersey Devil flicked its head, letting the lifeless woman slip from its grasp. Her body flipped end over end, landing into the waiting arms of several of her family. They fell hard onto the ground. The creature circled, then went into a blazing descent until it was practically level with the ground. More errant shots were taken. It didn't so much as flinch as it smashed into as many people as it could, snatching one of the children in its jaws. Ben saw a geyser of blood shoot straight into the air. It must have nicked the girl's artery. The child screeched until the Devil bore down on her. She fell from its maw in two pieces.

You motherfucker.

Ben burned the awful image into his brain. It would be fuel to fight the Devil and its diseased offspring, maybe the bit of anger he'd need when things looked their worst. And they would get worse. No one had expected this. How could they have?

"Just go, go, go!" he commanded his family. "Don't look back!"

His father went pale as another child was taken, flown a hundred feet up and dropped. "No!"

Ben pushed him forward. He knew that sometimes retreat was the best option.

"Keep running, Dad. We have to get out of the open."

And then what? Would the smaller Devils be lying in wait for them amid the pines?

It was a relief when they hit the trees, no longer able to see what was happening.

But the sounds, the terrible cries, they followed the Willets farther than anyone thought they could stand.

Norm Cranston ran the entire way with a protective hand over his head, knowing that at any moment, the smaller creatures were going to rain down on them. His heart almost burst with relief when they came to the clearing with their campground. Legs gone rubbery, his hip clipped the front fender of the minivan. He spun, landing on his ass with a heavy *whump*.

Chest heaving, he scanned the breaks in the branches overhead, looking for monsters.

While he sat, the Willet men went into the older van to get their weapons.

"We have to get the hell out of here and call the p-p-police," Norm said between burning huffs of air.

"You're free to leave, Norm," Sam said. The man had the stamina of a twenty-year-old. They had just dashed through the woods, stopping briefly a couple of times, but he looked as if he could go run right back to that awful place without missing a beat. "Go without feeling even the slightest bit of trepidation. You didn't sign on for this."

Somehow in the melee back in the field, Norm had had the presence of mind to record some of the Devil's horrid actions on his cell phone. He was afraid to even look at it now.

Norm said, "But someone in au-authority has to know about that f-family. They need help."

Sam shook his head. "People come out here because they don't want anything to do with anyone in a position of authority. I hate to say it, but I don't think there's going to be anyone left to save."

Just like the cows.

The image that popped into Norm's mind, the bodies of the backwoods family in place of the gutted cattle, made his stomach churn.

Daryl extended a hand to help Norm to his feet. He had to lean against the minivan to stay upright. His knees felt as if they'd been turned to water. "If you want, I can help load up your car," the youngest Willet said.

The kid looked scared, but also appeared to have complete control over his emotions. All of the Willets did, though Carol seemed a bit dazed.

"And what are you all going to do, go out and h-hunt those things?" Norm asked, raising his voice. Everyone was so busy arming themselves, they weren't taking a moment to stop and think things through. They'd all just watched a group of people who looked like they knew their way around firearms get wiped out in minutes. Was their desire to kill the Jersey Devil so great, their own lives didn't even matter? He held up his phone. "We have everything we need right here! All the proof every cryptozoologist and believer in the J-J-Jersey Devil has ever needed. We should get out of here now and show the damn world! They'll bring in the f-frigging Marines to capture these things and study them, dead or alive. In the end, you'll get your wish."

April handed him a bottle of water. She chugged her own, downing the bottle without coming up for air. She said, "No one, and I mean no one, will believe that video. Pictures and video are too easy to fake now. Come on, you know that kids can make clips of UFOs that look better than anything Spielberg ever did. You show that to anyone and they'll laugh you out of the country."

Carol, who had been staring off into the distance, arms folded across her chest, said, "What about the bodies from last night? You can't fake that."

She was right! Norm wanted to leap for joy. To have video *and* a few bodies, or at least parts of bodies. That was irrefutable proof! The goddamn holy grail!

"Yes, yes, yes!" he said, pushing away from the mini-van. "Everyone just hold on a sec. There may not be any n-need to rush off to war."

Bill Willet stopped checking the clip of his gun. His face was ashen. The rifle trembled slightly in his grip. "He may have a point."

"It's here, we're here, we can finish it ourselves," Ben said. Norm shuddered when he saw him pocket several grenades. *Where the hell did he get them?*

His father held out his hand, motioning for him to calm down. "Look, there are two things we came out here to do. One, find the Devil and hopefully discover what the mark means. And two, kill it so whatever hold it may have on us is no longer an issue. Boompa, what do you say? We didn't know it was going to be like this."

The old man removed his ratty cap, tossing it in the van. He wiped his head down with a black bandana he kept in his pocket. "I'm not going to lie to you. I'm out of my depth here. We're not just talking one creature. Who knows how many are out there? They need to be exterminated. There's no questioning that."

Norm felt, if given time and distance, he could question it. He'd dedicated his life to *finding* mythical creatures, not killing them.

Sam continued. "But if we can get someone else to do it for us, I think we should. There's no sense risking our lives if we don't have to." He sauntered over to the cooler where they had placed the most intact body last night. "Well, I'll be damned." Using the tip of his boot, he lifted the other cooler, reached in and grabbed a can of Schaefer beer. "I really need this right about now."

Norm and Carol scooted to the cooler.

It was gone! Someone had removed the plastic bag with the small Devil body.

"No, that c-can't be," Norm said, his head reeling. "Why would those hillbillies take it?"

"I don't think they did," April said, suddenly standing next to him, looking down at the half-melted ice, running red with the blood of the beast parts that had been inside. "We would have seen one of them carrying it. That thing was too big to just stuff in a pocket."

"So what are we saying, someone else has been here?" Daryl said.

"Or something," Ben said.

Norm shook his head violently. "No, not s-s-some-thing. For the Jersey Devil to d-do that, it would have to p-p-possess intelligence and dexterity far beyond . . ."

Carol looked to him. "Far beyond what?"

She was right. Beyond what? Beyond the abilities he *thought* something like the Jersey Devil should have? What was the baseline he should use to compare it to?

The real answer was that something like this went beyond what he *wanted* the creature to possess. Because if it was smart enough to know what they had done and able to reclaim the body of its brethren, the humans out here were in a world of trouble.

The closest Norm had come to being this afraid was the night he'd camped in a small cave in the Gilchrist State Forest in Oregon. He'd been there for three weeks tracking down sightings of a Sasquatch that had disturbed separate pairs of campers the week before. He'd found prints right off the bat, and was studying the plaster casts he'd made that night when he heard a strange, heavy moaning outside the cave's entrance. A powerful, wet animal smell wafted inside, making him gag. He'd grabbed his rifle, calling out, "Who's there?" It seemed even the night birds and wind outside the cave stopped.

Low mumbling between what sounded like two people speaking a foreign tongue whispered back and forth. Something about them didn't sound quite right. The stream of hard consonants seemed to come from a mouth and vocal structure beyond the capability of a human being. He pushed his back against the wall, staring at the small, open mouth of the cave, waiting for whatever was outside to clamber inside.

The mumbling stopped. He jumped, hitting his head on the low ceiling, when a palm-sized rock was tossed into the cave, hitting and breaking one of the plaster casts. Terrified, he fired a warning shot. The booming sound of the discharged rifle in the small space deafened him. Without that sense, he was left with only being able to see something coming at him in the dark. He never slept that night, expecting an angry Sasquatch to clamber into the cave.

That never happened, but he'd been so scared, he'd pissed himself that night . . . twice.

"We have to get the hell out of here," he reiterated. "Right now."

Daryl, April and their father had been scouring the ground around them.

"It's all gone," Bill said.

"What?" Carol said. She hadn't taken her eyes off the empty cooler.

"All the bodies, the bits, shit, even the leaves with their blood. Everything's been removed."

"It d-doesn't matter anymore," Norm said. "We have to l-l-leave. Proving to the world it exists is low on the p-priority list."

This was a creature smart enough to clean up after its deeds. It was most likely why it had remained undiscovered for centuries. Maybe it should be left that way.

Bill looked to Sam, the old man crushing the can of Schaefer, tossing it into the cooler that once held the Devil body.

"He's right," Sam said. "This has gotten too dangerous. We should go."

It appeared admitting defeat hadn't come easy. Norm was shocked to see his friend looking his age for the very first time. His entire body sagged, the lines in his face etching deeper.

"You all go," Ben said. "Just leave me a car. I'll meet up with you when I'm done."

His mother turned to him, saying, "No, we're all leaving."

"I'm not. I just need to bag one of those things. Then I'll leave."

"This isn't a debate," Bill said.

Ben cocked an eyebrow. "You're right, it's not. With any luck, I'll be with you all before you know it."

Norm tossed things haphazardly into his rental car. He'd be ready the moment they convinced their son to get the hell out of Dodge.

"I'll stay with him," April said. "Someone has to have his back."

"The hell you will," Ben countered.

"I'm with them," Daryl said. His brother looked like he wanted to punch him in the face for piling on to an already difficult situation.

"Enough!" Bill shouted. "No one, and I mean no one is staying behind! If I have to drag you, I will."

Norm didn't doubt the big man could do it.

Daryl pleaded with his grandfather. "Come on, Boompa, we got this close."

"No, this is too much. I think we know what those marks mean now. They mean that the Devil can find you when you're in the Barrens. There's no need to ever come back here. I see that now. Your grandmother wouldn't want you to be here like this."

"But what about the people these things have been attacking?" Daryl said.

"Norm's right. We'll report it to the police. Maybe

someone will be able to verify the video he took is real. They can handle it."

Norm was jumping out of his skin. He wanted to scream at them, tell them to get their asses in gear. They could debate the merits of staying or going when they were miles out of Jersey.

"This is bullshit," April spat, head downcast, kicking at the embers of last night's fire. Norm couldn't believe either the bravery of the Willet kids or their sheer stupidity.

Daryl went to the old Ford and placed his rifle inside. He took off his Mets cap, sweeping back his hair. "Boompa's right. Grams would freak if she could see us now."

That seemed to bring everyone back to the reality of the situation. Shoulders were lowered and protests cut short. Norm wanted to throw his arms around Daryl's hulking frame.

"All right," Bill said. "Let's see how fast we can pack this stuff up."

The loud whoosh from above stopped them in midstride. Norm watched in paralyzed horror as the big Jersey Devil from before, along with several of the smaller ones, swept down, heading straight for them. Guns were raised, but before a shot could be taken, Daryl was plucked and lifted away like a cheap prize in a crane game.

"Hold your fire!" Ben shouted.

The wind must have been knocked out of him, because Daryl didn't so much as make a noise as he was carried up and away, floating over the treetops until he was simply gone.

Chapter Twenty-three

"Daryl!" April screamed loud enough to bring a coppery taste to her mouth. It only took a few seconds for the Devil and its minions to rip her brother away. Hot tears stung her eyes.

Not sweet Daryl. Dear God, no.

In his anger, Ben smashed the butt of his rifle onto the hood of the Ford, leaving a big dent. Her mother ran into her father's arms, sobbing.

Boompa walked in a tight circle, eyeing the breaks in the pines, the grip on his rifle so tight, his knuckles were pale. "You goddamn son of a bitch," he kept muttering.

Even Norm had stopped packing his car. He leaned against it, deflated, a sail searching for a breeze.

April dug the small compass out of her pocket. "It was going northwest when it got out of the trees. We have to follow it."

Ben and her father dug even more weapons out of the van. April took a bowie knife, Beretta and pair of stun grenades, the kind that made brilliant flashes of light coupled with a nerve-jangling bang, along with her rifle. She then loaded backpacks with food, water and other provisions.

"I hope you can understand why we can't lead you out of here," Boompa said to Norm. "If you turn around and stay on course, you should hit the main road after a spell."

April stopped what she was doing when she heard Norm reply, "I'm staying with you."

"You don't have to. This is between my family and those things," Boompa said.

"No. I w-want to help. You're going to need all you can g-get. I can't just leave you all and be able to live with myself. Not after that."

"You'll need a gun. You know how to shoot?" Boompa said.

"I do. I grew up h-hunting with my father. I bring a rifle with me w-when I'm out in the f-field. People think I bring them to defend myself against the creatures I t-t-track, but it's the known animals that scare me the most."

April gave Norm a rifle and hunting knife. "Here," she said. "They're Daryl's." She felt the hitch in her chest and fought to keep it down. She tried picturing where he could be at this moment, what he was feeling. The terror must have been overwhelming. If she thought about it too much, she knew she would break down.

Turning to her older brother, for the first time fully appreciating his combat experience rather than blaming it for changing him, she said, "You think we can take the vans that way?"

Ben walked the perimeter of the clearing. "It doesn't look like it. The road, if that's what you call what we drove on to get here, stops here. Boompa, you recall what's this way?"

His jaw flexed from biting on his back teeth. "A whole lot of nothing. There may be some farms or homesteads, but just as likely there are bogs and empty flatlands. The way they were headed is strange territory."

Ben paced back and forth, thinking. "We need to split up, but stay close to one another. When we find where the Devil's taken Daryl, it would be better if we can flank it, maybe even take it by surprise."

Her father said, "If we do that, you stay with Norm and Boompa. I'll take your mother and sister." He tossed him a walkie-talkie. "Keep it low but check in every five minutes.

"Do you think it . . . it . . ." her mother sputtered.

Boompa put an arm around her. "No, dear, I think Daryl's okay. If it wanted to harm him, it would have done it right away, just like it did with those Pineys. It's smart as hell. It wants us to follow it."

April had that same feeling, and it twisted in her guts. Hunting a creature that acted on base instincts was one thing. Trying to track an intelligent animal that seemed to be one step ahead of them the entire time was the definition of a dire situation.

She gave a knife to her mother, helping affix the sheath to the loop in her jeans. "Just in case," she said. Her mother nodded, eyes vacant, and kissed the top of her head like she used to when she was a little girl.

"No more wasting time," her father said. He shoved three sticks of Big Red gum in his mouth, chewing loudly.

They separated the moment they entered the pines, Ben leading the way for Boompa and Norm, her father's enormous bulk making it clear for her and her mother to follow.

April couldn't shake the feeling that they were being watched the entire time. She imagined a tingle in her birthmark, the damned thing sending out a signal to the Jersey Devil that said, *"Here we are. See? We're right where you want us to be."*

Sean was starting to love the day shift. After a year of nights, always straining to see in the dark, his senses as raw as exposed flesh, he was finally able to relax . . . a little bit. At least he was able to see someone coming from a good distance and he wasn't jumping at every noise. At nights, he would swear Mother Nature was doing her damnedest to give him a heart attack.

"Yo, Louis, you got any of those beers left?"

His partner emerged from the small, two-man cabin, scratching at his head. Sean could see his dandruff floating in the shafts of early morning sunlight.

"Check for yourself," Louis said. "Are you that fucked up that you gotta start drinking in the morning now?"

They had an old, metal cooler, a real throwback from the '70s, beside the cabin. Sean pulled back the metal bar that kept the lid on. The ice had melted to tepid water, but there were still a few cans of Bud floating around like miniature life rafts. He took a swig of warm beer and belched, startling a bird perched in the tree over the cabin.

"You know what they say?"

Louis waved him off. "Yeah, yeah, it's five o'clock somewhere. But that doesn't make it five o'clock here."

"You can blame that damn graveyard shift. This is normally the time I spent relaxing with a few drinks so I could get some sleep. Give me a few more weeks to get my biorhythm back in normal mode."

"Biorhythm? You're full of more shit than a ten-ton

horse." Louis went back into the cabin to lie on the solitary cot. There was no need to have two sets of eyes on the marijuana plants. Not now. A person would have to either be demented or possess a death wish to traipse on in here in the cold light of day, looking to sneak off with a plant or two. This section of the farm had five hundred plants. Talking to some of the other guys hired to guard the farm, Sean had heard there may have been up to ten thousand plants across several plots of hidden land. Bruce Dyson, the big boss, wasn't about to tell any of them the full scope of the operation. That was fine by Sean. The less he knew the better.

"Shows how smart you are, dumbass," Sean said to the retreating Louis. "There's no such thing as a ten-ton horse."

Louis sighed so loudly, it could be heard outside. "I have a feeling you're going to wear me out real fast. Maybe I'll ask for the graveyard shift."

The cot creaked as he settled in, dropping an open *High Society* magazine over his face.

"You can have it," Sean said. "I'm never going back. If Dyson tries to screw me, I'm outta here."

He stepped off the narrow porch, tilting his face to the sun, enjoying the warmth as it spread down to his feet. It'd only been a week, but he'd managed to get a killer tan, though it stopped at his elbows. No matter. He needed all the vitamin D he could get. He heard on the radio that everyone lacked D and it was the reason people were so sick all the time.

The plants waved back at him as the wind skipped over the farm encased within the ubiquitous pine trees. Word was that Dyson had some men on the take in the local PD, which is why police helicopters somehow never reported the obvious pot farm when they flew overhead. This shit was big business, which was why people like him and Louis were on guard 24/7 with instructions to shoot first and bury later. No questions need be asked. What was the point?

Opening his eyes, the sun seared its image on his retinas. Wincing, he slammed his eyelids shut. "That was real smart." Rubbing at his eyes, he said with a chuckle, "I've been blinded by the light. Hey, you hear that, Louis? I was blinded by the light!"

His weary partner didn't make an effort to respond. Killjoy.

When he could open his eyes again, he had to wipe away a layer of protective tears. His vision was still blurry.

What the hell is that?

He caught a glimpse of something big flying over the eastern section of the farm. It couldn't be a hawk. It looked more like a helicopter in the distance, but he'd have been able to hear it if it was close enough to see.

Holy crap! What if it's one of those military copters? The ones that sneak right up on you and barely make any noise!

If that was the case, he and Louis would have to make a choice—try to shoot it down with the meager arsenal at their disposal, or run like jackrabbits into the woods. If they chose the latter, he'd stop at his apartment long enough to grab the gym bag where he kept his money and disappear. If the Feds didn't catch him, Dyson would.

"Louis, get the hell out here! We may have *federales*."

"I told you not to start drinking so early," Louis cried out from the cabin. It was obvious he wasn't moving his lazy ass.

Sean blinked hard, trying to get his eyes to focus.

Wait, that couldn't be a helicopter. Now he saw smaller things flying around it. Maybe it was the humdinger of all hawks with a bunch of birds doing their best to irritate it. He grabbed his rifle and jogged over to get a closer look. He wished he had a scope so he could get a better look and tell for sure what it was. It might have even been balloons twisting in the wind. Some kid was sure going to be upset when she saw her birthday balloons had up and left for good. Poor kid.

He stepped on a thick twig. The snap was remarkably loud. It must have been dry as ass to crack like that. It had been a while since he'd seen rain.

Sean froze when he noticed the things in the air had stopped moving. It was as if they had heard it, too, and were now very aware of his presence.

Stop psyching yourself out, man.

They started moving in his direction, flying lower. Shielding his eyes with his hand, he strained to see what the hell he was dealing with here.

All at once, everything came into focus. Sean felt last night's dinner struggle to make its way out his tail end.

The small things weren't birds. At best, they were deformed bats. But it looked like they had tails.

And the big one, holy Christ. It was carrying a person, some poor guy who looked dead, which was a mercy. The creatures were flying real fast now.

There was no doubt they were heading right for him!

Sean raised his rifle, pulling off several shots at the big one. It zigzagged with ease, evading the bullets.

"Louis! Louis!"

Sean turned and ran as fast as he could. Now that they were closer, he could hear the steady beating of their long, leathery wings. The cabin was just twenty yards away. He kept shouting for his partner. Any second now, they would be on him.

Louis walked out rubbing his eyes. "What the hell, man?"

Sean saw the look of horror on Louis's face and knew he was done. Something snipped at his ear, taking a chunk out of it. Sean screamed, clamping his hand over his ear.

It felt like a pair of ice picks stabbed into the front and back of his skull. Suddenly, he was no longer running. No, he was flying, blood pouring into his eyes. He dropped his rifle, swinging at the little serpent things as they nibbled at him, dangling in midair.

He heard the bone of his skull give way as the pressure built to an agonizing and final crescendo.

Louis saw the creature clamp its jaws around Sean's head and lift him into the air. The thing was already carrying another guy, his limp body dangling.

"Shit shit shit!"

Sean was a goner. He saw his partner's head cave in. There was nothing he could do to save him.

Louis ran back into the cabin, slamming the door and jamming the cot against it. He fumbled for his rifle, clutching it to his chest.

He'd be damned if those things didn't look just like the Jersey Devil. Being from Baltimore, he hadn't grown up with the legend, but he knew plenty of locals who believed in the creature whole hog. Now he was sorry he'd doubted them.

The Devils screeched for a while, their cries fading as they flew away.

There were no windows in the cabin, so he had no way of knowing where they'd gone or if they were still around, silently circling overhead.

I'll just wait them out, he thought. *Marv and Craig will be here around four. I can chill the fuck out until then.*

The one thing he did know was that he wasn't going back out there, not when he was alone. If those Jersey Devils or whatever they were didn't leave, he'd have a better chance with Marv and Craig around. They were both ex Special Forces and not exactly right in the head. They might even enjoy blasting them out of the sky like it was a duck hunt.

He'd just have to sit things out. Sure, it was dark as a tomb in here, but it was safe.

To kill time, he could play Asphalt 8 on his iPhone. Right now, his hands were shaking so bad, he worried that he'd just drop the phone.

"Just cool it. They got Sean, but you're okay. You're okay."

The roof exploded downward. Louis was hit in the shoulder by a heavy plank of wood. Something thumped heavily on the floor and made a sound like a watermelon exploding. Harsh light shot through the new skylight in the cabin. Louis fumbled for his rifle.

He recoiled when he saw Sean's mangled body twisted within the roof's rubble. The white of his fractured skull had split through his scalp. Louis felt something wet on the back of his hand. Looking down, he saw a smear of Sean's brain.

Flicking it off violently, he scrabbled to the farthest edge of the cabin.

A shadow passed over the hole in the ceiling. He fired wildly until he was out of ammo. He was starting to hyperventilate, and the periphery of his vision boiled with inky blackness.

The smaller creatures dove through the hole.

"No!" Louis screamed, covering his face with his arms. He felt the Devils pecking at his skin, biting and scratching, each fresh wound seeming to burn with infection.

Something heavy stomped on the roof. The cabin shook. Bits of dust and dirt rained down on him. The smaller Devils skittered away, jumping up and down all around the cabin.

"Please, go away!"

When he saw its satanic face, he knew for sure it was the Jersey Devil. It landed in front of him, its hard hooves clunking on the wood floor. It spread its massive wings, breathing foul vapor in his face. It smelled like the floor of a slaughterhouse. It dropped the man it was holding on the floor. Louis saw the Mets cap on the guy's head, assuming he was being kept for a snack later.

Before he could move to try to get out the door, it whipped its tail at him, slashing his throat. His hands went to his neck, desperate to stem the tide of blood that poured over his fingers.

He couldn't breathe!

Louis struggled to stand, fought to draw air, becoming woozy as his life seeped from the wound.

The little Devils swarmed over him, lapping up his blood. His vision clouded, saving him from watching the Jersey Devil bend forward, its long neck craning down until it buried its face in his stomach, tearing through his flesh and devouring the steaming organs within.

Chapter Twenty-four

"Give them a quick check," Ben said to his grandfather.
They walked as fast as they could in what he believed
was the direction the Devil had gone with his brother. It
was hard going, the ground being so uneven, the sandy
soil so soft, they'd all come close to turning their ankles
several times.

Boompa spoke into the walkie-talkie, "Everyone
okay, son?"

There was a brief crackle of static, then, "We're good."

It was a lie. Seeing Daryl taken by the Devil, none of
them was anywhere within the realm of good.

Unless he meant good and scared.

Or good and mad.

Because Ben was madder than he'd ever been in his
life. He should have seen the damn thing coming. At the
very least, he should have heard it and fragged its ass. It
wasn't as if he didn't know how to conduct himself in
enemy territory. Never let your guard down. Ever. How
could he have been so stupid?

When he found the Jersey Devil, it would pay dearly

for this. He'd come here knowing full well that the creature, if they ever found it, had a finite number of days left on this planet.

Now, when he came face-to-face with it, and he would, he'd savor every moment of its demise.

He was damned good at finding things. Back when he was stationed in Marjah in Afghanistan, his platoon had been tasked with ferreting out a cadre of Taliban that had the town on lockdown. On their second day, they'd nabbed one of the terrorists, a kid less than twenty, who turned out to be more of a coward than a killer. He'd given them enough intel to take the town back.

But then he'd disappeared. Tension was heightened, knowing the bastard could give their position away. He had to be found, fast.

It took Ben with two other men less than an hour to retrieve the informant, cowering under a bed in a house filled with small children. From that point on, Ben was known as the finder of lost souls, sent out to use what some joked was his sixth sense to locate men who'd made a living out of being able to vanish into thin air.

It was as if they were marked, carrying a beacon only Ben could hear. Just like the red stain on his own side.

If Daryl was hurt or worse, he'd make the Devil pray for a clean and swift ending—if it could even rationalize, which he was beginning to fear was the case. The beast was obviously intelligent enough to plan and strategize. For the first time since he'd been indoctrinated into the legend, he began to wonder if it was, in fact, partially human.

"Watch your step," he said, pointing to a depression. Norm and Boompa gave it a wide berth.

Ben did his best to keep to a path where the trees weren't so bunched together. His eyes were constantly looking up for signs of the creatures, and down for potential pitfalls.

"How do we k-k-know if we're on the right track?" Norm said, puffing hard.

"I just know."

Ben held up a hand, signaling for them to stop.

"You hear something?" Norm asked, nearly bumping into him.

"Shhh."

Breathing slowly from his mouth, he listened for his family. Leaves shuffled so faintly, he knew they were veering farther apart from one another.

"Boompa, tell them to change their course a little more to the north."

"Gotcha."

It was advantageous to have two groups, but not if they got completely separated.

"You holding out okay?" he asked his grandfather.

He clipped the walkie-talkie back to his belt. "Don't you worry about me. I don't think God kept me kicking around for eighty years just to have me drop dead from a walk in the woods."

Ben didn't like the look of him. He was as pale as fresh milk and sweating profusely. He'd worked with his grandfather on the farm all his life and knew it wasn't the heat. Old Boompa was worried to death about Daryl.

They started walking again.

"You remember when Daryl was little and said he could tip a cow?" Ben said, his head bobbing up and down, finger on the trigger guard of his rifle.

Boompa gave a short laugh. "He wasn't even as high

as that heifer's leg. I never saw someone so determined to do something that wasn't going to happen."

"And I told him he shook her up so much, he'd turned her milk into a milkshake."

"That was just so you could get out of milking her. Poor kid had to see for himself before you stole all the milkshake!"

"Hey, it worked."

Ben recalled his brother's disappointed face when he came back carrying the full pail. Two defeats in one day were more than the little dude could take. When he saw Ben laughing, he'd kicked that pail right over and stormed into the house, screaming how he hated cows and big brothers alike.

Their father had called Daryl Don Quixote Junior for the rest of that summer. Only the adults understood what it meant at the time.

Where are you, Daryl? Whatever it's done to you, keep fighting. Just keep fighting.

Ben felt heavy thumping coming up from the soles of his boots.

Something was on the move.

Something big, and heavy.

There was a mad flurry of wings flapping overhead. He looked up to see a roiling mass of birds shooting across the sky. What made it strange was that the mass was made of all types of birds, not just, say, a murder of crows or flock of geese.

The thumping got louder, the ground shaking slightly.

"Get ready," Ben said. "Something's coming this way."

Boompa cocked his ear toward the approaching rush. "Sounds like deer. A whole herd of them."

"This isn't the Serengeti," Norm said. "Wild animals don't rush around in packs in the Jersey woods."

"When those things are out there, they do," Ben said.

They had to find cover. Boompa was thinking the same thing, because he was on the walkie-talkie telling Ben's father, mother and sister to get behind the widest trees they could find.

Ben, Norm and Boompa pressed their backs against a trio of big pines.

"Here they come!" Boompa wailed.

Wild-eyed, hopping scared deer thundered past them, weaving around the trees in a ballet of barely controlled retreat. Ben tucked his right shoulder in a little closer, worried that he'd get clipped by one of the fleeing animals. He looked over at Norm. The man was as still as a statue, watching with rapt fascination as the deer flooded past. Boompa gave him a thumbs-up from his position.

It took less than thirty seconds for the frightened herd to peter out.

Boompa shook his head at the last deer as it bounded over a fallen tree. "Well, I think that proves we're going in the right direction."

Norm sighed, dropping his head toward his chest. "I've never seen anything like that, at least up close. I could even smell the fear coming off them."

He was right. The ripe odor hung in the air like a dense fog.

They heard more footsteps, but it was too late to duck behind a tree.

Four coyotes sped toward them, jaws snapping.

"You've gotta be shitting me," Ben grumbled. He shot one, missing the lead coyote. Two more shots yielded one more down, the coyote flipping in the air, yowling in pain. Keeping his calm, he caught the next two in the face, obliterating them from the neck up.

Both bodies continued their momentum, finally sliding to within a few feet of him, raw chasms emptying blood and exposed meat onto the forest floor.

"Damn g-good shooting," Norm exclaimed, cringing at the sight of the dead coyotes.

Boompa screamed. Ben turned to his right, just in time to see an enormous coyote take him down.

Carol couldn't believe what they were seeing. Deer after deer ran for their lives, just missing them as they cowered behind the tree trunks. April held her rifle to her chest, her forehead pressed against the barrel, eyes closed, waiting for the madness to pass.

The frightened animals kicked up great gouts of water as they fled. The gradient of the forest had taken a dip as they'd made their way, finding themselves in what Carol believed to be a scrub oak swamp. They waded up to their shins in dank water that smelled like frogs and rotten eggs.

Bill kept looking their way to make sure they were all right.

It felt as if she hadn't taken a breath, waiting for the last animal to go by.

When everything was clear, Carol said, "There's only one thing out here that could get them in a panic like that."

Her husband nodded. "That means we're getting close to the son of a bitch. We better keep moving."

"Come on, Mom," April said, giving her a gentle tug. They resumed sloshing through the thick water, hoping to find drier ground. She wondered if there were water moccasins here. It was best to put it out of her head.

Carol had been thinking about everything she'd ever

read about the Jersey Devil. She couldn't recall any reports of multiple creatures, or of it attacking people the way it had them, or worse, that poor Piney family. There was no denying that these things were the Jersey Devil, especially the big one. But their behavior was as mystifying as it was deadly. They seemed almost rabid. Rabid but smart. And strong.

For a creature that had done its best to elude people for hundreds of years, it was doing its best to announce to the world that it was here and in charge of the Barrens.

The closest it had ever come to being this brazen was in 1909, when the Jersey Devil had been spotted for a week straight from Trenton all the way down to Philadelphia. People saw it try to attack animals, heard it clawing at their windows and rooftops, and watched it dash off into the sky. It got so bad, men gathered into posses, beating down the woods to smoke out the creature. It was front-page news at the time, in legitimate papers.

But no one had died and, eventually, the Devil faded away. In fact, it had lain pretty low ever since then, popping up from time to time, but always retreating to wherever it called home. She suspected that it hibernated, like a bear, but for far longer periods of time.

What the hell had happened to make it so ruthless, reckless even?

It might be a good idea to find the place where this all started—the Leeds house.

She'd heard that the foundation at least was still there, but almost impossible to find without a guide. Once they found Daryl and took him somewhere safe, a few of them could try to make it out there.

Daryl.

Maybe Norm was right. Maybe they should have contacted the authorities. For a moment back at the vans, she'd hoped Norm would leave them, head into town and tell someone what had happened. When he volunteered to come help find Daryl, she was both thankful and upset.

Now it was early afternoon and getting hotter by the minute. They couldn't keep this pace up all day. They were tired and hungry and if they didn't watch it, they would soon be dehydrated.

The sound of gunshots broke her concentration.

"Where's that coming from?" she said.

Bill was on the walkie-talkie. "Dad, was that you?" There was no reply. "Was that you that fired those shots? Are you guys okay?"

April looked ready to bolt to where they figured them to be. Carol had to hold her back.

"You guys copy?"

He turned up the volume. All they heard was static.

Chapter Twenty-five

Daryl awoke with the mother of all headaches. Wherever he was, it was too dark to see and smelled like earthworms and mushrooms. He tried to move, his hand pushing through soft dirt.

"Where the hell am I?"

For a moment, he thought he'd been drugged, his senses were so slow to return. Gradually, he was able to piece things together despite the throbbing in his head.

He'd been grabbed back at the campsite. Before he knew it, he was in the air, but he couldn't breathe. Something had been tightly wrapped around his rib cage, making it almost impossible to suck in enough air. Panicking, he started to hyperventilate, which was about the time the lights went out.

The last thing he remembered seeing was his sister looking up at him, her rifle drawn, crying out his name.

His torso was a ball of agony. Every muscle and bone felt as if he'd been a human ball in a soccer game played by elephants. He didn't hear any wheezing when he breathed, which was one good sign. At least his lungs hadn't been punctured by any broken ribs.

His hands fluttered to his head.

His Mets cap was still there. He'd had it since he was twelve, calling it his lucky charm for the past eight years.

Was it still a lucky charm? He guessed it could be worse. He could be dead.

But this sure felt like something close to death.

"I guess this beats being dropped off in a giant bird's nest."

Daryl often wondered if the Jersey Devil, being a winged creature, spent most of its time within the thick canopy of trees. That would explain why people couldn't find it. People were earthbound. Even from above, it could still conceal itself. And who really had the money to fly helicopters and planes all over the Pine Barrens searching for a monster the majority of people thought was just a spooky story?

Maybe this was a place where the Devil kept its prey, a kind of outdoor pantry.

Whatever the case, he had to get the hell out of here.

Sitting up brought white sparks of pain in his head.

"Dammit, dammit, dammit."

He lay back down, feeling the cool ground at his back. Reaching up, he felt only solid earth. He was hoping there was some kind of board or door above him that he could work on moving aside once he got his strength and courage up to move again.

"And here I was worried about Boompa."

His breathing growing heaver as panic set in, the pain in his ribs and chest made his eyes roll in his head.

Wondering what had befallen his family, Daryl drifted off until he could no longer feel the pain.

* * *

"You guys copy?"

Sam struggled to get the coyote's limp body off him. His knife was buried to the hilt in the wild dog's neck.

The weight magically disappeared as Ben and Norm cast the cooling carcass aside. His knife dripped with blood. They each lent a hand to get him up.

"Much obliged," he said.

"You look like you went swimming in a slaughter-house blood tank," Ben said.

Giving himself a quick once-over, he saw his grandson was right. He must have caught an artery, because that crazed coyote bled every drop it had on him. Tossing the walkie-talkie to Norm, he said, "You better answer my son before he comes charging over here like one of those deer."

Ben handed him a small towel from his pack. "I'm not sure how much good this is going to do, but you can at least get some of the blood off your face. Use this, too," he said, handing him a warm bottle of water.

"It's good to see your old Boompa's still got it," he said, tilting the bottle over his upturned face. He closed his mouth tight. He didn't want to choke on any of that blood.

"You feel all right? We can rest up for a bit," Ben said.

"I'm fine. I look way worse than I feel. We have to find your brother and this old man isn't about to be the one to make us lag behind."

"You let me know if you need a break. In fact, maybe it's better if you and Norm head back to the vans. I can take it from here."

"The hell we will. I'll be worse off waiting than actually doing something. Besides, I have you to watch my back."

"Yeah, I'm great at that. Daryl got taken and you almost got killed by a coyote."

"Don't start talking like that. There isn't a man on this planet that could know what the hell is going on out here. You have us headed in the right direction, and when the time comes, I know you'll get Daryl back. Just keep doing what you're doing."

Sam's heart was doing a jig, but nothing to worry anyone about. That fall didn't do any wonders for his back, either. Again, old-man complaints that didn't need to be voiced.

Was there some bit of grim satisfaction from taking that coyote out by hand? He couldn't deny that. At least it showed he could take care of himself. The last thing the family needed now was for him to be a burden.

Lauren, if we only hadn't had that picnic, where would our lives have taken us? Would you still be here, your heart all the more lighter, free from the burden you carried all those years?

He looked over at Ben, motioning for them to press on.

If it means we wouldn't have our wonderful family, I guess we would have still gone out to the woods that day. I know you're watching over us, sweetheart. We'll be fine. I need you by Daryl's side now. Let him know we're coming.

Trudging farther through the swamp, Bill found the navigation increasingly more difficult. It didn't help that his legs felt like jerking out from under him. Was that exhaustion, or the damned Huntington's disease? His body hurt all over.

You can hurt all you want, I'm not stopping. And you don't even know if you have it, so quit worrying.

It was easy to say, but hard to shake.

The swampy goop puddled around their feet as the floor sloped upward. At least that was one thing going their way. Now if they could only get past the black cloud of gnats that buzzed in their ears and zipped up their noses and in their mouths when they took a breath.

"I see one," April said, pointing up and ahead of them.

"You sure?"

"Positive."

They'd noticed the smaller Devil watchers an hour ago. They kept to the trees, peering down at them. What gave them away was their size. They may have been miniatures compared to the one that took Daryl, but they were still about as bulky as two or three hawks combined. They had a tendency to make the branches they alighted on crack or sway.

He saw April raise her rifle and motioned for her to stop.

"Not yet," he said.

"So we just let them track us until there's so many of the fuckers around, we can't handle them?"

"April!" her mother said. It was the first time she'd spoken in a long while.

"They're not attacking for a reason," Bill said.

"Yeah, so they can overrun us when the sun goes down," April said.

"I can't explain why, but I don't think so."

What he didn't want to tell her was his suspicion that the Jersey Devil might know a thing or two about revenge. After his family killed four of them last night, the Devils took their anger out on that Piney family and their cows. Then they took Daryl. He worried that if they killed another one, Daryl would be the one to pay the price even further.

If it hadn't happened already.

Don't even think it! He's alive. You know it. You'd feel it if he wasn't. There's something more going on here.

April was right about one thing. Night wasn't far off. They were going to be at a major disadvantage in more ways than one.

As if reading his mind, Carol said, "We have to stop. My legs and feet are killing me. We haven't eaten. What good are we going to be if we're ready to pass out?"

Carol was covered in a sheen of sweat. So was April. He could only imagine how he looked to them. He wondered how his father was holding up. They'd checked in with him a couple of minutes ago and he sounded fine.

"We can stop for a while, but I don't like all the cover around us. Those things can easily hide. I know it defies logic, but I'd feel safer if we found open ground, but were close enough to run for some kind of cover."

They came across what looked like the last vestiges of several homes, the only solid thing left a massive stone staircase that was sunken halfway into the ground. It felt as if they had fallen into a time warp, depositing them in a world where man had long since been erased from the planet.

"I say we keep going," April said.

She called out for her brother. Just like the hundreds of times prior, there was no answer.

"We don't even know where we're going or where to look," Carol said, her voice breaking. Bill saw the tears spill from her eyes and ran to her.

"We're going to find him." He pulled her to his chest, rubbing her back.

"How? He could be anywhere. People have died out here, lost and wandering around until they can't take another step. You all saw how vast it is. When I think of Daryl out there, alone, and us on foot, following what? After those deer, we haven't seen a single trace to make us think we're even going the right way."

April came over and put a hand on her shoulder. "We can't give up, Mom. He'd never give up on us."

Carol turned on her. "I didn't say I want to give up! He's my son! I'll stay here for the rest of my life if I have to, searching for him. I just wish to hell we had a sign that told us we were on the right track."

April pulled back but didn't try to argue.

"I'm sorry. I didn't mean to say it that way."

Bill tilted his head up toward the trees. "Our sign is right there. If we weren't getting close, they wouldn't be here. Not just to watch us. We're going to find a better spot to rest a bit, then we're going to find him. Those things will eventually lead us to him, whether they know it or not."

Carol cupped April's face in her hands, kissing her cheek. "I shouldn't have snapped at you."

"Don't worry. We're all on edge."

They resumed walking, April spotting another Devil partially hidden in the trees.

They want us to see them, Bill thought.

But why?

Just as the sun was beginning to set, Carol spotted where they could finally sit down for a spell, but it seemed terribly ominous.

"How about it?" she said.

Bill looked ahead with his hands on his hips, chewing hard on his Big Red gum.

"It's in the open and we have more than enough places to take cover," Carol said.

Bill said, "April, call your grandfather, tell him about it. If this is our best option, I'd hate to see what our worst would be."

Chapter Twenty-six

It took them half an hour to find their way and reunite with Bill, Carol and April, but they'd finally made it. The darkness hadn't helped matters much. Now that they were here, Norm kind of wished they'd found a better place to meet.

"What the h-hell is a cemetery doing out in the m-middle of nowhere?"

It wasn't a sprawling graveyard, but it was much bigger than a simple, old-time family plot. Among the decrepit, crumbling tombstones were mausoleums and one crypt that had been built into the side of a small hill on the western edge of the cemetery.

A wooden church, its roof collapsed, windows broken long ago, sagged in disrepair beside it.

"This wasn't always the middle of nowhere," the old man said. "People don't realize there were thriving factories all over the Barrens just over a hundred years ago. I'll bet if we could look around, you'll find overgrown areas of foundations and either a farm, factory, or mill if there's running water nearby. This place has been abandoned for a long time. The forest is good at taking care of the rest."

Not for the first time that day, Norm questioned why he'd agreed to search for Daryl with the Willets. They were more than capable of handling this themselves. He wondered if he would only get in the way when things got bad . . . or worse.

Because despite everything, you fool, you feel alive for the first time in years. You have a chance to prove to the world that the Jersey Devil does exist, and if it's more than just some new species, what will it mean for the way we think of our place in it? If the Devil is real, what about all the other creatures like Bigfoot and lake monsters and big cats? And Jesus, after seeing the look on that kid's face when the Devil swooped down to get him, there's just no way I could turn back.

He found the white pill case in his pocket, popping one of his anti-anxiety meds. With night upon them, he needed something to take the edge off.

Bill said to his son, "Help me find wood for the fire. We'll get what we need in the church."

"This place freaking you out?" April asked Norm as she collected stones to build a fire ring.

"Everything's f-f-freaking me out," he admitted. "Here, take this. It'll help you see better." He handed her a mini camera, making sure to turn the night vision on.

"Thanks."

"I want it on now, anyway. We can use it to keep an eye on the trees."

He walked with her, holding the rocks in the tail of his shirt. She stopped at a pair of small grave markers.

"That's so sad. Look," she said, handing him the camera.

There was only one word on each of the markers— BABY. No name, no date.

"They might have been stillborn or d-d-died not long

after they were born. It happened a lot back then," Norm said. "Guess they weren't around l-l-long enough to even earn a name."

Some of the graves had dates from the late 1700s. The latest date they saw was 1923. It had been a long, long time since anyone had come here. The ground was uneven, as if the tenants below had been trying to rise up for the past century. In some places, weeds grew past his hip. Most of the headstones were cracked or simply a pile of broken stones. They made sure not to collect any of them for the fire ring.

"One good thing about the night," he said.

"What's that?" April seemed awfully calm and collected. She must have been a bundle of nerves beneath that cool façade.

"No more damn sun trying to sweat us out. I think I lost a-a-about ten pounds today."

"We'll have something to eat and drink to put a little back on."

"I . . . I know this m-must sound crazy. But I've got a strong feeling we're going to find your brother. Wherever he is, he's a-all right."

A wan smile touched her face. "I know he is. I'd feel it if he wasn't."

They made a big fire and sat around it, heating up water to pour in foil pouches of camp food. Wood from the old church burned hot. No one spoke much.

"Everyone should take fifteen minutes to sleep. We'll do it in shifts of two, the other four keeping watch," Bill said. "I know it's not much, but I think we need to keep moving. Right?" He looked to his son.

Ben closed his eyes, nodding, the shadows from the flames dancing across his face. "I think what we need to do before we start out again is take a warning shot at one of the things. When it takes off, we'll follow. We'll use Norm's camera to locate and track one."

April leaned back on her elbows, her feet dangerously close to the fire. "I can see two right over there. Saw them streak across the moon before settling in at the tops of those pines."

"You spot any more?" her grandfather asked.

"Just the two for now."

"Hopefully, they stay right there and watch us rest a bit. All we need is one for Ben's plan to work."

"Where exactly are they?" Norm asked, grabbing the camera. He needed to see if he could capture them on video.

April pointed to a tall pine tree to their left. He worked on the zoom, seeing nothing until a sharp movement caught his eye.

"I see it!" he said. "It's hunched on a couple of branches, kind of like a gargoyle. I swear it's looking right at us." His elation at seeing one without being attacked was tinged with cold fear that ran like ice down his spine.

"Try to keep your eye on it," Ben said. "It'll help to know where to shoot when the time comes."

"Don't worry, I will."

"Boompa, you and April should try to shut down for a bit," Ben said. "Then Norm and Mom, and me and Dad."

"I won't lie and say I'm not bushed," Sam Willet said, stretching out on the cooling ground.

Norm barely heard what they said. He was riveted by what was on his view screen. It would be great if he could get a better look, but he wasn't about to head across the cemetery on his own. He'd kill himself just from falling.

"Do you see just the one?" Carol whispered, suddenly next to him.

"Mmm-hmm."

The sound of stone grinding on stone put him on high alert.

"What was that?" Norm said.

Ben and Bill were on their feet, guns drawn.

"Could be one of those old headstones breaking some more. Hot day, chilly night, they get weak," Carol said.

Norm looked back to the camera.

The Devil was gone!

"Damn, it moved," he cursed.

He panned around the trees, but couldn't catch sight of it again. "I l-lost it."

"Don't worry, April will find it," Carol said. "She's been on them all day."

"You see anything near us?" Bill asked. "That sounded close."

"Let me check."

Norm tilted the camera down, scanning the cemetery. It looked spooky as hell in night vision. He'd spent a lot of time alone in the woods, but never in a forgotten cemetery. If this had been an assignment from a network, he would have turned it down flat. In fact, he hadn't taken on any job that had even a hint of danger for longer than he cared to remember.

Well, this is sure making up for all that, he thought.

"N-nothing walking about. Could have been a nocturnal critter rooting around."

They waited in tense silence for the noise to happen again. When it didn't, coiled muscles began to relax. Norm was about to retrain the camera on the treetops when he thought he spied something in the open doorway of one of the mausoleums. The thick iron-barred door lay on the ground, a victim of neglect or vandalism or both.

His stomach clenched into a painful knot.

The big Jersey Devil was in the mausoleum, looking back at him, its eyes piercing white through the night-vision display.

"It's over there," Norm said, afraid to speak above a tremulous whisper.

"What's over there?" Ben said.

"The big one." He pointed, but in the dark, there was no way any of them could see. "Everyone needs to act normal and take turns looking in my camera." Rummaging in his backpack, he found the small tripod he carried around. With one hand, he was able to extract the legs and affix the camera. The terrifying creature filled the frame. He could see its chest move in and out with each breath.

Ben casually came over and looked.

"Shit."

"That p-probably means the others are all around us."

"I wonder what they're waiting for."

"Maybe for us to f-fall asleep."

"Well, that's not gonna happen anytime soon," April said.

Ben walked away, his eyes locked on the mausoleum. Carol gasped when she saw the Devil. "It flexed one of its wings. It's just sitting there, watching us."

Each of the Willets looked through the camera, expletives and questions of what to do falling from their lips, all of them hoping to see Daryl somewhere close by.

"Looks like we have ourselves a standoff," Bill said.

"You think they somehow herded us here?" April said. "You know, like popping up every now and then, knowing we'd follow?"

"I wouldn't put anything past them," her grandfather said. Norm watched his fingers rub the stock of his rifle.

"They don't know we can see them," Ben said. "For the first time, we have the element of surprise. I say we don't let the opportunity slip away. We should still take our warning shots and follow the flock or herd or whatever you call it."

Bill took to a knee, making sure his rifle was fully loaded. "I think a warning shot will just get them to attack."

"Which is why we need to take out the big one," Norm said. All eyes turned to him. "It's the rule of Nature. That one in the m-mausoleum is very obviously the alpha creature. You bring it down, the others will scatter like birdshot."

Maybe it was the pill taking effect, but a burgeoning confidence was beginning to take hold in him.

"Norm's right," April said.

"I know I am. I s-spend most of my life watching animals. I'll bet the same rules apply here."

"What do you all say?" Ben asked, looking to his family.

His father rolled his neck, tiny bones cracking. "You have the bigger gun, son. You do the honors, and we'll do our best to suppress the others if they try to be heroes."

Chapter Twenty-seven

Ben had to get behind Norm's camera, lying on his stomach, to take the shot. The others talked around him in hushed tones. He zoned them out. He didn't want to miss, not that he could at this range. What was important was that he made it a kill shot. The last thing they needed was a wounded, enraged Jersey Devil. No telling what would happen then.

"Everyone in position?" he said.

His family and Norm were in a loose circle behind him, ready to take on any of the smaller Devils should they choose to attack. His father had thrown the remaining wood on the fire to increase the cone of light around them. The quicker they could pick the damned things out of the darkness, the better chance they had of shooting them.

"We're ready when you are," Boompa said.

"Once I take my shot, I'm heading to the mausoleum," Ben said. "If it took Daryl there, I need to search it right away. You all cover me as best you can."

He knew he might be running headlong into the biggest shit storm of his life. It didn't concern him one bit. If there was a chance his brother was in there, he'd go now with just a knife and slash his way through the Jersey Devil.

The beast remained in the mausoleum, only its head poking out every now and then. Ben felt as if he were looking into a portal to hell. Nothing about the Devil's existence made sense, yet here it was, stalking them. A long tongue flopped from its maw, curling up so it could lick its nose.

There was no need for a countdown. His AR-15 would be loud enough for anyone within a mile radius to hear.

Breathing regularly, Ben squeezed the trigger.

BLAM!

He must have hit it because the Devil was no longer standing in the mausoleum's entrance. Ben scrabbled to his feet, flicking on the flashlight Boompa had given him. The absence of gunfire behind him told him the little fuckers had decided to remain hidden. Or maybe they simply took off. If that was the case, he hoped to hell someone saw which way they went.

His foot snagged on a tangle of exposed roots from a downed tree. Spinning and off balance, he straightened himself out by smashing his hip into a tombstone. He heard the crumble of rock as he sprinted to the mausoleum.

Now that he was closer, he was able to shine his flashlight into the aboveground tomb. The beam alighted on a raised sarcophagus. Leaves and weeds and pinecones littered the floor.

Where the hell is it?

He'd shot it. He knew he had. He'd had its heart dead in the center of his sight. At least where he thought its heart should be.

Ben took a cautious step inside, his boot scraping against the grit on the cement floor.

Not possible. Nothing is that fast. If it's not dead, it should be wounded, and it should be right here.

There was one small stained-glass window, miraculously intact, at the back of the mausoleum. The pungent odor inside was enough to trigger his gorge. He swallowed hard. If he hadn't seen it before, he'd sure as hell know now that it had been here. He'd never smelled anything like it, and he'd often come upon dead deer and other animals on the farm.

This was even worse than the Afghani family he'd found: a mother, a father, and three children, all under ten. They'd taken refuge in their basement during a bombing raid three days earlier. It had been over a hundred degrees every day and the entire house had been torn away as if a tornado had ripped through the neighborhood. The family of five had been exposed to the sun for three days, waiting to be found.

He'd thrown up so hard, he'd thought he'd cracked a rib or two.

"It's not here!" he shouted, his voice echoing painfully in the stone chamber.

His father shouted back, "How is that possible?"

"I don't know."

"We're all clear out here. We can't even see any of the others."

Again Ben wondered how this was possible. Because his mother was a cryptozoology enthusiast, they'd all listened to her talk about creatures other than the Jersey Devil for years. He recalled a theory she once spoke about how Bigfoot and other cryptids were able to come and go because they had figured out how to slip through portals of time and space. There were no dead Bigfoots or grand discoveries because they had an innate ability to go places we could not follow.

Jesus, had the Jersey Devil been able to do something like that? As alien as the concept was to him, its very existence allowed him to consider anything was possible.

"We're coming to you," April said.

He heard them running across the cemetery.

"Don't come in until I give the all clear," he said.

The sarcophagus was wider than your typical stone coffin. The person inside was either someone of immense size, or there were two bodies inside, laid to rest next to each other. Maybe they were a husband and wife who had died together.

Whatever the reason for its size, it did present ample space for the Devil to hide behind. Ben didn't see any drops of blood on the floor.

Holding the flashlight against the barrel of his rifle, Ben slowly stepped around the sarcophagus. When he got behind it, he sucked in a deep breath, having to turn away.

A large hole had been excavated into the floor. Cool air that reeked of decay wafted from the hole.

"Holy crap, that's bad," he said, stepping back, eager to get outside.

It had to be down there. He would have seen it if it had tried to fly away.

"Everyone keep away!" Ben yelled. "Don't come in here!"

He grabbed one of the grenades he'd clipped to his belt. There was one surefire way to get the Devil now . . . unless it had built an entire underground warren with passages underneath the cemetery.

If that's the case, we'll just seal up one of its exits.

His thumb slipped under the pin.

"Fire in the—"

Before he could pull the pin, the Jersey Devil came screeching out of the hole, shattering through the roof of the mausoleum. Heavy stones rained down on Ben, knocking the grenade and rifle from his hands. A chunk of the ceiling caught him in the temple.

Falling backwards, the edges of his vision turning to black, he watched the shadow of the Jersey Devil streak past the stars into the night.

"Sweet Jesus!" Sam exclaimed when the mausoleum exploded.

They had been standing twenty feet from it, waiting for Ben to come running out when the Devil burst through, laying waste to the century-old structure as if it were made of Lego blocks.

The sky erupted with the piercing howls of the smaller Devils. Like a swarm of bats, they circled overhead. It was only a matter of time before they attacked.

"Bill, Carol, get Ben out of there," he barked. His son and daughter-in-law ran to the remains of the mausoleum, Carol shouting Ben's name.

"Don't wait for them to come to you," he said to April and Norm. "Let's give them a reason to reconsider their intentions."

The three of them opened fire on the flitting mass that filled the sky. There were a lot more here than there had been last night. It would be self-defeating to try and consider how badly outnumbered they might be.

April let loose with a hair-raising scream as she fired wildly into the sky. Sam followed suit, the only difference being his trying to find one and pick it off like skeet. It was very hard in the dark, and with his old eyes not quite what they used to be. He thought he might have nicked one, but there was no time to pat himself on the back. He looked for another shape, followed it for a bit and pulled the trigger.

Reloading, he saw one of the Devils on a collision course with Carol.

In an instant, it was a cascading mass of blood, flesh and bone.

He looked over at Norm, who had nailed the bastard just ten feet before it would have gotten her.

"You're turning out to be handier than a pocket on a shirt," Sam said.

Norm didn't show any sign of satisfaction. "I told you I used to hunt. Took down a lot of ducks and geese in my time."

April let loose with a steady barrage of fire. "Die, you fuckers!"

Something slammed hard into Sam's back, knocking the rifle out of his hands. The flesh between his shoulder blades burned as if he'd fallen on hot coals. The cool air kissing his shredded skin only made it worse.

"You okay?" Norm asked, shooting randomly around them to discourage another attack.

"I'll be fine." Sam crawled on his hands and knees to retrieve his rifle, joints popping when he got back to his feet.

Another Devil swooped between him and April. Sam waited for it to gain some distance, then shot it from behind. It went into a death spin. He heard its hefty body roll in the weeds, but it was too dark to see where it came to rest.

"They're coming closer," Norm said.

Sam saw that Ben was safely away from the ruins of

the mausoleum. He'd been knocked out, or at least he prayed to God that was why his grandson was being carried out by his father. Carol now joined in the fight, pulling off seven quick shots with her Beretta.

"I don't think they're getting the message that we shouldn't be fucked with," April said.

"I can't disagree," Sam answered. The Devils dove at them, one knocking the hat off Norm's head in a daring, almost playful gesture.

April dropped her rifle. She said, "Maybe this will make them think twice."

For the first time, Sam noticed that she had a small pack over one shoulder. She dropped it to the ground, tearing the zipper open.

"Ugh!"

She fell to her side as a Devil caromed into her. Landing beside her, it hissed, trying to stomp on her hands with its cloven hooves.

Carol ran and kicked the Devil like it was a football. It tumbled end over end until it was out of sight.

"Thanks, Mom."

"Watch out!"

Norm took another one down in mid-flight. Blood sprayed all over the two women.

"Dammit, that tastes awful," April groaned, retrieving the contents of the bag.

When Sam saw what it was, he silently thanked Daryl.

Improvised flamethrowers had been his specialty.

Chapter Twenty-eight

The small, cylindrical fuel tank was hot pink. Daryl had painted it for April, knowing it was her favorite color. She twisted the nozzle, looking for her lighter. The flame's range, once she got it going, would only be about twenty to thirty feet and wouldn't last very long.

All she needed was for it to last long enough to make a point.

When she had everything in place, she shouted, "Stop shooting! Let them come closer. Everyone get down!"

They did what they were told without question.

April wasn't thrilled about being the tallest target for the moment, but it was necessary.

"Come on, you little bug shits," she snarled.

They circled above, the rhythmic flapping of their wings sounding like an onrushing wave.

Just a little bit more.

She caught sight of many others staying away from the fray, a lurking battalion of reinforcements should things go south.

Or, if they were lucky, creatures that didn't have the instinct or balls to fight.

April preferred the latter.

"If this works, you all need to run to the fire," she said. "At least then we'll know what scares them."

Could creatures surely spawned from hell really be afraid of fire? She was about to find out.

A Devil snagged at her hair, almost tipping her forward. Another barreled straight at her chest. She turned away just in time, almost losing her footing.

Close enough!

Aiming at the densest mass of Devils, she lit the end of the nozzle and pulled the trigger all the way back. A geyser of flame licked at the low-flying bodies, igniting them. Their high-pitched howls of pain were deafening. The Devils flew in mad, frantic loops, little balls of light shining on the hidden parts of the forgotten cemetery like enormous, spastic fireflies.

"Yes!" April cheered, shooting the flame in a steady arc across the sky. Her father carried Ben in his arms, running with everyone else in tow to the fire they had made earlier.

She began to make her way there as well. Any second now, she was going to run out of fuel.

No matter, it did the trick. The Devils were taking off. Norm and Boompa resumed shooting at the retreating beasts. It was easy pickings to shoot the ones that were engulfed in flame.

The flame withdrew back into the nozzle, until it was no more. She threw the flamethrower aside, unslinging her rifle to blast the nearby creatures that were illuminated by the burning Devils.

"That was b-brilliant!" Norm exclaimed. "I'm almost a-afraid to ask what else your family has brought along."

"Be afraid when we run out of things to stop them," she said, taking one last parting shot at a fleeing Devil. She heard it cry out but couldn't tell if she got it or not.

"See where they're going?" Boompa said. "Back east!"

The forest was suddenly alive with the crash and whoosh of Devils that had remained hidden. April felt her resolve crumble. How the hell many were there?

"Shotgun!" her dad said. She grabbed one out of the bag Ben had been carrying and tossed it to him. Her brother was still out, his head in her mother's lap. They had to make sure the Devils didn't get to them.

The fresh wave of creatures flew low and fast. April's hair fluttered in every direction from the strong gust of their passing wake.

Boom! Her father's shotgun sprayed death in a wide swath. They could hear, but not see, several Devils crash to the ground. April, Boompa and Norm fired until her ears were ringing and she couldn't hear her own curses at the damned things. The hell swarm, overwhelmed by their sheer firepower, left their wounded and dead behind.

April's nerves tingled. She felt like leaping out of her skin. The adrenaline rush threatened to overwhelm her, now that there were no more monsters to fight.

"Check . . . check the hole," Ben stammered. He sat up with a dull groan, massaging the top of his head.

"What hole?" his mother asked.

"The one behind the sarcophagus. It . . . it was hiding there. I don't know how it moved so fast. I had it. I know I did."

April said, "I'll check it."

"I'll go with her," Boompa said, smiling at her in a way that told her he was prouder than he could ever express in words.

"Come on," April said before her father could object. She had to run some of this excess energy off. She knew she was in for a hell of a crash, but she might as well take advantage of it while she could.

As they walked to the demolished mausoleum, she said to her grandfather, "Norm's a real deadeye. Did you see that?"

"He's a man who's spent a lot of time outdoors. Funny how that usually equals being good with a gun."

The mausoleum had been reduced to ankle-high rubble.

Eerily, the sarcophagus was the one thing that had survived the blast. It was cracked and parts of it chipped off, but there it still stood.

"He said it was behind it," Boompa said.

"Watch my back," April said, gingerly walking over the jagged stones.

Sure enough, there was the hole, though it was partially filled with debris now.

"I see it, but it doesn't look like much," she said.

"Can you tell if it goes any deeper? Maybe that's where it lives." Boompa stood next to her, looking down.

"Only one way to find out."

April jumped into the hole, her head and shoulders remaining above the rim. Boompa handed her a flashlight. She dug around a bit.

"This doesn't look like a nest or anything. Just a hole that—"

She hadn't noticed the extensive damage to the sarcophagus on this side. The end facing away from the entrance had crumbled completely apart, taking a chunk of the wooden coffin within. A pair of skeletons slid out, the old, brittle bones cascading onto her.

Bone dust went down her throat and in her nose as

she batted them away, hollering at Boompa to get her out of the hole.

"Fuck, fuck, fuck!" she wailed.

The back of her hand swatted a skull. It turned to powder when it hit the edge of the hole.

"I've got you!"

Boompa grabbed her upper arms and lifted her the way he used to when she was a little girl, asking for a ride on his shoulders.

"Jesus shit crackers!" she shouted, wiping the dust from her clothes, her hair, her face.

"I'm sorry, April. I should have been the one to go in there."

She shook her head. "No way. That was all me. How was I supposed to know I'd take a bone shower?"

Her father came rushing over. "You all right?"

"Yeah, I'm fine. Just got a little surprise, that's all." He pulled her to him with one of his big paws. "One thing's for sure, that's not where the Devil lives. Too small."

Her mother, Ben and Norm stood around the ruined mausoleum. Ben was still holding his head, but he looked like he'd be all right. In fact, he looked downright pissed.

"I think I know where it lives," her mother said.

Norm said, "It seems too easy, don't you think?"

"Maybe that's why it's there, hiding in plain sight."

"There's an awful lot of them to h-h-hide."

"And plenty of space to do it."

"Where are you guys talking about?" April said, checking for cuts. If there were any, she'd have to disinfect them fast.

"They all went east," Boompa said. "Maybe back home. I guess Momma Leeds has a full house now."

* * *

When Daryl woke up again, he thought he was still in a dream. Or a coffin. It was so devoid of any light or noise, he wished it *was* just a dream he couldn't shake.

But a few minutes later with no change, his mind clearing despite the pain, he remembered that he was underground somewhere.

"I gotta get outta here."

Moving was a little easier this time. He first sat up, took some time for the dizziness to clear, then got to his knees.

"Baby steps," he huffed, remembering one of his favorite movies. In *What About Bob?*, Bill Murray played a man beset by more fears than a person could count. His shrink, played by that guy from *Jaws*, taught him the baby-step method to getting well. "Stop thinking about it." The last thing he needed was to laugh. He was pretty sure the slightest giggle would send fresh flares of pain to his rib cage that would knock him out again.

Trying to stand, he bumped his head against an earthen ceiling.

It buried me alive!

His heart went into instant overdrive, his breath coming in shallow gasps. His anxiety compelled him to move, to prove to his mind and body that as long as he could walk and talk, he was not going to die.

Holding his hands in front of him, he moved forward in a low hunch, wary of smacking his head again.

"Calm the hell down, man. Whatever this place is, it's big. See, you're walking. It's not a shallow grave. Just keep walking."

He did just that, one tentative step at a time, until he realized he was in some kind of underground tunnel.

Covering his mouth, he gagged. "Oh, crap, what's making that smell?"

Do I want to see?

Yes, if it meant he was one step closer to a way out.

There were no twists or turns in the tunnel, or what he'd come to think of as a gopher hole on steroids. Thinking of why the Jersey Devil would put him here didn't help his nerves. He had obviously been tucked away for a reason. He didn't want to be there when it came back to show him why.

Gaining confidence, he moved faster. Or was it the simple desire to get the hell out as soon as possible? Daryl didn't care. He just needed to find an exit, quick.

His foot snagged on a root.

"Dammit!"

He tipped to his side, feeling the tunnel pitch forward. He went into a roll, loamy dirt filling his mouth as he cursed his misfortune.

Slamming into something hard and unforgiving, he couldn't catch his breath. If his lungs hurt before, his tumble made him realize just how much worse the pain could be.

When he could finally take a few decent breaths, he turned his head and saw his Mets cap, streaked with filth.

Wait! I can see my hat!

Looking around, it appeared he'd ended up in a basement. Old jars and cans were stacked against the walls. A pile of rotted lumber was what had stopped his roll. Glancing up, he saw the remains of what had once been a home, three of the four walls of the house, along with the floors and roof now gone. The foundation of the basement was the only thing that had truly stood the test of time. The moon, so bright and beautiful he wanted to cry, shined down on him, as if it had sought him out, a spotlight of hope, a sign from God.

"I'm out. I'm out!"

Grabbing a plank of wood, he pulled himself to his feet. The stone basement walls were only about seven feet high. If he waited a few moments to recover from his fall, he could easily scrabble out. From there, he didn't know where to go, but it didn't matter. As long as he was out of that hole.

Taking stock in the light, he breathed a sigh of relief when he saw his hunting knife was still clipped to his belt.

"Maybe I should lean some of that wood against the wall and just walk up it."

It was an idea that could go south quickly if the wood split from his weight.

His head jerked toward the sound of something being dragged across the floor. He flipped the snap from the knife holder, extracting the thick, deadly blade as quietly as possible.

"Who's there?"

Yes, he had the moonlight, but there were all sorts of dark corners down here. Whatever it was had come from his right, over behind the rusted wheelbarrow. Maybe it was someone like him. It could even be one of his family members. If it was the Devil, he wasn't sure he had the strength to fight it. Swallowing hard, he said, "I know you're there. Did it bring you here, too? It's me, Daryl."

He recoiled at the maniacal peal of a woman. A dark blur knocked the wheelbarrow over, coming straight for him.

Holy Jesus!

The woman looked like a wild animal dragged from a mud pit. Her hair was an unruly mushroom cloud caked with muck. She was naked, her bones showing through her skin, with enormous eyes, the pupils so small they could barely be seen. Her lips pulled back to reveal jagged, stained teeth.

She leapt for his throat, throwing them both into the lumber pile, her jaws gnashing insanely as they were buried under an avalanche of termite-infested wood.

Chapter Twenty-nine

"It's where we would have gone eventually," Sam said. They'd put the fire out and started walking back to the vans. It was going to be a hell of a hike in the dark. The one shred of luck that had come their way was the almost preternatural glow of the sugar sand, casting a ghostly pall over the forest. There was no way they could walk to the Leeds homestead, or what was left of it. So even though the trek to the vans seemed unimaginable, it was their only choice.

"I know," Bill said, taking point, "I just don't like abandoning this whole area. Daryl could be somewhere right next to us."

"If he was, that boy would have found a way to let his presence be known. He knows how to use that big mouth of his." Sam wished to heaven and hell he'd hear that loudmouth right now.

"The L-Leeds house isn't easy to find. I've heard that locals can be very uncooperative if you ask them to take you there," Norm said.

"I may have an ace in the hole," Sam said.

"What would that be?" Ben said. He'd fully recovered,

but Sam worried about that head wound. If he had a concussion, the symptoms might not show up until later.

"One of the few people who knows where the actual house was. I'm not sure if he'll willingly take us there, but I'll burn that bridge when we get to it."

"There's another surefire way to know exactly where those Devils are headed," Ben said.

"What's that?" Bill asked, his breath coming in great, heaving gusts. If they lost sight of him, they could still follow him by the bellowing of his lungs.

"You saw how many there are. I think they were pretty confident that we weren't walking out of that cemetery alive. We just blasted the holy hell out of them. They're no longer the top predator out here. A group of creatures like that, frightened, maybe angry, they won't be hard to spot. By flushing them out, we may have set them on a path that will bring them in contact with other towns." He let that settle in a bit before adding, "We'll check the police scanner first thing when we get back to the van. If I'm right, we'll just need to follow the destruction they leave in their wake."

No one said a word. The weight of what Ben implied was enough to fold what were already dead-tired legs. Sam's soul suddenly felt weary. It was bad enough he'd put his family in danger. Now he may have upset what had been a peaceful coexistence, with everyone who lived in and around the Pine Barrens.

April said, "So you're saying that we may have just royally screwed the state of New Jersey."

Ben replied, "That very well might be the case. Or you could say we speeded up something that was already in progress."

"I guess the bright side is that if things get that bad,

we won't be the only ones hunting them down. At least we'll have help," April said.

Sam snapped, "Which means it's more important than ever to find Daryl. When the you-know-what hits the fan, no one in these woods is safe."

Heather Davids knew they were going to die out here. She pressed her body closer to Daniela, spooning her to keep warm. They'd covered themselves with leaves so nothing could see them, huddled at the base of an old tree.

Daniela had been sick ever since they drank out of that stream. To her credit, she pressed on, stopping every now and then to throw up. It got to the point where Heather was afraid that there was nothing left in her friend. Then what would happen?

She closed her eyes, only to replay what those monsters did to Tony and Justin. It had happened so fast. One second they were joking around, the next, running for their lives.

Heather opened her eyes, staring through the gaps in the leaves, spying very little. The trees were so thick, they could barely see the moon and stars.

How long had they been out here? She tried to recall how many sunsets they'd seen, but her exhausted, starved brain couldn't keep track. It could be days, a week or even more. She itched all over. Mosquitoes and ticks had been having a field day with them. They'd used the sharp end of a stick Daniela had found to dig the ticks out from under their skin. It hurt and there was the fear that even now, they had the beginnings of Lyme disease coursing through their blood, but it was low on the worry list at the moment.

Her stomach felt as if it had folded over on itself. The hunger pains had given way to a silent apathy that frightened her. The scent of wild herbs, conjuring images of fresh pasta and garden tomatoes coated with olive oil and spices, no longer affected her. Was this the kind of soothing numbness that preceded death by hypothermia, she wondered?

Before they'd settled down for the night, she'd spotted an old beer can, half-buried in nettles. The image had been faded from the sun, but she could make out that it was a can of Carling's Black Label. Her father talked about drinking it when he was younger. It was an old beer, and the first time she'd seen it, she thought of her father.

Seeing it again confirmed her suspicion that they had somehow been walking in a wide circle, which meant they were no closer to finding a way out. They'd come across several bogs and decrepit homes that hadn't seen an inhabitant for decades or more, but not a single person. It felt like being dropped in the middle of an alien world.

A coyote howled. Daniela flinched against her, but remained asleep.

I got her into this so Tony and I could screw around. Maybe I deserve whatever's coming, but not her. Please, God, help us find food or water or someone to get us out of here tomorrow.

Another coyote joined in the nocturnal lament. Their whines gave her a primordial chill.

Soon, a chorus of coyotes took to wailing, yipping and sounding increasingly distressed.

"Wh-what is that?" Daniela said, groggily.

"It's just coyotes. Something must have scared them.

Go back to sleep." She nuzzled her friend's neck, hoping she could somehow make her feel safer.

"Do you think it could be those things?" Daniela sounded like she was on the verge of tears.

"Even if it is, they can't see us. We'll be okay. I promise."

Will we? Those coyotes sound awful scared. And it sounds like they're getting closer.

"I want to go home."

"I know, sweetie. Shhh. We're going to find a road in the morning. I know we will. You ever hitchhiked before?"

"No," Daniela said. "I'm not that dumb. But I'll take a ride with an escaped convict if he'll get us out of here."

Heather heard a terrific rush of wind and the urgent flapping of wings. She'd watched a nature show once where a camera had been placed outside a cave somewhere in South America. At one point during the night, millions of bats had exploded from the cave, rushing into the night sky. This sounded spookily like that, only worse, knowing that this wasn't a TV show and all they had for protection was a thin layer of dead leaves.

"It's them," Daniela cried, her body going as stiff as a board.

"Just stay still and quiet," Heather whispered. "We can't let them know we're here."

Moving her head slowly, Heather did her best to let some of the leaves fall from the side of her face. She had to see what was coming their way. Shutting her eyes and hoping for it to go away only worked when you were a kid afraid of the monster in the closet.

Between the coyotes and the patter of wings, the calm of night had been shattered by a riot of sound.

Heather looked up, and there they were. Gliding

bodies, shadows of things that shouldn't be, passing over the treetops.

There were so many. She had to bite her lip to keep from crying out. A trickle of blood slipped across her tongue.

Aside from the creatures in the air, something else was running through the forest, too close to where they lay hidden.

"What is that?" Daniela whispered.

"I can't see."

There was no way she was going to shift her position to get a better look, possibly giving them away. Whatever it was, she prayed for it to move on.

Leaves skittered and she heard a low, warning growl. She clamped her hand over Daniela's mouth.

The animal resumed its dash, stopped again, and began sniffing at the ground.

When it finally came into view, stepping cautiously into one of the few shafts of moonlight, Heather cursed their luck.

She was no expert, but she was pretty sure it was a bobcat. It looked like a cross between a leopard and an overgrown housecat, with spotted fur, a wide face and a short tail. Heather guessed it weighed between twenty and thirty pounds and was about as big as a small to medium-sized dog. She was sure it had claws and teeth that would make it seem much bigger.

The bobcat slunk low to the ground, pausing as it locked its gaze on them.

"Slowly hand me that stick," Heather said so softly into Daniela's ear, she could barely hear herself. If it was going to attack them, their tick stick was their only weapon. There wasn't time to search for a large rock to use as a bludgeon.

"Why?"

"There's a bobcat sniffing our way."

It pulled its lips back, revealing a deadly smile.

"If it comes at us, you run while I try to slow it down," Heather said.

"I'm not leaving without you."

There was no need to really whisper now. The animal knew they were there. It could probably smell them from miles away.

Heather felt the stick as it was pressed into her hand.

After everything they'd been through, she wasn't about to get taken down by an overgrown cat.

She jumped away from Daniela as a pair of dashing shadows descended on the bobcat. It swiped at the air, missing its attackers. They made tight turns, diving back at the bobcat.

The leaves had fallen from Heather and Daniela. Both let out tiny yelps as they watched the strange creatures settle in to maul the bobcat.

"Quick, we need to get back under the leaves," Heather hissed. With shaky hands, they gathered the leaf pile back on top. All the while, they watched the creatures pull fur and flesh from the bobcat as evenly as if they had chef's knives for claws. The bobcat wailed in agony.

One of the flying creatures lifted it off the ground, and seconds later, they were gone. All that was left were a scattering of blood-soaked leaves and tufts of ravaged fur.

Heather and Daniela didn't dare move, speak or reveal themselves until the sun came up. At least then, they would be able to see their death coming.

Chapter Thirty

Daryl was surprised by the strength of the emaciated woman. No matter how hard he tried, she kept getting the best of him. She straddled his chest, nails digging into his arms, teeth gnashing dangerously close to his nose. He held her back as best he could, his fingers digging into her neck.

"What the hell's the matter with you?" he said, spittle flying from his mouth as he struggled.

Stop thinking of her as a woman! Holding back is only going to get you killed.

One of her nails pierced his flesh through his shirt. The wound burned immediately, like the world's worst case of cat scratch fever.

"Son of a bitch, that hurts!"

Twisting to his right, he broke her grip on his arm, using his lower half to buck her off his body.

Now that he had one arm free, he balled his fist, swinging as hard as he could. The blow connected with the side of her head, snapping it back. One moment she was snarling like a rabid dog, the next it was lights-out. She slumped on top of him, a deadweight that belied her slight frame. Daryl was careful wriggling out, making sure not to just toss her aside like a filthy rag doll.

When he got to his feet, he took several cautious steps back, massaging his knuckles. The woman was all skin and bone, and the bone part didn't feel good when he punched it.

"Who are you?" He knelt to get a closer look at her face while keeping enough distance between them that she couldn't strike him if she suddenly snapped awake. "And how did you end up here?"

She looked like one of those feral people that he'd read about—usually children left to fend for themselves in the wild, becoming more animal than man in the process. This woman was no child. If he had to guess, he'd say she was in her thirties, maybe forties. It was hard to tell.

Her skin was so dirty, it camouflaged her nudity.

Now the dilemma was, did he get back to the business of getting out of here, alone, or did he bring her with him? Sure, he could carry her now, but what would happen when she woke up, probably madder than a lovesick wolverine?

Their struggle made the pain in his ribs even worse. Getting her out wouldn't be easy.

"You know, I didn't need any more complications."

He moved some of the sturdier looking boards together so they were a ramp leading up to the surface. All he had to do was walk up them and leave this place in the rearview mirror.

Daryl looked down at the feral woman, her chest rising slowly, evenly. The side of her head was already starting to swell. She may have been bat shit crazy, but he felt bad for hitting her so hard.

"I don't know how I'm gonna do this."

Getting her into a fireman's lift almost took his breath, and consciousness, away. If she woke up kicking and screaming, he couldn't save her from hitting the ground hard.

Carefully, he placed his foot on the first plank—then the next on the board beside it. He took the first few steps slowly. Any sign of the boards breaking, he could easily bail. So far, they held.

Release from the underground was just a few feet away. Gaining confidence, he stepped faster, his balance tipping from the woman's weight.

At the midway point, the sound of wood cracking made him stop.

Oh, shit! Move your fat ass!

Daryl practically ran the rest of the way. One of the boards snapped, slipping out from under his foot. He lost his balance, attempting to fall forward. The woman slipped off his shoulder, rolling in the dirt. Free from her weight, he reached out, digging his fingers in the dirt as both ramps collapsed. It took him a moment to realize he'd made it. Only his feet dangled over the old basement.

He rolled onto his back, greedily sucking in fresh air until the ache in his lungs made him slow down.

I got us out of there. I should probably get going before she wakes up. When I find help, I can lead people back to her. If I take her, she'll just try to kill me again.

Resting on a knee, he checked her to make sure she hadn't gotten any cuts when she flew from his grasp. She was still out, but it was hard to find fresh wounds through all the grime.

She's obviously been out here a long while. She'll be fine. She's in her element. I'm the one that intruded on her. Nothing to feel guilty about.

He cast a wary glance at the trees, wondering if one

of those Jersey Devils was lurking about. He wasn't about to let them take him unawares again.

Stepping away from the unconscious woman, he spotted something just above her hip.

"What the?"

Licking his thumb, he wiped as much dirt as he could from the area, worrying that he might be coming in contact with some kind of open sore or disease.

But no, it couldn't have been that cut and dried.

The woman had a blazing red mark in the shape of a hoof.

The same one he bore above his own hip.

He sighed, hands on his knees, staring at her matching mark.

"I can't leave you now."

He lifted her again, not knowing how long he'd be able to carry her like this. Maybe when she woke up, he could reason with her.

"You showed me yours. Later, I'll show you mine."

Maybe then she wouldn't see him as the enemy. Because they certainly shared a common one between them.

It was dawn by the time they got back to the vans. Bill felt like he was seconds from collapse. The cooler was where they'd left it inside the old Ford. He gave each of them a bottle of Gatorade. Water just wouldn't be enough. There was also homemade beef jerky they all tore into. Protein was a necessity. Carbs would come from the package of hot dog rolls.

"Norm, I think it's best we leave your car here," he said, swallowing hard. "We need to stick together. The police scanner is in the old van. We can come back for your car and the minivan later."

Norm took a gulp of Gatorade, his mouth full of jerky. "That old thing c-can carry us all?"

"Don't you worry about my van," Boompa said. "Besides, it has a false bottom to hide our weapons. If we get pulled over in the minivan, we could be in big trouble."

"I'll drive," Ben said. Unlike the rest of them, he drank and ate sparingly.

"No, son, I'll take the wheel. You could use the rest."

Bill's hand did a strange flutter, an act of betrayal he didn't need now. He stuffed it in his pocket before anyone could see.

"Dad, I sometimes went three days without sleep in that goddamn desert, on high alert the entire time. Trust me, I'm fine."

As much as he wanted to father him, Bill knew he was right. Of all of them, his son was the best equipped to handle things now that they had gone to hell.

Ben slapped the side of the van. "Let's saddle up!"

April flicked a triangle of jerky at her brother as she stepped into the van.

Carol grabbed Bill's hand. "I keep thinking about what Ben said. Do you think it could get as bad as he says? The Jersey Devil has stayed hidden for over two hundred years."

"I guess they never had people like us around to royally piss them off," April quipped, taking the front passenger seat.

"Spoken with eloquence," Boompa said, settling in behind her.

Bill worried about his father. He was eighty, after all. He looked like eight shades of dog shit, but so did they all. He never complained once, but that didn't mean he was well.

A dark, terrifying suspicion crossed Bill's mind. *He's thinking this is a one-way trip. He's not going to leave anything in the tank.*

He patted his father's shoulder, feeling the solid muscle and bone.

In a sense, he was feeling the same way. Priorities had changed. If it meant losing his own life to get Daryl back, he'd do it without reservation.

Ben brought the Ford roaring to life. April turned on the scanner. Everyone in the van held their breath as they waited for the first report to crackle over the airwaves.

A sedentary retirement was never in the cards. When Jean and his wife, Rose, retired in the same year, they worried a lot about becoming too comfortable with days puttering around the house, tending the garden, mapping out what shows to watch on TV that week. Office dwellers their entire working lives, now that they had time, money and freedom, they wanted to explore all of the things they'd missed.

The problem was their friends had gotten old before their time. Diabetes, heart disease, bad joints, the litany of ailments that kept them either on the couch or in their doctors' offices was downright depressing.

When Jean left his job in Boston, he'd been diagnosed with early signs of diabetes. No way was he going to get on the medicine merry-go-round. He and Rose got off their asses, changed their diets, moved to New Jersey to be closer to their only child and grandchildren and got a new set of friends. They'd balked at the fifty and over community, but their protests were short-lived.

It was far from a cabal of aging retirees. Here were folks who wanted to get the hell up and do things.

Like this hike on the Batona Trail. Rose led the team of six couples on the trail after a night of camping. The goal today was to get to the Batona River and do some kayaking.

Jean admired his wife's newly sculpted ass, a perfect apple in khaki shorts. Neither had been this fit since their thirties.

He came up behind her, cupping a cheek, using his body to block his flirtation. "If more men had wives like you, there'd be no need for little blue pills," he whispered in her ear.

"Try to keep it in your pants," she said, chuckling. "You heard Jim and Dawn last night."

"We all heard Jim and Dawn last night."

"Exactly. You're gonna have to wait till we get home."

"Hey, newlyweds, how much farther to the river?" Eddie McClusky said from the middle of the pack. His wife, Edna, walked a few paces behind him, munching on a Snickers bar. Jean was astounded by the amount of sugar the woman consumed. And a little jealous.

"Not far," Rose said. "We should be there in under an hour if I've read the map and markers right."

"Anyone down for some skinny-dipping?" Jim said with a mischievous smile. Dawn playfully slapped the back of his head.

"I don't need the sight of your pale ass to ruin the beauty of nature around us," Eddie shot back.

It's amazing, Jean thought. *We're all grandparents, yet somehow it feels like we're back to being kids again, blazing trails in the forest with libidos that have somehow managed to turn back the clock. Maybe it's the weed Jim brought.*

Yes, they'd all sat around the campfire last night toking on what seemed an endless supply of joints that Jim had stuffed in his pack. Jean and Rose hadn't smoked in years, the last time being the day Mary had moved out to go to college. They'd both needed it to get through that night.

Rose said, "Does anyone need a break?"

Jean turned around to see if anyone looked too pooped. He tugged on Rose's arm. "Hold up a sec."

"Something the matter?"

He double-checked the headcount.

"Hey, where's George?"

George Howard was a retired Philadelphia cop with a chest as wide as a wine cask. He'd taken up the rear, behind his wife, Allison. She stopped and turned around.

"He probably stopped to shed a tear for the old country," Allison said. "George? We're all waiting for you."

Now everyone stopped, waiting for the telltale sounds of the burly Irishman to come lumbering out from behind the bushes, zipping up his fly.

"George?" A tinge of concern crept into Allison's tone.

"That's not like him," Jean said softly to Rose. "All those years checking in with dispatch. He always telegraphs every move he makes."

"Hey, George, quit pushing so hard and zip up!" Jim called out, his hands cupped around his mouth.

"I don't like this," Rose said.

"Me, either. Maybe we should double back. He might have passed out," Jean said.

Or worse. He could have had a heart attack. The man smoked like a chimney and wasn't in the best of shape. Plus the stress of being a cop all those years.

"Let's go," Rose said. She was about to tell everyone to head back when the sound of cracking branches made her instinctively cower, covering her head with her arms.

Something wet and heavy crashed to the ground between her and Jean.

Jean felt something hot and sticky on his face. Touching his cheek, his fingers came away crimson.

Looking down, he stared straight into George's dead eyes. The big man looked as if sharks had gnawed at him, flaying open his chest.

"Oh, my God!" Dawn screamed.

"Where the hell did he come from?" Rose said, grabbing Jean's hand to steady herself. "He couldn't have just dropped from the sky!"

"What happened?" Allison shouted from the back of the pack.

Everyone rushed forward, then instantly regretted it. People were, retching, crying out or both.

"How . . . how did, I mean . . ." Eddie was at a loss for words.

Jean looked up into the thick trees. He didn't see a thing.

"He . . . he fell . . . he . . ." Rose trembled, unable to finish her sentence. Allison saw her husband and went into hysterics.

For a moment, Jean heard nothing. Everything around him faded into the distance, a constant but unintelligible thrum.

So it was with deaf ears that he saw Dawn, then Allison, tears streaking down their faces, get pulled into the untamed edges of the trail. He knew Rose was digging her nails into his arm, but he couldn't register the pain.

Jim shouted something, and a huge, mottled wing sprang from behind a tree, wrapped him within the folds and pulled him out of sight.

One by one, all of the hikers disappeared.

But he could tell where some of them had gone.

Terrific spurts of blood erupted from the high foliage. It was like stepping through one of those fountain walks in the city, the kind where thin jets of water would spout intermittently from small holes in the ground.

He turned to his wife.

Two creatures, alien beings that reminded him of pictures of demons he'd seen in old Bibles when he went to Catholic high school, came out of nowhere, crawling over her like child-sized bugs. She collapsed under their weight, struggling, screaming, bleeding, but he couldn't hear or help her.

It wasn't until he felt something sharp rip into his back that his senses returned.

But by then, it was too late to even cry for help.

Chapter Thirty-one

They didn't get to a main road until eight in the morning. It was another hot and muggy start. Carol's bones felt as if they'd been liquefied. The only thing keeping her going, keeping any of them moving forward, was Daryl.

She used a map to direct Ben where to go. Navigation systems and cell phones were useless out here.

"How far a drive will it be?" her son asked, taking a turn a little too fast. The old van creaked like a battered warship. For a terrifying moment, she thought it was going to tip over.

"We can't find Daryl if you kill us," April said, clinging to the dashboard.

Ben didn't say anything in return.

Carol looked at the map. "It looks like a forty-mile drive, all southeast. We need to get to the coast."

Looking over at Boompa, she was glad to see he'd taken the time in the car to take a power nap. Norm's eyelids looked like they were getting heavy as well.

Her husband stroked her back, giving her shoulder a gentle squeeze. "We're going to find him," he said.

"I know we will."

It was hard to see the map through the blur of tears.

We got it all wrong, she thought. *We thought we knew everything, and it's cost us everything. Something's happened, and it has to have been recent. If not, people would have seen these things in droves. And the marks mean something more than we thought. They could have killed us all that first night, just like they did that Piney clan. They're saving us for a reason. Maybe the same reason they can find us so easily. But why did they take Daryl?*

The van hit a pothole. Carol bounced from her seat, the top of her head smashing the van's roof.

"To get us to come to them," she muttered.

"What's that?" Bill said.

"I think they're using Daryl as bait. Even if we make a wrong turn, they know exactly where to find us. They'll just corral us in the right direction. They need us for something."

"Maybe there's a chance we've upset their plans, made them change their minds after last night. We thinned their herd and showed them that we're not afraid," he said.

"Maybe."

What she didn't say was, *There's a good chance they think you're part of their family. We're all here now, and they want a reunion. But something had them stirred up before we came here. Did we really make it worse?*

She, Boompa and Norm didn't have the Jersey Devil

mark. She wondered what the Devils had in mind for them.

A quick burst from the police scanner caught their attention.

"I need you to stop over at one-nineteen Bevins Street. We have a report of someone's dog being stolen from the yard."

"Copy that. Did they see who took it?"

"This is going to sound weird, but they said it was some kind of bird."

"Could have been a hawk. Some of those toy dogs are awful small."

"The dog was a Saint Bernard."

Carol looked to the street listings on the big map. Bevins Street was three towns away, southeast of their location.

"We're headed in the right direction," she said.

She rubbed her forehead, closing her eyes tight.

Daryl was both grateful and unhappy about the sun. It was great to finally see where he was going—and what could be spying on him. So far, he and the deranged woman seemed to be on their own, Devil free. But it was already hotter than a bull's temper and he couldn't remember the last time he'd had a drink.

Maybe when she woke up, she could lead them to water. It was obvious she'd been out here a long time. She had to know places to find food and water.

Having her so close, draped over his shoulder, was no picnic. She stunk to holy hell and her flesh felt strange and oily.

"I need a break."

He bent to a knee, carefully placing her on the ground. Leaning back against a tree, he wiped copious beads of sweat from his forehead, shutting his eyes for a bit.

Birds chattered in every direction. Cracking his eyelids open, he spotted a squirrel leaping from branch to branch above him. Looking down, he fixated on the matching mark on the woman's side.

"Like it or not, you're one of us."

She must have been more fragile than she'd felt when she was attacking him. She'd been out for hours. He hoped he hadn't hit her hard enough to cause any kind of brain damage.

Leaning closer, he pushed a coarse, matted lock of hair from the side of her face. There was a time she'd been a pretty woman. He could tell by her high cheekbones, perfect sloping nose and full lips. Maybe under all that filth, she still was.

But it would take a team of doctors and shrinks to erase the crazy from her eyes.

He couldn't believe that the first time he'd see a woman naked was under these circumstances. This was definitely not what he'd fantasized about all those years. Sure, he'd gotten his hand up a few shirts with his brief relationships, but he was far behind most guys his age. He was hoping to change all that when he went away to college.

She moaned at his touch. He pulled his hand away.

"Please, if you wake up, be calm. I'm too frigging tired for round two."

Gritting his teeth, he let his fingertips brush against her face. "Hey, are you okay? It would be nice if I didn't have to carry you anymore."

Her mouth twitched and her legs stretched.

In an instant, she was awake, crouched on all fours, glaring at him.

Daryl flinched, immediately on the defensive.

"Hey, hey, hey, I'm sorry I had to coldcock you back there, but you went a little psycho on me. I'm not going to hurt you . . . again."

For some reason, he expected her to growl, maybe take a swipe at him. She didn't take her eyes off him, red-rimmed white orbs lost in a sea of grime.

He held his hands up, showing her his palms. "Friends?"

I wonder if she even speaks English?

A mosquito landed on his nose. When he swatted it away, the woman jumped to her feet, taking several steps back.

His stomach lurched when he saw her in the full light of day. The flesh of her stomach was a saggy pouch marred by deep stretch marks. Something leaked from her breasts. Her distended nipples were heavily scarred.

She's lactating!

Which meant that she'd had a baby recently. Where the hell was it?

"Do you have a baby?"

She cocked her head, studying him. He pointed at her leaking, mangled breasts. It didn't register with the wild woman.

"You know, a baby?" He made a rocking motion with his arms. A line of drool fell from the corner of her mouth. Maybe she'd lost the baby. It was easy to believe. This was no place to raise a child. Out here, without proper food, shelter or medical care, a common cold could be deadly

"This isn't working." He slowly stood up. "I have to

find someone and get the hell out of here. You're free to come with me, or go back to wherever you've been keeping yourself. But I'd prefer it if you stuck with me."

At least she wasn't attacking him. So, there was improvement.

"I know. Maybe you'll understand this."

He lifted the corner of his shirt, revealing his birthmark.

The woman's hands fluttered to her open mouth. She made a strange, strangled sigh.

He pointed to her mark. "See, just like you."

She looked to the sky, her eyes opening wider, if that was even possible.

She started walking. When he didn't follow, she stopped, motioning with her hands for him to follow.

"Where are we going?"

The woman resumed walking. She was headed in the direction he'd been going anyway, so it couldn't hurt to let her take the lead. Plus, he was curious. How did she get her mark? If she lived out here, she had to know about the Devils. The question was, how would they be able to communicate?

She picked up the pace, speed walking as she weaved through the trees.

Daryl did his best to keep up with her, his ribs aching with each labored breath.

"See, canoeing can be fun."

"Yeah, it's not so bad."

"Are we gonna hit any rapids?"

"Not here, and not in a canoe, no."

Chase Mincin swore that he was going to break out

of the rut with his biweekly visitation with his sons, and so far it was working out pretty well.

Dylan and Dean usually slept late on Saturdays, got up long enough to eat a late breakfast before settling on the couch, glued to their various electronic devices, sometimes texting each other even though they were two feet apart. Chase, not wanting to upset them, let them do whatever made them happy. The last thing he wanted was for them to go back to Maya bitching about their awful weekend with the dad who had abandoned them.

If only they were old enough to know the truth.

No matter, this was the weekend to try to change the dynamic. The divorce was now a year old and he needed to find ways to really connect with his sons.

Renting a canoe and taking them out on the Wading River, just like he and his father used to do, seemed like the perfect start.

Dean used his oar to splash water on his younger brother.

"Frig, that's cold!" Dylan said, retaliating. Chase caught some of the spray. Instead of scolding them, he laughed, dousing them both.

But he did say, "Okay, that's enough for the moment. We don't want to fill the boat with water."

"We have the canoe all day, right?" Dylan asked.

"Yep. We can take our time. I thought we could set ashore at one point and do a little exploring."

"Really?" Dean said.

"Sure, why not? You never know what you'll find out here. I had a nice Indian arrowhead collection when I was your age. I found most of them just by walking around the woods."

He heard a heavy splash ahead of them, somewhere past the bend in the river.

"What was that?" Dylan said.

"There might be an outcropping of rock ahead. People could be jumping off it to swim."

"Can we swim, too?"

"You guys don't have bathing suits."

Dean said, "That doesn't matter. Our clothes will dry in the sun anyway."

Chase was loving every minute. He'd spent all week worrying for nothing. Sure, they'd bitched about leaving their phones and iPods behind, but they hadn't asked about them once since they got on the river.

"You're right. We'll just have to make sure we take our sneakers off."

The boys seemed to paddle even harder, eager to get to the swimming spot.

As they coasted around the bend, Chase was surprised to see nothing but a long stretch of river. There was no outcropping, no sign of anyone around.

"Where is everybody?" Dylan said.

"I don't know."

"Can we still swim?"

"Sure, but we need to find a good place to park the canoe."

Strange. Maybe that splash was a heron diving into the water for a fish. But it had sounded awful big.

As he turned to tell his boys to be on the lookout for a good docking point, something exploded from beneath the water in front of the canoe. Dylan and Dean screamed. Chase pulled his paddle up, holding it across his chest.

A creature of unimaginable horror rose out of the water.

His first instinct was to strike at the animal with the paddle. He heard the *thunk* of wood on bone, felt the vibration from the direct hit. It squealed, diving back under the water.

The canoe rocked from side to side. His sons wailed in frozen panic.

"It's gone! It's gone!" he reassured them. They tumbled forward into his open arms.

"What was that, Dad?" Dylan asked between stuttering sobs.

"I don't know. But I think I scared it off pretty good."

He had to hold back a burst of hysterical laughter. His heart was trip-hammering.

"I want to go home," Dean said.

"Yes, yes, I'll get us back to the car. You both just sit right here and stay close to me."

With trembling hands, he dipped the paddle in the water to start to turn the boat around. Chase cried out when the paddle was yanked from his grip, disappearing under the water.

Before he had time to reach for the other paddle, the canoe was tipped onto its side. Chase, Dean and Dylan went splashing into the water.

Something smashed hard into Chase, flipping him in the air. He looked down at his sons, saw the naked terror in their faces as they flailed desperately to stay afloat.

"Daddy!" they cried in unison.

Chase saw a stream of blood pour down on them, realizing it was coming from him. He spun, now facing the clouds. What looked like enormous bats streaked to him like seagulls to chum. Jagged teeth locked onto his body and he was no longer falling.

No, he was going higher.

He could once again see his sons.

The world started going black when he saw the terrible thing wrap Dylan and Dean in its wings. He couldn't hear them anymore. When he tried to scream their names, he found he didn't have the strength to speak.

He sped over the treetops, his life bleeding away, carried by demons.

Chapter Thirty-two

They hadn't seen another soul for the past fifteen minutes on the small, two-lane road. Speeding past the famed pygmy pines, full-grown pine trees that only stood four feet high or less, Sam leaned forward, gazing out the front window. The landscape unsettled him, the tiny trees looking like a forest recovering from an apocalyptic event. He spotted something ahead.

"Slow down, Ben," he said.

His grandson saw the thing in the middle of the road at the same time. He eased the van to a stop several feet from it.

Sam hustled to get out of the van.

"Jesus Christopher Columbus."

It had been a deer. A pretty big buck.

Now it was simply an exploded bag of meat and blood. The splatter marks stretched to both sides of the road.

"That's disgusting," April said beside him. "It must have gotten hit by a semi."

"It wasn't hit by any car or truck," Sam said. "It was dropped here."

"You gotta be shitting me," April shot back.

"Either that or it strapped an explosive vest to its chest," Ben said, his eyes unblinking as he stared at the grisly remains. Dropping down, he dipped his finger into a particularly vile puddle of blood and organs. "It's still warm. That's one fresh water balloon."

Norm bent to get a closer look. "I think you're right. If it was hit, you'd see a blood pattern fanning out in the direction opposite from where it was h-h-hit. Looking at the c-circumference, I'd say it was l-let go from a tremendous height."

Sam reached into his pocket just to feel the Colt pistol he'd put there when they got in the van. What he wouldn't give to have one of those Jersey Devils right here in front of him. He'd leave one hell of a mess for the roadkill crew to clean.

Bill said, "I guess we all know how it got here. If it's a fresh kill, we have to be really close."

Ben said, "Let's get back in the van."

He made a wide berth around the carcass.

As Ben drove, Sam spotted more animals on the sides of the road, one of them a dog, impaled on a pygmy pine. It looked as if the dog's throat had been ripped open before it was unceremoniously ditched.

No one said a word, but the tension in the van was thick enough to reinforce steel.

The police scanner came alive with strange reports everywhere. People were seeing things in the sky and on the ground. Someone called in what he thought was a squadron of silent helicopters flying over his house. It seemed that witnesses couldn't come to grips with what they were seeing, so they equated it with things that made more sense to them.

During one dispatch about a winged creature that

was on someone's jungle gym in their yard, they heard the responding officer quip, "They have a Jersey Devil that wanted to go down their slide?"

The dispatcher chuckled. "Could be."

They may be laughing now, but not for much longer, Sam thought.

The Devils were riled up and mad as hell. April kept her head out the window, scanning the skies.

They were getting closer. The evidence of their recent passing was all too clear. He just hoped to God the beasts stuck to animals and left people alone.

"How much further to Leeds Point?" he asked Carol.

Carol looked at the map. "Maybe ten, fifteen minutes. I'm not entirely sure."

April slipped her head back inside the van. "I think I see them!"

"Where, where?" Ben said, straining to see himself.

"Just over there," she replied, pointing to the east.

Everyone moved up in the van, and huddled close to see out the window.

Sam saw the swirling black shapes hovering at least a hundred feet or more over the tree line. The Devils were snatching a flock of birds in midair, swallowing them whole, madly chasing any that made it through the gauntlet. In under a minute, they'd managed to track down and devour every single bird. "They're in a feeding frenzy. This isn't looking good at all."

The Sand Pit Bar and Grill had seen better days, but it was the only bar around, so business was always good. The building was starting to list to the left, and the outdoor bar concept that had been abandoned a decade ago still had rotted stools lined up against a chipped bar top.

Lynyrd Skynyrd blared from a lone, blown-out speaker fastened over the front door.

Gary parked his Harley right up to the front porch, the heavy bike sinking a bit into the soft sand. It was morning, but the lot was already half full with trucks and a couple of beaters. He'd been up since four in the morning working on repairs to his back deck and now he was tired and thirsty. The only advantage to insomnia was being able to get shit done early.

Gliding through the dented, metal front door, he was greeted by Sonia, the bartender. She had her hair in pigtails and wore a baggy sweatshirt and black yoga pants. "Hey, Gary, I wasn't expecting you so early."

A half dozen regulars were at the U-shaped bar, savoring the first beer of the day.

"Yeah, I couldn't sleep so I got an early start. The deck is done and I'm done."

Sonia reached into the cooler behind the bar and opened a bottle of Tecate for him. He put a twenty on the bar.

"I'm starving, too. You got any hot dogs ready?"

She shook her head. "I'll put some on."

"I'll have two with . . ."

"Chili and cheese. I know."

He nodded at Will Simons and Keith Lundy, cousins in their late fifties with matching handlebar mustaches and worn, leather vests. They headed up a local motorcycle club comprised exclusively of retired vice cops. These guys made the Hell's Angels cross to the other side of the road. They'd always been cordial to Gary, even when he beat them at pool at the warped table in the bar.

Across from him was Garrett Grandy, a middle-aged accountant originally from Connecticut who spent his Saturdays at the bar. He had a wife, but rarely spoke about her. He liked to read his paper and magazines while he drank.

Three other guys he saw from time to time but hadn't really spoken to much, sober at least, huddled near the end of the bar with their bottles of Bud.

Gary leaned back on his stool, tipping the ice-cold Tecate back. He could tell already it was going to be a long day at the Sand Pit. That was fine by him. He had nowhere to go.

"It'll be about five more minutes on that chili dog," Sonia said. She'd been two grades below him in high school and had been quite the cutie back in the day. Every now and then, she still captured some of that magic she used to weave on him and his friends. Most days, she was too tired and busy to give a shit.

Gary said to her, "You know, I'm still waiting for you to tell me when I can take you to dinner."

"You already did," she said, washing out a pilsner glass.

"Oh, yeah, when was that?"

"1989. You took me to the Sizzler. I still have dreams about the salad bar."

Gary laughed. "Hey, I'm a man now. I can take you to the Olive Garden for an even better salad."

"Hold your ground, honey," Will said, waving his empty bottle. "You don't say yes until he promises you dinner and gambling and a show at one of them Indian casinos."

Sonia rolled her eyes and went to the kitchen.

"Thanks for the cock block," Gary said with a wry smile.

"Hey, you get her there, you stay the night and get lucky. I'm only trying to help."

"With help like that—"

Whump!

It sounded as if something very heavy had landed on the roof. The entire bar shook. A couple of glasses shattered on the floor. Sonia came bursting from the kitchen, the swinging door hitting into her behind. "What the hell was that?"

"A tree maybe?" one of the trio said.

"That's probably it," Keith said, pushing away from the bar. "Get me another. I'll go check it out."

"I'll go with you," Will said. The cousins stormed out the door.

"If there's a tree sitting on the building, maybe we should leave and call the cops or fire department," Sonia said.

"You're probably right," Gary said. "This old place could be knocked to dust by an acorn. Before we go, can I get another Tecate?"

Garrett looked up from his paper. "Me, too."

"Men and their beer," she said, doling out another round and grabbing her cell phone.

The front door banged open, startling Gary. He spilled Tecate on his thighs.

Keith and Will ran into the bar. Will was covered in blood. Keith's left cheek flapped against his neck.

"What the fuck?" Gary shouted, catching Keith before he ran into the edge of the bar.

"It's . . . it's not a tree," Will said. He wiped the blood from his eyes with the back of his hand, flicking it onto

Garrett, who jumped backwards off his stool in a futile effort to avoid it.

"Who did this to you?" Gary said. Keith's eyes spun like pinwheels. His face was real bad. Gary could see the man's tongue and teeth through the ragged hole in his cheek.

Will strode to the pool table and grabbed a cue. Breaking it in half, he tossed the other to Garrett.

He looked out the open door. A shadow passed over the doorway.

"They're coming!"

Chapter Thirty-three

For a brief moment, Daryl thought he smelled salt water. He wanted to stop, maybe find which direction it was coming from, but the woman wouldn't or couldn't understand him when he asked her to slow down.

At least she's not trying to tear my eyes out.

The scent of the sea got him thinking about cool, running water, preferably from a tap into the biggest damn pitcher ever made. He was so thirsty, he could taste it.

"Hey, lady, you mind telling me where we're going?"

She cast a quick glance back at him, made a kind of grunting noise and plowed ahead.

He knew she wasn't going to answer him, but it felt good to pretend that he could have a conversation with another human.

Where is my family? Are they even near? I wish I didn't pass out when that thing took me. I should have kept my cool and paid attention.

There was no sense beating himself up about it. It wasn't as if he chose to black out. The lack of oxygen thanks to his constricted ribs was to blame.

"Why do I get the feeling we're not headed to civilization? Any chance you know where we can get a drink?"

The woods were getting more and more dense the farther they traveled . The only reassuring thing he'd heard all day was the passing of a passenger plane about an hour back. He couldn't see it through the thick cover of trees, but hearing it connected him to a more comfortable reality.

The woman stopped, going into a crouch. He pulled up a couple of feet behind her, peering into the woods.

"You see something?"

She didn't acknowledge him. After a few tense moments, she stood straight and turned to him. The milk was really flowing from her breasts now, carving through the filth in wavy lines.

If we go much longer without something to drink, that's going to start to look appetizing.

Daryl shivered at the thought.

Now she dashed away from him, arms and legs pumping hard.

"Hey, wait up!"

He tried to keep pace with her, but it just wasn't possible. The first deep gulp of air he took brought a dynamite blast of pain.

The distance between them was growing by the second.

"Come on, slow the hell down! Don't leave me stranded out here!"

She may have been poor company, and slightly dangerous, but she was all he had at the moment. Somehow, she had learned to live out here, and the closer he stayed to her, the better his own chance for survival.

It seemed like she was trying to lose him with the way she zigzagged around every tree she passed.

"I'm . . . I'm warning you. I won't be . . . be your friend if you keep this up."

Something fluttered overhead. Daryl looked up, grabbing his knife, expecting the worst.

He didn't see the huge pit. For just a second, his legs kept running over empty space, just like Scooby-Doo and Shaggy when they fled the monster of the week. Gravity reclaimed its hold on him and he landed hard on his knees. The knife spilled from his grasp. He heard it *plink-plink* as it disappeared into the darkness.

Winded and now with banged-up knees, he cried out, "Hey, you gotta help me! Hey! I'm down here!"

Tears blurred his vision. The fall hurt like a son of a bitch. If things kept up this way, he was just going to lie down and wait for death. It had to be more peaceful than this.

Despite the pain, he wondered, *why did my knife make that weird sound?* It was as if it had skittered across something hard. But this was just a loamy pit, a sinkhole in the middle of nowhere.

Wiping away his tears, he saw how dead wrong he was.

The pit was far from empty.

Bones, hundreds, maybe even a thousand, were stacked everywhere. Somehow, he had just missed being impaled on a yellowed rib cage.

"Aw shit."

He'd grown up on a farm. He knew what animal bones looked like.

That was not an animal's rib cage.

The woman's head popped over the hole. She wore a maniacal grin.

That crazy bitch just led me to a trap!

Daryl mustered a pained smile back at her. "You think this is funny? We'll see how funny it is." He looked for his knife amid the random scattering of bones.

When he found it, he wasn't going to be held responsible for what he did with it.

The abominations that flooded through the open door of the Sand Pit defied description. And there were so goddamn many of them!

Sonia ducked behind the bar while Gary ran to the pool table and grabbed his own cue. He, Will and Garrett swung like it was batting practice, clipping a few of the flying beasts, but doing very little damage.

The trio that had been at the end of the bar ran outside just as the creatures came swarming in. He could still hear their screams, though they were growing fainter.

Sonia shrieked. Gary turned to see two of the winged beasts nipping at her head, their wings flapping madly as they hovered over her.

"Hold on, Sonia!"

He jumped onto the bar, leveling a swing at one creature's midsection. It spun to the back of the bar, knocking a wood panel from the wall. The other got an uppercut and let Sonia go. The skin of his knuckles was shredded by its sharp chin.

"Just stay down. I'll do what I can to keep them away."

He was hit from behind and almost fell on top of her. Sonia was on her hands and knees, scrabbling away from him.

Will and Garrett were in serious danger of being overwhelmed. Just the sound of all the fluttering wings and unearthly screeches was enough to make Gary want to curl up in a ball and wish it all away.

Sonia suddenly popped up, now holding a shotgun. She took a deafening shot at a pair of creatures headed for Gary, shearing the head off one. Its body skidded across the bar like a frosty mug of beer, leaving a trail of blood in its wake.

She fired off another shot, but it went wild. Before she could reload, one of the flying demons clobbered her in the temple with its hooves. Sonia dropped like a bag of rocks.

"We have to get the hell out of here!" Will shouted.

"How?" Gary said, grabbing a creature by its long neck before it could bury its teeth in his face. It was one ugly bastard. He shoved the thick end of the pool cue in its open maw, pushing downward until he felt something inside its throat give way. It went limp instantly. He dropped it just in time to duck as another one went for his head. After seeing what they'd done to Keith, he was terrified of them lashing out at his face.

The blood that soaked Will through and through must have been Keith's, because the man was fighting like a champ.

Garrett yelped. Gary turned just in time to see him buckle under as a bunch of the creatures dog piled on the man, driving him to the ground.

How is any of this happening? He jerked his leg back when he felt something pinch the flesh by his ankle. A smaller monster tried to chew through his Achilles tendon. He drove his leg into the beast's mouth, and it gagged and let go, scampering away. Another one, flying in a drunken arc, plowed into his shoulder, spinning him around. The pool cue fell from his hand.

This is it.

Getting into a fighter's stance, he raised his fist. He had no idea what these things were or how they'd swarmed into the Sand Pit, but he sure as hell knew he was going down swinging.

The heavy rumble of an overworked engine caught his attention. The bar shook once again as a van nudged against the front door, blocking any hope of an exit. The side door slid open. The next thing he knew, incredibly loud booms and the sharp *rat-tat-tat* of gunfire erupted. The creatures shifted their attention, now concentrating on the people taking shots at them.

Sonia moaned. Gary got down next to her.

"Cover your ears and stay down, unless you want to catch a stray bullet."

Glasses and mirrors erupted. Shards of wood exploded as rounds hit the bar and walls. Gary covered Sonia the best he could. He doubted the wood of the bar was thick enough to stop a bullet. Especially the rounds these people were expending.

One of the creatures flipped over the bar, landing in front of them. Its chest heaved several times, then stopped. Gary saw that half its goat head was missing. Hot gore poured out onto the floor.

He dared to look up and see what was going on.

"I don't believe this."

"What's happening?" Sonia wailed.

Gary dropped back down. "It looks like a family of lunatics with more weapons than fucking Rambo. There's even a guy old as dust over there shooting away like he's at target practice."

"What are those things?" she said, pushing away from the creature's corpse.

"I don't have a fucking clue."

He heard someone shout, "Don't let them out!"

That was followed by a chest-thudding roar of gunfire.

It was like being close to a string of a hundred M-80s going off at once.

He got up again just to see Will deposited on the bar. His stomach was peeled open, a long neck tilted downward, the face of the beast buried in the man's organs.

"Get down!" a woman yelled.

He shrunk back as a bullet came exploding out of the thing's neck. It flopped about before crashing to the floor.

Gary looked back at the shooter, a very attractive, modern-day Annie Oakley who lithely spun to take out the next creature heading her way.

Dipping down to protect Sonia, he pulled back sharply. One of the beasts had slithered to the back of the bar. It had Sonia's head in its mouth. Her body convulsed as if it were being electrified. He nearly threw up when he heard the pop of her skull and the hiss of air and liquid escaping.

A stray bullet clipped his shoulder and he fell to his side, awash in blood, watching in horror as Sonia's head made its way down the monstrosity's long throat.

It had been Ben's idea to use the van as a barrier. Watching all the Devils as they soared inside the dive bar, he figured this was their chance to take as many out as possible—at least until they ran out of ammo. He had run over a man to get the van in place, but from the looks of him, his flesh ripped off in chunks, eyeballs ripped from their sockets, it was safe to assume he was already dead.

His mother and Norm stayed in the van, taking down any Devil that tried to enter. They were also on the look-out for the big Jersey Devil. If they spotted it heading their way, they would honk the horn to alert them.

He, his father, April and Boompa opened fire on the flying Devils at will. It was fish in a barrel time, there were so many.

There were a few people trapped in the bar who did their best to fight back, but a pool cue wasn't enough to beat down this horde.

"Keep behind me," he ordered his family. Ben pulled the trigger in quick, controlled bursts, using the points of the compass as a targeting guide for maximum effect. He clipped one flying against the low ceiling, caught one in the chest to his right, buried a bullet in the head of another straggling across the floor and finally blew through the wing of one fast approaching Boompa on his left. He heard and felt everyone's fire behind him, not worrying if they'd hit him by accident. Boompa had trained them well over the years. They may not have been planning for something as insane as this, but they knew how to handle themselves.

He missed one as it tried to fly out the blocked door. A hoof, hard as petrified wood, grazed the top of his head, unbalancing him. A hand pushed into his back, keeping him on his feet. He turned to see April smile.

"In a bar two minutes and you're already drunk," she shouted above the din. "Lightweight."

"April, look out!" Boompa barked.

Still dazed, Ben watched helplessly as two of the Devils swooped over her, knocking the rifle from her hands and dropping her to the floor. He couldn't shoot them without hitting his sister in the process.

That moment of indecision was enough for another creature to land on his shoulder, taking a bite from his neck.

"Motherfucker!" Ben spun in a circle, trying to dislodge the Devil.

There was a loud smack, and suddenly he was free. Boompa had brained it with the butt of his rifle. His hand went to his neck. Blood trickled between his fingers.

"April!" he shouted.

Her legs were writhing underneath the attacking Devils, but he couldn't see the rest of her.

A rumbling cry caught his attention. He spun to see his father drop his weapon, running to April. The man he'd always thought of as bigger than life in more ways than one jumped on the demons like a wrestler taking a leap from the top turnbuckle.

"Get the hell off my daughter!" he roared.

His massive hands grabbed each Devil by the back of their long, muscled necks. Snatching them away from April, he clapped their heads together with a snap that sounded like a two-by-four breaking.

When Ben went to help his bloody sister up, another Devil hit him from behind. He collapsed next to April. Somehow, he'd also lost his gun.

Now on his back, he watched as part of the roof collapsed. Instead of the trapped Devils using it as a means to escape, more came diving in.

"Come on, you sons of bitches!" Boompa wailed.

"Stay down!" his father said, covering Ben and April with his body.

"No, let us get up to help," April wailed.

Ben tried to slip out from under his father, but the man's massive body had him pinned.

He looked at them, and for the first time in his life, he saw fear in his father's eyes. That and a sadness that knew no bounds.

"Just stay still," he said calmly, wincing. His teeth ground hard on the stale lump of gum.

"No, Dad, we can get them off you," Ben said.

He shook his head. "Too many. I can protect you."

April was crying. "No, you can't. Not like this."

Blood ran down his neck, dripping on them. His body jerked several times as the Devils tried to pull him away, but his weight was too much for them.

"Please, Dad," Ben said.

"Just hold tight. I'm working on a theory here," his father said between gritted teeth. "They're not biting me. Just trying to pull me."

The sounds of gunfire increased and Ben heard his grandfather cursing up a storm. He and April lay there, unable to help, eyes locked on their father's as he desperately tried to protect them.

Miraculously, the madness began to recede. Ben watched as the remaining winged Devils flew out of the hole in the roof, circling in the sky above the bar.

His father's eyes closed, sweat running down his head like he'd just emerged from the shower.

"They're leaving," April said.

His father nodded, grunting as he pushed himself to his knees.

"Oh, my God, Bill!"

His mother came rushing from the van.

Ben and April scrabbled to their feet. Boompa and Norm's chests were puffing hard. Their eyes were on the sky, light filtering into the bar for the first time.

"Dad?"

Ben saw the blood pooling around his father.

It was bad.

Real bad.

Chapter Thirty-four

At first, Daryl thought he'd slipped into some kind of communal grave, like one of those potter's fields they had on tiny islands around Manhattan and the Bronx. Once upon a time, they'd been a fascinating and ghoulish subject for his teenaged mind. But the more he looked around, the more he realized it was some kind of feeding pit.

The skeletons belonged to all sorts of animals, from squirrels to deer and what looked like the remains of a big-ass bear. That he could deal with.

There were other bones down here that were most certainly human. He counted four skulls alone in the mass of jumbled bones. Some of them were yellowed with age.

The woman had intentionally led him here to serve him up to whatever gnawed the meat from these bones.

It didn't take a rocket scientist to assume what was feasting in this pit. The Jersey Devil was the number-one predator out here. There were enough of them flying around to fill this pit several times over.

I wonder how many other feeding pits there are in the Barrens?

And where the hell are the Devils?

Maybe they only fed at night.

The biggest question was, how on earth had this woman become their helper, like that crazy bug-eating guy who assisted Count Dracula?

Of course, he could be wrong and she was the one doing the killing for herself. He'd grappled with her and knew she was a hell of a lot stronger than she looked.

Daryl glanced up at her. She stared down at him with vacant eyes. Any hopes of being able to reason with her died the moment he saw those flat, emotionless orbs.

"If you think I'm going to sit down here and wait for whatever it is to add me to this collection, you've got the wrong idea."

He began piling some of the larger bones—femurs, rib cages, clavicles—against the wall. He'd use them to clamber his way out and hope she didn't swat at him with a large stick or something to knock him back down. He didn't want to stab her, but he would if he had to.

"I bet you thought I'd break something when I fell so I couldn't even try to make my way out. Is that how you work it? Or do those Devils bring their kills here? Maybe you're just the one in charge of luring *people* here."

As the pile grew, so did the look of concern on her face.

"That's right," Daryl said, taking a pained gulp of air as he hefted an armful of bones. "I'm not sticking around. Just need a few more solid ones and I can climb right on out of here."

There was an especially large leg bone protruding out from a tangle of bones at the farthest end of the pit. Grunting from the exertion and the agony, he tugged and tugged until it finally pulled free, sending him sprawling onto his ass.

The rest of the bones that had been on top of it cascaded onto the pit's floor like Death's dominoes.

Holding onto the leg bone, Daryl used it to prop himself up.

The bones had melted away, so to speak, revealing several industrial steel drums. None of them had lids.

"Don't look," Daryl said. "Nothing good can be in those things."

With their revelation came a noxious wave that made him stagger back until his back hit the earthen wall.

"Jesus, what the hell do you have in there?"

The woman looked to the barrels and became agitated. She scrabbled around the rim of the pit, pulling back, then peering over again.

"It's good to see something can scare even you, crazy lady."

As much as he didn't want to look inside, he knew he couldn't stop himself. The smell dissipated quickly, the first blessing of the day. Using the leg bone as a cane, he cautiously approached the barrels.

There was writing on the side, but years of filth had obscured most of it. He did see what looked like a Danger sign, a yellow triangle that lost its impact considering all he'd been through over the past two days.

Steeling his courage, he took a deep breath, held it and craned his head to look inside.

They were empty.

Not a thing in any one of them.

If she doesn't use them to put stuff inside, what did she take out *of them?*

Using his boot, he wiped some of the dirt away from the front barrel.

"Oh, crap."

Rubbing even more grit away, he was able to read everything. Someone had tried to scratch the name of the company away, but Daryl could piece it together. His heart went into overdrive.

GENODINE CHEMICALS
DANGER—TOXIC MATERIALS
HAZARDOUS
DO NOT BREAK SEAL!

For all he knew, just being here with those open barrels was taking years off his life with every breath.

He made a mad dash to the bone pile, scuttling up them on all fours, the knife in his teeth. To his surprise, the woman didn't make an attempt to drive him back into the pit. Instead, she cowered before him, her eyes wide and afraid. Her fingers nervously picked at a series of scabs at the bottom curve of her breasts. On her knees now, her head only came up to his thighs.

He took hold of the knife, flexing on the handle.

"I should just leave you here," he said.

Wherever here is, he thought. *I've got to find a way to mark this place so I can get the authorities to find it. Between the bones and the toxic waste, they'll have a frigging field day.*

He was startled from his thoughts when the woman spoke in a scratchy voice that sounded as if it hadn't been used in years. There was a passing cloud of clarity in her eyes when she said, "Please . . . help me."

Bill Willet knew something was wrong. He couldn't focus on Carol's face, or Ben's. They were close. He could hear them. But he couldn't speak. His body was betraying him. In fact, he no longer felt safely ensconced within his frame. His mind was like a kite, floating above, the tether to the man he was thin as a taut string.

He was dying. There was no denying it.

It wasn't painful. In fact, he felt nothing, at least physically.

He wanted to tell them that it was an accident. If those Devils wanted him dead, they could have easily chewed him to pieces. Something must have happened when they were straggling over him, trying to yank him away.

It was the mark that kept them from making him into their next meal.

But they desperately wanted his kids. He didn't know whether it was Ben or April or both they were after.

And he knew he never would.

Each breath became a laborious task.

Screw you, Huntington's disease. I beat you to the punch.

He wanted to tell his family he loved them.

He wanted to know Daryl was safe.

He wanted.

He wanted.

He . . .

Norm thought he saw a couple of people behind the bar before. One guy was on the bar itself, opened up like a butterflied chicken breast. The drip of the man's blood as it pattered on the floor was disconcerting.

He kept his eyes on the hole in the roof. Ben's idea had been on the money. They'd thinned the herd of Jersey Devils immensely. He saw only a few swirling above the bar before they flew away. That didn't mean there weren't stragglers left behind to take them by surprise. He was beginning to realize the scope of their cunning, and wasn't about to let his guard down.

The Willets surrounded Bill. Carol had broken out the first-aid kit and was trying to stop the bleeding around his neck. Norm thought it best he keep a lookout for them so they could concentrate on the big man.

"Anyone back there?" he said.

A man stood up clutching his arm near his shoulder. "I think one of you shot me," he said.

"I b-believe we did. Sorry."

"What were those things?"

Norm looked over the bar and saw the dead woman, He immediately pulled away.

"You from a-a-a-round here?"

"Yeah." The man opened a bottle of cheap Scotch and poured it over his wound.

"Then you know about the Jersey Devil."

"You telling me all those things were the Jersey Devil?" He sucked in a pained breath when the alcohol bathed the bullet wound. "If I didn't see it, I wouldn't believe it."

Norm looked at the bodies scattered all over the bar.

"People will h-have to believe it now. You know where they keep the garbage bags?"

"In back," he said, motioning with his head.

Norm made a quick trip to the less-than-hygienic galley kitchen. He found a box of lawn and leaf black garbage bags. When he came back to the bar, he handed the man his rifle. "Just keep a lookout for me for a s-sec."

The man stared at the gun as if it were a unicorn's horn. "Man, I need a doctor, not a goddamn rifle."

"P-please, just for a moment."

Norm shook out a bag, using it to wrap around one of the more complete Devil bodies. He tied it up tight, and did the same with a second. Flipping the lid of the cooler behind the bar, he emptied out the bottles of beer and settled the two bags inside. When they were ready to leave, he'd ask Ben to help him load it in the van. When the police came, the whole incident would be escalated to the state troopers, then possibly the Feds. Fearing a cover-up, Norm had to make sure he had proof. He'd held a long suspicion that there was a faction of the U.S. government that worked very hard to keep people in the dark about the strange wonders of the world. If he had a chance to break through that wall, he was going to take it.

"Dad! Dad!"

Norm took the rifle back from the wounded man. He ran over to the Willets.

Bill Willet leaned his head back, eyes closed, chest barely moving. Carol and Ben were covered in his blood as it continued to leak from the ragged gash in his neck.

April was trying to dial 911, but couldn't get reception.

"I think it nicked an artery," Carol said in a tone of cold certainty that these were her last moments with her husband.

"Is there anything I c-can do?" Norm asked.

Sam Willet slowly shook his head, watching his only child take his last, ragged breaths. Ben clung to his father, urging him to wake up, to fight it. Carol pressed wads of gauze on the wound, but they were quickly saturated. She pulled her husband to her chest, kissing the top of his head.

"It's okay," she whispered. "I'm right here, baby. I love you so much. I won't leave you. It's okay. It's okay."

Norm's eyes teared up. April launched her phone

against the wall, collapsing at her dying father's side. Wife, son and daughter held him long after he breathed his last.

Sam Willet gripped Norm's arm.

He said, "Did you see the big one at all?"

"No," Norm replied, feeling as if all of the wind had been driven from him.

"We have to find it. And we're not stopping until every last one of them is dead."

Chapter Thirty-five

Heather knew they were on the right path when she heard a car's engine in the distance. Daniela had been holding her hand so hard, she'd lost feeling in it about an hour ago.

"Did you hear that?" she said.

Daniela wore a quivering smile. "Yes! We must be getting close to a road!"

Heather wanted to run, but her body wasn't up to the task. She just hoped that once they got to the road, someone would pick them up. On the one hand, she knew they looked pathetic—they were filthy and exhausted. Then again, their appearance might scare someone from stopping to let them in.

We'll get a ride if I have to lie down in the middle of the road.

They came upon a small house that looked as if it had imploded decades ago. Oddly enough, the roof was still in pretty good shape, though now it was only protecting collapsed ruins.

"Why would anyone live out here?" Daniela asked.

Heather spied the detritus of late-night parties—

empty beer cans, a sweater, food wrappers and a busted Styrofoam cooler. She'd lay down good money that if she kicked the leaves around she'd find used condoms.

"Where was this place when we needed it last night?" Heather said, kicking a board. "I guess whoever lived here just wanted to get away from it all. I used to feel like that sometimes."

"When we get back home, I'm moving to New York. I don't want to see trees or open spaces ever again."

Heather nudged her shoulder. "You want a room-mate?"

"You sure you can take the whispering when I tell my family I'm gay?" Daniela gave a faltering smile.

Heather had to stop for a moment when her stomach cramped so hard, she couldn't take a breath. It was the dehydration. Her heart had been getting into funky rhythms all morning. It was going to be hard to control herself when she finally got something to drink. The urge to chug a gallon of water was overwhelming.

As the trees thinned out, she was finally able to see the road. It was just wide enough for two cars. There was no blacktop. Just hard-packed earth.

"Damn," she hissed.

"What?" Daniela said.

"That's some dinky side road. For all we know, one car a day drives on it. Probably leads to some redneck farm."

"Then we should follow it."

"But what if we go the wrong way?"

Daniela said, "There is no wrong way. If it leads to a farm, that's at one end. At the other has to be access to a main road."

Heather could have kissed her. "Thank God one of us is still capable of rational thought."

That was a small miracle, considering how sick Daniela had been. Since they woke up today, she'd rallied a bit.

Their boots crunched on the road. They looked both ways, deciding which direction to take. Now, out from under the cover of the trees, the full heat of the day hit them hard. Fat mosquitoes pecked at them, attracted by their sweat.

"Which way, Columbus?" Heather asked, trying to lighten the mood.

"I guess that way?" Daniela said, pointing to their right.

"Works for me."

A large shadow skidded over the road before them. It was gone in a flash.

Daniela pulled back.

"Maybe we should go the other way."

Heather bit her bottom lip. "How about we go back under the trees, but keep the road in sight and follow it that way?"

She wanted to believe the shadow was a passing hawk, but even her dazed brain couldn't buy that. Had it been following them all along, or did they give themselves away the second they stepped onto that damn dirt road?

Before they could head back under the tree cover, the shadow returned, this time sweeping across the road from the opposite direction. Heather looked up, her eyes catching the blazing sun. She blinked back tears, temporarily blinded.

"Did you see it?" she asked Daniela.

"No. It disappeared too fast. Come on, we have to get off the road."

Heather still couldn't see. Looking at the sun had driven a spike into the center of her brain.

"You'll have to lead me," she said.

Daniela tugged her arm. "Let's go."

Taking their first step together, Daniela screamed. Heather was momentarily lifted off the ground. Panicking, Heather let go of her friend's hand, dropping heavily onto the road. When she looked up, she could just make out a black blob wavering in the air.

"Oh, my God! Heather! Help!"

The blob came into focus. Heather froze.

The creature that had Daniela was five times the size of the ones they'd seen before. It held Daniela in the crook of a sinewy arm.

Heather looked into its terrifying face, reminding her of pictures of Satan, his face like that of a ram. She couldn't stop herself from peeing.

Daniela struggled to break free, but if she fell from that height, she'd be killed.

Better that than spending another moment with that monster!

"Hold on, Daniela!"

A rock! A rock! I need to find something to throw at it . . . if I can even reach it. Maybe if I piss it off enough, it'll come for me and let her go. Then we can both take off into the woods.

As Heather bent down to grab a palm-sized rock, something tore into her shoulders and she was carried aloft. The pain was excruciating.

Before she knew it, she was beside Daniela, both of them dangling in the grasp of winged creatures that would give the sturdiest person nightmares for life. Daniela reached out to touch her, but the big monster veered away. Whatever had ahold of Heather quickly followed. She watched with sickening dread as the tops of the trees swept by, the unbroken glare of the sun searing her skin as she and Daniela were carried like small prey.

They'd left Carol with Bill's body, promising to call the police once they found a spot with reception. April kept checking Norm's phone, looking for bars so she could make the call.

If there wasn't work to be done, Sam Willet would have happily laid down and died. In just twenty-four hours, he'd watched his grandson get snatched away by the creature that had haunted his entire life, and now he'd lost his son. Anger was the only thing keeping him going now. The need for revenge would have to be the blood that ran through his veins, the air that filled his lungs and the muscle that kept his heart pumping.

He turned to Norm. "You're the one that's spent years studying animals. What the hell was that back there? Why are these things out now, and attacking people without a care in the world?"

Norm scratched his wiry goatee. "I've been thinking about that. It's a-almost as if there's been some kind of m-mass hatching. They're newly born and they're hungry. Or, like a bird, they've been p-p-pushed out of the nest. There's also the possibility that some unknown catalyst has ch-changed their behavioral patterns. Whatever it is, they're not out just for sport. They were f-feeding back there. They saw those people entering the bar and it was like dropping birdseed into a feeder."

"You don't think it's our presence that's done it, do you?"

Sam had enough weight to carry on his old soul. He wasn't sure he could bear any more.

To his relief, Norm shook his head. "Sure, it's escalated since our arrival, but we came out here because it had already started." He lifted the cover off the cooler, looking at the sealed garbage bags. "These things d-don't look like newborns, so they've either come to m-maturity and are just doing wh-what comes natural, or we're left with the mystery of what's driving them to go m-mad. We took a hell of a lot out back there. That could either drive them back into hiding, or get the m-mother very angry."

"When you say mother, you mean the big one?"

Shrugging his shoulders, Norm said, "That could have been it . . . or the father. This is an unknown species. There's n-no way to tell for sure."

The van swerved sharply and they almost slipped off their seats.

"Sorry, there was a dead deer in the middle of the road," Ben said. It was the first time he'd spoken since they'd gotten in the van. Sam saw something wash over his grandson's face that frightened him after they'd covered his father's body.

"Can these things actually be demons?" April asked, breaking his thoughts.

Running his fingers along the stock of the rifle on his lap, Sam said, "I don't rightfully know. If you'd asked me before we came here, I'd tell you that was fairy-tale stuff. I'd always believed it was some kind of animal, but wondered how it put that mark on your grandmother and transferred it to your father and you kids. Your grandmother and I used to think—hoped is more like it—that is was a kind of benign infection, like psoriasis.

Now, I'm not so sure. Maybe Momma Leeds really did give birth to the Devil's child."

April's eyes were red and swollen. She'd said she would save the rest of her tears for when everything was over.

"You think there's a chance Daryl is okay?" she said, eyeing the phone.

"Before what happened back there, my gut was telling me he was all right. Now I know it for sure. Those things didn't intentionally kill your father. It looked to me that it just grabbed him in the wrong place. Think about it. There were so many in that bar, they could have easily overwhelmed us," Sam said.

Ben said, "Yeah, but we had guns. The dead people in the bar didn't."

"I don't think it matters. Even with our firepower, we were outnumbered and in a cramped space. What I saw was a couple of those Devils trying to make off with your father like they did with Daryl. He had the mark. That mark has to mean something. No, we're being saved for something, but I don't know what."

A chill ran up his spine.

How much worse could it get?

They'd find out when they got to Leeds Point.

"You can talk?"

Daryl's mouth had dropped open the moment he heard her speak and he hadn't been able to shut it since.

"Please," the woman said, her chin quivering, hands trembling.

He reached out a hand to her, but she scampered back.

"What's your name?"

The question stopped her trembling. She closed her eyes, seeming to concentrate.

"J . . . Jane."

"How long have you been out here, Jane?"

Daryl awkwardly sat on the ground so he wasn't towering over her. He needed to get her to keep talking. Other than his knife, knowledge was the only weapon he had out here.

"I don't . . . don't know."

"Why did you try to kill me?"

It was a rational question, at least to him.

"They're so . . . hungry."

"What's so hungry?"

She nervously looked around. For a second, he thought she might bolt. He wasn't sure he had the strength to give chase.

"The demons," she said in a hushed tone reserved for funerals.

He leaned closer to her, relieved that she didn't shy away. "You mean those things with the wings and hooves and tails?"

Her head bobbed up and down, dirt flaking from her hair.

"We call them the Jersey Devil," he said.

The name didn't register at all with her.

"What have they done to you?"

Again, nothing. He had to try another tack.

"Where do they live? I know there are a bunch of them."

She pointed at the ground.

"In that pit?"

"No."

"Is there a tunnel or something right under here?"

"No."

"Then what do you mean? They live underground?"

"Yes."

"Where, underground?"

"Not far. A very . . . big place. A building under the ground."

A building underground? Please don't tell me this is some government program gone wrong.

"How far is it from here?"

"Not . . . far. But we can't go there. Not now."

"Why not?"

"I'm not allowed when they're . . . not there. Not allowed. Not allowed."

He held out his hands. "Okay, I get it. You're not allowed. At least you can take me there, show me where they go."

When she'd first started to talk, he held out hope that she might be able to tell him how to get out of these woods. Now he knew she was fully gone, as part of the forest as the trees and the Jersey Devil. Why was she with the creatures, and why did they keep her around?

"No," she said, shaking her head violently. She stared at his knife. "You'll hurt them."

"I've seen them in action. There isn't much I could do with just this knife."

Her hand fluttered over her stomach. She said, "My . . . my babies. Can't hurt my babies."

Daryl felt the world slip out from under him.

"What do you mean your babies?"

She looked to the sky. "They fly with it right now. It ran out of food. They need . . . need to eat."

"I've seen those creatures. They can't be your babies."

The woman . . . Jane . . . must have had some kind of psychotic break. If she'd been out here, around the Jersey Devil and its minions, he couldn't blame her.

"I want it to . . . die," she sputtered. "Leave me and my babies alone."

"What do you mean by *it*?"

"The one that took me. The one that . . . rapes me. It hurts me . . . inside. You can make it go away?"

Daryl struggled to his feet.

Oh, boy, this one's gone. She doesn't know her ass from a moonbeam.

"Jane, I can barely stand at this point. Where do you get water? If I don't drink soon, I think I'm gonna pass out."

"Water?"

"Yes, water. I need some real bad."

When she stood, he saw a fresh gush of milk flow from her breasts. Talking about her babies had set everything off. She started walking, and he followed.

She has to be crazy. She may have a baby, but it's a human baby and either dead or lost.

Right?

Chapter Thirty-six

Erik Smythe had been planning the big event for five months now. He couldn't believe it was finally here. And the weather, though a little on the hot side, was about as good as he could have asked for.

He and several volunteers had worked all morning setting up the outdoor stage and running all of the electric cables so they could get the soundboard running.

Looking at his checklist, he flipped the page to the order of bands that would be performing for the charity benefit: fifteen bands in all, most of them local but some coming from as far away as Kentucky.

The anti-bullying benefit had been his idea, spawned by the death of one of his classmates, a quiet kid named Larry Quinto. Larry had killed himself after posting a video on Facebook, tears streaming down his face, saying he couldn't face another day of being ridiculed and literally pushed around in school. Time seemed to stop for a while at Erik's school when Larry's body was found at the Smithville parking garage.

When it restarted, Erik wanted to make sure no one forgot the lesson they'd all been tragically taught. He'd formed an anti-bullying club in school and this benefit was the culmination of all his hard work and passion.

His own band, Skeeter Beater, would be performing later in the day. It was going to be a blast, having such a big crowd, bringing punk back to New Jersey, if only for seven songs—four of them covers of The Dead Kennedys, The Ramones, Gorilla Biscuits and an obscure Boston band called Jerry's Kids.

"Dude, you need me to go up and do a sound check?" his pal Darren said. His band, Hippie Clipper, was set to be the next to last show for the day. It was a pretty important slot.

Darren was as thin as a pipe cleaner, black skinny jeans hanging off his sharp hips. He wore his orange hair over his face and was known to chew his bangs when he was nervous. Like right now.

"I hope you washed your hair, man," Erik said.

Darren stopped chewing, spitting out the wet strands. "This is huge. The most people we ever played in front of was like thirty at Bridget's sweet sixteen."

Erik shrugged, uncoiling some wires. "Thirty, a thousand, what's the difference?"

"How about like nine hundred and seventy!"

"Shit, when you say it like that, I guess it is gonna be weird." Erik smiled, punching his friend on the shoulder. "You got the girls in the ticket booth all set up?"

"Yeah. All's good. There are already people lining up to get in the park."

Initially, the idea had been to host the event in Atlantic City, but they decided it was better to do it right here where Larry had lived . . . and died. It would have more impact that way. The fairgrounds were right next to the beach. They'd get tons of people coming for the show, and once the music started, he was sure it would attract plenty of sunbathers as well.

"Let me just finish this and you can jump on stage," Erik said.

"Who's the first band?"

"Diana."

"She is so freaking hot. I can't wait until everyone sees her, all preppy until they hit that first sweet note and she goes total grindcore."

"Yeah, it'll be sick."

"What the heck is that?" Erik heard a girl say behind him. He didn't know her name, but she'd been helping get the refreshment stand together.

"What?"

She shielded her eyes from the sun, looking up at a clear azure sky. "I thought I saw something.

Erik looked up but didn't see a thing. "Probably someone flying a drone or something."

The girl had already gone back to stacking paper cups.

I should have thought of that. We could have had a drone with a camera filming the whole thing from the air. I bet we could sell copies of the benefit to fans of the bands. Damn.

Turning to Darren, he asked, "You know anyone with one of those camera drones?"

Darren's eyebrow arched. "No, but I can find someone."

"Cool. Forget the sound check. Go work your magic."

After jumping off the Garden State Parkway, they got on Route 561. Leeds Point was just a few miles away.

April worked hard to keep her mind on what needed to be done. The grief of losing her father kept trying to bubble up to the surface. Then there was Daryl, a big question mark that felt like a hundred-ton weight on her chest. Last, but miles from least, was the very real horror of the Jersey Devil that had to be faced and overcome, or else many more people would lose their lives before the day was done.

Boompa handed her a piece of paper with an address on it.

"Is the GPS working?" he asked.

She checked. "Yes."

"Plug that in. It'll take us to the one person who I know will help us find what's left of the Leeds house. People who come out here usually go to one of two purported houses. Neither is the real McCoy."

April's fingers had a hard time entering the address. Ben hadn't spoken in a while now. She saw the hate simmering in his eyes and in the way his jaw kept flexing.

She'd thought it would be hard to face down one Devil when it was seven of them. Now they were down to four, and one of them was Boompa, who they probably should have left back at the bar with her mother. Her mom had been too distraught for words, urging them to go with her wet eyes. April shook it off, stopping the ball from jamming in her throat.

Norm had turned out to be a pretty damn good shot and would come in handy. She'd worried that he'd cut bait and run when the shit hit the fan, but he'd proven himself.

"What if we're wrong?" she said, watching the road pass by in a blur.

"Then we sit and wait for those bastards to come to us. And they will. I know it."

"And if they come and we still haven't found Daryl?"

"We'll report he's missing to the police. After everything that's happened today, the Barrens will be crawling with them. We'll find Daryl. Don't you worry."

She felt his reassuring grip on her shoulder. April laid her hand over his, the skin tough and rough as burlap, his knuckles swollen from years of toiling at the farm.

Looking down at the GPS, she said, "Ben, take the next exit and bear to the right. We're less than a mile away."

He gunned the overworked engine, rocketing toward the exit.

"Slow down or you'll get us all killed," she snapped.

He didn't even look at her, much less take his foot off the accelerator. The GPS guided them into a residential, suburban neighborhood, the streets lined with tidy Cape homes.

"You have arrived."

Boompa slid the side door open before they came to a full stop.

"You might want to come and lend a hand," he said. "This might not go so easy."

They walked through a creaking, metal gate and up a few short steps to a wide, peeling porch. He rang the bell, giving the door a few raps for good measure.

"I suppose Gordon's hearing isn't what it used to be," Boompa said.

The door flew open. A man as old as her grandfather, if not older, stood in the doorway, his full head of gray hair askew as if he'd just been woken from a nap, the lines of his face deep as wells.

"I can hear you just fine," he said. "That rust bucket you came up in can be heard across the damn Atlantic. Now who the hell are you?"

"We don't have much time for formalities," Boompa said. "Are you Gordon Leeds?" The man narrowed his gaze at them, not answering his question. "I'll take that as a yes. My name is Sam Willet. This here is my grandson, Ben, my granddaughter, April, and a friend, Norm Cranston. I need you to come with us."

The old man tried to slam the door, but Boompa shot his foot forward, keeping it wedged open.

Gordon Leeds! April thought. *Boompa said he knew someone special out here.*

To her surprise, Leeds's face softened.

"I know who you are," Gordon said, wagging a finger at Norm. "I seen you on TV, right?"

Norm touched the brim of his hat. "That w-would be me. No TV crew around for this one."

Gordon's mouth pulled in to a rigid line. "I bet you wish you had. I know what you're looking for. You won't get any assistance from me. People like you have done enough exploiting of my family as it is."

Boompa pulled back the hammer on his Colt. The heavy click stopped Leeds cold.

"Now, I'm not here asking you to take me to the Leeds home. An old drunk like you, here's your chance to do something good for a change. The Devil that your family birthed has company. Lots of company. I just lost my son to them, and I'm in no mood to debate with you. They also have my grandson. I aim to get him back."

Leeds scratched his wiry hair. "What do you mean, *company*?"

"We killed a few dozen of them just an hour ago. And there's more. They're tearing through the Barrens like locusts."

The door opened wide.

Gordon Leeds rummaged around his couch. It was

covered, like every other piece of furniture in the small living room, with old clothes, books and garbage.

April said, "Is he from the same family that started the legend?"

Boompa kept his gun trained on the man. "Eleventh generation, if I recall correctly. There's quite a few Leedses still milling around, and they're not hard to find. Old Gordon here is the black sheep. I was afraid he'd be dead by now. Hard to fathom how people can still believe that the Jersey Devil ate the entire family when they've been living and procreating just fine for over two hundred years."

"He knows where the original house is?" Ben asked, startling April just a bit.

"Yep, and we're the only ones outside of his family that will see it. Rumor has it that he's one of the few who remembers. I've heard that the family steers clear of him because of his belief in what the rest consider their curse. I came down here twenty years ago on the sly, looking for Leeds. Found a couple nice enough to let me bend their ear. After a few drinks, one of them slipped about old Gordon here. They used the word *eccentric* when they didn't say he was outright crazy. He wasn't around then, but I saved his address just in case. Somehow, I knew he was would be our man when the time came."

Gordon Leeds returned with a wool cap on his head and a shotgun. "I'm sorry about your loss," he said. "Seeing as I don't have much say in the matter, we better get going. How're your legs?" he asked Boompa.

"Still moving," Boompa said, his gun pointed squarely at Leed's forehead. The ancient man didn't even seem to notice.

"Good, you're gonna need 'em. We can only go so far in that van of yours."

"Point that shotgun the wrong way and it won't go well for you," Boompa said.

They ambled into the van. April took Leeds's shotgun from him for safekeeping. As Ben started the engine, Gordon said, "I spent a lifetime worrying about something like this. Everyone thought I was crazy, but I guess now they'll know better. You say he has children. That's not a first."

April saw her grandfather's face turn ashen. He quickly looked away.

Leeds continued, "But a lot of them, that's not how it works. You say you've killed *dozens* of them? That I find hard to believe."

April turned around in her seat to face him. She kicked the lid of the cooler off. "Open one of those bags if you need goddamn proof."

He did just that, whistling with amazement as he peered at one of the bodies. That one had a face that disturbingly bordered on human. He looked to Boompa. "Maybe if you showed me this first, I would have come without you having to point that gun at me."

Boompa exhaled, the Colt firmly in his grip. "That's a chance I didn't have time to take."

To Daryl's chagrin, Jane the wild woman didn't take him to a water source. Cramps knifed his stomach. When he tensed, the pain in his cracked ribs intensified. All he wanted to do now was lie down and sleep until the next day.

They came upon a six-foot high column of stones. Jane pointed.

"Down . . . there."

He looked at her dubiously. "What's down there? I'm not in the mood to be lured into another pit."

She savagely shook her head.

"Down!"

He cautiously moved closer to the stones. They looked like they could have been part of a wall or chimney about a hundred years ago. Green moss grew in patches.

"You stay in front of me," he said.

For once, she did what he asked of her. She kept giving furtive looks to the sky, which made him think she was expecting company, and not the good kind.

This was no pit. He looked down at the remains of what was probably once somebody's home. The sunken foundation was a perfect square. It was old, redolent with the scent of centuries of abandonment. There was what looked to be the opening of a tunnel across from him, an opening into pitch blackness.

"Is this where the Jersey Devil stays?" he asked, pointing at the shadowed recess.

Jane nodded, her eyes wide and frightened.

"Where is it now?"

"Away."

"With your babies?"

Again with her furtive head nod.

What happened to her to make her think she had a bond with these creatures?

If she was right, there was a chance, a slim one, that he could end things right here.

You're out of your mind. You're hurt, exhausted, thirsty, starving and all you have is a knife against the Jersey Devil and all those other ones. You wouldn't stand a chance.

But what if an opportunity presents itself when I can maybe get at the big one? Would the rest fall back? Or would they have me for lunch as revenge?

"So, what do we do now?"

Jane went still, her eyes rolling in their sockets as she either saw something in the sky or was on the verge of a full-on seizure.

Without warning, she slapped him across the face with the back of her hand.

"Go!" she said in a harsh whisper.

"Go? Where?"

She jabbed her finger at a pair of fallen trees, time and the elements melding them into one decaying mass.

Daryl grabbed his knife.

This time, he could actually hear something—the flapping of wings. He still couldn't see where it was coming from, but he agreed with her plan. He didn't want to be caught out in the open.

Ducking behind the trees, he peered over the top, eyes locked on Jane.

She raised her arms as if in a greeting. He looked up and saw the big daddy Jersey Devil slowly descending. It held a woman, her body limp.

Some of the smaller Devils touched down right next to it, another woman in their clutches. Both women lay on their backs, unmoving.

All Daryl could think was—*dinner?*

He did not want to watch that. If they started gnawing on those women, he'd have to do something.

Jane suddenly screamed. "My babies!"

The Jersey Devil glowered at her, its crimson eyes soulless. It snorted at her, blowing her hair back. Its tail whipped out, catching Jane at her ankles. She tumbled into the sunken foundation without so much as a yelp of surprise.

Daryl's heart galloped faster than a frightened mare. His breath came in short, shallow gasps.

The Jersey Devil was only fifteen feet away.

And he had no idea what to do next.

Chapter Thirty-seven

Daniela awoke screaming. The last vestiges of a nightmare, of being carried away by what looked like Satan's pets, soaring so high she stopped struggling for fear of falling to her death, clung to her with desperate tendrils.

It was made worse when she saw those same creatures standing above her, heads inquisitively close, sniffing her, lips pulled back to reveal small, sharp teeth.

"Get away from me!"

She swatted at one, connecting with its slick, oily skin. Daniela had to swallow back hard to keep from retching.

The beasts stepped back. She turned and saw Heather a few feet from her, unconscious.

"Heather! Heather, wake up!"

Daniela shook her friend by the shoulders. Her back was to the creatures, but for the moment, she didn't give a damn.

Heather's eyelids fluttered.

"We have to get out of here, now," she said, casting

wary glances at the trio of creatures. Their necks craned forward, horrid horse faces too close for comfort.

Pulling at Heather, Daniela said, "Come on, get up."

Snapping fully awake, Heather scrambled to her feet. "Daniela, where are we?"

"I don't know."

The creatures took a small step towards them. Heather grabbed Daniela's hand.

"Where's the big one?" Heather asked.

"I . . . I haven't seen it. I think it left."

One of the creatures opened its maw, emitting an ear-piercing shriek. The girls covered their ears, legs trembling. It was as if the monster had issued a harsh warning—*don't think of moving!*

Looking at the forest floor, Daniela searched for anything that could be used as a weapon. Even a stick would do at this point. If all they had were their hands, they were in deep shit.

"Stay away from us!" Heather shouted. She feinted a run at them. They didn't move an inch, instead scrabbling closer, opening and closing their wings in preparation to take flight, or maybe just to scare them.

The girls continued to slowly back away.

"We'll just have to run and hope we can lose them," Heather whispered, as if the monsters could understand her. Daniela wouldn't be surprised if they could.

"On three?"

"Yeah, on three."

"One," Heather said.

In unison, they took another backward step, eyes never leaving the agitated creatures.

"Two," Daniela said.

Before Heather could say three, Daniela bumped into something hard.

They both turned and screamed.

The big creature had somehow crept behind them, the fetid stench of its breath washing over them, making Daniela light-headed. It swiped at them with its massive wing, knocking them to the ground. Two of the creatures leapt onto Heather, pinning her to the ground.

Daniela couldn't move. She lay on her back, panting, crying so hard her ribs ached, now the creature's sole focus.

For a brief moment, she thought for sure it smiled at her. Something swished in the leaves. She saw its thick cord of a tail snapping back and forth. Looking up between its spread legs, she cried out in unmitigated terror.

A thick, red, dripping penis protruded from the gray and brown folds around its groin. Droplets of drool from its open mouth splashed on her thighs. Daniela started seeing spots, her vision dimming as her fear took control. She didn't need to be held down. She couldn't rise from the earthen floor. Every muscle was locked.

The creature bellowed, gaining the attention of the smaller ones.

It dropped to its knees, its hideous, corkscrew penis dangling over her.

Oh, my God! It's going to rape me! This can't be happening!

She thought she heard Heather scream something, but nothing was registering. All she could see was that thing between its legs, all she could hear was its labored breathing, and all she could feel was its bony hands on her as it ripped her jeans to shreds.

The bag of weapons was so heavy, the strap dug into Ben's shoulder deeply enough to practically dislocate the bone. He didn't give it a moment's thought. They were close. He could feel it. For the first time since coming home, he felt like himself again, the new Ben Willet. At the farm, nothing had changed while he'd been away. Well, Daryl had grown, but everything and everybody was exactly the same.

Not him. And he knew it. Worse, he knew they knew it, and he'd had no idea how to turn back the clock.

Reliving the past had never been a want of his. Until now. He'd give anything to have his father and brother back.

Gordon Leeds led them through some exceedingly thick brush. They could have used a machete, but that was the one thing they hadn't packed.

"It doesn't look like anyone's been here in years," Ben said, eliciting a sneer from the old man. For a man being forced by strangers at gunpoint, Leeds was being very cooperative. That got him to worrying. So he kept him close, letting the man know his gun was locked and loaded.

"They haven't, and we've liked to keep it that way," Leeds said. The old codger angled his wiry frame between two closely packed tree trunks. "The less people out here, the better."

"Have you ever seen the Jersey Devil?" April asked. She pulled a tangle of nettles from the hem of her shirt.

"No, but I've heard him. And one time I knew he was close, because I could smell him, and it's not something you'd ever want to smell again. Anyone comes out here, they feel watched. That's how I know he's still here. Oh, he has places all throughout the Pines that he goes to, but this is home. It's always been home."

"You keep calling it a he," Ben said. "We've seen it up close. It's not even remotely human."

"I agree," Norm said. A stray branch knocked his hat off his head. He bent to pick it up. "Those things are some animal sp-species gone wrong."

Gordon Leeds shook his head. "We'll have to agree to disagree. I'm not proud to say that thing is my kin, but he is."

"Are you saying the Jersey Devil we're tracking now is the very same one that your many times great-grandmother gave b-birth to? That s-seems impossible."

Leeds stopped, turning on Norm with a look of pure incredulity. "Mister, does anything you've seen seem possible? You come across any textbooks that have pictures of what you have in that cooler? I watch you go out looking for Bigfoot and lake monsters and all sorts of hogwash. Are you telling me that's all just for show, that you don't believe the impossible can exist? Because if that's true, you're one hell of an actor."

Norm blushed. "No, I c-couldn't act to save my l-l-life."

"Well, okay then."

"Do you feel it now?" Boompa said. He kept his rifle pointed at the ground, finger resting on the trigger guard.

Leeds nodded. "He's here. I can't tell you about the young ones. That's new to me. How many you figure you saw?"

"Dozens," Ben said.

"We took a shitload out at the bar, though," April interjected. "So it's either in mourning or pissed."

"You killed its kin," Gordon said. "You can bet it's mighty pissed."

"It killed one of mine, and took another," Boompa said. "Now we're both in the same state of mind."

Ben thought he heard something, a voice, and raised his hand for everyone to stop.

"What's up?" April whispered.

He narrowed his eyes. She pulled her lips tight.

There it was again. Definitely a woman. It sounded like someone crying.

"Any people actually live out here?" he asked Leeds.

"No. Locals won't come near it and we have ways of discouraging outsiders from laying down stakes."

He waited to hear the woman again, cocked his head to the west, and said, "That way."

"That's where the old homestead is," Leeds said. "The real one."

It was impossible to make their way with any degree of stealth. The crackle and snap of traipsing through the overgrowth was like gunshots out in the middle of nowhere, making it hard to proceed as quickly as Ben would like.

When the woman screamed a bloodcurdling wail that could raise the hairs on their arms, a wave of calm coursed through Ben's veins.

I'm coming, you goddamn monster.

Chapter Thirty-eight

Jane lay in the dirt, listening to the women's cries.

You'll be crying a lot harder soon. And again and again and again. It will never get easier.

There was a time when she used to cry like that—tears of pain, terror and confusion. So many times, she willed her heart to simply stop, to put an end to the madness, but it kept right on beating, forcing her to endure the unendurable.

She began to see it as a just punishment, for what she did to her husband.

It had been so long, she couldn't remember if she had been the one to kill Henry or if it had been an accident. It was so hard to focus, to remember anything with clarity.

There'd been his body, she recalled that, wrapped in a rug or bags or something. *Like a burrito.*

God, what did a burrito taste like? That memory, too, was gone, wiped clean.

But she did try to bury him out in the Pine Barrens. Problem was, she'd picked the wrong spot. It took her, dropping her with the others. Were there four women, or six? Shit. She'd been with some of them for years and couldn't even recall their names. Sometimes, in her dreams, it all came back. All it took was her waking up for it to slip away.

It didn't matter. They were all dead now. They'd served their penance.

Jane assumed her sins were greater.

She must have been one awful bitch to be dealt this hand.

Birthing the creature's offspring was a painful affair, more so than the conception. She'd had to chew through the umbilicus, tend to her own afterbirth—time and time again over the years, and never pushing out just one. No, it was always multiples, for Jane and the other women. They were monster factories. The three who'd tried to leave had their Achilles tendons severed. So they crawled in mud, lay in their own shit and bore the creature's children until their hearts just gave out. Even then, their job wasn't done, their flesh feeding their own offspring.

They were the lucky ones.

Jane forced herself to look at the deformities as her babies, though they bore no resemblance to anything that had ever passed from a woman's birth canal. It made coping easier.

That thing showed them where the barrels were. Her mind may have flown the coop, but she had enough sense to know whatever was in those steel jugs was bad— poison. They ate, and they grew, fast, turning violent.

Feeding was everything now. Their brains had been rewired by the poison, or maybe they were always meant to be this way.

Jane knew what they wanted with those women.

She wanted to cry out to them, "Stop your worrying! They won't kill you!"

Oh, but you'll wish you were dead.

Daryl couldn't sit and watch what was about to transpire. The Jersey Devil had completely removed all of the woman's clothing, while her friend watched, struggling against the smaller demons.

It spread its wings as wide as they could go, blocking everything from view. The creature dropped to its knees, and the woman's blubbering cries escalated into the mother of all wails.

His jaw ached from grinding his molars. Glancing at the knife in his hands, he knew it wouldn't be enough. If he was lucky, he'd take it by surprise, maybe put a nice gash in its wings. But then all bets were off. It would tear him to shreds. There was no avoiding it. Maybe he'd buy the women some time, give them a chance to run.

What if Jane tried to stop them? Once she realized he was no longer any help to her, would she feed these sheep to the wolf?

She will and you know it. Jane's long gone. She'll do whatever it takes to survive. Just have to hope she can't get out of that damn hole.

"Fuck it."

Daryl sprang from behind the fallen trees, rushing at the Devil with the blade held over his head. If he could somehow sink it to the hilt in back of the thing's neck, they all might stand a chance. He just prayed he didn't hit bone.

One of the smaller Devils screeched like a wounded bird just as he was about to plunge the knife.

The Jersey Devil whirled around, wings spread wide,

accepting him into a foul embrace. The knife connected with its shoulder. Daryl felt resistance. The blade fell from his hand just as the creature put him in a bear hug, bringing him face-to-face with a vision of hell's own nightmares come to life.

Its eyes blazed crimson with an eternal light that came from someplace far, far away.

Daryl stared into a face that was at once that of a horse, but with the ability to convey human emotion, the muscles working in ways that no animal's could—or should. It didn't appear frightened or surprised or even angry.

No, the Jersey Devil instead flashed an unearthly smile, the way a parent would look to a child that had done something wrong and just needed a light scolding. It had no fear of him. He saw in that gaze a creature that had never known fear because it *was* fear, a beast so horrible, even the boogeyman would run screaming from its sight.

It snorted at him, a sick smell blasting through its wide nostrils, reeking of rotted roadkill and brine from a diseased sea.

For the first time, Daryl also saw the flaking stumps of horns on its head, the rounded ends discolored and chipped.

Its grip was like being pinned between two cars. Daryl's feet no longer touched the ground. It was almost impossible to breathe. He couldn't tell if the girls were trying to make an escape. He was entirely entombed in the Devil's embrace.

"Go on, kill me," Daryl spat. The pain was excruciating. "I'm not afraid of you."

But he was. In fact, his terror was so complete, he'd rather die than spend another moment in its presence.

A black tongue protruded from its long, curved mouth.
Oh, Christ, don't touch me with that thing!

Daryl turned his face away, no longer able to stare
into the abyss of its glare.

As its tongue traced a wet trail over his cheek, starting from his jawline and slithering up to his forehead,
Daryl felt something vibrate through the Devil's body.

Its hideous face turned away from him. Daryl saw a
thick branch lash out, catching it right on its nose. It
wailed an inhuman cry, dropping Daryl.

As he hit the ground, he saw the naked woman swing
again, missing. One of the smaller Devils jumped on her
back, claws digging into her skin. Blood trailed from the
wounds as she twisted under its weight. The woman on
the ground tried to wrestle herself out from under the
Devil on her chest. Desperate, she smashed at it with her
fists, voicing her desperation with a primal scream.

The crack of a gunshot brought the melee to a mo-
mentary stop.

"Get down!" he shouted at the naked woman. She
stared back at him with a blank expression, eyes darting
every which way, searching for the shooter. The creature
on her back stopped tearing at her flesh.

Even the big bastard paused, sniffing at the air.

When Daryl saw his brother push through the brush,
his AR-15 pointed right at the Jersey Devil, Daryl looked
to the beast and said, "Oh, man, are you fucked."

April's mind reeled at the scene before them.

To see Daryl not only alive, but not bleeding or severely wounded made her heart do triple beats.

There was a naked woman, a creature latched on to
her back. It looked like it must hurt like hell, but the

woman had the faraway stare of someone who'd checked out, not registering the pain.

Another woman was pinned to the ground by two more Devils.

And then there was the life-size Jersey Devil itself in all its twisted and formidable glory.

"Holy sh-sh-shit," Norm sputtered.

Ben's warning shot had given them time to assess the situation.

"I've got the ones on the ground," she said.

"I'll take the big one," Boompa said.

"No," Ben said. "If I hit it with this, it's not going anywhere this time."

The Jersey Devil let loose with a mix of a roar and an eagle's screech. Before anyone could take their shot, it flapped its wings, heading straight up.

"No, you don't!" Daryl shouted. He charged at the Devil, wrapping his arms around one of its legs. The sudden weight shift put a stop to its ascent. Daryl looked to Ben. "Shoot it!"

The moment Ben pulled the trigger, the Jersey Devil veered to the left, dragging Daryl with it. The shot missed by inches, taking out a chunk of a tree trunk behind it.

"Dammit!" Ben cursed. He darted after the creature, Daryl clinging to it, tugging on its legs and trying to skew its equilibrium.

"I . . . I can't believe it," Gordon Leeds said beside her. "I've spent all my life knowing he was out here, but I never imagined . . ."

April ran to the women, worried about using her gun now that the smaller ones were all riled up and in full motion. If she could get close enough, she'd deliver a nice head shot to the beasts.

Her grandfather and Norm were at either side.

"Go on, get! Heyaaah!" Boompa bellowed, the same way he got animals on the farm to get moving. It worked, because the Devils scampered away from the women.

April pulled the trigger and watched with delight as the knee of one of the Devils exploded in crimson gore. It twirled in the air before collapsing in a writing tangle.

She kept advancing, reaching down to pull one of the women to her feet. The naked one stared upward as the creature that had been on her back flew away. Boompa and Norm took shots but missed.

The remaining Devil had flown away as well, but it came roaring back, heading straight for April.

"Down!" she shouted, dragging the woman back to the ground. The Devil went for April this time, its jaws open wide, speeding to wrap around her face.

She held her Beretta with both hands and fired. Its head became a red mist two feet before it reached her. Its body continued on its path, hitting into her shoulder hard before tumbling to a dead stop. Her shoulder made a loud pop as the bones dislocated from the impact, slipping back into place the second she rolled over in pain. Her mouth filled with dirt as she howled from the pain.

"Go help Ben," she wheezed, momentarily winded.

"Are you all right, honey?" Boompa said.

"Right as fucking rain," she said, grabbing her shoulder.

The three men ran to where the Jersey Devil had flown.

"Stay right there! We'll be back!" Boompa shouted as they slipped out of sight.

April glanced at the two women. They looked like they had been to hell and back, then hell again for shits and giggles. "Stay close to me in case one of those things returns."

"Are you sure you can shoot with that arm?" the one with the clothes said.

April nodded. "Trust me, if I need to, I could shoot an elephant gun."

Chapter Thirty-nine

"Daryl, just let go already!" Ben shouted, leaping over a crumbling log.

His brother kept tugging at the Devil's leg. He wasn't a small guy, and it was doing the trick of keeping the creature from flying away—at least for now. The last thing Ben wanted was to watch his brother get taken away again. The odds of finding him amid over one million acres a second time were too infinitesimal to even consider.

"Just kill the damn thing, bro!" Daryl barked.

"I can't!"

Any shot he took carried the risk of hitting his brother. The Devil jerked in the air, up and down, left and right. It was impossible to get a bead on it.

"If you let it go, I can try!" Ben barked.

"If I let go it'll get away!"

Daryl's body smashed into a tree. He and the Devil spun in a crazy circle. Still, he held on. Ben was about to yell at him again that this wasn't a fucking rodeo when he watched his brother's body sail free, tumbling through the brush and out of sight.

To his relief, it didn't turn to have a go at Daryl. It knew it had to get away, fast.

He squeezed the trigger—once, twice, again and again. The Jersey Devil swooped between the trees. Ben watched as bits of bark filled the air like snowflakes. The creature was fast, almost impossibly agile, as if it knew where each bullet was going to be a split second before it arrived.

How the hell am I missing it?

It was just like back at the cemetery. His military career was chock full of commendations for his marksmanship. Even on a bad day, he could shoot out the eye of a passing pigeon. This creature was almost as big as a man, and no matter how hard he tried, he couldn't even wing the damned thing.

A pair of blasts behind him had Ben ducking.

His grandfather, Norm and Leeds had arrived, out of breath and trigger-happy. Their shots didn't even come close—and it was getting away, sailing up farther and farther toward the canopy.

Ben ran to get closer. Maybe, if it was concentrating on getting so far overhead they couldn't see it, much less shoot at it, the Devil wouldn't expect him to get right underneath it and send a parting gift its way.

Something snagged his foot and he skidded to one knee.

"Son of a—"

He looked up.

The tail end of the Devil was still visible, the wide, leathery wings pushing hard, reaching for the blue sky and freedom.

Only one chance left.

Using pure instinct, he swung the AR-15 upwards

and fired. There was no time to line up a shot. He was at the mercy of blind luck.

He almost shouted in triumph when he heard the Jersey Devil's pained screech. It pulled one wing to its side for a moment, slowing down its retreat.

He'd hit it! But where? Was it the wing, or the beast's side?

No matter, it was wounded.

Before he could take another shot, it broke through the canopy, turning sharply to the east and out of sight.

Someone groaned to his right. There was a rustling of leaves, and Daryl stood up, holding his head with both hands.

"I think you winged it," Daryl said.

"I hope I did more than that," Ben said. "I hope the fucker is bleeding out right now."

"You're starting to sound like April."

Daryl made a pained smile. He wobbled a bit, his knees threatening to buckle. Ben rushed to hold his brother up. "You break anything?"

"Maybe a rib or two. If they weren't before I took that fall, they are now. Other than that, I'm fine."

Slipping his arm around Daryl's waist, he said, "Just lean into me."

When he saw the relief in Boompa's eyes, he almost smiled. Their grandfather dropped his rifle and ran, clutching them in a tight embrace.

"I thought we'd lost you," he said, his voice shaking, on the verge of tears. Ben had always considered Boompa someone who was larger than life, both in size and personality. He'd never seen him cry, not even at his grandmother's funeral.

Daryl adjusted his Mets cap. "It's more like I lost all of you. I don't even know where the hell I am right now."

"It took you back to its home," Ben said. "We're at Leeds Point."

Daryl's eyebrows rose. "I know exactly where it hides out. There's an old foundation back there. I think it dug under it and stays there. It . . . they have other places, too." He looked at Gordon Leeds. "Who's this guy? And where are Mom and Dad?"

Boompa said, "This here is Gordon Leeds. And before you ask, he is a descendant. That foundation is all that's left of the real Leeds homestead."

Leeds said, "You say that it's tunneled its way under there?"

Daryl nodded.

Leeds scratched at his head, pondering.

"And there's a woman down there, too. I think she's been living with the Devil for some time. She keeps calling the smaller ones her babies. You don't think it's possible, do you?"

Norm cut in. "No, it can't be. Interspecies p-procreation isn't possible."

"I told you, despite appearances, that damn Devil is not an animal," Leeds said. He looked to Ben. "Now you know why we call it a *he*. And it looks like he's been very busy. I hope that woman is still there."

Daryl winced with pain when he said, "There's a good chance she's run off. If she hadn't spoken to me, I'd have sworn she'd gone full-tilt feral. She's strong as hell, too, for someone that looks like they've skipped a year's worth of meals."

"Was she that naked woman back there?" Boompa asked.

"No, a different naked woman. She got shoved into

the foundation by the Devil. She could still be down there."

Ben shifted his body to take on more of Daryl's weight as they walked. Now there was another woman involved? And the monster had been able to mate with her? But no one woman could give birth to so many of those things.

Unless there were others.

Chapter Forty

April learned that the two women were Heather and Daniela. She gave her shirt to Daniela. It was just long enough to cover her privates, but it was better than the nothing she had.

"But what about you?" Daniela asked, her voice sounding far away, circling out where April was sure her mind had flown.

"Don't you worry about me. It's summer. I'd be in my bikini now anyway."

Heather filled April in on everything that had happened to them—from their boyfriends being slaughtered in front of them all the way to the Jersey Devil trying to have its way with Daniela. No wonder her friend had checked out. The words poured out in a torrent. She rarely stopped to even take a breath. April waited for Heather to break down at several points. She could hear the hitch in her voice, see the film of tears, but Heather never stopped. It was as if she knew something terrible was moments away from befalling them, and this was her only chance to tell their story before the shit hit the fan.

That feeling may be right, April thought.

She didn't have the sense that any of those things were around, but she was no expert.

"There's another woman," Heather said. April tried to take Daniela's hand, but the dazed woman walked in circles around the sunken foundation.

"Was she with you, too?"

"No."

"She's down there," Daniela said, pointing.

April ran to the edge of the deep depression. A woman lay on her back, her body streaked with grime and bruises. Her eyes were closed, her chest rising and falling in irregular spasms. She was naked, too.

Sighing, April said, "I'm running out of clothes." She turned to Heather. "You think you could haul her up if I bring her over to you?"

Heather kept glancing at the sky. Waiting.

"Yeah, I can do it."

Looking to Daniela, who now sat cross-legged, watching them, April wondered if a small slap to the face would snap her out of it. The woman in the hole would be deadweight. Heather looked ready to collapse. If she couldn't grab hold of the woman and pull her out, April was going to buckle under her weight.

"You can't always get what you want," she murmured.

"What?" Heather asked.

Waving her off, April said, "Nothing."

But we did get Daryl back, so quit complaining. I just hope they're all right. I heard the shots. Please let them be on their way back, preferably with a monster's head on a damn stick.

Her father's face flashed briefly in her mind, but she

quickly shut it out. If she lingered, she'd break apart. She had to hold herself together.

The woman stunk like she hadn't bathed in years. Judging by her appearance, that most likely wasn't far off. A bright red gash on her forehead trickled blood into her hairline.

"Hey," April said, bending close to her face. "Can you hear me?" She brushed the woman's cheek with the back of her hand.

"Is she okay?" Heather said.

"I think even if she wasn't unconscious, I wouldn't exactly say she was okay."

What had happened to her? How did she get like this? And how was she connected with the Devil?

April elevated the woman's head, tapping her cheek. The wound on her head was pebbled with dirt.

"April!"

It was Daryl!

Gently laying the woman back down, April ran to where Heather was perched.

"I'm down here!"

Daryl and Ben's heads poked into view. Her older brother looked tense enough to turn to stone.

"Hey there, Hag," Daryl said with a lopsided grin.

April's face brightened. "Welcome back, schmuck. Where's Boompa?"

"We're all okay," Daryl said. "Big brother here clipped the fucker."

"But it still got away," Ben said, his jaws flexing.

Daryl's eyes went as big and round as baseballs. He shouted, "Jane!"

Before April could turn around, a pair of hands wrapped around her throat. She was thrown off her feet, struggling for air.

* * *

Norm ruminated on everything that he had seen and done over the past two days, wondering what the hell had possessed him to follow the Willet family to the brink of hell. Then he remembered those creatures in the cooler and the frenzy that would follow when he unveiled them to a world that had lost its sense of wonder. He was contemplating the potential windfall that would come his way when he heard the screams.

Sam Willet and Gordon Leeds were tending to the stunned girl staring off into nowhere. Well, not nowhere. Norm was sure she'd never be able to close her eyes without seeing the Jersey Devil.

He ran to the old foundation where the Willet boys and another woman were shouting. April was in the clutches of some wild woman.

Without a second thought, he leapt into the pit.

The events of the day had ceased to surprise him. Now he was simply torqued off that everywhere they turned, something or someone was out to get them.

"Let her go!" he shouted at the woman. Her eyes narrowed into hawk's slits. Her hands tightened on April's throat.

There were two heavy thuds behind him, presumably Daryl and Ben entering the fray.

Norm saw the filthy woman with the crazy eyes was out to lunch, orbiting a planet galaxies away from the one sitting topside. There was no point trying to persuade her to let April go. He was on her in several quick strides. Grabbing her wrists, he exerted all the pressure he could, feeling her bones grinding on one another. She gasped, letting April go. Daryl was there to catch his sister before she could fall and hit her head. Ben came up behind the wild woman, wrapping her up in a sleeper hold. She struggled against him, but it was no use. He had her in an iron grip. The veins on his forearms popped out, angry vines delivering more strength to taxed muscles.

When her eyes rolled up in her head, Norm said, "Ease up. You'll kill her."

Ben didn't look at him, nor did he let the woman go.

"Stop it! She can't breathe!"

"That's the idea!" he snapped.

The woman started to go limp. Her eyelids fluttered and closed. "She's out. She's out."

"Enough already," April said, massaging her throat. Her voice snapped him out of his angry fugue. He let go, allowing the woman to slump to the ground in a boneless heap.

"That's the woman I was talking about," Daryl said. "Her name is Jane. She's the one the Jersey Devil's been doing stuff to. She asked me for help before when she had one of her lucid moments. I think she's gone schizo or something."

Ben walked away from Jane's body. He stood behind his sister.

"Everybody all right?" Boompa asked from above.

"We're f-fine," Norm said. "We just need to get out of this h-hole."

With everyone helping, they made quick work of getting Jane out. Boompa covered her in his flannel shirt.

Daryl was trying to wake her up when Gordon Leeds said to his grandfather, "Why didn't you tell me about that?"

"How was I to know there was a woman out here?" the elderly Willet said.

"I don't mean her," Leeds said. He gestured toward Daryl. "I mean him. And her. Those marks."

Norm tensed. The woman had the same red hoofprint mark on her side as the Willets.

"I needed you to take us here. I didn't have time to recount my family's history," Sam said.

"If you'd told me, things could have been different," Leeds said, shaking his head.

Sam squared his shoulders. "How so?"

Leeds, refusing to be intimidated, replied, "I would have told you to stay the hell away from here! If you'd have listened to common sense, you all could have avoided a world of trouble."

Ben got close to the man. "And I may have shot you someplace non-vital to convince you otherwise."

"Common sense?" April huffed. "There is no common sense out here." She had finger marks around her neck. She turned so Leeds could see her own mark. "You telling me you know what this means?"

Leeds broke her icy gaze. His hands gripped his rifle tighter. Norm could see his knuckles whiten. "You all should never have come to the Pine Barrens. Never."

"We didn't have a choice!" Sam roared, startling everyone. "You have no idea what it did to my wife! Not just that day it took her, but every day after. And to see that same thing on our son, then our grandchildren. It broke her. The rotten branch on your family tree broke her. She died afraid. We're here to put her soul at rest. And to make sure it stops now."

Gordon Leeds slowly backed away.

"Take me home. Now. I showed you our place. You took your best shot. Take me home and leave New Jersey and never look back. You hear?"

"Not until you tell us what this means," Daryl said.

The old man raised his gun, pointing it at Daryl. "I said take me home!"

Norm didn't see how Ben had gotten behind the man, pressing the barrel of the AR-15 into Leeds's ear. "You have two seconds before I turn your head to cherry Kool-Aid. One."

Leeds dropped his gun. He lowered his head in resignation.

Everyone was too personally involved in this. Norm knew he had to step forward to try to make sense of everything.

"Look," he said, "I don't think you'll find a group of people with a greater working knowledge of the Jersey Devil than wh-what we have here. For myself, I've never come a-across any part of the legend that mentions a Devil's mark."

"You ever see a *legend* do what you just saw, Mr. Cranston?" Leeds said. "Your legend and my family's truth are entirely separate things."

Sam Willet grabbed Leeds by the arm. "So what the hell is your family's truth, Mr. Leeds?"

Leeds jerked his arm away. "If I knew your family had the mark, I'd have never taken you here, even with your guns pointed at me."

A cold realization hit Norm. He said, "You've been protecting it. Despite everything that's been going on around the Barrens, and I don't for a m-minute believe you're ignorant of the killings, you p-protected it. That's why you're an outcast in your own family. Without those marks, the odds of us ever coming across the Jersey Devil out here would have been sl-slim to none. No harm, no foul. But I've seen what happens. It's dr-drawn to them. How does it work? How can it pass it on to others?"

When Leeds didn't answer, Ben put the rifle to his chest.

Drawing a deep breath, Leeds said, "I've never seen the mark myself, but stories of other people with it have been passed down in my family for generations. The last time we heard about it was back in 1907. A woman was found wandering in the woods. She was catatonic. No clothes, no way to identify her. They said she had a bright birthmark on her side in the shape of a hoof. When the doctors examined her, they were shocked she was even alive. They assumed the mark came from a fall. She'd been tore up bad inside. She died a week after they took her in. Never once spoke a word. No one thought much about it at the time.

"Two years later, you all know that Jersey Devil sightings hit an all-time high. Folks saw it all the way from Jersey to Pennsylvania—sometimes being spotted in two distant places at the same time. That's when my family realized what had happened to that woman. She'd bore his offspring. The mark was his brand, in case he'd need her again. You see, in his eyes, the women are breeders, and any human male child that comes from her has the potential of giving birth to a new breeder. The mark is a way for him to find his kin when he or she is near. Only certain parts of my family even know about the mark. Until your family, the mark hasn't been properly passed down because the women either kill themselves or die. And whatever child they bear, well, they're not exactly like you or I. You see, every hundred years or so, he mates. But the children that come out, the devil children, they have to be put down. They're wild, untamed, a danger to everyone in the Pines."

Norm said, "And if they draw too much attention, they become a danger to *him*."

Leeds shook his head, looking to Sam. "Your wife must have been a hell of a strong woman. I don't expect you all to understand. He never harmed anyone."

"Except the women it's taken," Sam said, his anger near the boiling point. His face was red as a fire hydrant, his hands balled into fists. Norm had a feeling Gordon Leeds wasn't going to make it home.

Leeds continued, "My grandfather, father and uncles waited right here in 1909 for the children to return. They always come back. It's said there were two of them that time. They were shot down right quick, and burned on a pyre. That's what we do! We take care of our own, and the Barrens."

"And that's what we're doing—taking care of our own," Sam grumbled. "My family isn't cattle, or breeders."

Sam strode over and punched Leeds in the gut, folding him in half.

April stared hard at the man as he struggled for breath. "My grandmother may not have had one of its devil children, but we're here to sever the bloodline, just the same."

"That's not entirely true," Sam Willet said.

He looked to his grandkids, his eyes sparkling with tears.

"Your grandmother did," he said. "It died, stillborn. The doctors said if it had lived, it would have been severely deformed. They couldn't make heads or tails what was wrong with it. This was a long time ago. The body was incinerated, written off as a cruel twist of fate for a young couple. But your grandmother and I, we knew. We had to hide our joy that the child was dead. For a while, we actually thought we'd been saved."

Norm looked down at a groaning Gordon Leeds. It was all almost too much to bear. What he thought was an impossible legend was a truth so bizarre, he was stunned into silence. As long as the mark was passed down, future generations would be at risk if they ever came near the Pine Barrens. They would never be entirely safe.

Norm slipped his arm over Sam's massive shoulders. "You're doing the only thing you can to save your family, and any others that bear the stain. You have to k-kill it."

"But can it even be killed?" Daryl wondered. "If he's right, this thing has been alive for centuries. How do we know it's even mortal?"

Sam looked up at the empty blue sky. "Because it bleeds. If it can bleed, it can die."

Chapter Forty-one

The first two bands took the stage later than scheduled with minor audio issues, but Erik Smythe had gotten a handle on things midway through Mankiller's set list. The turnout was phenomenal. The perfect summer weather helped, but so did the cause. It was incredible to see so many people in the community giving their support and having a good time in the process. They'd taken a moment of silence in between the second and third bands to remember everyone who had lost or taken their lives because they'd been bullied. Erik had noticed quite a few tears. He hoped the feeling would last beyond today.

"How many you think are out there?" Darren asked.

While Erik checked the soundboard for the next act, he scanned the crowd. It was hot, so there were a lot of people in bathing suits. The smell of fried dough and sausage and peppers wafted over the fairgrounds, making his stomach rumble. All he'd had today was coffee. He needed to get something in his stomach soon.

"Maybe five hundred," he said. "Which is about four hundred more than I thought would come."

Darren laughed. "You're such a fatalist."

"My worldview keeps me full of surprises when things go right. How are you doing with that thing?"

Darren was fiddling with the controls of a drone that he had borrowed off their ninth-grade earth science teacher, who was at this moment staring at a couple of college girls in cutoff shorts, eating frozen bananas. Erik figured if he charged guys to watch them eat their treats on stage, he'd raise enough money to launch anti-bullying awareness campaigns twice around the world.

"It's not as easy as I thought it would be," Darren said. "When I look at it in the sky, I'm okay. The moment I check the video feed, I get disoriented and screw up the flight pattern."

There was a small video screen on his lap, displaying the concert from a hundred feet above. The near silent drone circled the event. To Erik, it made the concert look even bigger.

"That is just so cool," Erik said. "And it's recording?"

"Yep." The tip of Darren's tongue poked out of the corner of his mouth as he maneuvered the drone to sweep over the stage, capturing the tops of the heads of the band as they plugged in their guitars and assembled the drum kit. "I'll have to recharge it later because I want to get some night shots. With all the lights we have set up and everything, it'll look awesome."

"Just don't break it. Mr. Berenson will kill you."

"That I can live with. As long as he can't flunk me."

"Those days are behind us, brother." Erik shielded his eyes to look at the drone. It was pale blue, so hard to pick out in the clear sky. It looked like something out of *Star Wars*, a round flying droid hovering over them. The video it was taking was going to sell like crazy.

"I'm going to take it out over the beach," Darren said.

"Don't go over the water," Erik warned him. "If something goes wrong, you don't want to lose it in the friggin' ocean."

"You worry too much. Check this out." He handed Erik the monitor.

He watched the fairgrounds disappear in a blur as the drone turned toward the beach. Soon it was sand and sparkling water, rippling waves foaming at the shore. The drone dipped, getting closer to the beach. Erik could see people sitting in beach chairs and lying on blankets, soaking up the sun. He watched a particularly busty blonde apply sunscreen to the back of a tan brunette in perfect clarity.

"Sweet." As much as he'd like to stare at girls all day from the safety of the monitor, he had work to do. "Bring it back around here."

The angle tilted up as a gust of wind buffeted the drone.

Erik saw something big and brown zip across the screen. "What the hell was that?"

"What? What?" Darren said, concentrating on controlling the drone.

"Turn it so the camera is pointing that way," Erik said, showing his friend which way to go.

"Why? What did you see? Was it some chick who lost her bikini top?"

The drone leveled out, but all he could see was blue sky and the tops of the buildings to the south of the fairgrounds.

"No, I have no idea what it was. Maybe it was a kite or a balloon or something."

Someone on the microphone on the stage said, "Erik to the stage. Erik to the stage."

He looked over to see the girl lead singer of the next group waving him over. Handing the monitor back to Darren, he wove his way through the crowd, every now and then glancing up at the sky.

Joanne and Noah were down to their last fifty fliers. After the visit from Norm the cryptozoology dude, Noah said they had to get their asses in gear now. The music fest was packed. When people took the time to glance at the flier, saw it was a weekend Jersey Devil tour, she could tell a lot were interested. Some even asked for extra fliers so they could give them to their friends.

Noah chucked the empty box in the garbage. "This is a good sign," he said.

"What's a good sign?"

"I don't see any of our fliers in the trash can."

"Come to think of it, I haven't seen them littering the grass, either."

He pulled her in for a kiss. "What do you say we hit the beach after we hand the rest out? Might as well take advantage of it before tour requests start rolling in."

"Good thing I have my bathing suit on under here," Joanne said. "Always prepared. But first, I'm hungry. You mind getting me some sausage and peppers?"

"By your command," he said with an exaggerated bow. "I'm sure you'll be out of fliers by the time I get back."

She watched him disappear into the crowd, heads bopping to a techno band she'd never heard of but was pretty good considering everyone in it looked to be twelve.

All the fear of going back in those woods had been replaced by excitement the past couple of days. Noah's enthusiasm was contagious, and she was having fun riding with it. Today being so beautiful seemed like a good sign.

"Jersey Devil tours," she called out above the unceasing beat. Two people in their early twenties turned around.

"Cool, let me check that out," a guy with a scraggly mustache and hipster fedora said, plucking a flier from her grasp. A girl next to him did the same.

Noah was right, she was going to be out before he got back.

Gordon Leeds hadn't said a word since they'd crammed into the van. The first step would be getting Heather, Daniela and Jane to a hospital. Sam wondered how many orderlies it would take to get Jane in the building. She was still out, but from what Daryl told him, she could fight like a hungry tiger.

For a moment back there, he thought he'd be taking Leeds to the emergency room as well. Lord knows he'd like to give Gordon Leeds a reason to end up on a gurney. The man had been protecting the Jersey Devil, along with some of his relatives, past and present, while covering up what it had been doing to young women all along. The fact that the Devil out there now was the same one born into this world over two hundred years ago worried Sam. Despite what he'd said, there was a niggling of doubt. Maybe it couldn't be killed. Or perhaps it had only survived because it could hide in the

Barrens seemingly forever while being protected whenever it sought a mate to procreate. And this was the first time, if Leeds was to be believed, that an entire family had grown with the mark. Three generations were gunning for it now.

What kept Sam from hurting the man was knowing that he'd held on to his own secret as well. He'd never told his family about the child Lauren had lost, because they were both ashamed and terrified of what had come out of her that day—Lauren's shame that a monster had been her first. Sam's constant worry was never knowing the full extent of what it meant not just to Lauren, but their healthy children who came into this world branded by a beast.

Every family had their secrets.

The Leeds family had harbored what to most people was an amusing legend.

Until now.

Something was different this time around, though. Even all the Leedses in the world couldn't sweep this under the rug.

Rocking in his seat, Sam looked to him and said, "You just wanted us to weed out the young ones, didn't you?"

"Your anger and desperation seemed a good fit to the task that had to be done. Look, I'm sorry about what's happened to your family. I really am. But you have to remember, this is *my* family we're talking about. You can't erase three hundred years. Things run too damn deep for that."

Sam leaned in close so the others couldn't hear, lowering his voice to just above a whisper. "If you were the last of your line, I'd kill you right where you sit,

Gordon. Wipe everything clean. Short of that, I'll just take care of your family's dirty little secret. Future generations of the Leeds family will thank me."

Leeds returned a cutting glare. His rifle was safely stowed away. If he made one menacing move, there'd be hell to pay before he could draw a breath.

"You won't find him now," Leeds said, leaning back in his seat with a look of grim satisfaction. "He's smart. He knows enough to hide now. All you'll find out there are what's left of his twisted kin."

"I think you're wrong," Daryl said. He was holding his side, a sleeping Jane leaning against him. "This isn't like all those other times. First, as long as we're out here, it'll be drawn to us. We have Jane and the girls, which it wants. And there's one more thing I saw that I think explains what's been going on."

April turned around from the front seat. "What was it?"

"Jane tricked me into falling into this pit. It was deep and filled with all kinds of bones—animal and some human. I think it's where these things have gone to feed. In that pit, I saw empty barrels, you know, the kind of steel drums that factories use to seal up and transport liquids and stuff. They had all kinds of signs about the contents being toxic. If I'm right, the Jersey Devil and all those other things have been feeding from it. Maybe it's done something to their brains. The Devil's never killed before, but that's no longer the case. I think whatever was in those barrels altered them. It may also be why there are so many of them. You know when doctors mess with women at fertility clinics, a lot of times they have twins or triplets? Maybe that's what's been going on here. Whatever was in those barrels is creating multiples."

"Even with that, she couldn't have given birth to all of them," April said. "There's just no way."

Jane murmured something, her eyes still closed. Daryl bent his ear closer to her mouth.

"What did she say?" Heather asked. She and Daniela were wrapped in a foil shock blanket April had found in the first-aid kit.

"I said there were five of us," Jane grumbled. She still leaned into Daryl, looking like she was asleep.

Sam, wanting to seize on one of her lucid moments, asked, "There were five of who, honey?"

"Women. It kept us there. Whenever we tried to escape, it's like it knew ahead of time. We'd be punished. It got to where we were too scared to even try anymore. But I knew, it was sent for me. For what I did to my husband. I had to endure, to set things straight. Hell is here, not after we die."

Everyone held their breath, waiting for her to continue. They'd be at the hospital pretty soon. Sam had to know the rest before they let her go.

"Where are the others?" he asked.

She flicked her hand. "Dead. They couldn't handle it. The babies. So many of them. They hurt when they come out. Sometimes you bleed a lot. Not me. I was stronger. Always twins. One time, triplets. It wasn't so bad. They didn't stay in for long. Not long at all. They grow so fast, inside and out, you know? Nursing was harder. Too many mouths. When the others died, it was only me. But I miss them. And I'm afraid of them."

Her eyes flew open and she clutched Daryl's arm. "Take me to them! Take me to my babies!"

Heather and Daniela backed as far away as they

could from Jane, afraid of what she might do. Norm did his best to pry her hands from Daryl. Sam saw the wild look returning to her eyes. They could take her from the forest, get the docs to patch her up, destroy the monster that had done this to her, but she would never be free. If she was lucky, she'd spend her days in an institution, too drugged up to remember.

"I knew something was wrong," Leeds said, shaking his head. "Toxic waste. And here all I thought people dumped in the Barrens were bodies."

"You still feel the need to protect it?" Sam asked. "Knowing that its brain may be fried?"

"I don't rightfully know. He comes from a power greater than anything on earth. We've safeguarded him mostly out of fear—fear of what he could become if we didn't keep him to the shadows. Maybe he's impervious to whatever we can cook up. The same can't be said for his offspring and, because of that, I hope you can finish what you started. But I don't think you'll get him in the end. We'll be dust and bones before he ever shows his head again."

"Don't be so sure," Sam said. "It appears your rule book no longer applies."

The van swerved hard to the left.

"We're here," Ben announced, coming to a shock-rocking stop.

He pulled right up to the hospital's emergency room entrance, the front bumper just missing a cement pole. "April and I can get some wheelchairs."

"I'd prefer to walk," Heather said.

"It's better if we wheel you in," Ben said, jumping out of the van with his sister close behind.

Jane was wide awake now and struggling. "No! No! Take me back! Take me back!"

Daryl tried in vain to soothe her. "You asked me for help. Remember? They're going to take good care of you and keep you safe. We'll find your babies. You're going to be all right now."

It took Sam, Daryl and Norm to get her out of the van. Sam held on to her wrists. She kicked at his balls, her foot just missing. When the hospital staff saw the struggle, two male orderlies came rushing out.

"She's not in her right mind," Sam said. One look at the dirty, wild-eyed woman confirmed it. The orderlies were wide and strong, providing the needed muscle to get her in the wheelchair.

They had just strapped her arms to the chair when the sound of breaking glass brought them all to a stop.

Sam looked to the source of the sound and felt his stomach fall to the floor.

Chapter Forty-two

Heather watched the Jersey Devil smash through the glass enclosure above the emergency room entrance. Its thrashing wings pelted shattered bits of glass at them like studded hailstones. Landing between her and April, the monster emitted a soul-quaking shriek, then cast its horrid gaze to Jane and the men working to keep her in the chair.

A security guard and one policeman burst from the doors, guns drawn, shouting something that she couldn't make out.

We'll never get away from it.

Heather's heart sank. Daniela dropped to the ground, curling up in a ball, head turned away from the creature.

"Don't shoot," April screamed. "You'll hit one of them."

"Just stay back!" the cop commanded her.

The Jersey Devil slowly stomped toward Jane, its hooves clomping on the hard concrete. The heat of the sun bounced off its leathery skin in undulating waves.

Heather saw that a portion of one of its wings had been punctured. It was covered in dried blood.

"Stay away from me!" Jane wailed. "Don't touch me! Please, leave me alone!"

The orderlies, seeing the image of a true devil from their childhood textbooks, turned to run back into the hospital. The Jersey Devil swiped at them with a wing, clotheslining them at the neck. They fell backwards, their skulls crunching. At the ghastly sound, two of the smaller creatures came swooping down, eager to clamp their mouths on the soft tissue of their faces.

One of them had the face of a miniature horse, the long face shortened somewhat, leather stretched over sharp bone, stained crimson. The other looked almost human, with a flatter face, elongated nose and chin that were the beginnings of a deformed snout. Its eyes were closer together than the others she'd seen. The sight of it made her skin crawl.

"Boompa, Norm, get the hell into the van!" Ben shouted, rushing to the other side of the van.

Daryl took wild shots at the creatures as they sped overhead.

"We can't leave her," the old man said, facing the creature. His left hand flexed into a fist.

"What the hell are those things?" the security guard stammered. His gun jittered wildly.

The cop pulled the trigger, the bullet grazing the monster's shoulder. Specks of blood and flesh filled the air, along with a noxious odor. With lightning speed, the creature spun, diving at the man like a torpedo. It rammed into his midsection, the force so great, he was cleaved in half. To Heather's eternal horror, the bottom half of the cop spun into her, bathing her legs in gore.

The Devil circled around, landing in front of Jane, who was strapped to the chair.

Ben emerged from the side door of the van, brandishing the biggest gun Heather had ever seen.

"We have to get out of here," Heather said to Daniela, trying to lift her up. "Come on. We'll be safer inside!"

The sound of a man screaming in pain brought Daniela back to her feet. Ben's arm was in the Devil's grip, the gun on the floor. It twisted his arm, bringing him to his knees. April brushed past Heather, almost knocking her down. She let out a guttural cry, launching herself onto the back of the creature, taking it by surprise. It spun in a circle, wings extending, hitting April, trying to break her free.

Of everyone out here, the crazy woman, Jane, was in the most danger. For one, the creature was fixated on her. If what everyone had been saying was true, it would need her to make more of those horrible monsters. Second, she was tied down to the chair, unable to defend herself or even run away.

Heather had to help her.

"Stay right here," she said to Daniela.

While the creatures were distracted, she ran to Jane, getting behind the wheelchair.

"What are you d-doing?" the TV crypto guy said. He had a rifle aimed at the spinning Devil, but didn't dare take a shot.

"Getting her inside!"

Heather pushed the chair around the struggling monster, April still on its back, now biting at its neck like a wild animal.

When Daniela saw her coming, her face hardened with lucidity. She ran to hold the emergency room door open. To both their disappointment, the way was blocked by a throng of people—patients, doctors, nurses and other personnel—all of them too stunned to step aside and let them in.

"Get the hell out of the way!" Heather screamed.

No one moved. Not a single one.

Shots were fired. She jumped, twisting to see if the heavily armed Willets had done what they'd come to do.

The old man and the TV guy were on the ground, pinned by the smaller creatures. Daryl was bounced off the hood of the van by one of the creatures, holding his head, dazed. April was on her knees as well, blood running down her arm. The Jersey Devil turned to Ben, who had broken free and now stood in the doorway of the van, holding a gun with his left hand. The beast rocketed into the van, it and Ben disappearing from sight. The van tilted, close to landing on its side from the impact.

In a flash, the creature was back, leering at Jane, Heather and Daniela.

It walked past April without giving her so much as a passing glance. She swiped at it, missing.

"Let me out of here!" Jane screamed, her arms struggling to be free. Heather backed away, her eyes never leaving the advancing creature, but avoiding its dead eyes.

"Everyone move aside!" Daniela shouted at the people clogging up the entrance to the emergency room.

But it was too late.

April watched, helpless, her arm numb from the bullet that had passed through her bicep, as the Jersey Devil grabbed the wheelchair with Jane in it. It shot straight up, high over the hospital while people poured from the building to see where it had gone.

Jane's cries faded the farther it flew, until they couldn't hear her at all.

The smaller ones left Boompa and Norm, circling around their father in the sky.

It was eerily silent around the emergency room entrance ramp, despite being crowded with terrified people. April saw one old woman, holding a bloody bandage to her hand, totter and almost fall from craning her neck so far back to watch the creature. She got up to steady the woman.

"You need to go inside and sit down," she said.

"It . . . it took that poor woman."

"And it'll take you, too, if you don't get to safety." April spoke sharply to the crowd. "That goes for everyone. You need to get inside before it comes back."

Ben placed a hand on her shoulder. "I'm sorry, sis. I thought I had it."

He took a rag and tied it over the wound. The pain wasn't as bad as April thought it would be. "You could have shot me in worse places."

"Look out!" someone shouted.

Suddenly, people were running in every direction.

Boompa looked up and muttered, "Christ in heaven."

The wheelchair, with a screaming Jane, came plummeting back to earth. It landed on top of several people scrambling to get out of the way. They came apart like overripe fruit, juices squirting everywhere. The wheelchair, and Jane, flattened. The loud crunch of bones sounded like a lumberyard of wooden beams snapping at once. Jane's head landed in her lap, still attached to her body, no longer encumbered by a solid bone structure to keep it in place. Both eyes had exploded from the sockets.

The Devils plunged within the melee, raking at

heads, biting at limbs. In seconds, the area had been turned into a bloodbath. Boompa grabbed April's good arm, dragging her into the van.

"We can't hide in here," she said.

"We're not hiding," he replied, handing her a Beretta. "We have to clear those bastards out of here."

She noticed Gordon Leeds on the floor of the van, blood leaking from his ears. Boompa felt his neck for a pulse.

"He's dead. Must have borne the brunt of Ben and the Devil's weight when they crashed in here."

One of the seats had been ripped from its mounting, half of it on Leeds's chest.

"One less person to defend that damn thing," April said. As much as she wanted to hate Gordon Leeds, there was a part of her that pitied the man, sworn to a family oath that was bigger than he'd ever be.

April, Boompa, Daryl, Norm and Ben emerged from the van with enough firepower to turn the Devils to paste.

The only problem was getting a clear shot would be next to impossible. The Jersey Devil was fast, unnaturally so, making quick work of everyone around it. Heads were twisted ninety degrees, throats slashed, limbs torn off. All the while, its mad children took turns feasting at the human buffet.

April could swear they were getting bigger the more they ate.

Heather and Daniela were on the ground, dazed. It looked as if they'd been swarmed over by a stampede. The doors were closed tight, others pounding on the glass to be let inside. Whoever was left alive ran up the ramp, screaming, casting wary glances behind them, waiting for the monsters to pursue them.

Norm took a shot at one of the smaller ones, but it jumped away, taking to the sky. The bullet buried itself in the cooling carcass of a woman in a bloodstained nurse's uniform, most of her face missing.

"Dammit!" he cursed, aiming for the other, the one that looked like a cross between a child with Down syndrome and a goat. It took to the sky, disappearing over the hospital.

The Jersey Devil remained grounded, savaging anyone in its path. When it spotted Heather and Daniela, it bounded atop them, dragging them to their feet by their hair.

They raised their guns at the creature, not daring to pull the trigger lest they hit the women. Both twisted under its grasp, trying to pull free. Daniela went limp. The weight of her body, married with gravity, caused her hair to pull out at the roots. The tearing sound set April's teeth on edge. Daniela rolled free, the bloody ends of her scalp dangling in the Devil's grip.

Instead of running, she faced the monster, bringing her knee up hard into its groin.

It didn't affect the beast in the slightest.

Instead, it smiled, revealing hideously rotten teeth, before tearing out her throat.

Daniela staggered back, hands at the raw meat of her neck, blood hissing between fingers.

"No!" Heather screamed, reaching out for her friend.

Daniela's eyes turned up in her head and she collapsed, her life pumping out of her in syncopation with the last beats of her heart.

Boompa and Ben opened fire at the right side of the

monster, now that it no longer held Daniela. With an easy flick of its wings, it zipped aside unscathed.

It clutched Heather directly in front of its body.

What April saw next made her throat burn with volcanic bile.

The Devil's coarse, mangled penis rose from between Heather's legs. She was lifted inches off the ground by its turbid protrusion.

Boring its vile gaze into April, it said in a voice as deep as a canyon and old as time itself, "For you."

Chapter Forty-three

Sam Willet felt lightning bolts of pain arc across his chest.

Not now, you son of a bitchin' heart!

The Jersey Devil spoke!

Maybe Gordon Leeds was right. It was as much human as it was monster.

The poor girl in its arms looked about ready to faint, and he couldn't blame her. They were at a standoff. At this close range, with five people with their fingers on their triggers, even by chance, one of them was going to hit their mark. And it knew it, which is why it was using the girl as a shield.

"Put the girl down," Sam said, his voice even, stronger than he felt. He didn't know if it was possible to will a heart attack away, but he was damn well trying his best right now.

The beast hissed back, its eyes locked on April.

"You're not taking her," he said, nodding toward his granddaughter. To her credit, she didn't seem the least bit fazed by the Devil's fascination.

The Jersey Devil turned its deep-set eyes to him.

Sam felt a hand squeeze his heart. His vision wavered, but he refused to put his rifle down.

April started with a low chuckle. She said, "The joke's on you. You could try, you ugly fucker, but you'll never get what you want out of me. I can't have normal kids, and I sure as hell can't have whatever shit stains will come out of that diseased-looking thing you seem to think is so impressive."

In its anger, the Jersey Devil flew at April, stopping just short of bowling her over. Heather screamed, still in its clutches.

When April moved the Beretta to the Devil's forehead, it lifted Heather higher so the gun was to her mouth

"Your mark doesn't mean shit," she said.

There was a loud explosion. Sam staggered, kept on his feet thanks to Norm.

The Jersey Devil wailed, taking to the sky with Heather. Blood came down in tiny droplets, staining the ground.

"Shit!" Ben spat, dropping to a knee and aiming at the ascending creature.

"You n-nailed it!" Norm shouted, staring at the blood.

"Not good enough," Ben said, keeping the Devil in his crosshairs. "It still has Heather."

The girl was yowling in a mix of agony and unbridled fear.

Sam heard the desperate wail of police sirens.

The Devil must have as well, because it hovered over them for a moment, looking where the emergency vehicles would be coming from. The other two creatures came from wherever they'd been hiding, now flying on either side of it. All three took off, vanishing in seconds.

Ben punched the van's hood. "Dammit! Dammit! Dammit! I had it!"

April grabbed his shirt, pulling him to the open door. "Come on, we have to follow them and get out of here before the cops arrive. Once they block us in, we'll be stuck for the rest of the day, if not the week, trying to explain what the hell happened here."

Norm looked in the van and said, "What about L-L-Leeds?"

Despite the heaviness in his chest, Sam grabbed the dead man's feet. "Help me get him out. We'll leave him here with the rest of the casualties."

Shooting him a wary glance, Norm said, "I didn't sign up for disposing of bodies, Sam."

"Then you're free to stay here with him."

He didn't have time to give a rah-rah speech or assuage Norm's concerns. They had to get their asses on the road and hope they could spot the damned things.

He could hear Norm's teeth grinding, but the man wordlessly helped him extract Gordon Leeds from under the interior wreckage and laid him down next to an orderly who was missing his head.

They made it out of the single road leading to the hospital just as a flock of cop cars and firetrucks came screaming in.

As they tore down the road, Sam noticed the gunshot wound on April's arm. "Go back!" he yelled.

Ben hit the brakes. Everyone fell forward.

"Did you see them?" Daryl asked.

"Your sister's been shot."

"I'm not going anywhere," April said. "Keep driving.

That thing has Heather and we all know what it's going to do to her. We have to stop it."

"It won't go back to the old Leeds house," Norm said. "B-Because we know about it. But that leaves over a m-million other acres for it to lose itself."

Ben kept the van idling. "It's not going to violate Heather." His face was grim, but there was the beginnings of a smile at the corner of his mouth. "It took Heather knowing we would follow it."

"What the hell are you talking about?" April said. She looked ready to jump out of her skin.

Now Ben put the van back in drive. "Because I just shot its dick off."

Heather watched in horror as the world sped beneath her.

I don't want to die! I don't want to die!

She didn't want to end up like Jane and she sure as hell didn't want her throat slashed like Daniela. Her terror had taken total control. She couldn't even feel sad for her friend. Not now, dangling from the clutches of this nightmare, hundreds of feet in the air.

The Jersey Devil emitted a constant stream of rumbling groans. It was hurt. She could see the blood spattering the bottom half of her legs.

As much as she wanted to be free from its grasp, freefalling to her death was even less of an option.

All she could hope for was that the wound was so severe, it would have to drop down to land either out of exhaustion or the inability to keep flying.

I hope you bleed out!

The ability to speak her feelings aloud had been

robbed by cold fear. She wished there was some way to see where it had been hurt. Maybe, if she could apply a little pressure to the wound, it would force the creature to land.

Or let me go.

No, that wouldn't do. Unless it flew low enough over some trees that could break her fall, if not her neck.

The two smaller creatures swooped back and forth, snapping at her, just missing taking portions of her flesh.

And then she heard something that seemed so out of place, she wondered if she was hallucinating.

Music.

It sounded like a live concert, or someone with some really big speakers out to piss off the neighbors.

When she looked down, her head spun. The Devil had climbed even higher. Vertigo punched her in the solar plexus. She was sure she was going to black out. It would be a mercy.

But she stayed conscious, long enough to see they were soaring over a shore, blue waters stretching on for as far as she could see.

And on the shore, there were tons of people milling around the green grass of a giant park. She saw the stage, heard the clapping and cheering as the music cut off.

What she wouldn't give to be down there, a cold beer in one hand, maybe a corn dog in the other, jamming out to any kind of music—all that mattered was that she was safe and surrounded by people having a good time.

She had to look up. If she stared down at the event any more, she'd vomit, and she wasn't sure she had anything left to come up.

Something flew just ahead of them. It wasn't another creature.

It looked like a giant Frisbee, but one powered by four propellers, like a helicopter.

The Jersey Devil banked hard, heading for the flying object the way a hummingbird went after insects.

When the object dipped away, making a fast descent, the Devil and its minions followed. The ground rushed up toward her. Heather closed her eyes and screamed, wondering who would be waiting for her on the other side when she died.

Norm's body buzzed from head to toe, so much so that his ears even felt stuffed, the steady thrum of his heightened heartbeat drowning out most of what was said around him.

He kept looking to the cooler, remembering what was inside. That was going to be small potatoes compared to everything that happened. If the Jersey Devil did manage to slip away once again, at least they had proof right here, and back at that bar. And it would be hard to explain away the massacre outside the hospital.

I hope Carol's holding up. I can't imagine the look on the faces of the police when they walked in that bar. I'm sure the same thing is happening right now at the hospital, only there are no creature corpses left behind to lay blame. Just the frantic words of all the witnesses.

Witnesses who would alert them about the van full of crazy people who pulled out a cache of weapons to drive the monsters away—or attracted them in the first place.

He buried his face in his hands, wishing it all away.

I should never have come.

But you did! And you proved you're no coward. It's gone beyond the Willet family needing you or any notoriety that will surely come after all of this. As long as those things are out there, crazed and angry, every innocent person in New Jersey is depending on us whether they know it or not. With Ben disabling its ability to procreate, Lord knows what state of mind it's in.

April had her head out the window again, searching the sky for the Devils.

He shook the pill case out of his pocket, contemplating tripling his dose of anti-anxiety meds. The way his heart was hammering, he could sure use them.

But the damn things made his head feel like cotton, dulling his senses. He needed to be clear. If they got another shot at the creatures, he needed to see straight.

He threw the small case across the van. It bounced off the dented wall, hitting Daryl.

"What was that?" Daryl said.

"Pharmaceutical courage," Norm replied, chewing on his lip.

Despite all they'd been through, Daryl Willet smiled.

He said, "Bet you never thought it would be like this, did you?"

"N-no, I certainly didn't."

"We're gonna kill it." He wiped his nose with the back of his hand. "If not for us, then for my dad. That mark doesn't mean a thing to me. I just won't pass it on. And you heard April, she can't. No, it's all going to end here and now. And you have a front-row seat. You'll be famous after this."

Tugging at the end of his goatee, Norm replied, "Or infamous. Not many cryptozoologists go out killing the very things they've spent their lives trying to prove were real."

Daryl tapped him on the leg. "When this is over, everyone will see the truth, and they'll know it had to be stopped. Then you get to write it up in some textbook, probably get a movie deal, too. Make sure Chris Pratt plays me."

Norm watched the youngest Willet, in obvious pain, shift in his chair, wiping down his rifle. His wasn't the calm before the storm—it was the calm in the eye of the hurricane.

Sam looked pale and haggard. He was thumbing through a box of old cassettes. Handing one to April, he said, "Can you please pop this in?"

Frank Sinatra's smooth as silk voice crooned from the van's speakers. It was jarring, listening to him sing about the summer wind after all they'd been through. Sam closed his eyes, his head resting back. Sweat trickled down his face. Norm thought he heard him mumble, "One last time." He was about to ask what he meant, but thought better of it.

Besides, there was something that had been nagging at him. Norm thought hard before speaking. "When it spoke, I started to re-rethink every single theory about the Jersey Devil. If it can talk, it can think and reason. That, in a way, makes it human. If we k-k-kill it, does that make us murderers?"

Daryl's expression turned stony.

"No, that makes us saviors. Whatever doubts you have in your mind, bury them deep. We can't have that getting in the way of doing the right thing when the time comes. And you know what the right thing is."

Norm looked to the rifle on his lap, images of Bill Willet, Jane, Daniela and so many others paining him.

The boy seemed years beyond his age, a hardened man who had accepted a fate that would crush most others.

"I do," Norm said softly.

April slapped on the door.

"I think I see it!"

"Where?" Ben said, his forehead almost pressing against the windshield.

"Not far ahead of us. I saw something big swooping down real fast."

When Norm moved forward to look for himself, his foot slipped in something slick. It was Gordon's Leeds's blood.

All he saw was blue sky and a few puffy clouds.

"You sure?" Sam said.

"I'm pretty sure."

There was a break in the trees lining the road. Ben slowed down, easing the van to the side of the road. He and April opened their doors, scanning the horizon.

"Is that music?" Daryl said.

"Yeah," April said. The bullet's blackened exit wound on the back of her arm looked horrendous. Norm didn't know how she was still functioning. At least most of the bleeding had stopped. He realized that the Willet kids would stop at nothing now to avenge their father. It was no longer about proving the Jersey Devil was real or discovering the secret to the mark that had forever altered their family's fate.

Now, it was simply a matter of an eye for an eye.

Chapter Forty-four

"Erik, get the hell over here!" Darren shouted, his eyes transfixed on the monitor, hands working the controls for the drone.

"What?" Erik had a headphone covering one ear. The steady thrum of the ska band on stage forced Darren to shout until his throat hurt.

"I said get over here now! You have to see this!"

Handing the headphones over to their friend Taylor, who was helping run the soundboard, Erik sidled up to Darren.

"What the heck's got you all excited?"

Nodding his head toward the monitor, Darren barked, "Look!"

At first, there was nothing but sky. Darren forced the drone out of its dive, gaining altitude and banking to the right.

"I don't see anything," Erik said.

"Just hold on a second."

Darren looked up. The sun was so bright, it made seeing anything difficult without his sunglasses.

But it didn't make it impossible, especially for this.

The three objects he'd seen before were in pursuit of the drone. The camera was mounted on the front. He had to turn it around so Erik could see. His thumbs worked the toggles, legs tapping to the beat of his nerves, not the music.

"Almost there," he said.

"Look, man, I got a ton of shit to do," Erik said impatiently.

"Just keep your eyes on the screen, dude."

Darren forced the drone into a near ninety-degree turn, sailing over the pursuing objects until it was right behind them.

"Holy shit!" Erik squealed, jumping back from the monitor. "What the hell are those things?"

"I don't know, but I think that's a woman the big one is carrying."

Moving the drone closer, his stomach felt like lead had been poured into it when he saw the struggling woman. Her mouth opened in a scream he couldn't hear. The thing that held her looked like a bat, until it turned to face the drone.

That face! No, it couldn't be!

Erik's finger wagged at the screen. "No way. No freaking way. You know what that looks like?"

Darren had lived in the Pine Barrens, though on the southern, outer edge, all his life. If there was one thing he knew, it was the creature leering at the drone.

"That's not possible," Darren said, having to move the drone away quickly as the three creatures altered their trajectory until they were hot on its trail.

Both boys looked to the sky.

And there they were, streaking over the fairgrounds. Darren noticed other people casting glances skyward, some pointing.

"You have to get them away from here," Erik said, looking at the crowd. "They want that drone for whatever reason. Let them have it, but not right here."

"What about the woman? Shouldn't we tell the cops or something?"

Erik slapped his back. "Right. Right. I gotta go find someone." His friend was breathing hard, his face gone pale despite the sunburn that had been creeping up on him all day. He stood frozen in place, eyes on the monitor.

"Hurry, dude. Get the cops over here," Darren said, breaking Erik from his paralysis.

Erik ran. There were cops everywhere, so it wouldn't be hard to find one.

Darren looked back at the monitor and saw clouds spinning.

What the . . . ? Clouds don't move like that.

Glancing up, his mouth went dry.

One of the creatures had gotten to the drone. It spun, powerless, heading to the area around the stage, the very place that had the highest concentration of people.

The rest of the world thought people from New Jersey had been off their rockers, claiming to be the home of the Jersey Devil, a creature spawned not far from here.

Darren wondered what they would say when this was all over.

Heather flinched when one of the smaller monsters nipped the speeding drone, tearing off one of the propellers. That seemed to put the entire craft in a stall. It fell in long, looping arcs. The Jersey Devil's hell spawn followed it as it made its helpless descent.

As the children went, so did the father. Heather's

stomach did backflips as the Devils rushed to the falling drone.

Seeing all those people directly below them, she was helpless to warn them to get out of the way. No matter how hard she screamed, they would never hear her.

But some did spot them. More and more faces turned toward the sky, hands blocking out the sun, fingers pointed their way. As they got closer, Heather could even begin to see their expressions, happiness turning to curiosity, then abject fear. Bodies jostled to get out of the way. In seconds, panic had taken control. She saw people fall in their mad desire to flee, others trampling over them, the next wave of humanity dropping in turn.

The drone was on a direct trajectory toward a family trying to get a small girl to her feet. If they didn't move, it was going to land right on top of them. She knew what would come next.

She twisted as much as she could, making it difficult for the Jersey Devil to keep its hold on her. Her only hope was that she could somehow break free as they got closer to the ground.

The music stopped, the band casting their instruments aside. Heather saw the girl and her mother screaming, but couldn't hear over the fervent cries of the dispersing crowd. She wanted to close her eyes and save herself from witnessing what would happen to the family, but she needed to be aware of her proximity to terra firma.

To her dismay, the Jersey Devil slowed its descent, using its powerful wings to buffet the air, pulling them back. They were at least a hundred feet up. If she fell from here, she would die for sure.

Heart thrumming, she shouted in vain. A half-second before the drone would have crashed onto the family, one of the creatures zoomed over their heads, snatching it from the air. The other one joined its sibling, both of them tearing the drone in half as they soared over the crowd.

Knowing it wasn't something they could eat, they would head back to wherever they'd planned to take her. She couldn't let this opportunity slip through her fingers. It very well could be her last shot.

Better to die here than go through what Jane and the others did.

Heather's mind calmed, then her body.

The Devils had let the pieces of the drone sprinkle among the scattering people, snapping at the heads of anyone close by.

One of the Jersey Devil's wings brushed against her as it worked to hover over the scene, screeching to its children, most likely urging them to come back.

She could see the intricate pathways of veins in the membranous wings. As much as the thought sickened her, she knew what she had to do.

When the wings brushed against her again, she grabbed one with all of the strength she had left in her body. Letting out a wild shriek, she opened her mouth wide, clamping down on the foul-testing flesh of its right wing. It tried to pull away, but she held fast. The Jersey Devil had a hard time maintaining its balance, and she felt herself tipping.

It dropped closer to the ground, frantically trying to free its wing from between her gritted teeth.

Don't let go. Don't let go. Not yet. Just a little farther.

She felt its grip around her waist weaken.

The Jersey Devil enfolded her in its wings, pulling back with enough force to pull her teeth from her mouth. Heather watched in horror as white flecks

stained red at the roots, *oh Jesus, her teeth*!—pelted off
its wing, tumbling away.

She'd never imagined there could be so much pain.
Her mouth quickly filled with blood. The Jersey Devil
lost its grip and she started a free fall, hoping she
wouldn't land atop someone, her only satisfaction
seeing the beast was also falling, a hole torn in its wing
big enough to ground it, hopefully forever.

Ben slammed on the brakes. There was no way he
could navigate through the crush of humanity headed
their way.

"It's definitely that way," he said. "We're going to
have to fight against the tide."

Boompa and Daryl had already opened the secret
compartment in the floor of the van, extracting as much
firepower as they could all carry. Ben parked the van on
the shoulder of the two-lane road.

He looked back at his grandfather, whose face had
taken on a gray, death mask pallor. "Why don't you stay
here, Boompa?"

The old man snapped, "Just get your gear. We don't
have time to waste."

They spilled out of the side door.

The moment they stepped out of the van, they were
buffeted by a steady stream of people, most of them
screaming for their lives. They heard shots fired in the
distance, which only got the frightened crowd moving
faster, getting deadlier in their stampede. Of course.
There were always police at outdoor events. And if they
were shooting, it meant the Devils hadn't up and disappeared.

Ben told everyone to get behind him. It was easier

to cut through the scrum in the formation of a knife. He pushed forward, batting people away as kindly as possible, though he knew he'd hurt some with the stiff arms he had to employ to keep from being bowled over.

Boompa fired his rifle in the air. The crowd stopped for a moment, saw that the crazy people running to the madness were carrying weapons, and parted like a Biblical sea.

"Thought that might make things easier," Boompa said.

"With age comes w-wisdom," Norm said, pushing his straw hat harder onto his head.

"Stay close to me," Ben said to April. He knew she was hurt more than she was letting on. For now, the numbness that followed shock was keeping her from howling in pain.

"I'm with you," she said. "Come on."

As she brushed past him, blood from her arm streaked across his shirt. He hooked a finger into her belt loop as they ran to the center of the storm.

Chapter Forty-five

The Jersey Devil made a sound that caused Heather's heart to miss several beats. No longer screeching, it was bleating like a wounded goat, then whinnying like a crazed horse, both sounds blending into one another to produce something otherworldly.

This was the sound of the Devil, not just the *Jersey* Devil. When Armageddon came and souls were swallowed up, it would be to this siren call, a bleating for the damned to come home.

She was on her back, unable to move, watching the creature hit the ground hard, tumbling into a couple of teen boys, one with a guitar strapped on his back. As it scrambled to regain its feet, the Devil's talons and hooves tore the flesh from the boys, leaving them a shredded pile of remains.

Oh, God, I think I broke my back!

Heather couldn't feel her legs at all, and her arms were afflicted with painful pins and needles. It was a chore just to lift her head off the ground, in time enough to see the Jersey Devil stalk toward her.

Its two diseased children jumped from person to

person, tackling them and taking chunks from necks, faces and arms thrown up in helpless defense. They were gorging like there was no tomorrow, the feast of terrified humanity too much to pass up.

The world spun. Heather had to lay her head back down, closing her eyes tight. Someone stepped on her hand but she couldn't move out of the way.

Hot, foul air blew across her face.

Her eyes snapped open.

The Jersey Devil loomed over her, its hideous face inches from her own. It twisted its long neck until its head was between her legs, sniffing loudly. She willed her legs to draw up and kick it, but they were completely detached from any commands her mind could give.

The creature's head rose up and it sneered at her.

She was too tired to scream, incapable of even getting up.

"Go on," she said, finding it hard to draw enough breath to be heard above the wails of the people and creatures around her. "Finish me."

If there was one speck of luck left in her fleeting life, the Devil would bite her in an area that had already gone numb. She wouldn't feel a thing. She'd simply grow tired as she bled out, dying in her sleep. After everything that had happened, it seemed almost too much to hope for.

The sound of gunfire crackled behind her. She was flipped onto her stomach as the Jersey Devil, perhaps with its tail curled under her, leapt away to avoid being shot.

She saw a man in police uniform, legs spread apart, both hands on his gun, pulling the trigger again and again until he was out of ammo. She couldn't turn to see if he'd hit the demon.

"Thank you," she muttered, sure he couldn't hear her.

Just as she was about to pass out, either dying or her body's response to remove itself from the severe trauma it had endured, she saw a look of panic wash over the cop's face. There was a brown blur, and after it had passed, the man's head was no longer there. Jets of blood pumped from his open neck like sprinklers on the back lawn. His knees gave out, his body collapsing, blood washing over her. She could feel it pooling around her head.

Heather tasted the bitter copper of his blood. She tried in vain to turn her head away from the river of crimson, slipping away as some settled into her open mouth while most of it was absorbed by the lush earth.

The scene unfurling before them was beyond April's worst nightmare, and she couldn't help wondering if it was all their fault. Food stands were overturned, bodies were everywhere, some writhing in agony. When she saw a baby strapped in an overturned stroller, her blue eyes vacant, deadening with each passing second, she wanted to cry until her heart gave out.

No. You can't blame yourself. Those things were moving outward before you got here. Just think of all the ones we've killed so far. What would this place be like if there were more of them?

Whatever toxic waste that was in their systems had driven them completely mad, filled with an insatiable lust for food and mayhem. They were like a pack of rabid dogs.

The Jersey Devil ran—no—galloped toward a group of people running for the beach about a hundred yards away. The two smaller ones were diving at people and taking back to the sky, up and down as if they were on an invisible trampoline. They no longer looked so small. It appeared as if they had gained mass, bones stretching taller, since they'd first appeared at the hospital.

"Norm," she said, "do they look bigger to you?"

They watched as one plucked at the back of a woman lying in the grass, tearing some meat from her shoulder. She didn't move or make a sound.

"Sweet Jesus, I think they do. There's no way their metabolism could speed up like that."

"Maybe with all the feeding they've been doing . . ." April's thoughts trailed off when she saw the Jersey Devil spread its wings, using them to smother a running man and woman, driving them to the ground. Its head flicked up, blood splattering in a spreading arc.

"Not knowing what th-these things really are and what toxic sludge they were f-feeding on, I shouldn't say no to anything at this point."

The few police that were standing were talking frantically into mics clipped to their shoulders. It was a safe bet to assume they had spent every bullet they had, unable to stop the slaughter.

"We need to come at them rationally," Ben said. "April, Daryl, Norm and Boompa, you concentrate on the small ones. I'll sweep behind Big Daddy and take it out before it even knows I'm there. It's bleeding pretty bad. That should slow it down just enough."

Boompa shook his head gravely. "I've got him, son. I didn't come out here to hide behind you."

"You can't. You're better with moving targets anyway, and those two are moving pretty damn fast."

"This is not a debate, it's an order. Now hurry before more people get hurt."

April shouted, "Wait!" but her grandfather was running away before anyone could stop him.

Daryl followed after him, as she knew he would.

"Goddammit!" Ben hissed, punching his AR-15.

"You want to help Boompa? Then let's kill these fuckers fast," April said. She took quick aim at a swooping Devil, fired but missed. Norm, taking her cue, did the same, with the same results. The beasts were getting faster, smarter. It was as if they could hear the bullet the moment it left the barrel of the rifle, making impossible moves to avoid being a target.

The only mercy now was the fact that most of the people from the fairground were gone. But that also meant the Devils might move on from here, so they had no time to waste.

The recoil of the rifle, though not much, brought fresh waves of pain to her arm, waves that went straight to her head, making her vision and balance waver. She tried firing in places where she thought the Devils would be next, but even then, they seemed to read her mind, zigging left when she fired right.

With sickening dread, it dawned on her that even they might not have enough ammunition to keep going like this. And when they were done, the creatures would flit away, unscathed, growing deadlier by the kill. If the Jersey Devil could no longer procreate, what was left but to feed along with its diseased offspring?

"If we're going to nail them, we have to get closer," April shouted over the sharp crack of gunfire. "Like right on top of them. Literally."

"Watch it!" Norm shouted just as a Devil swooped over their heads, knocking the hat from his head.

This was insane. When it came back around, April flipped her rifle in her hands, swinging at it with the barrel like it was a flyswatter. Her palms burned from the piping hot steel. She missed and dropped it, waving her hands to take the sting away.

"You're not going to be able to beat them to death," her brother said.

"We have to do something before they move on!" April said, scrambling for her rifle.

Norm tapped her shoulder. "I d-don't think they're going anywhere soon."

She looked to where he was pointing. People in bathing suits were running from the beach directly into the hell that the fairground had become.

"What the hell are they doing?" she said.

It only took seconds to answer her question.

A half dozen more Devils flew low enough to knock the sunbathers over.

"The fucking cavalry," April said, feeling all of her energy flee her body like air from a popped balloon.

In all of the madness, she'd forgotten about the creatures that had gotten away from the bar. The bar where her father's body was now, his last dying act saving his children.

It was now five against nine in an open space. Nine creatures that moved faster than their bullets could travel.

They were royally screwed.

Somehow in the mad panic, Erik Smythe found himself trapped under the fallen zeppole stand. He was pretty sure his leg was broken. He didn't have the strength to lift if off his midsection. Maybe staying put was his best option. Those Jersey Devils—wasn't there only supposed to be one?—zeroed in on anyone on foot. They'd passed over him a couple of times, so he'd been relegated to watching the event he'd been so proud of turn into Grand Guignol theatre.

He heard people shooting but couldn't sit up enough to see. Now there was a new wave of screams, and he wondered if he'd died and was in hell or some kind of purgatory for people whose good intentions went bad.

Something clutched at his shoulders and he screamed.

"Dude! It's me! We have to get you out from under there."

Erik breathed a sigh of relief. Darren crouched over him, his face streaked with blood.

When Darren noticed him looking at his face, he said, "Not mine. But it will be if we don't get the hell out of here. More of those things just arrived. The cops are dead, but there are some crazy asses shooting at them."

"I think my right leg is broken. Go and get help. They've been ignoring me. Maybe they think I'm dead. I'll be all right."

Darren shook his head savagely. "No, you won't. They go back to the dead ones and pick at them like prehistoric vultures. I'll carry you if I have to. When I lift the stand, use your arms to pull yourself out from under it."

The veins stood out on Darren's neck as he lifted the cart. Hot oil spilled out, singeing Erik's chest. He wailed in agony.

"Holy shit! I'm sorry!"

"Keep . . . keep lifting."

Despite the blinding pain in both his chest and leg, Erik dug his hands in the grass and managed to extricate himself far enough for Darren to drop the cart. Powdered sugar puffed out into a thick cloud, choking them both.

Erik looked down to see his right calf at an angle it was not designed to be in.

Darren hooked his arm over his shoulder and lifted. He stumbled and almost dropped him, but managed to recover in time.

Now that Erik could see the total destruction, he wished he were back on the ground under the perceived protection of the cart. So many people dead. And so many more being attacked as they fled the beach. He saw too many of his classmates, bodies torn open, limbs missing. His gorge barreled up his throat.

"Come on," Darren said, hobbling under his weight. "My car isn't far."

Erik's burned chest smelled like barbecue. It reminded him of a pig roast his family went to on their vacation to Hawaii when he was twelve.

The stench made him vomit, chunks splashing his feet.

He saw Darren's car, a beat-up Nissan, several hundred feet away. So close.

Spotting something from the corner of his eye, Erik said, "Hold up."

Darren stopped. Erik's foot caught against something, twisting his leg. He bit down hard enough on his lip to draw blood.

"Why are we stopping?"

"There's a kid over there."

A boy no older than four, tears streaming down his cheeks, walked in a small, stunned circle, crying for his mother. Erik saw a woman's body not far from the boy, the head missing.

"We can't leave him," Erik said.

He felt Darren tense. "I know. You all right if I put you down?"

"Yeah."

Darren laid him down as gently as he could and ran to the boy. Without saying a word, he scooped him up in his arms.

"Darren! Duck!"

His friend never saw the flying monster as it craned its neck down close enough so it could clamp its jaws over the top of his head. The boy spilled from his arms. Darren's arms swung wildly, hitting the creature's legs to no effect. When it did fly away, it did so with a section of his skull in its maw.

"No! No! No!"

Erik scrambled across the dirt, skin pulling free from his fingers as he fought to make his way to his friend. The little boy was on his knees, crying harder than ever.

He saw the gray and red of his friend's brain. Darren's body twitched, his legs and arms gyrating. Erik looked up to see the creature coming back for more.

Only it was coming for the boy.

"Stay there!" he shouted. The boy looked at him, his crying momentarily stopped, eyes wide as he stared at the fast approaching monster.

Erik draped his body over the boy an instant before the creature was able to snatch him away. He felt the skin flayed from his back.

With his mouth right next to the boy's ear, he said, "Don't move, kid. Just stay right here. You got me?"

His head nodded, his body hitching with sobs.

Erik's shuddered as more of him was claimed by the beast. His vision darkened and he could hear his galloping heartbeat as if it were a bass drum beside his head.

"Just . . . don't move."

His lungs felt like they were filling up with water. But he knew it wasn't water.

Before he closed his eyes, he told the boy he'd protect him. What he didn't say was—alive or dead.

Joanne held onto Noah's hand for dear life. What was happening was impossible. Even covered in the warm blood of other people, her mind couldn't handle what she was seeing.

The sky was filled with monsters. The fairground was cluttered with bodies, both the dead and the maimed. She tripped over the shredded torso of a man. Noah jerked her arm to keep her from falling.

"We have to get to the car!" she shouted.

"It's too far. We need shelter."

He pointed at a squat brick structure. It looked to be a public bathroom. They weren't the first to think of it. A swarm of people struggled to push their way inside.

Tears stung her eyes as she ran.

Noah pulled her along.

"Almost there, baby," he said. He sounded calm but she saw the terror in his eyes.

They should have dropped the whole Jersey Devil tour idea the day they found their gear strung along the top of the pine tree. She thought she was scared then. It didn't hold a candle to the raw panic that gripped her heart right now.

The closer they got to the restroom, the more she realized it was a dead end. More and more people were outside the doors, pushing to no avail.

No room at the inn, she thought, feeling like her mind was going to shatter into tiny, irretrievable bits.

"We can't," she said, daring to look back, seeing a creature sweep inches from their backs.

"I'll get you inside," Noah said.

And then his grip was gone. Joanne stumbled over him as his feet slipped on one of their fliers, sending him into an erratic tumble.

"Noah!"

Before he could even get to his knees, a monster pounced on Noah. It tore the flesh from his face. Noah's scream turned Joanne's muscles to jelly. She collapsed next to him.

The monster turned to her, part of Noah's cheek slipping from its mouth.

"Please, please, leave him alone," she said, sobbing.

Its arm shot forward, sharp talons burrowing into her neck. Holding her quivering body in place, she watched helplessly as it continued to feed on Noah. Each breath was harder to take than the previous one. Her vision faded, but not before she saw it split her boyfriend's stomach open, feasting on his organs. She knew it would do the same to her, and was grateful she'd be dead before it could.

Chapter Forty-six

Sam Willet was stunned when the first bullet tore off a chunk of the Jersey Devil's calf. Ben was right, it was getting slower. It whirled around to face him, a trio of torn bodies revealed underneath it.

"Surprise."

The next shot went into the stage as the creature leapt skyward. He flinched when gunfire erupted beside him. Daryl fired shot after shot at the Devil as it made serpentine maneuvers above them.

"I told you I'd take care of it alone," Sam said.

"You didn't think I'd let an old man do all the heavy lifting, did you?"

He wouldn't say it, but he was grateful. During the run across the fairground, Sam's heart felt like it was being tightly compressed, making it harder to pump much-needed blood to his legs and arms.

"Crap, there are more coming," Daryl shouted. Looking past the stage, Sam saw a fresh stampede of people driven to the killing field by a new wave of Devils.

"Come face me, you son of a bitch!" Sam shouted at

the Jersey Devil. If it could speak, it should be able to understand him. "Are you afraid of an old man?"

Daryl's rifle clicked empty. "Dammit. I'm out."

"Then stay close to me."

He watched as the Jersey Devil eyed its returning children, howling something that could be best equated with a cry of victory. It then turned to face them.

Sam didn't bother raising his gun. Now that it was aware of his presence, it would evade any shot he took.

Instead, he let it fall to the ground.

"Boompa, no!" Daryl said.

His grandson bent to pick up the rifle. Just as he did, the Devil lasered in on him, knocking them both down, spinning ass over heels.

The Jersey Devil stood over Daryl, a cloven hoof on each side of his chest. Daryl may have been bigger but he was hurt. The creature snapped at his throat. Daryl was quick enough to get his forearm up in time. A section of meat was torn away, revealing bone. Daryl screamed. Sam, his chest feeling as though someone had stabbed him with a sword, rose unsteadily to his feet. The Devil once again went for Daryl's neck. He moved out of the way, and it snatched his Mets cap instead, tearing it to shreds.

Daryl reached up and grabbed it by the throat, his big hands wrapping all the way around it.

There was fire in his eyes, the whites the same color as the blood seeping from his arm.

"Hold it there!" Sam yelled, staggering to them.

He only had one chance left. If he missed, he knew he wouldn't be around to try again, and neither would Daryl.

Reaching into his pocket, he lurched at the Devil.

* * *

Fucking guns were useless!

Ben knew there was no point anymore. Whatever these things were, they had a preternatural ability to evade them. They'd need a damn army in order to take them down that way.

He, April and Norm stayed close together.

"We have to lure one in," he said.

"Are you c-crazy?" Norm said.

Ben extracted a thick knife from the holder on his belt. "Put your guns down, let them think they've got us."

"No way," April said, just missing one that was feasting on a body with an open chest cavity.

"Just do what I say for once!"

She shot him daggers, but even she wilted under his gaze. Slowly, she lowered her rifle.

And sure enough, being the few people still standing, they were now an open target.

One of the Devils came screeching straight at them.

"Get down!" Ben shouted.

April and Norm dropped to their knees.

He sprang at the flying Devil, catching it by the throat. He was lifted off the ground, sailing toward the beach.

The creature had a hard time keeping its balance with him around its neck. Before it could go any higher, he buried the knife to the hilt in its back. Gouts of thick blood and a hellish aroma poured from the jagged wound.

The creature squawked, plummeting to the ground. Ben rolled with it, the sound of his left wrist snapping lost in the dying squeals of the beast.

He stepped away from the Devil, his hand dangling loosely at his side.

"Looks like I won't be doing that again," he said, staring at his wrist, the bone pressing hard against his skin.

Another Devil, seeing its sibling dead, came for him. It was reckless in its anger. Ben locked his knees, waiting for the inevitable, knife held steady at his hip.

A second before impact, a shot rang out and it tumbled away from him.

Ben looked across the field and saw Norm tipping his cap.

"Keep their f-focus on you!" Norm shouted. "I'll do the rest!"

It was a good plan. Only six more to go. He hoped Norm could keep up his Wild Bill precision.

Then he realized April was nowhere to be seen. Where the hell had she gone? There was no time to think. A couple of teens in bikinis ran past him. Another Devil paused in midair, gazing at the two dead creatures. Ben sneered at it, waving his knife in the air. "Next!"

When April saw Boompa and Daryl struggling with the Jersey Devil, she took off after them. Ben was right, the best way to kill them was up close. And her brother and grandfather couldn't be any closer.

She made it halfway to them before she was spirited away, her rifle fumbling from her grasp. One of the creatures had grabbed her by the bullet wound in her arm. Everything went fuzzy in an instant. She spewed a string of curses, but her body was too shocked and weak to fight back.

In moments, she was soaring over Daryl, Boompa and the Jersey Devil. Daryl looked like he was trying to choke the beast out. Boompa was clutching his chest, moving toward them on unsteady legs.

She saw the red sand of the beach, bodies lying in mangled heaps.

In an instant, everything changed.

The roar of gunfire swallowed up the sounds of the shrieking Devils and screaming survivors. She watched as the flying creatures were torn to ribbons, pinwheeling in the air before colliding with the hard earth.

April felt the Devil's body vibrate. The ground was coming up fast. Closing her eyes, she braced for impact.

Smacking sideways into something hard yet forgiving, she tumbled free, lying on her stomach. Looking down, she saw Ben's face, his eyes glazed, one hand over her back.

Somehow, he'd caught her just before she hit the ground. His head must have hit pretty hard, because his eyes were swimming in jittery circles.

When he mumbled, "Jesus, you weigh as much as Daryl," tears sprang to her eyes.

Norm came to them at a crouch. His rifle was gone. But the heavy gunfire continued.

"Are you both all right?" he asked.

"No," April said, trying to help Ben sit up. "Who's doing all the shooting?"

For the first time that day, Norm smiled. "They had their backup, we have ours." He pointed to the parking lot. "Looks like your mother was able to convince every cop in the state to get here and save our asses."

Gunfire crackled like the crescendo of a fireworks display. There must have been dozens of people shooting at the creatures. Even they couldn't evade that much firepower.

April saw her mother shielded behind a pair of cops in riot gear with Plexiglas shields.

"Mom!"

The Jersey Devil fought like a bucking bronco to get free of Daryl's grip. If it weren't for the damage to its wing and leg and groin, Sam was sure it would have been long gone by now.

Drawing in a breath made his ribs felt like they were cracking and set his lungs on fire.

Sam jumped the last couple of feet, landing on its back. It beat at him with its wings, but he held on, locking an arm around its throat.

One of its horns nicked Sam's temple, drawing blood. This close, the stench of the creature was overpowering. It reeked of death, both fresh and decayed.

"Daryl, I need you to let go!"

"No! I've got him."

The Jersey Devil thrashed, making wounded horse sounds that would weaken any man's resolve.

With his free hand, Sam showed his grandson what he had in store.

"Now let go and run like hell!"

Daryl reluctantly released the Devil's neck, rolling out from under it as it tried to stomp him to death. Sam bore his weight down as hard as he could. When Daryl was out of range, Sam reached up toward the creature's mouth, its teeth snagging on his hand.

The Jersey Devil snapped its head round, staring into Sam's eyes. He saw hatred in its purest essence, a hatred he was sure he was giving right back.

"You . . . dare . . . to hurt me," it said. "You will . . . all die."

Sam was past being surprised or afraid.

"This is what you get when you fuck with my family!"

Sam flicked the pin free on the grenade, ramming it down the Devil's throat. He used both of his hands to squeeze its mouth shut, preventing it from spitting the bomb out.

The look in the Devil's eyes morphed from pure animus to raw fear.

Just a few seconds, he thought, willing his heart to pump just little bit longer.

He pictured Lauren. Imagined Bill standing next to her.

And he thanked God for giving him just enough life to finish what had been started sixty years earlier.

Chapter Forty-seven

The explosion made everyone duck for cover. Carol heard policemen shouting, "What the hell was that? Where did it come from?"

She knew right away. She'd spotted Daryl, her boy she thought she'd never see again, running from the Jersey Devil, her father-in-law strapped to its back.

When both the creature and Boompa exploded into a horrid mist, she was both sad and happy.

It was only right that he be the one to take down the demon that had nearly destroyed poor Lauren and haunted their family ever since.

Maybe now, they could lead normal lives, without the specter of the unknown hanging over them, wondering where everything was eventually going to lead.

Maybe now, they were free.

The last shots were fired as the final creature was brought down. With the big creature dead, the others seemed to simply give in.

Carol pushed past the police that had kept her protected, ignoring their orders to stop.

She ran, tears flowing like rapids, to her family. Her kids were hurt, but they'd be all right.

"Mom!" April and Daryl cried out at the same time. Norm stepped aside to give her free access to her children. Even Ben smiled, pulling her close to him.

"You know, Ma, I had everything under control," he said.

She grabbed them all, laying their heads against her chest the way she used to when they were little. When she looked down at April's arm, she noticed her shirt had been torn, revealing her torso.

The mark on her side was gone.

As he'd predicted, it had been too big to cover up. Norm Cranston ended up not needing the two bodies he'd stuffed in the cooler. There were plenty of others for the scientists to dissect and examine. Unfortunately, there wasn't much left of the true Jersey Devil. There had been video, taken by people on their phones, proof that the big bastard did exist.

The speculation was that it couldn't have been the very same Devil that sprang from Momma Leeds hundreds of years ago. It obviously procreated, as evidenced by all the smaller creatures. It only made sense.

Norm wasn't so sure.

The mystery of the Jersey Devil had been solved, but in a way, it had only deepened. What exactly was it?

Neither he nor the Willets mentioned in the dozens of interviews they went through that it had spoken. That would have been too much. Maybe someday, Norm would talk about it, but by then he was sure most people wouldn't believe him. He'd just be an old cryptozoologist looking to gain a bit of the spotlight one last time.

Getting out of his rental car, he thought of all the people who'd been lost. Papers had listed their names the way they did after 9/11. Of the hundreds, he only recognized Bill and Sam Willet, Heather Davids and Daniela Robards. Jane turned out to be Jane Moreland, a woman who had gone missing five years ago, along with her husband.

The ME was still going through all the remains found at the pits that Daryl led them to. There was a chance they could give a sense of finality to families of the missing.

The Pine Barrens held many secrets.

Now it held one less.

The tiny bells chimed as Norm walked in the door. Just like before, the general store was nice and cold, a perfect refuge from a sweltering day.

The same old woman still manned the register. She looked up from a book she was reading and nearly fell off her chair when she saw him.

Norm smiled. "I told you I'd come back to let you know I was all right."

She grabbed his hand over the counter. "I saw you and that family on the TV. It's a miracle you all survived."

"Mind if I grab a s-soda?"

"You can have all the soda you want. It's on me."

She truly looked happy and relieved to see him. He wondered if his cat Salem would look at him the same way when he got back home.

Probably not.

The bottle of birch beer was about the most refreshing thing he'd had in weeks.

"Was everything they said true?" she asked, offering him a seat beside her.

His phone vibrated. Norm looked at the screen. It

was his agent . . . again. He had big plans for Norm, plans that would make them both rich.

The only problem was, Norm wasn't sure he ever wanted to revisit the nightmare. He did promise himself that he would give half of anything he made to the Willets. He and Carol vowed to keep in touch. Money couldn't replace what she'd lost, but it was only right that they have it.

He swiped the call to Ignore.

"It was pretty bad," he replied. "But it's over, and I guess that's what matters most."

She cut him off a large hunk of fresh fudge.

"Only if you share with me," he said.

They ate in a perfectly comfortable silence